The Verderer

Pitch & Sickle

Book Two

THE DIABOLUS CHRONICLES

D K GIRL

The Verderer © 2021 by Danielle K Girl
Cover Art by Deranged Doctor Design

Edited by **Inspired Ink Editing**

ISBN: 978-0-6453274-2-7

CHAPTER 1

Silas clung to Lalassu's reins with the fervour of a man grasping a lifeboat in a savage ocean. His shoulders ached, as did his stomach, and his thighs positively screamed for relief.

'Head up, Silas.' The shout stirred him from his misery. 'Raise yourself in the stirrups, lean forward, eyes fixed ahead of you. I have a good feeling about this run.'

Sybilla rode alongside him on a stunning dapple-grey gelding, without benefit of saddle or bridle. Silas had not yet worked out how she communicated with her steed. She moved neither legs nor arms in any obvious way, totally at ease upon her galloping mount.

Quite unlike himself.

Silas pressed into his stirrups, his eyes set on the obstacle ahead: a gorse hedge that Sybilla insisted was quite low, but to Silas's eye might well have been the tallest peak in the British Isles. He grit his teeth, and the flutter of panic rose anew. Dear god, how long would this torture continue? Lalassu thundered beneath him, her massive bulk sinking her hooves into the grass, the gorse looming impossibly large. He threw himself forward, pressing his hands into the warmth of Lalassu's thick mane. The horse gathered herself, muscles bunching, launching herself at the jump. A frightened squeak escaped from Silas as they rose drastically upwards.

'Lift your arse!'

1

But the cry came too late for Silas to heed. Lalassu's back legs lifted from the ground, sending her powerful haunches into the air. The saddle met Silas's backside with a solid thump, and at once he was airborne too.

He cried out, a pitiful sound even to his own ears, and soared over Lalassu's near side, clearing the jump a fraction ahead of the horse herself. Arms flailing at the fast-approaching ground, Silas braced for the impact. It was as solid and unpleasant as it had been the last time, and the time before that, knocking the air from his lungs. He was conscious of Lalassu's hooves close to his head, and he rolled himself into a bruised and mortified ball. Lady Satine may have named Silas one of her Horsemen, but the title did not come with instant horse mastery. Dear god, he was dreadful. His frustration grew with each attempt, and not only with regards to his lack of riding skill. He had no clue what being one of Lady Satine's Horseman entailed, nor when the service would begin in earnest. The waiting, the uncertainty was making him irritable beyond words.

Laughter, delicate and dreadful, filled the air.

'Oh shut up, Pitch!' Silas pushed himself to seated and punched at the hapless ground. 'Do you not have something better to do than laugh at my expense?'

For ten long days the daemon had snickered at Sybilla's attempts to imbue Silas with the basics of horsemanship.

'Well, I have *someone* better to do, of course.'

Pitch stood over him, coming as he did so often out of nowhere. When the ride began he'd been near to the farmhouse, watching from where he lounged upon the back of a straw-laden cart; and yet here he was, in the blink of an eye right at Silas's side. Far too close as usual, and discomfortingly fetching in snug-fitting moleskin trousers, a pair of heeled shoes utterly impractical for walking in a field, and a loose-fitting smock, which gaped to reveal his brazen bare chest beneath.

'But I do truly relish the daily amusement you provide, dear Sickle,' he continued. 'Have you any idea how delightful it is to see that wonderfully oversized body fly through the air?'

The late morning sunshine was too kind upon his emerald eyes. It continually astonished Silas that such a cruel tongue could rest within such a beautiful face.

'Leave me be, Pitch. I'm in no mood for you this morning.' He refused the slender hand offered to assist him to his feet, but took note of the bruises upon Pitch's knuckles. Grey-green against his pale skin. 'Be on your way.'

Silas dusted himself off, adjusting his trousers, which had slid low upon his hips.

'Unless of course, Tobias, you'd prefer to be soundly beaten once again in some swordplay?' Sybilla sat astride her horse, her light brown riding skirt structured like a pair of baggy trousers so that she could straddle her mount and forgo side-saddle niceties. Her dapple grey and Lalassu grazed upon the vibrant green grass of the paddock. 'It makes you far more interesting to look at.' She touched at her chin. 'Flawless skin is ever so dull. I rather think my nicks add some character.'

Pitch's smile was caustic. 'Do not flatter yourself. Your skills with the sword are reasonable, but you'll only inflict injury if I'm in the mood for such things. You cannot lay claim to these marks, my dear.'

With a clearer head, Silas saw that there were indeed some cuts at Pitch's chin and several more lower on his neck. But if these injuries were not made by her able blade during one of their endless tarries, then how?

'Then might I cause some injury I can name my own?' Sybilla scratched at the short, tight curls of her pearl white hair. 'How about it then? Silas is almost done for today, I fear. Take up a sword, Tobias, I am quite looking forward to seeing my point at your throat once more.'

The woman appeared fearless in many matters, not least of all when it came to goading Pitch. A pleasant turn of events that Silas welcomed, for it took the daemon's attentions off him.

'Oh my sweet Sybilla,' Pitch said. 'I see quite clearly what all this appetite for roughness truly means. It is *my* point you wish to have at your throat, stuck deep into your mouth, if I am not wrong.'

Sybilla's laugh nearly rocked her off her horse. 'Gods,' she sputtered. 'I don't know if I should be laughing or throwing up.' Her night-black cheeks glistened with wept tears. 'I imagine I'd do both if I had your cock anywhere near my lips.'

Silas choked on unexpected laughter and hurried over to Lalassu, where he might find a hiding place behind her to allow his smile free, safe from Pitch's temper.

But the daemon's smug expression did not falter. He too laughed, though not as heartily as Sybilla had done. 'Sunset then?' he said. 'Blades at the ready?'

'Of course.' Sybilla wiped at her mirthful tears. 'We shall work up an appetite for supper.'

The pair fought daily, going at one another as though enemies at war. Training only, Sybilla insisted, but Silas tried not to think on what enemies required such fierceness. Each was a remarkable master of the blade. Pitch and Sybilla pirouetted and swung at one another like ballerinas in battle, so light of foot and graceful of motion that Silas at times forgot about the sharp blades they held, mesmerised by the sway of Pitch's hips, the stretch of his elegant shoulders as he parried a blow. Sybilla too moved as though upon a dancefloor. That she was a gifted swordswoman was to state it too plainly. The blade was an extension of her, her quick step astonishing to behold. She was a soldier, Silas did not doubt it, but in what army could a woman do battle? And what war did she wage?

Sybilla's blade was a rather old-fashioned rapier, but stunning nonetheless, with an intricate hilt that reminded him rather of an elaborate crown shielding her hand. Each time he watched her manoeuvre it so deftly through the air, he was reminded how little he knew of Sybilla. Or the Lady Satine for that matter. His mysterious mistress was hardly one for fireside chats. She'd not appeared again since using Clarence as her mouth-piece, and Sybilla and Pitch had brushed off his queries.

'Very well then. Our date is set.' Pitch's smock was too large for him and had slipped down over one bare shoulder. 'Now, I shall leave you to continue bruising our dear ankou.' He nodded at Silas. 'Feel free to break your neck so that we might end this ridiculous union sooner.'

Silas busied himself with unnecessary adjustments on Lalassu's girth and did not reply. He heard no hint of Pitch's retreat, but when he raised his head a few moments later, the man was already far across the paddock, headed towards the farmhouse.

Sybilla sighed. 'I wonder if you do need a guardian, Silas, or was the Lady Satine simply desperate to rid herself of a daemon?'

Silas watched Pitch leap over the wooden fence at the paddock's edge. 'I dare say it is probably a touch of both.'

Sybilla laughed shortly and her smile bared stark-white teeth. 'You are rather amusing when you find it in you.'

'I can't say I've found all that much to jest about of late.' He ran his hand along Lalassu's pale coat, the brush of his fingers stirring that strange hue of green hidden in the strands. 'This waiting, it's leaving me in knots. I do not know where I will be led to next, or what I'm to face. I am in the dark and it's keeping me awake at night.'

He had not intended to disclose so much to Sybilla, but without Jane to speak with and air his concerns, Silas was going mad with trepidation. And he certainly would not rely on Tobias Astaroth to ease his mind.

'Well then, how about you mount and we attempt the jump one last time before we head into Bishop's Castle and get some ale into you?' Sybilla said with notable kindness. 'Tobias has certainly not kept himself secluded here, as you have done. In fact I'm quite certain he's probably bedded half the town by now, and eaten them out of cakes and sweets. The company might do you good, Silas. Keep you away from your thoughts for a while. What do you say?'

Until that moment he had declined every attempt made by both Pitch and Sybilla to have him step foot beyond the borders of Lower Broughton Farm. He'd been recuperating to begin with, the wounds from Black Annis healing fast physically but not so within his mind. The vision of the desecrated bodies of the children haunted both his dreams and his waking hours. His reticence to leave the place grew with each day he lingered, strolling the paddocks, toiling with the feeding of the horses and cleaning of the stables, and enduring the seemingly endless training, in both horsemanship and fighting. He'd not been allowed a sword, merely a crude imitation of the already rudimentary scythe with which to be battered about as Sybilla played the role of an attacking teratism. When not taking punishing lessons Silas was left to his own blissful devices, which was not as comforting as he might have liked, for he was constantly on edge. Waiting for the summons to ride that he knew would come.

But now, with the sun's uncharacteristic November warmth upon him, and thoughts of fresh ale on his mind, he nodded. 'Yes, you're right. It is perhaps time for an outing.'

He grasped hold of the reins and readied his aching thighs for the mount, hoping that Bishop's Castle was as dull and commonplace as Pitch bemoaned. Normality was a delightful prospect. He may be going half-mad not knowing when the call to set out on the Lady Satine's mysterious quest would come, but that did not mean he craved another day of horse falls and sword nicks.

'Right then, one more try.' Sybilla urged her mount into a trot. 'Then we shall have that delightful arse out of the saddle and onto a barstool.'

CHAPTER 2

S ilas sipped at his second pint, an ale with a sharper bite than he preferred, but it warmed his belly well enough; and as Sybilla was providing the shillings required, he would scarcely complain at her selection. They sat at a small round table by one of the front windows, just out of reach of the full force of the fire that dominated the far wall with its stone hearth. Considering the warmth of the day, the blaze was unreasonably large and Silas had soon removed his coat upon entering the establishment.

The Three Tuns Inn was saturated with the odour of working bodies, the sweat tangible upon the air and mingling with the less unpleasant reek of ale. At times, the murmur of the patrons rose into swells of raucous laughter and flurries of curses, before returning to quieter conversations. Upon arrival Silas and Sybilla had drawn much attention, few bothering to conceal scrutinising stares. Several patrons had nodded a greeting towards Sybilla and raised eyebrows Silas's way before hands were lifted to conceal whispers. He was quite sure that a table of ruddy-cheeked gentlemen took it upon themselves to depart as soon as Silas and Sybilla had entered, their half-full pints abandoned, muttering as they went.

The bartender, a slight man with spectacles and a cleft chin, seemed rather more enthused at their arrival, and he had raised a hand in greeting, gesturing towards the single empty table by the window.

Now, a serving woman set down two plates, each graced with a golden-crusted pork pie and two round baked potatoes. 'There you go, luv. Though I told Cilla I think you'll need the two plates just for you to satisfy the appetite of a burly man like yourself.' She winked at him, her hazel eyes full of mirth. Her light brown hair was tied in a messy bun at the nape of her neck, and her thin lips brought forth a bright smile.

'Thank you, Clare.' Sybilla touched at the woman's arm. 'Mr Mercer, this is a good friend of mine, Clare Williams. Mrs Williams runs the inn with her husband Tom.' She gestured to the bespectacled man behind the busy bar. 'Clare often comes to the farm for eggs, and the like.'

Mrs Williams played at her lips with her tongue, and her gaze flitted ever so quickly to her husband.

'Very nice to make your acquaintance, Mrs Williams,' Silas said, his stomach growling at the pleasant scent of the meal before him. 'This looks wonderful.'

'Well, if it's not, you be sure to let me know. Cilla certainly doesn't mind letting her feelings be known, do you, my luv?'

'I didn't think that bothered you?' Sybilla's smile was rather coy, her glance from beneath dark lashes equally so. Clare's cheeks reddened, and she could not seem to keep her eyes upon Sybilla, who regarded her intently.

'Tell me,' Clare said. 'What do you think of those beautiful horses, Mr Mercer? I hear you are riding Lalassu?'

Silas could only assume she had heard such a thing from Sybilla herself, and he thought he now understood the strange vibrancy in the air between the two women.

'I've never seen such fine horses, I'll say.' Silas breathed in the tang of rosemary and pork, longing to lift his fork and dig into the sun-gold crust. 'Though I'll admit I do Lalassu no justice with my riding.'

Clare laughed lightly. 'I'm sure Cilla will soon have you set right with your horse mastery. She has a very fine way about her...with horses, that is...' The flush of pink upon her cheeks deepened. To Silas's consternation she leaned her hands on the table so she might speak closer to his ear. 'And don't be paying any mind to those about here who'll talk all sorts of nonsense about Lower Broughton Farm. They might spread all kinds of nasty rumours, but you can be sure as soon as they're needing a new cart horse, or are looking for a cure for an ailing flock they'll call on her soon enough. Be assured, any acquaintance of Sybilla's is welcome at The Three Tuns Inn.'

Sybilla slipped her hand over Clare's, and for a moment the two women seemed frozen in position. Though they did not look at each other, Silas felt terribly uncomfortable, as though he had happened upon them in a state of undress in their boudoir.

'Those are quite delightful,' he blurted, gesturing to the delicate bunch of pale pink flowers set in a crude pottery vase on the window ledge. 'Milkweed, if I'm not mistaken?'

Clare straightened, and Sybilla reached for her fork.

'They are indeed,' Clare replied. 'I didn't pick you for a gardener, Mr Mercer.'

'Oh no, I'm certainly not...' He hesitated. For perhaps he was. It was true that the names of plants and trees and flowers came to him with a clarity that little else did. 'They are quite lovely,' he said simply.

'Indeed. Well, I best be off then,' Clare sighed. 'I'll be bothered enough for gossip now as it is.' She rolled her eyes. 'The town is positively humming with talk of you this past week, Cilla, what with your two gentlemen callers. That young one, Mr Astaroth is he called? He's finer than half the princesses in England, I'd wager, and having no trouble finding a bed to lie in thanks to it.' She winked once more at Silas. 'I'd bet you'd have no trouble yourself, but I've not seen you in the town before now. Has Sybilla been having her way with you out at the farm?'

'I beg your pardon?' Silas said, quite lost.

Clare laughed gently. 'According to the blacksmith, Sybilla has you both doing all manner of terrible things to her while you worship at the altar of the devil himself.' Her voice dropped low, and notably husky, but her eyes danced with amusement. 'Maisy Greenwood offered up prayers for you at last Sunday's service. I thought Father Taylor's eyes were going to pop from his head with him imagining you sandwiched between two fellows, Cilla.' She laughed softly, shoulders shaking. Her hand slid to where Sybilla's cupped the base of her pint glass, and their fingers met. The contrast in their skin tones was both startling and beautiful. 'I've been sending up my own prayers, you know. Hoping the angels keep you safe and forgive you all your sins.'

Sybilla chewed at her lip, a stifled smile contorting her mouth. 'I can assure you, the angels keep me very safe. And I regret none of my sins. Do you?'

'Not a one.'

Silas stared down at his pork pie. Dear god let this be over with so he might enjoy his meal while it was still warm.

Clare straightened and rested her hand on Sybilla's shoulder. 'Go on then, eat your food. You best keep your strength up for your dark rituals. Very nice to meet you, Mr Mercer.'

'And you, Clare.'

At long last, they were left alone. Silas touched his fingers against the sides of the bulky slab of pie. There was no fear that it had cooled, the pastry comfortably warm and promising even steamier insides to come.

'So they think you a witch?' He bit deep into chunks of pork and rich, thick gravy. Asking Sybilla *what* she was directly seemed far too common, though his curiosity quite ran away with him. There was little doubt she was far more than an able horsewoman, considering her mistress.

Sybilla still watched Clare as she made her way through the tables, exchanging cheerful greetings with each of her patrons.

'I've been called a witch, a sorceress, the devil's whore, I've rather lost count of the names sent my way.' She cut into her baked potato, the cracking of the skin delightful. 'They fear a woman like me, one of dubious origins, living out there all alone on a farm owned by a mysterious foreign gentleman who has never once visited. Tending to her herb gardens and her horses, strangely masterful with both. What else could I be but Satan's mistress?'

Silas cleared his throat. 'And might I –'

The door to the inn swung open, and the breeze carried in the scent of dense, moist soil. An all too familiar smell. One did not forget the grave one rose from. A peculiar sensation came over him, not unlike a shiver of delight. He set his feet more firmly upon the wooden floorboards, seeking to quash the sudden urge to traipse out of the inn at once.

'Silas?' Sybilla frowned. 'Is everything all right?'

He swallowed a generous mouthful before he spoke. 'Quite.' Coughing against a resilient crumb that clung to the back of his throat, he added, 'It is nothing.' He'd forgotten entirely what he'd been about to ask and scrambled for another question. 'You mentioned that the farm belongs to a foreign gentleman? I had thought that the Lady –'

'Mr Mercer' – Sybilla waggled a finger at him, voice lowered – 'best keep that name to yourself. So far as the registry is concerned, the farm is owned by a wealthy businessman who spends all his time in deepest India. Our mutual friend prefers to keep her affairs to herself wherever possible. She rather favours Lower Broughton. You were quite fortunate to have been brought there. She must deem you rather important to risk such attention.'

'Oh, I see.' Silas was not so hungry as he had imagined. The heat of the room was most unpleasant, and his nostrils still held the scent of the earth.

'Come now, your face betrays your fears so readily. But it is misplaced, I'm sure. Whatever is in store for you, I have no doubt you shall face it admirably. You've met a friend of mine in London, Tyvain. Do you recall her? Short as a dwarf, quite the church bell. Some call her the Hag of Beara.'

'I recall her well. She's rather hard to forget.'

Sybilla grinned. 'Never a truer word was said. Well, she thought quite highly of you, though to be fair, I wasn't sure if she was referring to your potential, or your...' She swept her hand towards him. 'Rather striking appearance.'

Another bite of pie was in order, and Silas took his time with the chewing. He sniffed, seeking to dislodge the dense odour that would not abate, and found his thoughts drifting, wondering at the location of the town's graveyard. How he longed to dig his fingers into the coarseness of the dirt there.

'Anyway,' his companion continued, 'she's not the only one who has a good feeling about you. Mr Ahari is most enthusiastic, the Lady Satine tells me.' Sybilla belched into her sleeve.

Mr Ahari. The very man who had dug Silas from his resting place. The strange but affable man who had tested Silas with his curious pub, The Atlas. Silas had passed whatever queer test he'd been subjected too, finding his way through the maze of hallways and staircases that led him eventually to Mr Ahari's cluttered quarters.

He swirled the few inches of ale remaining in his glass. How distant both the public house and the ever-grinning man with his pleasant heavy-lidded eyes and full cheeks now seemed. His gaze shifted to the doorway, through which new patrons arrived and inebriated ones departed. The dank allure of earth sang to him like a siren. He considered asking Sybilla whether this affliction fell upon all ankou, for such a longing was decidedly unnerving.

Before he could ask that, or the dozen other questions he had, Sybilla shoved back her chair. 'Another?' She jabbed a finger towards his glass, which Silas handed to her with a nod. 'Good man.'

Sybilla made her way to the bar quickly but took her precious time in returning. Clare stood behind the bar now, and the two women fell into deep conversation, despite the furrowed brows and nosy glances sent their way. A space formed around Sybilla, as though the menfolk who had dominated the bar area feared standing too close.

For long minutes Silas sat alone, cursing the door every time it opened. His eyes fairly watered with the richness of damp earth. His chair grew more uncomfortable with each passing moment, his buttocks, suitably ruined by the horse riding, were much displeased with the lack of movement. He let his gaze wander the room, hoping for distraction. Instead, he found himself the centre of unsettling attention. A solitary gentleman stared hard at him from a neighbouring table, and a heavyset couple seated near the fire leaned into one another as they very evidently spoke of him.

Silas edged his seat around so that he faced the window. He shrugged against the eyes boring hard upon his back. The outdoors had never looked so appealing. The sun shone yet, though clouds were creeping their way across the sky. A man pushed a cart laden with firewood past two women clad in dirt-stained smocks, flapping their arms about as they sought to shepherd a flock of geese down the street. Silas glanced at the bar. Sybilla had settled into an abandoned seat and sipped on a dark ale, her shirt sleeves pushed to her elbows as she leaned against the bar. There was no sign of his own promised brew.

'Wonderful,' he muttered.

He considered crossing the crowded space to order his own pint, but as the doors swung open yet again, and that scent of grit and dirt beckoned.

His mind was quite made up. Silas gathered his coat. A walk was in order if he was to manage another pint after the heaviness of the pie and potato. A flushed-cheek serving girl was rubbing a cloth over a recently vacated table. Silas caught her attention, and she jumped, her eyes widening as they traced his full height.

'How-how can I help you, sir?'

He gestured to Sybilla. 'Would you be so kind as to tell my companion I am just taking a short walk?'

She nodded with too much vigour. 'Of course, sir.'

'Thank you.'

Rushing for the door, past the lingering stares and curious glances, Silas stepped out into the daylight. And only there did the air finally find its way deep into his lungs.

CHAPTER 3

S ilas, following the lead of his nose, passed by the stables as he made his way along the street. He could just make out the silhouette of Lalassu and Sybilla's mount, whose name she had never uttered, dozing in the stalls. But he'd not stop to visit the horses. Even the deep richness of hay and horseflesh could not overwhelm the bouquet of the earth. A low whinny floated from the stalls, and Silas would have wagered the bandalore itself that the sound came from Lalassu. He knew it without a shred of doubt. Just as she knew to call out to him at that precise moment. Despite the ache of his body, he found himself looking forward to being upon her broad back once more.

He continued down the road. As the waft of the horses faded, the gritty heaviness of hallowed ground dominated the air and guided him as surely as a lantern through a snowstorm. There was no such storm of course, rather the opposite was true. This autumn day was enormously pleasant, made even more so by the fact that Silas was, for the first time in such a long time, on his own. After his arrival at Lower Broughton Farm, as he'd recuperated from Black Annis's ministrations, Sybilla had kept a discreet distance but seemed to hold an uncanny ability to know when he required assistance. He'd only so much as think of food, and she'd be at the door with a bowl of porridge or a fresh boiled egg, tapping gently to ask his permission to enter.

Pitch, however, was far less obliging of Silas's privacy. Once he'd woken from a restless slumber to find the covers pulled away and Pitch wiping a damp cloth against his bare legs. The intolerable man had made his way far up Silas's thigh before he was stayed with a firm hand and a harsh word.

'What are you doing?' Silas had fumed.

'Is it not obvious? You reek, but are refusing the tub. I'm simply assisting.' Despite Silas's grip on his wrist, Pitch had rather too easily continued pushing the washcloth up Silas's thigh.

'Good gracious, man, I can bathe myself. I do not need your assistance.' To add to his mortification, Silas was aware of the morning's hardness between his legs, and the notion that Pitch might spy the stiffness and assume himself responsible made Silas's throat clench. 'Get out. Now.'

He'd snatched the cloth away and lunged for the bedcovers. The daemon, damn him, merely pursed his bowed lips and watched Silas from beneath his lashes.

'You are so terribly tense, Sickle.' Pitch had risen, unhurried, to his feet. 'Do let me know when you'd like some release. I have rather the talent for it, and I do believe you have the need.'

Silas had held his breath long after Pitch left. And sleep, when it came again at last, was fraught with the most unsettling dream. His dream self had partaken in the most unspeakable acts with the man, opening himself wide to the daemon's every whim. On waking, horrified and abashed, Silas had decided then and there that he must find a bedfellow before too long – a woman, for he preferred them, did he not? – so as not to be so vulnerable to Pitch's nefarious, daemonic manipulations.

A divot in the road sent him stumbling, wrenching Silas free of the troublesome memory of the dream. The odour of packed earth was sublime upon the air. He stepped off the main road and moved to follow a narrower beaten path that meandered past a ramshackle cottage and on into a thicket. He knew not where the certainty came from, but he was sure that the grounds he sought lay directly south, and this footpath would take him there far quicker than the road. He passed along the back of several properties, larger detached houses built on open land with vegetable gardens and some livestock. A goat's bell chimed lazily at its neck as the animal worked upon the grass, a full udder heavy beneath its belly. It stopped for a moment to regard Silas, green strands hanging from its mouth.

'Good day to you.' Silas touched a finger to his forehead.

The goat lowered its head to the grass, continuing as though Silas did not exist at all.

Several strides later, the high rise of an imposing building with multiple pitched roofs appeared across the way, a jutting spire holding aloft a simple cross. A church, unless he was very much mistaken. Always the grandest of structures no matter a place's size. He quickened his step, brimming with a strange rumble of excitement. The lure of the soil of the dead was quite overwhelming, he would have broken into a run if not for the unevenness of the ground and the certainty of a turned ankle. A cautionary whisper reminded him of the last time he had set foot in a cemetery alone. He'd been attacked by insidious creatures, in need of rescue from his predicament by one who was arguably just as insidious. But surely Silas was not in danger here? Mr Ahari had said it was Holly Village's preternatural barriers that were responsible for luring in such beings, like moths to the flame. Lady Satine's farm, which might also hold such a lure, was miles away. Still, Silas mused, Mr Ahari had also said such an attack was virtually unheard of, and that the times were indeed strange. With a grunt of frustration, he stopped at the end of the pathway.

A wide dirt road stood between him and what he saw was without doubt the church. A grand dark-slated roof pitched its angles to the sky, and its bulk took up a space of land equal to at least three inns the size of The Three Tuns. Silas had intersected with the grounds exactly where he hoped he might, where the lay of the land was dotted with headstones.

The very sight of the cemetery brought on the oddest sense of contentment. Several magnificent oaks formed a barrier of sorts between the graves and the road, but there was no fencing to speak of. His entry would be unhindered. But Silas shuddered at the sight of the robust trees. They would forever hold such dismal memories. He squeezed his eyes closed, forcing back the image that came unbidden – a child's skin, denuded from its bones, caressing the breeze amongst the high boughs. Silas blinked into the sunshine once more. He set off across the road and stepped onto the hallowed ground. A great calm washed over him, the torment of Black Annis's deeds swept away. It was as though the sounds of the world quietened. Only the gentle rub of crickets disturbed the welcome silence. He inhaled deeply and then released the breath in a long, slow exhale. Black Annis's wounds had long since stopped bothering him, his ribs free to move, the scars on his belly so faint as to barely exist. He stood by a handsome gravestone topped with a weeping angel, her head buried in grief-stricken hands, the tinge of moss upon the stone's surface. All around him, similar works lay. And the bandalore did not stir. The trinket rested quietly in the depths of his pocket.

Souls were at rest here.

No one lingered, no one was lost. Stretching his arms skyward, Silas tilted his head to and fro, relieving the clench of muscles there. How settled he felt. At ease with his surroundings. He strode through the graveyard, hands clasped behind his back, admiring the markers of the dead as one might admire works of art in the National Gallery. How terribly odd to be imbued with such a consoling sense of place here, but he could not deny it. To be amongst the dead soothed him. Here was his release, not in the arms of a woman, or god forbid, a man as beautiful as one, but amongst the departed. At ease with those resting in eternal slumber. He had but one gripe: he could not read the engraved epitaphs. He would speak with Mr Ahari of this when he next shared the old man's company. It seemed a more than fair exchange: Silas would take on the teratisms, and the Order would teach him to read.

He leaned down to run his fingers along the grooves in a lopsided stone. A sudden movement drew his eye.

Silas gasped.

Bounding through the headstones, coming from the direction of the church, ran a huge scruffy black dog. An Irish wolfhound he decided, in somewhat of a fluster, as the creature picked up pace, all flying fur and slobbering tongue.

'Stay back!' Silas shouted, warding off the animal.

Should he run from such an animal? Or was it best to stand his ground? He could recall nothing of any experience. The dog moved rapidly towards him but did not utter a sound. No maddened barking that might note it as being in a rage. But then, perhaps rabid animals were rendered mute. Was it rabid? He saw no white foam at its mouth. Silas hurried in behind a nearby headstone, one that reached high as his chest, taking what shelter it could offer.

'I said stay back,' he repeated.

'Is everything all right there, sir?' A middle-aged man had appeared as though out of nowhere. He wore all black, with a brimmed hat to match. The dog bounded by him, not wavering from its path set for Silas.

'Is that your hound?' Silas clutched the curved stone.

'My hound?' The puzzlement in his reply was clear.

The dog drew ever closer.

'Yes, blast it. Right there.'

The shaggy creature leaped, hurtling over the very headstone Silas sought paltry protection behind.

'No!' He raised his hands to shield himself. The mass of fur crashed into him, and Silas was sent tumbling backwards. But it was not a gnashing of teeth that found him, or the strike of claws. Instead, the dog whimpered in snippets of excited delight, and a lolling tongue slid across its face before a wet snout burrowed into the curve of Silas's neck.

CHAPTER 4

'Is everything quite alright there, dear boy?' The man asked, unhelpfully.

Silas stared up at the dog that stood over him, a bulk of long matted fur and curiously gentle wide brown eyes. Of course everything was not alright. Why did this confounded man offer no assistance, for surely this creature belonged to him?

'Get off, get off, I say.' Silas shoved his hands against the damp black nose thrust at him. Oddly, for such an unkempt creature, there was no foul smell to match it. Swinging its narrow tail madly, the dog moved back, affording Silas view of the man once more.

'I beg your pardon?' His questioner was a priest, the white collar at his neck marking his faith. The man's face was squeezed with a concerned frown, his ginger-dusted beard cradling pursed lips. 'Have you partaken of the devil's liquor, my son?' He offered a hand to assist Silas to his feet. An offering Silas did not accept.

'No. At least, no more than is reasonable.' He rocked onto his knees, eyeing the hound at his side. The moment he set eyes on the creature, its tail wagged so rapidly that it was a black blur. 'You do not see that?' He pointed to what appeared most obvious: the large panting dog at his side.

Knitting his bushy eyebrows, the priest stared earnestly at the spot. 'Archibald Spencer's grave? Did you know the man?'

'No – that is...' Silas halted his protest, his eyes tracing the ground at the dog's feet. Not a hint of shadow.

He'd been quite a fool. The ghost of a hound stood before him, and he had carried on like a lunatic. The priest was liable to have him trundled off to the nearest facility. Silas glanced at the gravestone. 'Yes...Archibald...was a family friend...I'm sorry...this is my first visit to his resting place and I have acted rather uncouthly. The emotion has done me in.'

'I understand.' The priest gave him a solemn nod. 'We all react very differently to grief. And he was so terribly young, wasn't he?'

Maybe. Silas couldn't read the headstone to know.

'Oh yes, awfully young.' Silas frowned at the long-settled mound of dirt where autumn leaves had gathered. He himself was not an old man. The wild-haired chap he'd seen in the mirror could not be more than thirty, if that. Did anyone mourn his youthful demise? 'I do apologise again for my untoward behaviour. I'm not sure what came over me.'

The dog tilted its head side to side, its gaze shifting between Silas and the priest as though following the conversation.

'Think nothing of it, my dear boy. The grass here grows on salty tears I'm afraid. But the greatest honour I believe we can do the dead is remember them, as our Lord God remembers us. Grieve your friend however you see fit, but do not forget him.'

A twinge of melancholy struck Silas. He was all but forgotten. Not even a name upon his grave.

There was nothing to be seen upon your marker, I'm afraid. No birth, no death, certainly no names. So I gave you two I hope you shall enjoy. Silas comes from the Latin for woods or forest, and seeing as you are large as a tree I thought it most suitable. Mercer is simply because I once had a barber with the name who was a master at the close shave.

This was what Mr Ahari had told him. Which was as close to nothing as it could be. What sort of man died so lonely a death?

He stood up, flicking at grass that clung to his coat.

'Goodness,' the priest exclaimed, 'you're quite the grown lad, aren't you?'

On every occasion that question was uttered, Silas grew increasingly perplexed as to how to answer. For was it not obvious he was a man of grand height and broad shoulders? When the awkward pause stretched, the priest rubbed his hands together. 'You have much upon your mind, I would wager. I see the weight of it upon your face. Perhaps some time in the Lord's house might soothe you?'

'Thank you, but I must decline.' What might happen should a man like himself, barely a man indeed, step foot inside a church? Silas harboured no desire to find out. 'But I wonder if I might linger here? Spend some time walking with my thoughts?'

'Of course, you are most welcome, take all the time you need.' The priest gestured back towards the church. 'I must head out now to attend one of my parishioners with the last rites I'm afraid. George and I are most unfortunately kept busy by the ills and misfortunes of the parish.'

Silas glanced around, seeking out the priest's companion. So far as he could see, it was just he, the priest, and the salivating hound that now sat on its haunches.

'Oh, George is my gravedigger,' the priest said, noticing Silas's wandering gaze. 'Hardworking lad, though I wish he did not need to be. Still, with all life there is death, I'm afraid.'

'Indeed,' Silas said.

The priest clasped his hands behind his back and nodded. 'I shall leave you to your prayers and considerations. The church is always open, should you change your mind about a visit.'

'Thank you, you've been most kind.'

He stood watching until the priest was almost returned to the church. When the black-clothed man stepped into a side entrance, out of view, Silas at last turned his attentions to the dog. The animal began to whimper and dance upon its feet under his gaze. The hound barked, and Silas jumped. The animal dropped its shoulders low to the ground, its back end still high in the air and its tail ever feverish in its to-and-froing. Again it barked. Squeaky cries of high-pitched excitement that stirred the waft of damp earth ever richer upon the air. He stared at it in some confusion. Partly because he had no idea what the peculiar display might mean, but mostly because he was at a loss as to what to do now. Should he use the bandalore upon the soul? Was an animal capable of being a lost soul to begin with?

'Quiet now.' He glanced back at the church, fully expecting to see the priest marching back towards them. But the graveyard was empty. The headstones silent witnesses.

The shaggy creature loped around him in a ludicrous display, diving at the ground with its front paws, while it continued to hold its backside skyward. Barking all the while. The hound was as solid and real to life as Black Annis had appeared, though unlike that monster, this beast's presence made no visible impact upon the world around it. The dog's substantial claws made no mark upon the cut grass.

'Do sit, be quiet.'

The hound paid him no mind at all, continuing its energetic display, barking in snaps of hoarse sound. All at once it danced away from him, whirling in a circle before barking once again. The animal repeated the motion, moving yet further away. This time the barking faded into a whimper. And if Silas was not much mistaken, it was a sound knitted with frustration. The animal turned its head to peer at something over its shoulder, and then barked once again.

He frowned. 'What is it?' He was acting every bit the lunatic the priest might suppose, speaking to an animal as though he expected an answer. But then, these were strange times. 'Do you wish me to follow?'

Another round of barking, whirling, padding, and manic tail wagging ensued. Quite astonishingly, Silas had indeed received a reply. He should follow. Giving the bandalore a consoling pat where it lay in his pocket, he did as he was bid.

The dog led him through the main section of the cemetery, the area in full view of the church's impressive double oak doors. There was a moment when Silas feared he was being led right up to those doors, but then the hound shifted right, past a splendid mausoleum whose brass plaque was green and unreadable with age, and on towards a low stone wall where a gateless gap would allow passage. The dog made its way through, its long needling tail sweeping low to the ground but not disturbing any of the leaves lying there. A sensible voice told Silas perhaps he should return to Sybilla at the inn and advise her of this odd encounter, but the richness of the graveyard's soil lured him on as readily as roast duck fresh from the oven. Besides, the dog had done him no harm, aside from dribbling upon his coat, and the graveyard was Silas's domain.

Beyond the wall were yet more headstones, stretching on for a considerable distance across a flat expanse of land. A handful of rowan trees grew along the wall, forming a leafy barrier between this section of the cemetery and the area closer to the church. An interesting choice for a church garden, Silas mused. Rowan trees, with their red berries, were said to keep witches and evil at bay.

The hound kept watch on Silas's progress with regular backward glances as it padded through the headstones with brisk certainty. Silas noted several fresh mounds of dirt, some still strewn with floral tributes. New additions to the cemetery's membership. But his fingers did not tingle, nor the bandalore stir. Izanami's work had been done most completely. The goddess of death's ankou was not required, here at least.

Hurrying along, he tried to outpace his own thoughts, which spread like fine ivy into areas of his mind he did not wish to touch upon. Silas was not ready to think too deeply on the goddess he served, nor the fate that might await him in one year's time when his servitude was done. It was taxing enough to endure a day at a time.

He coughed against the grittiness of the air, the perfume of soil and rot growing altogether more potent. And for the first time, unpleasant. Up ahead, the land swelled into a rise that concealed what lay beyond, and it was towards this knoll that the hound bounded. The smattering of graves were not so carefully tended here, nor lined so tightly in a row. The layout was far more haphazard, the tilt of the stones more pronounced now that the church rested beyond sight.

Silas negotiated a fallen marker, its chiselled words all but rubbed clear by years of exposure to the elements. A sharp snatch of muscle in his chest gave him pause. He pressed a hand to his coat front. The spasm eased, and then returned once more, its tempo strangely regular. One that matched all too perfectly with a new sound upon the air. The steady, dull thump of a shovel digging into the earth.

He winced, pressing his fingers into his chest. The clench of muscle was uncomfortable rather than unbearable, but it was the oddness of it that concerned him. He'd thought himself safe from the perils of reanimation that Mr Ahari had mentioned, leakages and such. Had he been too quick to think so?

The black dog lifted its long, hairy nose and bayed at the blue sky. The forlorn howl distracted him from his own discomfort. The animal pushed to all fours and galloped up the slope of the mound. Silas followed quickly after, scrambling up the short rise, with the steady tempo of the digging continuing, and the pangs against his ribcage thundering ever harder. He reached the top of the mound in just a few forceful strides and found himself staring down upon a distressing sight. A disturbed grave, the soil all but cleared from around a dark wooden casket, a headstone lying flat upon the ground. Cold, hard fury flickered to life within Silas's gut. The gravedigger, George he presumed, was awash with sweat. It clung to the straw-like lengths of his hair and darkened the armpits of his shirt. He was too busy at his task to notice Silas at all, heaving a shovelful of soil onto the pile beside him and readying for another.

His rage boiling over, Silas thrust his hand into his pocket. The bandalore was ready for him, the string slipping around his finger instantly. He raced down the mound. In once graceful arch of his arm, Silas gathered momentum and hurled the bandalore through the air.

'You will stop,' he roared.

The wooden discs, still retaining the mahogany stain of the Black Annis encounter, flashed past George, brushing the man's shoulder. Silas drew back his hand, thinking his aim had been poor. But the bandalore pulled against him, moving in a wide arc around the back of the gravedigger's head, before racing forward once more, and wrapping the string about the man's neck. The bandalore flew in a circle again, sending another coil around the panicking chap's throat. George collapsed onto his knees, releasing a strangled, startled cry, clawing at the string fastened around his neck.

'Help me,' George gasped, spittle bubbling on his lips.

Silas had slackened his hold the moment the bandalore wove its second coil, but the grip of the string about the gravedigger's neck held tight. With his burst of anger winnowing fast, Silas dashed to the man's side. He attempted to slip his fingers in behind the string, but it was sunk deep into the man's skin.

'Stand still, I'll free you.' Silas grabbed the bandalore, trying to unravel the noose it had made, but it were as though the string had become one with flesh. Whichever way he pulled at the discs, he met the tug of resistance.

George fell into a panic. 'Can't breathe...' The man's lips were a disquieting shade of bruised blue. A terrible gurgle came from him.

Silas dropped to his knees, grunting with the effort of trying to release the bandalore from its stranglehold. His fright rose with that of the stricken man. The bandalore was rebelling against his wishes.

'Enough, enough,' Silas hissed under his breath. 'Stop it, damn you.' His heart raced, his own throat tight with panic. How was this possible? Mr Ahari had told him the bandalore was a weapon against the dead, not the living. But he'd very soon count this man amongst those needing burial if the bandalore did not relent. George's eyes rolled back in his head, his body jerking as he madly sought breath.

'Oh god!' Silas cried. 'Stop, damn you. This is not what I want. Release him.' The cold grip of terror had him firmly in its hold, his own breathing haggard and shallow.

A dark shadow pushed past him, and a great snout snatched the bandalore from his grasp. The hound tossed its head, the wooden discs held fast between its canines. The animal shook its head back and forth, foam flecking from its thick black lips. All at once the string slackened. Silas clawed at it, dragging it from George's neck. It came away so easily now, as though the incident had been imagined, but the nasty red line upon George's throat was clear evidence this was not the case. The hound dropped the drool-covered bandalore at Silas's side.

George collapsed onto all fours, sucking in enormous gulps of air. Before long the man regained enough of his senses to fling a punch at Silas.

'Get the hell away from me, devil,' he croaked.

'I'm sorry...' Silas gathered the sodden bandalore with shaking hands.

George shrank away. 'No! Don't be striking me down again. I'll send word I'm done with this. The resurrection men can find their corpses elsewhere.'

'You must understand, I did not intend to hurt you.' Silas wound the rebellious string quickly and tucked the wayward trinket into the dark folds of his coat.

'Intentions or not, you bloody did.' He touched at his throat, wincing. 'That black witch sent you, didn't she? That's where you're from, ain't ya? I've heard tell she's keeping company with a giant of a man, and a right dandy. Tell her she can keep her devils off me, I'm done with grave robbing.'

Silas stared at the ugly welt left upon George's skin. The horror of it still roiled within him. He'd nearly killed the man. 'She did not...' He hesitated. What harm would there be in allowing him to think Sybilla wished a stop to this harvesting of the dead, if it meant it would be stopped once and for all? 'If she should learn of this happening again in this parish, you can rest assured I will be told.' He paused. 'And my wrath shall bear down on you once more.'

Fanciful words, nothing more, but they had the desired effect. Poor George paled and looked set to burst into tears. His nod was most unsteady.

'Who put you up to this?' Silas asked. 'Why do they seek these bodies?'

George shrugged bony shoulders. 'Buggered if I know why. I got word of it through another digger from up Shrewsbury way. He'd met a tosher in the Old Bell pub who was asking for corpses and paying damned well for it. Safe to wager it isn't the tosher who is handing out the coin, you don't make your fortune wading about in the sewers, but that's where you could start if you are that bothered. I'll let you know though, you're going to take some good coin out of needy hands if you cut it off.' He flicked an anxious glance at Silas. 'I means to say, I care mostly about keeping my family fed, that's all.'

'The church doesn't compensate you well enough?'

The gravedigger scoffed. 'How can a man who has never dipped his wick know what it takes to keep three babes and a wife? Father Taylor does well enough, 'spose, but what's being offered up in Shrewsbury would have seen my family through winter with full bellies and warm beds.' His eyes were still widened with panic and now he'd started talking he couldn't seem to stop. 'The tosher's master, whoever he is, is paying well 'cause they be wanting a specific kind of corpse, see. Can't have been

26

struck by disease or bloody accident. They need a young body, intact, and can't have been dead more than two months. Fresh buried gets you the highest fee. Whoever it is, they want clean bodies, like. This youngun here, he was only seventeen. Farmer Bennett's boy. Fell into a swollen river not three months ago and drowned. Not a mark on 'im. I knew 'e wasn't fresh enough but I was gonna give it a go. Winter's not far off you see...'

'I see.' Silas stared at the coffin at his feet, light-headed. Not least of all because he stood over a victim of drowning, the cause of his own demise. It struck Silas that he had no idea how long he'd been buried before Mr Ahari pulled him from the earth.

'I will say nothing of this to your priest,' he said, 'and I'll speak with Sybilla about sending some coin your way for your family if you will swear to me this is the end of it.'

Colour at last returned to George's sullen cheeks. 'I promise you, sir, you have my word on it. But you'll send the black...Miss Sybilla, fairly broke if you think you can pay off all the diggers who are heeding the call.'

'How many bodies are being sought?'

'As many as we can bring.'

Bloody hell, he had stepped into an appalling situation. Silas could only hope that Sybilla would be as reviled by it as he was. 'I'll leave you to your work then.' He pointed to his own neck. 'Again, I do apologise for that. You might wish to clean that before long –'

'The wife will tend to it right enough.' George picked up the shovel. 'I'll keep to my end of this deal so long as you keep to yours.'

'Of course. I'll be seeing Sybilla shortly and she is a reasonable woman. You will have your money. I promise.'

George considered him and seemed to decide he believed what he was told. 'Right then, goodbye, Mr...'

'Mercer.'

'Mr Mercer.'

'Goodbye, Mr...?'

'Walker.'

'Mr Walker.'

Silas turned away from the uncomfortable farewells. The hound jumped to its feet, ears pricked and tail mad with movement, and Silas decided to level one last question at the gravedigger. 'Have you ever noticed a large black dog on these grounds?'

George finished dumping another shovel load before he ran his hand over his dirt-flecked ginger beard. 'Black dog?'

'Large animal.' Silas gave the hound a furtive glance. 'Spindly tail, long fur, a hunting hound I believe.'

'Who was with it? Might know the owner.'

'No one. It appears...appeared to be quite alone.'

George regarded him for a long moment. 'Are you seeing it now, witch's man?'

With a frustrated sigh, Silas waved off the question. 'Never mind.' He walked away, but the gravedigger was not done.

'I reckon a man like you'd be seeing the church grim.'

Silas turned back despite himself. 'The what?'

George flicked a thumb back towards the church. 'When a place like this is built, a poor bastard dog gets buried alive under a cornerstone so its spirit can guard the place. I've heard Father Taylor say it was a wolfhound. There's even a carving of it in the altar somewhere. Don't like dogs meself, so I ain't seen hide nor hair of it. But you, Mr Mercer, seem to be the sort of man it would show itself to.'

The hound whimpered, wide eyes upon Silas.

'Thank you, Mr Walker. A good day to you.'

Silas returned to his departure, leaving George to the grave. The sound of digging grew distant, the whole distasteful affair fading with it. He spotted a rickety wooden gate across the way that would allow him to escape the cemetery entirely. He reached it in a handful of strides. The hound followed all the way, but now dropped to the ground, settling itself as though curling up before a fire.

'That's it then?' Silas asked. 'You will go no further?'

The hound's tail wagged but its snout remained resting on its paws.

'Very well.' Silas nodded. 'And thank you. You were most helpful.'

The dog's brown eyes closed, and it released a contented snort.

Silas stepped through the gate, leaving behind the ripe smell of the soil. Despite the misadventure, it still pained him to remove himself from the calm of the graveyard.

He stood, gathering his bearings. The wind carried the distant clamour of raised voices, and a tune. Silas frowned, trying to catch the notes. He made his way further along the lane, spying a richly painted red barn which stood sentinel in front of a bare field. The raucous sounds grew louder. More defined. A crowd of some kind, he would wager, with someone among them finding time to belt out a most unfortunate ill-tuned melody.

'Oh dear,' Silas sighed.

It seemed he had found the daemon.

CHAPTER 5

S ilas hunched his shoulders, trying to make himself small enough not
to be seen over the crude rock wall that ran along the right-hand
side of the lane. He arrived at the wide entrance of the barn just as the
excruciating singing stopped abruptly, and the jeers and shouts grew
louder. The crowd, he heard to his horror, were baying for blood.

'Fuck 'im over!'

'Another kick!'

Silas broke into a brisk walk, crossing the exposed area between road
and building and, with an exhale of relief, positioned himself in behind
an enormous pile of chopped wood which rested against the barn wall.
The pile was high enough that he did not need to crouch nor bend to
keep himself hidden. A cheer went up, and Silas shrank away from the
timber palings that separated him from the mob. Christ, what had Pitch
gotten himself into here?

'Now that's a right batty-fang.' Someone laughed cruelly.

'Bastard is done.'

'If it ain't over, I'm a hairy whore,' another bellowed.

Snarls and unlikable laughter wound about one another, as though
beasts and man mixed within the confines of the barn. That interminable
singing, as pleasurable as nails being dragged upon a plate of tin, soared
overhead once more. If Silas had harboured any doubt as to who was
amongst the rowdy bunch, it evaporated now.

'For fuck's sake, close his bloody sauce-box for good, Simpson,' came the call.

'Break his jaw and be done with it. I want my fucking lunch.'

Silas found himself at a brawl it seemed. Or a boxing match. One in the same. And certainly explained the bruised knuckles Pitch so often bore.

'Damned lunatic needs to stay down.'

'Your wife doesn't mine 'im staying down on her. Saw Flora all kinds of tickled pink yesterday with the dandy, behind the grocers.'

'Bullshit, that fucker ain't looking for pussy. Your brother Ned reckons he's a mandrake. Likes it hard up the arse and Ned would know, wouldn't 'e?'

A snorted laugh was cut short by the unmistakable thud of fist against face. A second later something heavy slammed against the wood not two steps from where Silas huddled. He stumbled away, his heartbeat a mad hare beneath his ribs. Bloody hell, stepping into this den of ruffians seemed an unwise decision. Besides, Tobias Astaroth was hardly going to need his assistance. Silas straightened his coat. He should be on his way and leave the daemon to his strange amusements.

The insult-borne squabble on the other side of the palings was short-lived. Before Silas could step away the murmur of the crowd died down well enough that the slap of flesh against flesh was audible. Great thuds of fist against bone. Grunts of stifled pain followed before the crowd erupted once more. Cursing under his breath, Silas turned back to the wall, searching for a gap generous enough that he might see what was truly going on within. A short investigation revealed a gnarl in the wood perfect for an inquisitive eye, but with it so low on the wall, Silas was forced to kneel. He pressed his forehead to the wood, peering through the opening. Light filtered through slats in the barn roof, highlighting the haze of dust in the air, and spotlighting a makeshift arena constructed at the centre of the barn.

He could not make the ring out entirely due to the number of men around it but the sections he could discern were crude in build. A haphazard assembly of items: some barrels to form a barrier here, a wheelbarrow to block a gap there, lengths of fencing stacked in between. The men, for it seemed to be males entirely, bunched around the perimeter. Two portly fellows blocked Silas's direct view of the small arena, and each clutched strips of paper in their hands, waving them about in their enthusiasm. The burliest of the two sucked on a cigarette. He stepped aside to cast the butt onto the straw-covered ground, giving Silas his first clear view of the fight. And what an unpleasant sight it was.

His assumption that Pitch was present was entirely correct. At least, Silas was all but certain it was Pitch beneath the coating of blood covering his fine-boned face. His wavy hair was plastered against his skull, richly drenched there too by blood. Trickles of crimson ran onto his bare shoulders and chest. The man was stripped to the waist, his corduroy trousers tattered and torn, his right eye so swollen that the glint of fixating green was all but hidden entirely. Pitch spat at the ground and gave his opponent a bloodied grin. He was on his feet but swayed dangerously as he raised his fists.

'Christ.' His opponent danced lightly on his feet, a giant barrel-chested man with a rumbling voice of thunder. 'You want more, you bloody maniac?'

He was easily Silas's height, but far broader of shoulder and chest. For the very first time, Silas found himself not the most imposing man in the vicinity. This brute could be none else but a fighter, and a professional one at that, with arms to rival a tree trunk and barely a neck to note beneath his square jaw. His brow was a jutting ridge of bone over his eyes that gave him a most unpleasant appearance. 'You can take a beatin', I'll give you that.'

Pitch gave him a desperately unsteady bow, his head wobbling upon his shoulders as though it were at risk of coming away entirely. He was delicate as a china doll compared to his competitor.

'And you, my fine sir, can deliver,' Pitch slurred. 'I'll not deny *you* that, but there is little wonder your mother abandoned you, for you're an ugly fucking bastard.'

The brute coughed, or laughed, Silas could not tell. 'You like to bleed, don't ya, you fucking Mary. Didn't think you'd show your face again after your last beatin'.'

'It's a dull town.'

There were various shouts from the crowd, calls to 'Finish the prick off, his number's up,' and 'Send 'im back to the black witch with a crack in his skull. See her work her foul magic on that.'

Pitch wiped his mouth upon his arm, smudging the blood running from his nose more horrifically across his face and forearm. He held the fighter's stance too, though with far less prowess, staggering as he performed the circle. The enormous tattoo upon his back, the strange pitchfork design, flashed momentarily into Silas's view, the undulation of muscles there glistening beneath a layer of sweat. Pitch's trousers hung low against his hip bones, as though the merest tug would see them tumble. He swayed back to face the fighter, taking a step in towards him so they were less than an arm's length apart. His all too familiar grin rose, its hint of wickedness stretching his Cupid's bow lips.

'I think you are holding back,' he said in an overly-loud whisper. 'You can't fuck me again if I am entirely broken, isn't that right?'

The fighter ceased his dance, planting his feet and tensing his fists. 'Shut your bloody mouth,' he growled. 'He's talking his bullshit!' he shouted at his audience. 'You've 'eard him do it before.'

Pitch raised his hands in the air. 'He didn't mind me opening my bloody mouth a night ago. Just as soon as our last fight was done and you good gentlemen had left us, he was upon me.' There were snickers amongst the crowd. The fighter's face darkened. 'He didn't even give me a chance to clean up. I had a cock up my ass before I could blink. Took me on the floor, right where you are there, fine sir.' Pitch lifted his arm to indicate exactly where the sordid deed had taken place.

The fighter bawled up a fist, drew back his solid arm, and pummelled it straight into Pitch's gut. The daemon cried out, laughter tangling with pain, and slumped to his knees. But the fighter was not done with him. Another fist flew, this time striking Pitch under his chin. Silas winced at the crack that came. Pitch dropped onto his back and was stolen from Silas's view. The crowd roared back to life, fairly manic with the lust for the fight. The heavy-browed thug knelt on one knee and drove strike after strike into the supine man beneath him. The crowd closed in around the brutal assault, and Silas lost his view of it altogether. Above the shouts and cries for more blood, more injury, came the most unsettling sound of laughter, light and carefree. Easily mistaken for a woman's mirth if Silas had not recognised the sound so well. Pitch was laughing, as he was being beaten quite to pieces.

Silas pressed his nails into the wood. The daemon could easily overpower his adversary. Silas had witnessed the raw animalistic way he fought when the harpies attacked, so why on Earth did Pitch do nothing here? He goaded the fighter to strike him, but put up no fight of his own when the punch was thrown.

A muscle twinged in Silas's calf. With a grimace he rose, shaking the offending leg to seek reprieve. Upright as he was, he caught sight of a man rushing in from the laneway, running at a brisk pace towards the barn doors. Silas shifted down behind his wooden shield. But if the runner had caught sight of him, he showed no interest. Ignoring the protest of angry leg muscles, Silas dropped to peer through the hole once more. A shout rose over the hubbub of the crowd, all still intent on the fighter who had not yet relaxed his attack on Pitch. The call rose again, and this time Silas, along with all the men within, heard it loud and clear.

'Pigs are comin'.' The messenger was not a man but a mere boy. Freckle-faced, and red cheeked from his exertions. 'Close it down. You've been ratted.'

A few swore hard and fast at the intrusion to their amusements, and several others waved their tiny shreds of paper at a bespectacled man, who waved them off as he hurried towards the entrance.

'Come see me at the King's Head this evening,' he called over his shoulder. 'No time for all this now.'

'The witch's man threw the bloody fight, the cunt is half-mad,' said another man with deep-set eyes and rubbery lips. 'And if Simpson doesn't kill him, I bloody will.'

The fighter, Simpson, was in the process of being pulled off Pitch. No easy task for those who tried to stay his fists, one of the men copping a sharp rap across the nose as he shouted at the fighter to break it off. Silas could only make out Pitch's legs, and they were far too still upon the straw.

'Blast it, what am I to do?' Silas peered out from the woodpile. There was no sign yet of the authorities. Only the departing men were evident, some headed out across the field, others sauntering up the road in little rush or bother. He supposed that was sensible enough. They could hardly be arrested for walking the laneway. Simpson strode past the woodpile with a companion, and Silas shifted back into hiding. The fighter tugged on a striped shirt, while the other man, a slim but muscular fellow with a shock of light brown curls, fussed at him with a rag, trying to wipe clear the blood upon Simpson's cheeks. They muttered in low tones as they passed by, oblivious to Silas's presence.

'Is he still alive?' said the curly-haired man. 'Christ, Simpson, this wasn't one of your bloody London fights. These folk don't need a dead man to make them happy.'

'That tosser asked for it. That fucking mouth of his. Should have ripped it clean off.' Simpson snatched the cloth from his companion and rubbed at his knuckles. 'You know it was all tripe, don't ya? I didn't do a bloody thing with 'im.'

'Of course.' The man touched at the broader man's back. 'I know you wouldn't do that to me. And he damned well knew it too. He played you Simpson, like he's done the rest. The man is a snake all right. And a bloody strange one at that. Stirring you up so you'll lay the punches in harder.'

They moved beyond Silas's hearing, heading across the field which lay beyond the barn, perhaps deciding the fighter's bloodied state warranted a more clandestine escape. The entire crowd had dispersed with an efficiency that suggested this meeting was not the first of its kind. But not a one of the attendees had deemed it necessary or proper to attend to Pitch, who had not moved from where he lay.

In the distance, ever so faintly, Silas heard the fast clip of hooves along the laneway.

'Sod it.' He hurried out from behind his makeshift fortress and raced to the open barn doors. It surely wouldn't do to have Pitch arrested. Sybilla faced enough opposition in the town as it was, and what if the summons finally came for Silas to meet the next teratism? What point in having a guardian if he was behind bars? Silas strode into the barn, where the brightness of the day was dulled. The stench of sweat and tang of blood were rife. Up in the rafters a dove cooed, its gentle sound in great contrast to the brutality it had just witnessed. The dust was still settling, and Silas coughed against the irritation. He made his way past an overturned barrow that had been pushed aside in the evacuation and stepped into the makeshift ring. The daemon lay with arms splayed above his head. Silas could barely make out the man's face for the blood that formed a grisly mask upon it. His right eyelid was a dark and ugly mound, completely sealed shut, and the crookedness of his nose spoke of a break. Pitch's lips, usually such ripe full things, were slashed and swollen. Great welts made a patchwork on his torso, and storm-cloud bruises marked his breast. He lay deathly still. Silas could make out no rise of his chest. With the amount of hay that clung to him, stuck fast in his blood, Pitch might have passed for a terrible scarecrow.

'Pitch?' Silas knelt beside him. 'Do you hear me?'

A bubble of blood formed at Pitch's lips. Perhaps the man breathed yet. Silas lowered his ear closer, so he might hear.

'You there, stop!'

Silas sat up with a start. The clatter of horses' hooves rang out.

'I'm not blind,' a gruff voice scoffed. 'I see you hiding beyond the wall there.'

The cry came from outside the barn, and was not intended for him at all. A small relief, but the authoritarian voice was much too close for any real comfort. There was little doubt an officer of the law was nearby, and Silas feared his time for unnoticed escape had likely come and gone.

'Head into the barn, Stevens, check if anyone is stupid enough to hang about. I'll deal with this fellow.'

'As you say, sir, Constable Lewis,' came a shakier reply.

The sharp clip of a trotting horse sounded, entering the courtyard in front of the barn. The rider would be upon them in moments.

Silas thrust his arms beneath Pitch, and uttered a silent prayer the man would not wake in a pain-fuelled rage.

CHAPTER 6

Pitch did not stir, and cold pricks of dread pressed at Silas. The daemon had spoken of fighting upon the fields of hell itself, how could it be that a ruffian might fell him? Silas searched keenly for a place to hide them both. He found it in the shape of an overturned hay wagon at the very back of the barn. Three of its four wheels had been removed, indicating that perhaps repairs were underway. Whatever the case it was the only thing large enough in sight to conceal them. Silas pinned his hopes on the police deciding no one would be truly foolish enough to remain here and would not search the barn with any real vigour. He pressed Pitch against him and heaved himself to his feet. He did so with too much gusto, expecting a heavier burden, forgetting how subtle the daemon's weight was when last he'd carried him, in the Forest of Dean. Silas rocked back on his heels, in danger of overbalancing. Steadying himself, he hurried out of the arena, greatly regretting his failure to close the barn doors on his own arrival.

Silas hurried in behind the wagon. The equipment had been resting in this place for some time and cobwebs were thick about it, clinging to his coat as he set about manoeuvring both himself and his passenger to the ground without making a sound. A rich, musty smell clung to a nest of hay bales set around the end of the wagon. If Silas could just shift a little to the right, they would afford him extra protection from prying eyes. He was near to a squat, and only one step short of his ideal resting place, when his heel clipped something beneath the hay. He gasped, and

Pitch's legs slipped from his hold. There was a chaotic moment where Silas did not know whose limbs were whose as the floorboards rushed up to meet them. When all was said and done, he lay sprawled with Pitch atop him, the daemon on his back. His bloodied, sweat-drenched hair was unpleasant against Silas's chin. He raised his hand to Pitch's chest, searching for sign of a breath taken. His fingers met the firmness of muscle on smooth skin. The daemon was slight, but his body was hard with muscle, as though he were carved from marble. The distant thump of a heartbeat made itself known against Silas's palm, and a wave of relief swept him.

'Anyone about? I'll ask you to step forward.' There came the creak of leather and the faint grunt of a rider as he dismounted. Silas thought he detected the tremble of uncertainty in the young man's directive.

Footsteps sounded their way into the barn. Silas clutched tighter to the battered, half-naked man who lay on him. The dove cooed and the dust toyed with Silas's nose.

'I'll say it again – anyone about in here?' The officer held his silence only a moment before he muttered, 'Not bloody likely. Waste of bloody time.'

Silas breathed into Pitch's hair.

The clatter of wood came then, loud enough to stir the dove from its perch. Silas suspected the young man had just vented his frustrations on a section of the arena, none too pleased with his lot.

'Let them bloody kill each other if they want,' the officer grumbled. 'I've got better damn things to do.'

'Find anything, Stevens?' The constable had returned.

'Blood everywhere, sir. There was a match for sure, just as Tindle said. But they're all long gone.'

Barely had Silas dared imagine they might be safe and Pitch stirred in his arms, uttering a weakened moan. Silas slapped his hand to the man's blood-slippery mouth.

'Hush,' he breathed against Pitch's ear. 'Do not make a sound.' He adjusted his hold around Pitch's middle, preempting any attempt to sit up. Pitch fell, most thankfully, silent. Though if it was because he'd once again fallen unconscious, Silas could not say.

'Third one this week we've missed.' The constable sniffed. 'I don't like it, don't like it one bit.'

'We'll catch them eventually, sir. You always do.' The praise held a note of fatigue. 'Besides, if they're holding that many matches at the moment, their luck's got to run out sometime.'

'No thanks to that bloody woman and the company she keeps.'

'Sybilla? You think she's got that big bloke bringing in some cash for her in the fights? I've not seen him at all before today.'

'No, not him, though she might have plans for him at some point. Tindle says it's the other one that's been causing a stir. The dandy.'

The dandy shifted in Silas's arms once more. This time with more vigour, his sigh a thing of pleasure rather than discontent, as though he were waking from a pleasant dream.

'Pitch, do not move.' Silas dared not press his hand any tighter against Pitch's face for fear of exacerbating his injuries. 'Stay still.'

Pitch suddenly raised his arm over his head to find Silas's face, cupping a hand to his cheek.

'Morning,' he mumbled.

'Quiet,' Silas hissed.

Pitch wriggled against him. Swaying his body in such a way that his backside brushed hard against Silas's crotch.

'Relax, Raph,' the daemon said sleepily. 'You're tense.'

Abandoning his concerns about Pitch's damaged face Silas clamped his hand hard across the daemon's mouth. But the gagging only seemed to encourage him. Pitch arched his back, pressing his shoulders hard into Silas's chest, intimate whimpers escaping him. Wherever the man believed himself to be, and whomever with, it was not here on the dirty floor of an old barn with Silas.

'Pitch, I beg you.'

Pitch tossed his head, smacking his crown against Silas's chin. The impact was sudden and painful, and Silas's hand fell from Pitch's mouth. With Pitch's body slippery with sweat and blood, Silas struggled to keep his grip upon the man. A task made no easier by Pitch's sudden desire to roll over. Their clumsy struggle saw Pitch slide off Silas entirely and land against the hay bales. Luck was not with them that day, for whatever rested on the other side of the bales now fell. The clanging of metal suggested milking pales. Many, many milking pales. Pitch, facedown in the straw, his trousers dragged so low that the crack of his buttocks showed, burst out laughing.

'Who's there?' the officer shouted. 'Present yourselves.'

'Oh god.' Silas searched hopelessly for a way out, a weakness in the timber sidings that might afford an escape. But even if he found one, there was no time to gather up the man at his side.

Two faces peered over the hay bales. And eyeballs swept over Pitch before landing hard upon Silas.

'What the bloody hell do you think you're doing?' The constable was a sinewy man with a remarkable moustache that clung to the width of his cheeks. 'On your feet.'

The other man, clad in clothes more suited to the field than law enforcement, shoved at the hay, managing to remove one of the musty bales.

'Christ, what's going on here?'

'Public indecency I'd wager, Stevens. I've heard enough said about that one.' The officer's moustache wriggled with indignation, and he jabbed an accusatory finger at Pitch, who still laughed into the straw. The tattoo upon the daemon's back was half concealed by the blood and muck that clung to him, but the mess did not hide everything. The pale hint of his arse cheeks was far too evident, peeking from trousers dragged low. With so much of Pitch's clothing missing, he played them right into the constable's accusation. 'Celebratin' your win, is it? You'll go down for this. I won't have that vulgarity in my town.'

Silas shook his head. 'Sir, you are quite mistaken.' And a fool. What man in his right mind leapt to such accusations, considering the bloodied state of both Silas and Pitch? 'I object to –'

'Object all you like. Get on your feet.'

The younger man, with sun-marked skin and pale blue eyes, frowned down at Pitch. 'He doesn't look much of a fighter, sir. I've got a sister built bigger than him.'

'Tindle says he fights hard when the fancy takes him. A right bruiser.'

This Tindle was fast growing upon Silas's nerves. Whoever he was, he was a certified tattletale first and foremost.

'I said on your feet, boy.' The constable landed a kick to Pitch's ankle, which only served to elicit another round of gutsy laughter from him. 'What's so bloody funny?' The second blow was less gentile and met nearer to Pitch's knee.

'Don't.' Pitch kept his face to the ground, the wavy lengths of his stained brown hair hanging like a dirty shroud about his head.

'If you don't want more of that, get to your feet, you mug.' Undisguised disgust showed on the constable's face. 'I won't ask you again.'

Stevens appeared less disgusted and more irritated, gesturing at Silas to stand. 'Come on then, you too. Don't be causing no trouble.'

As he had no intention of any such thing, Silas levered himself to his feet, using the overturned wagon's axle as a crutch. The screech of long-rusted metal against weakened wood echoed unpleasantly. Stevens took a step back.

'Christ,' he said. 'You're a bloody giant. Sure you didn't get your hands dirty here too?'

'I can assure you, I am no fighter.'

Silas held up his hands, surrendering as added assurance, and edged slowly out from his failed hiding place. The young officer (if that's what he was, though Silas suspected he was likely just keen to earn some coin by assisting the lawman) moved with him, leaving the constable standing over Pitch.

'My dear Sickle tells no lie. He's quite useless, truth be told.' Pitch rolled onto his back, and the movement put a further strain upon his trousers, the V-shape of muscle between his hips visible almost down to its point. He was not quite exposed, but he had strayed well from decency. 'I'm rather capable though. I could demonstrate, if you like?'

Barely had Silas time to groan at Pitch's inflammatory words than the constable delivered his reply. It was as violent as it was rapid. He tugged his baton from a holster beneath his ill-fitting jacket.

'I said' – he struck Pitch once – 'get on' – he struck again – 'your feet.' He struck a third time.

Pitch uttered not a sound, merely draping his arms over his face as the blows rained upon him.

'That is too much,' Silas cried. 'He offers no resistance, can you not see?'

'Then he best get on his feet.' The panting officer stalled a moment in his vigours, pausing with baton raised.

Silas stood a good head and shoulders taller than the constable. He suspected it would not take much to overpower the man, and the farm boy officer fairly quaked in his boots. This could be done within a moment. But then what? He carried Pitch all the way back to the farm? For they could not risk returning for the horses if they wished to stay out of a cell.

'Sir, I suggest you best give him a chance to follow orders.' Silas attempted his most menacing growl.

The constable eyed him, taking in the massive contrast in their builds, and his baton lowered. 'He better be quick about it then.'

Silas feared that Pitch had fallen again into unconsciousness, lying still, the baton marks evident upon the sides of his ribs. But then he sighed, light and carefree, and slapped a bloody hand to the bale nearest him. With an exaggerated groan, he pulled himself unsteadily to his feet. He caught at his descending trousers, rescuing them all from a most unpleasant viewing, and tugged the corduroy back into place over the sharp curve of his hips. As he straightened, the air about him shuddered as though a candle's light framed him.

Silas clenched his fists. Unease burrowed low and deep inside him.

Pitch brushed the hair from his face. In the eye not nearly sealed shut by the swell of bruising, his iris gleamed like polished jade, and at its heart was the glow of flames.

'No, Pitch!' Silas cried.

But it was too late for the constable standing before the daemon.

The man lifted off his feet and shot into the air with a terrified scream.

'Constable Lewis!' Stevens staggered back, eyes locked skyward.

His superior streaked towards the roof, another pitiful scream launching itself from the constable's lips. The man's legs and arms flapped about, as though he sought to fly himself from the situation.

'Pitch, stop this,' Silas shouted.

He received only snide laughter in reply. The angles of Pitch's face, normally so tenderly treated by the light, were harsh and razorlike now, the glow that encased his body placing him in a spotlight of his own making. Silas had seen but a glimpse of the daemon when the harpies set upon them, but it was fully revealed here. Pitch's skin clung to his bones in a frightening way, and it was as though the lids of his eyes had vanished entirely, exposing horrendous widened orbs of flame.

Stevens's courage escaped him, and the pale-faced young man ran from the barn, screeching for help.

Pitch stared up at the constable with eyes of fire. The desperate man wailed, beseeching them for help.

'Pitch, you'll kill him.' Silas's heart pounded.

'Then he should have stopped when I said so.'

The constable's body hit the wooden shingles with a sickening thump, cutting short his cries. Broken slats of wood rained down upon the arena.

'Please, Pitch. Think of Sybilla.' Silas considered using Lady Satine's name but feared mention of her might well stoke the fires hotter. 'She would not want this.'

'Why would I care an iota for what the Valkyrie wants? She is Satine's dog and, just like her mistress, is intent on making my existence disagreeable.' He cocked his head, eyes still upon the constable, who he held fast against the shingles. The roof creaked at the pressure laid against it. 'What's that you say? You wish to come down? Very well.'

The constable fell. He tumbled from the rafters, peculiarly quiet as he gained speed.

'No!' Silas cried. He raced to catch the stricken man, all reason fleeing from him. A body coming from such a height and at such speed would most likely see him injured. But he could not watch on.

'You idiot,' Pitch snarled.

The constable's body jerked, his head snapping forward, and he jolted to a dead stop in midair, just beyond reach of Silas's outstretched arms.

The man's lips were pressed tight, but his cheeks bulged with his attempts to speak. Pitch had him muted, utterly without recourse. Cold shivers ran up Silas's arms. This poor man was at a daemon's mercy.

'Enough, Tobias.' Silas shouted. 'Your point is made.'

'Not quite.'

At some point in the struggle, the constable's baton had fallen to the ground. It lifted now and flew unaided across the barn. Both the constable and Silas saw what was coming. The wide-eyed man's face was crimson with his imprisoned screams.

'Stop!' Silas roared.

Pitch's grin was a callous smear across his stained face. 'No. I decide when I am beaten.'

The baton struck at the hapless man's shoulder, then the other. It darted to his stomach, tilting vertically to land a vicious strike there. All the while the constable could only grunt and gag against the unseen pressure that held his lips shut fast. He was splayed wide in the air, as vulnerable as a man upon the rack. His own weapon brutalised him, striking so fast it was but a blur in the air. Pitch directed it to land upon the small of his back, the swell of his buttocks, and the crook of his arms. Heavy strikes that might well be breaking bone.

'Enough!' Silas's voice cracked with his distress. He buried his hand in his pocket in search of the bandalore. It was a last resort; he doubted the effect would be quite so stunning upon a daemon as upon a gravedigger, but what else was there to do? His fingers met the smoothness of the wood.

A thundering of hooves disturbed the unsettling quiet. Framed in the open doors and backlit by the afternoon light, Lalassu rose on her hindquarters, front legs lashing at the opening. Another mount was just visible behind, this one's rider propelling themselves from its back. A brilliant flash of white light saw them disappear in the glare. The streak of radiance flew through the barn. Silas dove for cover, the light hissing as it passed frighteningly close by him. It struck Pitch square upon his chest. He uttered a cry and was sent hurtling back against the wagon. The impact was ferocious, the wooden structure collapsing beneath him, burying him in a covering of shattered timber and bent metal.

'Tobias, you imbecile. Control yourself.'

Silas peeked around the barrow he'd taken hasty shelter behind.

Sybilla held the constable in her arms. Behind her Lalassu dug at the earth with quick hooves, while Sybilla's own dapple-grey watched on from beyond the doorway. 'Silas, are you all right?'

'Yes. But the constable?'

'Who bloody cares?' Shattered pieces of wood flew helter-skelter through the air, curses rising with them. Pitch stood up, rubbing at the smear of black that marked the skin between his nipples. His glow was entirely extinguished, and the delicacy of his features was evident once more, though his eyes still glimmered with gold. 'Touch me again, Sybilla, and you will find your nag with four fewer legs to walk upon.'

'Touch a finger to Hastings, and Satine will render you with two fewer legs to walk with, I dare say,' she replied, setting the constable down with his back resting against an overturned barrel. The man was frighteningly still.

'You are quite pale, Silas. Did you think it your turn next?' Pitch's grin was tilted, and his swollen eye was a grotesque mottling of colours, bruises and blood alike.

Silas shook his head. 'I held no such fear.' Strange as it was. But he had feared most desperately for the life of the officer.

'Well, you would be the first. I'm told I go rather berserk on occasion, and it is quite the spectacle.' He might have been far more frightening if he'd not tried to walk just then. The leg of his trousers snagged upon a length of timber, and he swayed about like a tightrope walker in danger of slipping his rope.

'Gods, Tobias, you are pathetic.' Sybilla sighed. 'Get out of here. And I shall clean up the mess you've created.' She jerked her head towards the door. 'You were fortunate. I caught the other one before he could scream his lungs out to the town.'

Silas did not enjoy the sound of that but decided against enquiring too deeply. 'And what is to be done with the constable? Does he live?'

'Of course he fucking lives. If I wished him dead, he'd be very dead.' Pitch tossed his chin, his balance returned. For all his bloodied skin and ugly bruising, he managed to appear quite striking, holding himself like a one-eyed king upon his balcony, peering down at his subjects.

Lalassu nickered softly, her soulful eyes upon Silas. She wore her saddle but no bridle, just as he had left her in the stables. Had she made her own way out and found him here? If so, he could not have been more grateful for it.

'Come, Sickle. I must bathe. I'm positively filthy.' Pitch rubbed at his belly. 'I've got quite the appetite I should say. Our precious little Valkyrie will be sure to make everything better now, won't you, Sybilla dear?

Satine's glorified chambermaid comes in ever so handy for such trivial duties.'

'Silas, I would thank you to take him away from here before I rethink my loyalty to duty.' Sybilla pressed her hands to the constable's head, covering his temples. A soft light, the glisten of a fresh snow, shone between her fingers.

A Valkyrie? A warrior of Nordic legend. They should have been quite unreal, but then so should daemons, and dead-men with scythes. It was not so hard to imagine Sybilla as a fierce soldier. He had witnessed first-hand her prowess with the sword, and marvelled often at her effortless control when mounted. But a creature of myth?

He was so busy staring in wonder that he did not notice Pitch move to Lalassu's side until the horse stamped her feet, tossing her glorious mane.

'Hurry along then, Sickle,' Pitch said. 'I wish to go.'

'Where is Sanu?' Silas asked. 'Did you not ride here?'

'In a manner of speaking, yes,' Pitch replied. 'Just not on a mare with four legs. But you won't mind if I double with you, I'm sure. I promise I'll keep my hands to myself...for some of the journey at least.'

Sybilla gave him a look that might have seen a lesser man piss his trousers. 'For the gods' sake, be gone with you.' She settled kinder eyes on Silas. 'Mr Mercer, I'm sorry to burden you with this, but there is only so much time we can delay before others come searching. I will tend the constable, and his officer's memories of this, as best I can. Make your way back to Lower Broughton, quickly now.'

Silas nodded, dragging his eyes from the cloud-like glow coming from Sybilla's hands. He joined Pitch beside the pale horse and took some pleasure in shouldering the man out of the way so he might mount. He had reins gathered, and one foot in the stirrup before he hesitated. With a grunt he set his foot down and shrugged off his coat.

'Put this on. If we are to try to escape notice, it will hardly do to have you so bloodied and undressed.' He thrust it at Pitch before the man could return a lewd reply, which was undoubtedly being readied, and swung himself up into the saddle, settling well before it struck him how easily the movement had been made. As though he'd ridden for years and not just mere days.

'Come on then,' Silas said. 'Ride with me if you must.'

Silas's coat was far too large for Pitch of course, and had the effect of making him appear ever more delicate in its oversized folds. Still, the shade of blue suited him well. Pitch smiled up at him through lips swollen with trauma. He raised his arms, with only his fingertips visible from the bunching lengths of material.

'I've been so very viciously assaulted, will you not assist me?'

He ain't happy till he's hurtin'. Gilmore's words returned to Silas. Why did Pitch despise the skin he was in so thoroughly? What caused such angst in a man?

With much irritation and grinding of teeth, Silas leaned down and offered his arm.

'Be gentle with me, won't you?' Pitch simpered, laughing with delight at his own ridiculousness.

'Do be quiet.'

Silas stared straight ahead as Pitch grasped his arm and pulled himself aboard, finding his seat upon Lalassu's haunches. There was small doubt the man needed any such assistance. He rose light as a leaf caught in the wind, Silas's coat flaring about him like a rippling pond.

'How very kind you are, Sickle. It's rather sickening.' He shifted against Silas's back, pressing in as close as the saddle's cantle would allow, and set his hands low upon Silas's waist.

Silas urged Lalassu homeward, and the daemon stayed blessedly quiet. They had not travelled far when Pitch rested his head against Silas's back, and began to snore in lilting, gentle breaths. Certain that he was deep in slumber, Silas laid one hand upon Pitch's own. He assured himself it was only to guarantee the man did not slip from his seat. The daemon's hands were softer than he imagined, as though made of velvet, and warm as a steeping cup of tea. After a time Pitch muttered and nestled in closer. Silas stiffened to begin with, conscious of how close they pressed to one another. But after a while a revelation struck him. This was the first time in his new life he had been held this way. There had been the dreadful dancing at the ball, of course, but that had not been the same. The warmth of another's body had been missing, the sense of being...well, needed, had not been evident there.

For the length of this journey Silas would pretend that it was someone precious who embraced him. Someone who cared for the man he might once have been.

As long as Pitch slept, Silas would imagine his companion to be someone other than a daemon, something other than a creature with a taste for violence and chaos. And he himself not so awfully alone.

CHAPTER 7

L alassu took them swiftly along the back roads, thus avoiding the village altogether. The horse picked her path surely, and as Pitch slept, Silas rode along in wonderful silence, his hands light upon the reins, his hips finding a pleasant rhythm in the saddle as they moved at a brisk walk. It felt altogether quite wonderful, as though he had at last learnt the tune the animal played for him. The pale horse was solid beneath him, sure and strong, granting Silas the illusion of being equally as steadfast. He was at ease. Prepared to continue on this way for as long as Lalassu saw fit. She bore him away from the befuddling encounter with the gravedigger and the bloody chaos of the barn. It was a shame she could not remove him from Pitch's company.

The man's arms were wrapped around his middle. Silas's coat draped from his slender limbs like some elaborate costume, and he leaned his full weight upon Silas's back. Light as he may be, after some time it made for an uncomfortable ride. Silas pressed into his stirrups, raising his backside from the saddle, seeking to stir Pitch.

'Gods, tell me we have reached out destination,' Pitch groaned. 'I can no longer feel my balls, and I fear greatly for my cock's survival.'

Silas only just managed to curb his laughter. As intolerable as Pitch may be, it could not be denied that on the rare occasion he could amuse.

'I do not control Lalassu,' he said. 'She is choosing our path and knows her own mind. How are you faring, aside from the indignity to your privates?'

Pitch's peal of laughter startled Silas, and Lalassu. She tossed her graceful head, and Silas patted her storm-cloud neck, whispering words of ease.

'You are so dull at times I think I might die, and yet, at others you are quite bearable.' Pitch squeezed Silas's thigh, as though he'd just delivered the jaded compliment to a child.

'You received quite the thrashing.' Silas ran his tongue around the question that had bothered itself free. 'Though I do not understand why. I suspect you are capable of winning any such fight easily.'

'Bloodletting is good for a man...and me,' Pitch replied, with rather too much flippancy. 'Perhaps you'd like to try it?'

'I would not, thank you.' He stared ahead, considering his next question. In the distance paddocks stretched along either side of the road, and the rise of the farmhouse roof was evident. 'I see no need to cause myself pain intentionally, and I do have to wonder...well, that is...I do wonder why it appeals to you?'

He considered mentioning the name he'd heard fall from Pitch's lips. Raph. Perhaps there was a story there that might account for his blatant need for violence. He'd seemed irritated in his mumblings, distressed at times. But if Silas had learnt anything these past days, it was that one must take steps with great caution around Tobias Astaroth. The twitter of birds echoed in the silence.

'A fist makes for a release from other pains,' Pitch said quietly. 'I have a veritable list, and at times require more than an apple pie, a fuck, and pint of ale to stave off the twinges.'

His hands tight upon the reins, Silas said, 'Might...might you tell me...what it is that ails you?'

'No. I might not. And it does not concern you, or my guardianship of you.' The warning was there in Pitch's tone for Silas to recognise, the faint flicker of his anger.

Silas cleared his throat. 'I would say...that it does perhaps concern me. You could not have helped me, should I have needed you.'

'Oh gods.' Pitch was irritated, but not furious. Much to Silas's great relief. 'You have returned to frightfully dull again, my dear Sickle. Speak of something interesting, or I may find you as disagreeable as I did the constable.'

50

Silas rolled his eyes, safe in the knowledge that Pitch could not see. 'Fine. I have another question that begs answering, and I see no reason why you cannot speak of this. Sybilla...' How did one ask this question of a lady without vulgarity? 'Might I know what form of supernatural she is? For it is clear she is far more than the farm's caretaker.'

'I believe you heard very well what she was when I said it.'

'You called her "Valkyrie."'

'There you have it. Your ears work fine.' He touched at Silas's lobe. The touch brought on an involuntary shiver.

'Stop that. Will you not give me a straight answer to any question?'

'No, I don't believe I will. You are far too amusing when you are frustrated.'

Silas slumped in the saddle, and he could not say if it was his obvious dejection that swayed Pitch to say more but he did so.

A sigh came first. 'I called her a Valkyrie, because that is what she is, or was at least. And no, before you think of asking, she is not an imaginary Norse god's chosen warrior. How the humans got wind of the name I do not know, nor care, but I do enjoy that their stealing of it vexes the Archangels, being the pompous arses they are. For the title of Valkyrie is their invention, given to an elite few soldiers who are tasked with the more distasteful of wartime missions. From what I understand, it seems poor Sybilla did not have the stomach for it and found herself more suited to shovelling horse shit for Lady Satine.'

Silas played his tongue against his lips. 'So she is...you are saying that she...is an angel herself?'

'Oh gods, are you going to go all weak-kneed at the mention of such a word? It is pathetic.'

'I can assure you I am not weak at the knees.' In fact, he rather felt he was being admirably stoic about the entire situation. 'I simply have questions, as we humans are wont to do.'

'You are not human.'

'I was.' Silas dug his chipped nails into the leather reins. He had been human once, with a life he could not recall. It sickened him to think on his nameless grave, with its simple wooden cross. Whoever he had been, no one appeared to mourn his loss. 'And however you might despise it, this all comes as quite the shock to me, to learn such creatures exist. Daemons...and angels, actual angels...it is astonishing.'

'Oh by Lucifer's asshole, spare me the breathless awe. I can assure you the Angelics are nothing like what humans imagine them to be. Their Halos in particular are a case in point. Pretty circles of light above their heads? What an utter load of tosh.'

'But wings then? Do they have those?'

Pitch thumped his forehead against Silas's back. 'So what if they do? Such an appendage is no great marvel in Arcadia, I can assure you.'

'Everyone has wings?' Silas marvelled at the image that formed in his mind. An entire world of glorious winged creatures.

'Don't be daft, you idiot. Of course not. Does every human have yellow hair, or pale skin?'

'That's hardly the same thing, surely.'

'You would know of course, being the scholar in all things Arcadian.'

With an ever-improving finesse, Silas ignored Pitch's sarcasm-laden words. 'Did you know Sybilla in Arcadia then?' That mind-boggling place where Pitch claimed daemons and angels lived side by side, and a most horrendous war was being fought.

With a cluck of his tongue, Pitch replied, 'As though I would have deigned to spend time with Valkyries. We may have passed one another on the Hellfield I suppose at some time, but I would not have paid her much mind.'

Silas found himself trying to imagine such a sight. Pitch and Sybilla fighting upon this Hellfield. The images he conjured were terrifying, but, he would admit most grudgingly, also rather thrilling.

'Is there such a group...amongst the daemons?' How easily the word left him nowadays. 'Are there Valkyrie among them?' He could well imagine Pitch being amongst those tasked with undertaking the most sordid of missions, but could see less well how the man's mercurial temper would fare under such conditions.

'Gods no. We are called many things, but Archangel dogs is not amongst them.'

With Pitch seeming amiable to conversation, Silas pressed further. 'And you? What of your place on the Hellfield?'

'What of it?' Therein rumbled the distinctive tremors of Pitch's temper. 'It is long done with.'

Silas trod carefully. 'You will not return there?'

'I cannot. And am all the happier for it.'

His current battered state would suggest he lied about such happiness. 'You must face a formidable foe on the Hellfield. If angels and daemons cannot drive them back. Who - '

Pitch's hand suddenly slipped south, down between Silas's legs. He grabbed at the sensitive flesh there and squeezed, hard. Silas cried out, the shock of it driving his heels into Lalassu's sides. The horse launched them into a riotous trot. The jarring movement nearly unseated him and thankfully dislodged Pitch's hand. Silas's balls throbbed and his eyes smarted with tears. He eased the pressure of his heels, and with gentle coaxing, Lalassu returned to her amiable walk. She snorted and tossed her head with displeasure, despite Silas's muttered apology.

'Why would you do such a thing?' He shoved his shoulders against Pitch, who still leaned in uncomfortably close.

'You were being dull again, and I wished to be entertained. Gods, I'm famished. Will this interminable journey never end?'

As though those gods he spoke to had taken heed, Lower Broughton Farm appeared in its full glory some ways up ahead, a generously sized house upon a rise in the landscape, not more than a few minutes ride away.

'There it is. Can you not have this nag move faster?' Pitch said.

But Silas's balls still pained him; he'd not push Lalassu into a trot if the daemon held a knife to his throat and demanded it. 'If you wish to move quicker, then I suggest you walk.'

'Very well. I prefer my arse to ache for more pleasurable reasons anyway.'

Pitch slid from Lalassu's haunches, taking his dangerous hands with him. Although his stride was no greater than when at a casual walk, he drew ahead of them. Each step taking him much further than seemed likely, just as Silas had witnessed with Jane on many an occasion. Pitch moved like the air elemental in other ways too, a teasing sway of hips that drew the eye to pert buttocks. Only here Silas could not seem to keep his gaze lifted, as he did so when around Jane. The temptation was greater, more encompassing. Silas shook his head, putting a stop to where his thoughts were drifting. Pitch was a masterful seducer. Silas must not be led astray.

The daemon reached the low wooden gates of Lower Broughton Farm well ahead of Silas and Lalassu. Pitch's chestnut mount grazed alone in one of fields that bordered the roadway leading up to the house. Sanu raised her head to consider them, ears flicking. There was no denying the creature held none of Lalassu's regal stature, with a barrel-girth, swayback, and short narrow neck. The horse turned its rump to the passing traffic, returning to grazing. Pitch did not spare the animal a glance.

'Will you join me in the pond,' he called. He held Silas's coat draped over one shoulder, and it dragged through the dirt behind him. 'It's a pleasant enough day, and I'd say we are both in need of a thorough cleansing.'

Even if the very idea of dipping a toe into the waters did not send a shrill of alarm through Silas, he would not have joined Pitch in such an endeavour if the very world depended upon it.

'I am not in as dire need of cleansing as you,' he replied. 'I'll tend to myself indoors.'

'See, there you go again. Being ever so tedious. I could have given you a scrubbing down you'd not forget.' Pitch flung Silas's coat over a fencepost. The man was a dreadful mess of dried blood and dirt. 'Thank you for the loan of your coat, though I dare say I have stained it beyond repair.' He carried on, disappearing around the corner of the farmhouse and out of sight.

Silas relaxed into the saddle, releasing his feet from the stirrups, and drew in a deep breath. There was some relief to be had at returning to Sybilla's residence. He had little idea of what time it might be, but the growl of his stomach suggested it was a long while since the pork pie. He leaned down to reach for the coat where Pitch had discarded it.

And Lalassu's mane began to act in a most unusual way.

There was no wind to speak of, and yet the thickly layered strands along her neck rose into the air. The silvery-green threads, many as long as Silas's arm, curled and twisted in upon themselves, as though a hundred serpents hid in their midst. Silas snatched up his coat and straightened himself in his seat, unsure whether he should release the reins entirely. Lalassu continued on with her great plodding steps, but he was now blind to the way ahead, the lift of the mane had reached so high. The strands wove into one another, their pace quickening like a misplaced storm cloud hovering above the horse's neck. Silas was considering dismounting when the curious display grew still.

'Oh my,' he whispered.

The mane had woven a most wondrous sight. A diorama sat before him, a perfect replica of a castle, derelict as it was, made entirely by the bruised green hairs. He could barely breathe for the intricacy. A deep gully lay around the castle's ruinous exterior, a moat perhaps, with a narrow bridge connecting the structure to the grounds beyond its walls. Those walls, thick as they were, were in a dilapidated state, uneven at their top where the stonework had collapsed. The roof was gone entirely, exposing the interior to the elements. It appeared long since abandoned.

Goodrich Castle.

It was not a voice, or a whisper, or even a conscious thought that brought the name to him. He just knew it. Silas stared at the marvellous construction, certain of its name. He knew without consideration that this was the sign he had waited on.

The pale horse was guiding him, just as the Lady Satine had said. Silas gripped the pommel, absorbed by the shimmering grey and green display before him. The detail within the loops and folds of horsehair was astonishing. The urge to set out was overwhelming.

'Is everything all right?'

He started, and the diorama collapsed. Lalassu's voluminous mane fell down the side of her powerful neck. Sybilla had drawn up alongside him, right outside the farmhouse. He found himself at a standstill though he had not felt Lalassu halt. He lifted his gaze to Sybilla. It was just as well he was so distracted by Lalassu's display, for he might not have been able to look on the Valkyrie, the angel, so easily otherwise.

'It has happened.' He ran his tongue against the back of his teeth. 'The sign Lady Satine said to expect. I believe it is time for us to go.' Silas ran his hand down the length of Lalassu's mane, and with the shift of the strands, the mossy green accents rose to the surface.

'All right then.' Sybilla was measured and calm.

'Goodrich Castle. Do you know of it?'

Sybilla nodded. Sweat glistened on the dark skin of her upper lip, and a smudge of blood stained the cuff of her shirt. 'I've heard tell of it yes. It's a ways south of here. A couple of days ride I'd say, in the Forest of Dean. When do you plan to leave?'

Silas's nerves fairly danced with the idea of setting off. 'This day.'

She frowned but nodded. 'Very well. I cannot say I mind the idea of Tobias being removed far from here, but do you think you are ready, Silas?'

He did not answer straightaway. 'I'm not sure it is possible to be truly ready for something one does not understand.' He wrapped strands of mane around his fingers. 'But I do know that we should not delay.'

And knew it with conviction. A meal, a wash, and he would set off. They *must* set off.

'Very well then. But you are going nowhere without supplies.' She peered about. 'Where is the daemon?'

'Bathing, in the pond,' Silas said.

'You handled it well, in the barn. You were not as frightened as I might have expected when his rage took hold. Have you seen such a display from Tobias before?'

'I'm afraid so.' Silas nodded. 'Though I must say he likely saved my life on that occasion, so I cannot begrudge him. You were not long with the constable...were you able to help him?' He recalled vividly the white glow rising between her fingers as she nursed the injured man.

'I've tidied up as best I can.' A muscle tensed in Sybilla's jaw. 'He will recover, there is no doubt. And it was easy enough to work on the memories of both men. They will not recall your faces but rather think themselves victims to some seedy stragglers of the fight. It will be tiresome to see the constable search for his assailant over the coming weeks, though he's a rather unpleasant man, so perhaps it will be more amusing than I imagine. Silas, I shall say it, you will be missed, but Tobias far less so. I do not understand Her Ladyship's reasons for placing him with you, and it is not for me to question such things, but take care, won't you? At times I fear he is not in control of himself at all.'

'Is that the way of all daemons?' Silas released the reins, eager to begin the preparations for their departure. 'To be so taken by their rage?'

'To some extent, yes. They are born for conflict, for strife. He's told you a little of Arcadia?'

'He has.'

'And of me?'

He busied himself with the reins so he did not have to meet her eye. 'He did indeed. I am quite overwhelmed, I must say, to hear that you....to learn that...well, to be told of your true nature.'

'Don't be, for it leaves much to be desired.' Sybilla alighted from her horse, moving with swift gracefulness. She exuded strength in the way she held herself, sensibility in the way she spoke. Pitch was wrong when he said angels were not what Silas might imagine. Sybilla could slip easily into his vision of how such a creature might be. As Pitch fitted the idea of a daemon: that was to say, cruel and manipulative, coarse and crude and vile. 'But it seems you are able to coax conversation from Tobias at least. That is impressive, Mr Mercer. Perhaps I should not be too concerned about you after all. You may well know more of the daemon than I do. He's rather opposed to idle chatter about his days past.'

'I fear I do not know much at all.' Silas followed Sybilla's lead and dismounted, with much reluctance. His place felt to be in the saddle now.

'Well, you and I share that much at least.' She clapped her hands. 'Enough of Mr Astaroth, let us ready you for the task ahead.'

CHAPTER 8

I t was several hours before Silas would find himself in the saddle once more. And all the while it was as though two parts of his mind warred against one another, the more practical of the two suggesting it was much safer to remain here at the farm, whilst the other – and it was the stronger of the pair – urged him on with such an impatience and appetite that he could barely stand it.

As he watched Sybilla sort out supplies for the journey, stuffing an assortment of gingerbread, shortbread, and sweets into a pair of saddlebags, he said, 'I must tell you that Pitch may not be the only one to have upset some of the townspeople.'

She glanced at him. The rich brown of her eyes was brightened by the kitchen fire. 'Really? Have you set jealousy amongst the ladies of the village, Mr Mercer?' Her smile was gentle. 'I saw the eyes you drew when we were at the inn. Did you take your pleasure, perhaps?'

'No, no. Nothing like that.' His cheeks warmed. 'I had an unfortunate encounter with the gravedigger, I'm afraid. He was not doing as he should. Instead of burying a body, he was digging it from its grave.' He shuddered at the unseemly memory.

'George?' Sybilla paused in her attempt to fit a loaf of bread into the bulging bag. 'Are you certain it was him? His wife is one of the few who is not afraid to make her visits to me evident, and she does speak ever so highly of her husband.'

'I'm afraid I'm very certain of what I saw.' Silas had not yet decided if he would include all the violent details of the encounter. 'And I spoke with him at some length, after I' – he paused – 'interrupted what he was doing.'

'And what did he say?' Sybilla had abandoned her packing.

'That he had been offered very good coin for his work. Apparently, there has been a call for a very particular type of corpse.' He swallowed. To even imagine the dead being disturbed left his mouth dry and stomach weak. 'Young is preferable, and they need to have died in such a manner that the body is unharmed. No disease, no injury.' Again he shuddered, though this time it was for thought of his own death. No disease, no injury, save for the starving of his lungs.

Sybilla frowned at him. 'Did he tell you who called for such a thing?'

'He mentioned something, yes.' Silas nodded. 'He spoke of a tosher in Shrewsbury. The Old Bell pub, I think he said.'

'A sewer-hunter can barely feed themselves, they certainly aren't paying for bodies. Did he know who was the master of this plan?'

'No. He didn't. But if George is to be believed, then towns across the country are digging up their dead to receive their coin, of which the sum is substantial.'

Sybilla watched him closely. 'If they are wanting such pristine corpses, likely it is for the universities or the medical schools. It happens, I'm afraid.'

'And nothing...more?' The bandalore's behaviour had shocked Silas, and he'd since been entertaining the idea that it was more than simple indignation towards the treatment of the dead that drew its ire. 'There is not a more...shall we say...preternatural reason for such theft?'

There was some time before Sybilla answered. 'Are you filling your head with thoughts of necromancy, Silas?'

'I just thought...well, perhaps if that is what brought me back to life, then maybe...'

'The goddess raised you, Silas. Not a sorcerer. Those skills are not for this world. It is quite impossible.' But she frowned as she said it. 'I will be sure to tell Lady Satine of what has occurred though, believe me.'

'Thank you.' He considered mentioning the large wayward dog that had barrelled its way into his personal space and decided against it. 'Oh, I'm afraid I might have promised you to something in the exchange.'

'You did?'

'George said that he undertook such things to feed his family. He thought I had been sent by you to put an end to it.' In the light of day his promise to the man seemed quite ludicrous, and he rushed his words. 'I said that perhaps you could assist him with the coin he would lose with having to rebury the body as I demanded. He has a family to feed, you see...'

Sybilla smiled at him, her white teeth as brilliant as the light that had streamed from her fingers. 'Silas, it is all right. Please, don't work yourself up so. It was kind of you to see to him in such a way, rather than have him dragged before the police. Though, admittedly that may have suited us better, for it would mean the constable would have been kept too busy to fall into Tobias's company.' She sighed but her smile did not waver.

Silas took his leave to see to Lalassu for the journey.

An hour later they were, at long last, on their way. Pitch's hair was still damp from his bathing, which had drawn on so long preparations were done by the time he reappeared. His transformation was astonishing. The bruises upon Pitch's high cheekbones had morphed from fresh blue-grey to older, yellowing marks. His right eye was no longer swollen shut, and his lips too were repaired, retaining only the merest hint of cuts and bruising upon them. Now he settled himself upon his bow-backed horse with much grumbling and talk of glue factories, and helped himself to the rations before they had even left the front gates.

Silas waved to Sybilla, who stood watching them until a rise and slope in the road stole her from view. Already he missed her steadying influence.

Pitch was the first to rouse his horse into a trot, the dull chestnut mare taking some convincing to lift her hooves. Lalassu broke into her loping gait with small urging from Silas. The horse danced light upon her massive hooves, appearing as excited by the beginning of the journey as Silas himself. His trepidation remained of course, with a touch of fear to join it, but overall he would say his mood matched that of his steed.

He wished to be on his way. He wished to set eyes upon Goodrich Castle. His skin fairly tingled at the thought of it.

Silas adjusted the length of his coat so that it lay spread over Lalassus's wide haunches. Sybilla had done a commendable job in cleaning the fabric, considering the short time on offer to her. She'd tried to have him wear another piece of clothing, a solid black jacket that fit him well enough but simply would not do. Silas could imagine abandoning his royal-blue Inverness coat as readily as he could imagine abandoning the bandalore. In other words, neither was a possibility. Regrettably though, there had been no time for the coat to dry through before they departed, so he sat within its somewhat damp folds.

'Which way?' Pitch had no trouble slowing his mount at the intersection with the main road, Sanu immediately lowering her head to sniff at the long grass that grew on the edges. 'Oh mighty Horseman, show us the way.'

His words were so heavy with sarcasm, it was a wonder they escaped his mouth. He had dressed in a rather ludicrous ensemble: patterned red trousers, tightly-fitted; a velvet black jacket that pinched in at his waist; and a vest imprinted with images of butterflies. A straw boater topped the outfit. Pitch appeared ready to step onto a stage, not provide guardianship.

'This way.' Silas and Lalassu trotted past the distracted Sanu, and as they made their way east back towards the village, they were serenaded by Pitch's curses as he struggled to follow.

'Pig's cock, I might as well bloody walk.'

But that was hardly the case, and before long they had bypassed the town entirely and headed south, following along Brampton Road for a while before Lalassu led them off onto narrower, less worn roads through the Shropshire countryside. They rode for several hours, passing only the merest of conversation between them. At times Pitch took to his god-awful singing once more, only increasing the volume if Silas dared ask him to cease. Silas learned quickly that the man was but a mere child, and as a child might grow quiet with lack of attention to bad behaviour, so too did the daemon. Within ten minutes of Silas's silence, Pitch amused himself with some other distraction. Mostly raiding the saddlebags. Silas had glanced back to see his mouth dusted with sugar or jam more than once. But if devouring their supplies meant precious quiet, he did not intend to stop him.

Early evening saw the sun sink low behind the horizon, leaving them in a dim but not unpleasant light. In a short time it would grow dark.

'Where do you intend to stop for the night?' Pitch asked between hissed threats of the knackery for his mount if the animal did not hasten her pace. 'I do hate to disappoint you, but if you intend to reach Goodrich this night, it shall be without me and the red turtle here.'

Silas stifled a smile. It would do no good to allow Pitch to see that, at times, he was rather amusing.

'I'm not sure it is my decision to make, I'm afraid.' He rose in his stirrups, allowing his legs to stretch. Truthfully, he hoped Lalassu might halt them rather soon, for his ankles ached and his tailbone murmured with discomfort. 'Lalassu guides us. I do not know the way to Goodrich Castle.'

'A bloody abandoned stack of rocks in the middle of a godsdamned forest,' Pitch grumbled. Which is not quite how Sybilla had described it when Silas told her of their intended destination in the Forest of Dean. She did say though that the castle had fallen into disrepair and had not been occupied for many a year. 'Why would anyone want to know the way? I can't imagine anything more unworthy of visitation.'

'I understand you are not an admirer of the natural world, you've made that abundantly clear. But Lalassu is our guide.'

'So we are at the mercy of a great pile of hair and bone that shits while it walks. How delightful.'

Lalassu's tail swished the air with a hiss, her ears pulled back as though the animal listened in with much disapproval.

Silas settled his shoulders. 'Would you rather Lady Satine herself guide us?'

'Gods no. That miserable bitch could bore the arsehole off a statue,' Pitch said, bright with the warmth of the sugar he'd consumed. 'Besides, she would not deign to cavort with her chained monkeys. Well, I suppose I am her singular monkey. You, my fine, sturdy friend, are death's whipping boy, are you not?'

Silas supposed he was, but he turned in the saddle and redirected the conversation back upon the daemon. 'I understand you've been with the Lady Satine barely a year. What brought you into her service?'

When Pitch had attacked Gilmore in Holly Village, the gnome had screamed that it was little wonder Arcadia had thrown the daemon beyond its borders. Pitch himself had made mention of the Lady Satine having a hold upon his leash, as though he were bound to her. But Silas was still yet to have any clue what mighty fault had thrust him into servitude.

Pitch considered the cinnamon bun he held. 'A terrible mistake.' He bit into the bun. 'What brought you to heel alongside death then?'

'A fair question, and one I have no answer to. Serendipity, it would seem.' Silas paused, waiting until Pitch took another bite. 'What was this terrible mistake that saw you thrown from your homeland?'

How bold Silas felt upon Lalassu's back, his fear seemed stripped way. He doubted he'd have asked such a question anywhere else. It was some comfort as well to see the massive height difference between Sanu and Lalassu. Pitch might as well have ridden on a miniature horse.

Pitch regarded him from beneath narrowed lids, his fine pink lips pressed shut. Silas had just begun to doubt his sudden courage, and was quite certain the daemon would refuse to answer him, when Pitch spoke.

'I do believe I've explained this to you already.' He stuck out his tongue and ran a finger down its length. 'It is not so much *speak no evil*, as *speak no truth*, for me.'

Silas frowned, recalling the occasion in the carriage on the way to Black Annis's bower. 'That's right, you cannot speak of certain things. But how is that possible – ' Silas halted his enquiry. He had seen enough already to know all manner of things were possible. Instead he asked, 'Why would such a thing be done to you?'

'They would tell you it was done for other reasons, but I suspect they were most aware of how painful it would be, and are enjoying my punishment all the more for it.' His voice drifted low as he spoke, the remainder of the cinnamon bun forgotten in his hand.

'They?'

'The powers that be, of course. The makers and destroyers, the kings and the judges. No matter how high you might fly, Sickle, you are never more than what they make you.' He hiccoughed and followed it with a sizable belch.

'They punish you...for your mistake?'

'No worse than I do myself.'

Though Silas's neck ached with the angle he held it, he could not look away from Pitch's face. His eyes were glassy with the influence of the food he ate. Sugar had the most curious effect upon him. If ever there were a moment he might wring some truth from the daemon, it may well be now. Drawing upon Lalassu's reassuring presence, Silas pushed on.

'Was it...anything to do with that man you speak of? Raph, I believe you called him.'

Pitch grew rigid, his jaw set hard. He dug his heels unkindly into Sanu's side. She broke at once from her plodding walk into a cantering lope and drew alongside Silas and Lalassu.

'Tell me what you heard,' Pitch said.

'When you were beaten near senseless in the barn, you spoke it again.' Silas coughed, reliving the physicality of the last occurrence, the grinding of Pitch's body against his. His cheeks reddened with the flush of blood, and, damn it all, a pressure between his legs. 'Though this time you did not sound anguished...'

'What then?' Pitch demanded.

'Well...it was...'

'Damn it, man –'

'Intimate,' Silas rushed. 'There was an intimacy in the way you spoke of him.' And not that between brothers. At least, not in this world.

This was another of those rare occasions when the hardness seemed to lift from the daemon, and a rawness came over him, a shadow of uncertainty where none had dared exist before. Pitch's battered face lent him an air of fragility.

'I don't...'

For a shocking moment Silas thought Pitch about to declare he did not understand. The first time any such uncertainty would have been evident. Pitch dropped his reins and bothered at his straw boater, which, so far as Silas could tell, needed no such adjustment.

'I would guess him to be, quite important to you.' Someone he desired. Silas fought back the image of Pitch with just such a lover. A partner he sought to please, rather than conquer in a fleeting encounter as seemed his way.

'Do not guess at anything.' Pitch tilted his boater low so that his eyes were hidden from Silas's view. 'You truly heard this name from my own lips?'

'Well, yes.' Silas was not sure whose lips might have been the alternative. 'Pitch, what is this about?'

The evening had deepened around them, the trees' shadows more indistinct, the road a lighter streak against descending darkness. Lalassu's steps quickened towards what Silas, saddle weary and needing refreshment, hoped might be accommodations for the evening.

'Allow me to show you something.' Pitch held Sanu alongside Lalassu. He lifted his chin so their eyes could meet and opened his mouth wide.

'What are you doing?'

Pitch's body jerked, as though he were about to vomit. Silas squeezed one leg against Lalassu's side in the hope the animal would distance them, which of course she did not, allowing him full, clear view of what was occurring. Pitch's mouth was a wide circle, the very back of his throat visible to Silas, and he pointed a finger wildly at his lips. His body shuddered with spasms but not a sound came from his throat. Not a gurgle, not a hiss.

All at once it occurred to Silas that something was very much amiss. 'Dear god.'

Pitch had no tongue between his jaws. A nub of flesh sat at the back of his throat, the hollow of his mouth empty but for his teeth.

He heaved once more and at last, and thankfully, closed his deformed mouth. A moment later, the tongue Silas was so certain had been missing suddenly darted to wet Pitch's lips.

'You saw it then?' the daemon said.

Cringing, Silas nodded. 'Your tongue...was quite gone.'

'And that is how it is when I try to speak of things that should not be said. Just then I told you the reason why I have no place in Arcadia, but I dare say you did not catch a word of it.'

Wiping the sight from his mind would take some time. 'I'm sorry,' Silas said, and truly he was. Even for a man such as Pitch. 'Does it pain you?'

'Yes. But only as it should.' He returned to his cinnamon bun, nibbling at it.

'You did not expect I would hear that name, did you? Raph, I mean. It is a piece of your past that I shouldn't have heard.'

'Handsome, and moderately intelligent. Good man.'

'Why did I hear it, then?' Did it endanger him to know?

Pitch released a grand sigh, spreading his arms. 'No idea. Perhaps it was because I was sleeping when you heard it the first time –'

'And barely conscious the second.'

Pitch squinted into the gloom. 'I have an idea, Sickle. You should lie with me so you might watch me sleep and report what is said.'

'I do not think that is a practical solution.'

'I care little what you think.'

'But very much what I might hear.'

Pitch tossed his head, the crack of his smile appearing. 'A feisty reply, Sickle. Becoming the Lady's Horseman has quite changed your weak-boned self. Perhaps you are not in need of a guardian after all. They will be done with me sooner than I could have hoped.'

The cocksure lift of his shoulders had returned, as had the imperious tilt of his chin. Sanu might be diminutive beside Lalassu, but her rider was far less so. He urged her on, and the chestnut found a turn of foot that took them, for the first time, well ahead of Lalassu and her rider.

CHAPTER 9

Lalassu's energy appeared endless. The hours stretched on and the night sank deep beyond midnight. The great horse beneath Silas preferred the canter, no matter how uneven the ground became or how difficult a path they followed. Lalassu led them off the obvious road many a time, plunging through fields and bracken and meadows before returning them to a discernible path through the forest. Silas had only the moon's position to base his general direction upon. It sat always up above and to the right.

The night was clear and crisp enough to keep Silas's coat from drying entirely. The collar touched damp material to his neck, keeping the skin there prickled with gooseflesh. He did not enjoy the press of the woods, the bleakness of the night-sodden trees reminding him all too well of Black Annis's own woods.

He ran a hand against his belly. Though the wounds no longer bothered him, he was doubtful he would ever forget them. If he closed his eyes too long, there she lurked in all her dripping foulness.

His first teratism.

His first nightmare.

Yet he longed to arrive at Goodrich Castle and put paid to what awaited him. Silas had considered his compulsion over the journey and thought he understood it. As haunting as Black Annis may be, he had destroyed her. He alone had prevented her from bringing further misery to those such as Clarence and his family. Silas had set the balance right again. And he could not ignore the deep satisfaction that came with it.

'Don't blame me should I fail to come to you when you are most in need.' Pitch and Sanu had long since returned to second place behind Lalassu, and his voice was faint behind Silas. 'This fucking nag shall be entirely at fault when I arrive an hour too late to haul your generous arse from danger. I'm not certain the cretin has not died beneath me already.'

Silas's smile rose unbidden. 'Lalassu sets a formidable pace.' Though his thighs ached, and his tailbone still muttered its discomfort he no longer desired to halt, enjoying too much the soothing regularity of the horse's rhythm.

Pitch returned to his near-constant berating of the hapless Sanu, describing in graphic detail how she would be fed to ravenous-sounding creatures called nuckers. Silas had no intention of asking about them, for they sounded rather unpleasant.

They travelled another half hour or so, Silas in quiet contemplation, spotting some quite delightful dancing points of light within the foliage at one point. He supposed them to be fireflies of some kind, though his innate and strange sense of knowledge of such things whispered that such a creature was rare to behold indeed, and near on impossible at this time of year. Still, he admired the display weaving about the tall grasses as Lalassu slowed into a walk to negotiate a narrow gutter that served as the pathway. With the moon barely half-full and the night so velvet rich with darkness the lights made for a pleasant distraction, Silas raised his brow at the generous size of the insects. Several were as large as a lantern's flame. They swirled high, as though startled by the passersby, looping around one another in a mesmerising display that was sadly short-lived. Settling into a large group, their combined light so great it could rival a gaslight in the London streets, the insects sped off deeper into the surrounding woods, and once more Silas rode in shadowy darkness. Lalassu, refreshed, broke into a trot.

He had begun to wonder if perhaps the pale horse intended to continue until dawn, when her chosen path led them towards a thicket of hawthorns, their shapes reminiscent of large leafy green umbrellas, with their short bare trunks taking the place of a handle. Thoughts of umbrellas led Silas straight to the curious bartender, Kaneko, and Mr

Ahari's assertion that the man was in fact a tsukumogami: an inanimate object become sentient with time. In this case, an umbrella.

Silas grinned at the thought of it now. What a curious conversation that had been. 'Mr Ahari jested, did he not, when he insisted that Kaneko was somehow a former parasol?' He laughed, expecting Pitch to laugh as well and declare Silas ridiculously gullible to believe such a thing possible.

There was only silence. Silas gathered up the reins to slow Lalassu, but the horse heeded his request before he'd made it, dropping from a trot to a slow walk.

'Pitch? Where are you?'

But the road behind was empty. Ahead, the path swept to the left, allowing a view of a simple stone bridge some yards distant. He could not make out the river it traversed and hoped fervently that it would be a riverbed dried to dust. Ever unsettled by the thought of water, Silas was happy to turn his attentions elsewhere for now. 'Pitch, this is not amusing.'

A snap of wood came from beyond the cluster of hawthorns. 'This is no time for pointless torment. Hurry yourself, Pitch. I'll not wait on you.'

A bald-faced lie of course.

'I'm taking a piss, you idiot,' came the faint reply. 'Should I have invited you to hold my cock for me?'

'Must you always be so vulgar?'

'Yes. I must. It alleviates the boredom.'

Silas blew out his cheeks, not gracing Pitch with a reply. He readied to squeeze his legs into Lalassu's sides to urge her on, but the mare broke into her trot before he could tense his muscles. He was beginning to wonder if he needed to use his body at all to relay his desires. The animal seemed to read his thoughts. Lalassu had them at the bridge before long, and Silas eyed it warily, the familiar twist of his stomach coming at the sight. A strong current flowed beneath the low-set bridge, with barely a handspan to separate the two. The flow was utterly silent, its movement only betrayed by the pale touch of the moon upon the surface. For the first time Silas was grateful for the concentration demanded of him to stay unified with Lalassu's tempo, for it distracted him as they moved across the expanse of the bridge. In truth the crossing was hardly worthy of consternation. The stream was no wider than Lalassu's length doubled, and it was doubtful it held much depth, but Silas sat rigid, hands clenched upon the unneeded reins. Barely had Lalassu stepped hoof upon it than the animal was carrying him off the bridge.

Silas exhaled and laughed softly. Had he been a little less anxious this time? There was no sweat upon his brow, and the knot in his stomach was quick to unravel. Once again, settled upon Lalassu's back, he found himself a braver, surer man. It would be quite wonderful if he was able to slay the next teratism while seated in the saddle. Silas was picturing such an encounter when something struck him directly in the back. Hard fingers dug into his shoulders.

'You great clod.' A shrill voice spoke close to his ear, and another solid blow landed between his shoulder blades.

Lalassu reared and the extra weight upon Silas's back threatened to spill him from the mare. He threw himself forward, grabbing handfuls of her lustrous mane.

'Get off me!' he shouted, working hard to keep his seat.

But his passenger had no such issue. A hand slapped at the back of Silas's head, then at his right shoulder before returning again to his head. All the while the painful grip dug deeper into his left shoulder where his assailant steadied himself. Silas flailed one arm, trying to reach behind him and lay hands upon his attacker. His fingers met with air alone. But it could not be. He could feel the pressure of a body against him, the heat of their breath as they shouted at him.

'Wakin' me up, eh? Think you can bring that beast here at this time? I tell you what, you're a madman to think it.'

Slap. Slap. Punch.

But as rapid as the blows were, they were feeble. Sharp and sound, certainly, but potentially harmful they were not. The smacks were something a child might be capable of. A child with the speed of a fox evading the hunt, darting this way and that, eluding Silas's efforts to stay them. Lalassu thumped her hooves to the ground, snorting her displeasure at the unwelcome guest.

'Wake you up? What are you talking about?' Silas grunted, smarting from a precise slap to his cheek. 'Stop this at once. I intend no harm.'

Another slap landed over his ear, causing it to ring. Now more enraged than fearful, Silas thrust his arm once again behind his back. This time his aim was true. He took hold of what felt to be an arm and locked his grip tight. He wrenched his attacker from his back, the load far lighter than he might have imagined, and found himself the captor of a maddened, queer creature.

Silas held fast despite the creature's vigorous protest. It bore the familiar attributes of a human body, with a head, legs, and arms all evident, but its skin was like nothing Silas had seen. It held a silver pallor for the most part, save for those sections where darker pieces flaked away, reminding Silas of a birch shedding its bark. The creature was quite large, at least the size of an adolescent child, but light as a feather. It had rounded, lidless eyes set deep in its bulbous head, and its mouth was a slashed opening below a pointed chin and sleek, sharp ears. It was quite naked. Which was far from the most disconcerting feature. The creature displayed no sex organs at all between its legs. The space was smooth and flat.

'Don't be touching me,' it screeched.

'What on Earth are you?' Silas grimaced, the struggling curiosity dangling before him like caught game. 'And it was you who touched me. I've done nothing to you –'

'Disturbed me rest with your damned horse,' the creature hissed.

It struck out with a spindly but fast-moving leg, catching its heel upon Silas's chin, and snapping his mouth shut so quickly that Silas bit his own tongue. He cried out and loosened his hold. The creature landed lightly on its feet. Lalassu pranced sideways, edging back onto the bridge proper.

'Steady there,' Silas murmured. 'Steady.'

The hairless creature did not rush to put distance between them. Instead, it held its ground, and with its pale shadings and oddly inhuman appearance looked not unlike how Silas might have imagined a ghost, before he learnt better.

'Get on with ya,' it demanded, sweeping its hands towards Silas as though it were an innkeeper attempting to extricate a drunk patron.

Silas frowned down at the diminutive creature. It was difficult to be much concerned when one was seated as he was upon Lalassu, not to mention Silas's own considerable advantage in size.

'I was on my way, it was you who stalled us.' Silas spared a glance back the way they had come, and mild consternation rose as he saw no evidence of Pitch's arrival.

'Speaking back to me, eh?' The creature's too-wide glare was rattling, and Lalassu appeared eager to move on, restless beneath Silas. 'Seems a good time to teach you some manners.'

'You had best be on your way before my companion arrives.' No harm in letting the creature know that Silas was not entirely alone, just in case the spindly, sexless being was more ferocious than its blows accounted for.

'On me bloody way? Born a fool, was ya?' The creature wiped a hand beneath its beak-like nose. 'This is me 'ome. So just you be leaving now without making so much bloody noise as to drive a boggart near mad.'

'A boggart?' Silas frowned down at the creature.

'Don't be screwing up ya nose at me, boy. I see ya now, for the witless lump ya are, if the stink of grave dirt didn't give it away already. You're an ankou, ain't ya? And newly hatched I'm betting. Your type don't know nothing about nothing for the most part. Except throwing that blade of yours around. Ain't my problem that they wipe ya clean to begin with. Let me tell ya what a boggart be.' The creature smacked its lips in a most repulsive way. 'I'm a nasty sort I am, me bite's a vicious one. How's about I show ya?' The creature darted at him, squealing with a most untoward laughter, lips pulled back to expose gums devoid of any teeth at all.

Still, Silas cried out and threw himself away from the small ball of unpleasantness that leapt from the ground to reach for him – quite forgetting he sat astride a towering equine. Silas's feet slipped from the stirrups and his arse left the saddle. He thrust his hands forward too late to find purchase, and with little ceremony, tumbled off his mount. He fell against the low parapet. His hip took the brunt of the blow, but the angle at which he struck cast him over the side of the bridge. He landed in the water with a thunderous crash. Down he went, quickly submerged into a place of his nightmares. The water poured in over him, forcing its bitterly cold way up his nostrils.

Terror rushed in, fresh and new and all-consuming. Not again.

He could not endure this again.

Silas screamed into his liquid grave. It was dark as a tomb beneath the surface, the moon so rapidly extinguished by the waters.

Down he went. Ever deeper.

The water tore down his throat, searing into his lungs, and weighing him down with icy hands. Silas reached skyward, clawing at the water as it flowed around him. Over him. Through him. Taking him over. Claiming him for its own.

But he did not wish to be claimed. He thrashed with renewed vigour, the sting of dirty water paining his eyes and rubbing his throat raw. His lungs held not an ounce of air and stretched to what must be breaking point by the fill of water.

His body jerked, his heart pounded against his ribs, desperate to continue its beating. Silas thrust himself one last frantic time upwards, legs kicking at emptiness.

His head burst through the surface of the deathly waters, and his agonised lungs sucked greedily. He gasped and spluttered and cried with the relief of it all. Through the blur of tears he searched his surrounds. The bank must be nearby, the bridge overhead.

But there was sign of neither. No boggart leering down at him. No pale riderless horse.

Silas squeezed his eyes shut. Opened them.

He kicked his legs beneath him, struggling to keep afloat in a great lake.

This was no insubstantial stream; it was a wide body of water ringed on one side by snow-capped mountains. Grunting and kicking, he managed to turn himself around and his heart lifted. He floated not a few yards from a long wooden jetty, which led back to a boathouse on the shore. Though his body felt soaked through with the weight of the water and his breath escaped him in ragged gasps, Silas sought to move himself towards the solid structure. Yearning for it with a longing that ached its way into his bones.

'Help me,' he rasped. 'Pitch, help me.'

But the weight of his clothing was too great, his body too fatigued to cooperate with the commands his mind screamed at it.

The icy grip of the water covered his shoulders and rose up his neck, marching fast towards his mouth. Jerking like a trout upon a hook, Silas used what was left of his reserves and found them wanting.

He was going to drown. Again.

As the gritty water marched against his lips, he laid eyes upon what could well be the last thing he would ever see. Towering, swaying pines stood sentinel upon the shore of the body of water that sought to consume him. Beyond the trees there hulked a grand castle, a flag upon its highest tower slapping hard in a silent wind. But it was the woman in a white and lilac dress who held his true focus, her flaxen hair catching the late afternoon sun. Her dress was simplistic, a white skirt that hugged her body and whose waistline was lifted to just beneath her breasts, where a fitted lilac jacket with puffed shoulders accentuated her fine figure. It was not a style of costume he'd seen the like of since waking in Holly Village, and yet he had the oddest sense, even as his senses were being wrenched from him, that he knew exactly what fine stitch-work the bodice held: gold thread in diamond shapes upon the lilac. She lifted the hem of her dress as she ran across an open lawn towards him. Her mouth was open, but if she called to him, he did not hear it for the roar of the water.

Silas thrashed and kicked and swore. He could not go now. He would not go. He must hear her voice. He must. There in the dappled light beneath the oak trees, he thought he noticed another figure running some distance behind her. If only he could keep his damned head above water he might see more clearly who came for him.

But nature had no time for his wants and needs. She did not care for his desires. The waters claimed him, dragging him ever down into that frightening abyss. He lost sight of the woman and the other figure just as they reached the shore. They stood desperately far away and Silas only had time to recognise that it was a man who stood with her before he was sinking once more.

Silas screamed into the waters. 'Help!'

And nature replied. Grabbing him by the collar, and slapping him square across the face.

CHAPTER 10

C areless, delicate laughter flowed about him. Silas was hauled off his back and forced upright by rough hands. He could not see straight for the sting of the water, his world a dark blur of movement, but he didn't need his eyes to tell him who handled him.

'Well, you certainly can amuse one, dear Sickle,' Pitch said. 'Gods, man, if she could see you now.'

For one fleeting, painful moment Silas thought Pitch spoke of the woman on the shore, but as his vision cleared so too did the fog that clung to his senses. He found himself returned to the real world. A world devoid of snow-capped mountains, grand castles, and whimsical visions of a woman in lilac. Instead, there was only the daemon.

'So, have you succumbed to madness?' Pitch stood over him, one leg planted on either side of Silas's own, the lengths of his hair pulled back from his face and tied at his neck. The bridge was a smudge of darkness behind him, and the structure was not nearly so formidable as Silas had supposed. 'I'm not sure what else accounts for your showmanship right now. You did ever so make a fool out of yourself.'

Silas blinked down at himself. He sat in water that barely reached high enough to cover his hips. The riverbed was shallow. Even if he were to lie down, the water would struggle to cover the tip of his nose, let alone submerge him completely in coal-black darkness.

'Knew there was something wrong with 'im, I did.' The boggart crept over the side of the bridge like a lumbering spider, and dangled gaunt legs over the edge. If Pitch had so desired, he could have reached up and tapped the creature on its knobbled knee, that was how low the stone structure was set to the water. Silas's fall could not have been nearly as dramatic as he recalled.

'I don't understand,' he whispered.

Pitch groaned. 'Are you returned to your perpetual dumbfounded self again? I was beginning to enjoy it when you did not look quite so bamboozled. You're not entirely unpleasing to the eye, if I'm honest, but your wide-eyed bafflement does you no favours. Come on, get up, for my boots are wet and my stomach empty. I'd like to get to some accommodations before long if you don't mind.' Pitch held out his hand.

Silas stared at the slender fingers but saw only the image of the lake. 'This was not where I thought I fell.' He swept his hand through the water, brushing the murky bottom, and froze with a stunning realisation. Though his heart still raced, he was not held tight in the grip of fear despite the fact that he sat in the water. Certainly, he did not wish to be here, soaked through entirely, but nor was he set to tear off his own skin so as to launch himself clear. 'I was not here...I was not here at all.'

'You weren't here all right,' Pitch sniffed. 'You were dancing mad with panic. Thrashing about like a babe in a washbasin. Your screech could have deafened a banshee, and whatever else might be watching us in these woods. Now do be a dear and get off that lovely arse of yours, won't you? For I won't ask again quite so nicely.'

Silas did not doubt it, but even Pitch's threat did not rouse him from his wet seat. He sought the bandalore in his pocket, finding some comfort in the smooth touch of the wood. The scythe had not roused during his misadventure.

The boggart shifted into a crouch upon the parapet, cracking the bulging knuckles on its bony hands together. 'Stay right where you are, ankou, for I've a mind to see a daemon lose his temper. I've 'eard tell it's quite a magnificent sight.'

Pitch still held out his hand to Silas, but at the boggart's words his fingers curled into a fist. 'You shall see it soon enough, boggart,' Pitch said lightly, 'if you don't close the gaping hole in your face.'

The boggart shrieked, the sound like a crow caught in a wagon's wheel. But it was not fear that took the creature. As the high pitch subsided, Silas realised it was laughter, broken and awful, that leaked from him.

'You don't smell right, you.' The creature fixed bulbous eyes on Pitch.

The daemon only sighed, as he did so often and so well. As though exhaling were barely worth his effort.

'Can't say I've met many daemons,' the boggart continued. 'But those I have usually don't make my nose itch and my eyes water. You're makin' my head hurt with the whiff of you. Strange, it is. Like you've rolled in somethin'.' It paused, slapping its lips together wetly. 'You coverin' something up beneath that stench, then?' It didn't wait for a reply and Pitch showed no signs of delivering one anyway. He was statue still. 'Heard tell there's a good number of daemon soldiers on the run, deserters from his legion. Scattered after the mess he caused. I hear the naiads talkin' beneath the bridge. Bring me stories, they do. Things haven't settled, they say, since *he* fell. What did they call him? The Beserker Prince? He tore up one of his own. A Seraphim, so they say. Now that's a powerful daemon, if he can bring down the likes of that type of angel. Word is even the Daemon Kings lost control of him. Couldn't stop the prince when he clipped the Seraphim's wings well and good. Tore a mighty angel from the sky.'

Pitch moved like the swiftest bird of prey. He rose from the ground, his feet clear above the water and rushed at the boggart, taking hold of its neck and wrenching it from its higher perch. Pitch slammed the struggling creature against the wall of the bridge, pinning it there like a butterfly upon a display board. Several pieces of its flaking skin fluttered away free. The boggart hissed and spat, and Silas saw first-hand just how fast the creature could move, its legs and arms as blurred as a hummingbird's wings as it sought to free itself. The boggart had got its wish. Now it saw a daemon's temper, and it did not seem to be enjoying the experience at all.

'I do not like your fanciful tales,' Pitch hissed in the creature's face. 'They bore me, and I do not like to be bored.'

Silas pushed himself free of his watery seating and stumbled to his feet, the sodden weight of his coat dragging at his shoulders. 'Pitch, calm yourself. It is purposely seeking to rile you.' It was hard to say whether something the creature had said struck a chord, or if Pitch were truly just bored. 'Do not waste your energies upon it. We should continue on and leave it to annoy other travellers.' Silas didn't seek to defend the boggart, not entirely. It was to blame for his current drenched state, but that hardly warranted the type of punishment he knew Pitch capable of dishing out.

'Did the boggart not say it wanted to see me lose my temper?' Pitch held the flailing creature easily. 'I am simply accommodating the request.'

Silas was soaked through, and the night air touched at him with cold fingers. On the riverbank Lalassu and Sanu grazed, with their broad ends shifted towards the spectacle in the water. 'I think you have made yourself quite clear.'

The boggart wheezed and squeaked, its struggle quite frantic now. 'Set...me...down,' it coughed.

'Tell me what you think of a daemon's temper now?' Pitch brought his face close to the boggart's own. It was impossible that the creature's eyes could get any wider, but the mouth had done so, stretching to reveal inner workings that were so white as to glow in the darkness. 'Could you imagine me in this legion you speak of? They all went mad along with him, so the tales go. Do you think I would fit in?'

The boggart appeared to try to nod, but Pitch held him fast. A breeze swept down the shallow stream, ruffling the surface of the water. Every inch of Silas's drenched skin rose with gooseflesh, his teeth chattering. If the boggart had not had enough of Pitch's anger, then Silas certainly had. He strode up to Pitch and grasped hold of his shoulders. 'Enough.' He pulled at the man, hauling him backwards.

Perhaps the unexpectedness of such a move worked in his favour, because Pitch let out a gasp and released his hold on his prisoner. He swore his displeasure with the gusto of a weathered seaman, and the boggart squealed its delight, scampering up the stonework, settling there to glare down at them.

'You could have been spat from old King Lucifer's cock just as that prince was. I'll give you that.' The creature seemed delighted by its own tirade, its laughter akin to a marble-filled jar rolled upon the floor.

Silas had to admire the creature's foolish courage. He was not sure he would linger after such an encounter, let alone throw insults. Pitch stood before him, silent, his back to Silas but his head hung too low for his eyes to be set upon his lost prey.

'Go on with you,' Silas called out to the boggart, who had still not yet deemed it wise to flee. 'And bother us no more.'

'This is me bloody 'ome. And even the likes of him won't see me movin' from it. 'Specially not now the world's going all topsy-turvy. It's the pair of ya who should be getting on. Take your death and your violence far from 'ere, for there's enough of it around.'

Silas scowled. 'Now listen here, it was you who attacked me to begin with and –'

'Let us go, Sickle.' Pitch turned to face him. His eyes were illuminated, emerald dancing with flecks of flame, bright in the darkness. Silas's pulse thudded. 'Did I not say I was hungry? And you do know how I dislike being hungry.'

He spoke in a strange, flat tone, and Silas could not decide how to decipher it. Calm, perhaps? Or the contrary, a bubbling pot within a moment of boiling over? The ambiguity was disconcerting.

'I am merely waiting on you.' Silas sought to lighten the mood. 'I will quite happily leave this place immediately if there is a decent stew in it.'

Pitch grunted, smoothing at the sides of his black jacket. The cloth was cut to hold tight to the curve of his body, but his waist seemed so defined and narrowed that Silas would not have been surprised to learn that his butterfly-embellished vest was boned. He drew his eyes away, conscious they had lingered too long.

Lalassu waited at the edge of the stream, her grey eyes fixed on him, her pale coat seeming to catch the moon's rays. Silas made his way to her and readied to mount. He thought he might struggle with the added weight of his heavy clothing, but he pressed into the stirrup and swung his leg over the broad back easily. He settled into his saddle, silently praising himself for the trouble-free mounting, and enjoying the brush of calm that came with being upon Lalassu's back. Up here, he was nicely out of reach of Pitch's still-radiating displeasure which was not dampened any by the fact he was forced to traipse much further to regain his mount. Sanu had grazed her way deeper along the road. Her red haunches vanished in behind a willow that hugged the edge of the road like a swaying curtain.

Silas spared the boggart one last look, and the creature met his gaze with a raised chin. A section of its peeling skin there dangled like the pendulum on a grandfather clock.

'Do not bother us again,' Silas said, awash with the courage that came with being astride the pale horse. 'We leave you to your bridge.'

''Tis not me who'll bother you next.' The boggart grinned its wide white grin and scurried over the siding to crawl into the shadows beneath the bridge.

With a sigh Silas urged Lalassu back onto the road. What a curious encounter it had been. Shaking himself, as much to dislodge his shivering as to cast off the strangeness of the bridge crossing, he urged Lalassu into a trot to bring them alongside Pitch who glared at the willow.

'What do you suppose the boggart meant when it spoke of the world being topsy-turvy? Do you think it might know something of the Blight's rise of late?' Silas had put good effort into not thinking too deeply on the troublesome energy seeping from the heart of the Earth. His days were worrisome enough as it was, his dreams well-addled.

'The little bastard is as old as the rocks. Of course it knows something.' Pitch kicked a booted toe into the mud. 'And so soon as it knows you want the answer it will go out of its way to keep it from you. That cretin could not care less if the very world itself were to explode into pieces. It would just crawl out of one of those pieces and continue on.'

He pressed two fingers to his lips and sent forth a whistle that tore Silas's ears near in two. Sanu trotted out from behind the willow like an encroaching shadow. The sharp prick of her ears was evident.

'Huh! The bitch listened to me.' Surprise lit Pitch's face, vanishing a second later. 'As it bloody should.'

Though the horse had returned, it took Pitch several attempts to remount. Try as he might, Silas could not stifle the grin that rose each time. It was dangerous to stir the daemon's ire so soon after it had been placated, but there was something so incredibly amusing about a finely-dressed man with the elegance of the grandest of aristocrats nearly being set on his arse each time he sought to throw a leg over. Sanu flirted more dangerously with demise than the boggart had done, shifting her bulk away at the most inopportune times, causing the daemon to declare a torrent of awful things he would do to her if she did not keep still.

Pitch at last found his seat and took a moment to smooth at his hair. Silas pondered what the boggart had said about the Berserker Prince, and his deserting soldiers. And what of talk of Lucifer? The name had sent a shudder through him at the time, and it did so again now.

They moved on, the deepness of the nighttime shadows swallowing the bridge behind them. Lalassu and Sanu walked side by side, both animals seeming content to make their way in unison despite urgings from both Pitch and Silas to do otherwise. Pitch pulled a tin of shortbread out of the saddlebag and nibbled on the contents. He did not offer any to his companion, and that was fine by Silas. He watched the daemon as he ate. Pitch slouched deeper into his saddle with each golden morsel, his eyes taking on that glazed look that came when the daemon consumed foodstuffs laden with sugar. As Pitch swayed in his seat, Silas dared venture his question.

'Was anything that foolish creature spoke of true?' He cleared his throat. 'The Berserker Prince, was it? And the Seraphim?'

The daemon's eyes were locked on the way ahead, his body stiff with tension. 'Why don't you go drown in your puddle again, the naiads seemed to know it all, perhaps they'll tell you.' He ever so faintly slurred his words, sugar doing as much to impede him as whisky did, but that caustic note of warning had returned.

'You don't wish to speak of it?'

'As I said to the boggart, the tales bore me.'

It was not boredom that had caused his eyes to gleam, and his body to grow still as a gravestone when the boggart spoke. Perhaps it was true then. Pitch *was* a deserter from this mad prince's army. It did not seem too far-fetched an idea. The daemon had already admitted to being upon the Hellfield. He was a solider. And this may account for why Pitch was being silenced. Lady Satine had taken in a deserter and wished none to know. When Silas had asked Pitch how he had come to be in her employ, he had replied only with, *a terrible mistake*. The death of a Seraphim, an angel he presumed, sounded terrible enough. Especially when it appeared the daemon and angel had been on the same side.

But there was one question above all others that he could not suppress.

'There is truly a king called Lucifer?'

Silas waited anxiously as Pitch tried to cram the empty shortbread tin back into the saddlebag. When he failed for the third time, he threw the tin into the woods.

'There is such a cockheaded fool as he.' He flourished his hand. 'Daemonkind's most vainglorious King Lucifer. Never puts a cloven hoof wrong, so far as he is concerned.'

Silas's eyes widened. 'Cloven hoof?' he whispered. 'You're talking of the devil.'

'Oh fuck, Sickle.' Pitch lolled in the saddle. 'Tell me you do not put weight in those bloody tomes the priests bandy about, otherwise I'll be forced to slap you. They may have some of the names right, but much else is utter dribble. Including cloven hooves. Gods, Lucifer would no sooner oversee a human pit of misery than he would shove his precious vestige up his royal arsehole. He abhors humans. Watching over them, delivering paltry punishments for all eternity would be his hell, not theirs.' He laughed so hard at the idea that he threatened to tumble from his slow-moving steed. 'But oh how I should like to see it.'

Silas found none of it remotely amusing. 'Lucifer... is he, the King of Arcadia?'

Pitch released a mighty belch, and Sanu tossed her head. 'He should so wish. No. He is King of Daemonkind but he does not rule alone.' He rubbed at his flat stomach, as though the hastily-consumed shortbreads did not agree with him. 'Lucifer is not nearly so special as he'd like to believe. Three kings rule Daemonkind, while their seven princely spawn do all the actual hard work upon the Hellfield.'

'The Beserker Prince was one of these?'

The question hung lonely and unanswered, until finally Pitch spoke.

'He *was*, you're right. Now there are only six Princes of the Hellfield.' He chewed at his bottom lip. 'Shall we move on from rancid kings and abominable princes and talk of you instead, my Sickle? I'm at a loss as to how a mere boggart could frighten you so that you threw yourself off a bridge –'

'I did not throw myself off the bridge. The rascal attacked me, and the fall was quite accidental.' Silas shuffled against the uncomfortable rub of wet clothing. Blast it, he was not ready to move on from talk of Lucifer but pushing the daemon was foolish.

'Hmm,' Pitch said. 'And what of the fit that came over you, once you were in such desperately deep waters? Accidental as well, I presume?'

Damn the man and his mockery. 'I can hardly be blamed for an innate fear of water.'

'Fear of water? Oh my mistake, I thought you'd been overcome by a terrible aversion to standing upright, seeing as there was so little water to speak of.' His giggle was girlish and ever so infuriating. But at least his eyes no longer glowed. 'Oh come now, my lovely Sickle, is it not a little amusing? You can face and survive the likes of that Black Annis hag, you prance about on that monstrous steed and call yourself the Lady's Horseman, and yet you are terror-stricken by a puddle?'

'It was absolutely not a puddle,' Silas snapped. 'And I call myself no such thing. That is Lady Satine's word, whatever it may truly mean.'

Pitch made a dismissive sound. 'Well, it's a tiresome fear to have. I shall endeavour to push you into any body of water I find and cure you of it entirely. I suppose that is why you would not join me in the pond then. How disappointing. The sooner we rid you of this affliction, the better I say, for I imagine you look fine in a lather, and I am said to have a fine arm for a thorough scrubbing.'

Silas screwed up his nose. 'If you are suggesting I will ever bathe with you, you are set for greater disappointment I'm afraid. Even if I were to rid myself of this phobia once and for all, that shall not happen.'

He did not much enjoy the sideways glance Pitch sent his way, with his lashes lowered demurely and his bowed lips parted. Even with the shadows upon him, his profile was disturbingly pleasing.

'We shall see,' Pitch said.

'There is nothing to see at all. And do not think to use your influence upon me,' Silas said. 'For I am wise to your daemonic ways now and will not be led astray.'

The forest ended abruptly, and Lalassu and Sanu stepped out into a landscape filled with rolling pastures. The peach blush of morning hugged the horizon.

'But what if you wish to be led, Sickle? I've told you, I merely turn a head that wishes to be turned. Whatever you may do, you do so because you desire it.'

'I can assure you,' he said firmly, 'I do not wish to bathe with you.'

Curse Pitch's crooked smile and the wave of hair that fell ever so perfectly down the side of his face. Many a thing about Pitch turned Silas's stomach: his unseemly appetite for violence, his grotesque talk and blatant lust, but damn it all, the man was difficult to look away from.

'Gods, Sickle,' Pitch said, 'You must be quite frightened of that dastardly water if you will not consider such an offer. You have seen me naked, haven't you?' Silas was not about to answer that question. Pitch chuckled, and the sound found its way into Silas's chest, toying at the tightness there. 'Tell me then, how such a paltry thing as water can render you so senseless?'

Silas chewed at his answer, debating the wisdom of revealing too much to the daemon. A crossroads lay up ahead, and wooden signposts declared the destinations on offer. He was grateful then for Lalassu's guidance, as it would spare him from having to request that Pitch read the signs. Much mockery of Silas's inability to read would have been inevitable.

'I have reason to believe I may have died in a body of water.' Silas stopped short of describing what he had seen in his panic-stricken moment in the stream. The vast lake with its rim of mountains and rather magnificent castle. The woman with flaxen hair running to him, the man travelling in her wake, a blur Silas could not determine. Was there a chance that castle had been his home? That woman his friend...a wife?

So lost was he in wondering that Silas did not realise Pitch had not replied, and had managed to push poor Sanu into a generous trot. When he blinked himself clear of his thoughts both horse and rider were some ways down the road ahead of him. It seemed that Pitch did not care much for Silas's cause of death.

'Where are you going?' he called.

'To determine if my eyes deceive me, or if salvation lies ahead,' Pitch cried, pulling Sanu up short alongside the signposts. 'Aha! Salvation is afoot. We are not long from Mordiford.'

Lalassu broke into a trot, her greater stride bringing them to the crossroads in just a few lengths.

'Mordiford? If that is not where Goodrich Castle lies, then we have no time for it.'

'You have no time for it perhaps.' Pitch wheeled his horse around. 'Are we not deserving of rest? It is fine for you on your steed, but Sanu is set to collapse beneath me. Come, there is a delightful place called The Moon Inn where the landlord's daughter is rather a charming lass, and far more agile than she may appear on first sight. I'll introduce you. It wouldn't do you any harm to have your wick dipped after your frightful encounter with that puddle.' What Silas would not do to wipe that smirk from the daemon's face.

'We cannot deviate.'

'We can always deviate.' Pitch winked at him. 'So long as we return to the true path eventually.' He flapped the reins against Sanu's neck. 'Ha!'

The horse, most astonishingly, set off at a vigorous trot before breaking into a canter. Sanu seemed as much pleased by the idea of Mordiford as Pitch himself.

Silas cursed as he watched them take the well-worn road that led northeast. Lalassu had kept them headed in a mostly southeasterly direction since leaving Bishop's Castle. It was hardly likely Mordiford was anywhere near their destination. 'Damn that man. Pitch! Come back at once.'

Lalassu nickered. She swung her head towards the southerly path, then back to the road where Sanu and Pitch grew smaller every moment. He couldn't deny that Pitch's idea of a stopover was appealing. They had ridden through the night and for hours before that. Silas was far too weary to even consider a dalliance of any kind, but he would not mind a chance to dry his clothes and lay his head upon a pillow. Still, which path they chose was not Silas's decision to make. Pig-headed daemon or not.

He stroked Lalassu's broad neck, the shimmer of moss green evident in the coat no less mesmerising. 'Are we to set off without him?'

The mare turned them towards the village of Mordiford.

CHAPTER 11

A formidable stone bridge stood between Silas and Mordiford, far grander than the one where he had the misfortune of meeting the boggart. This one was wide enough that three horses might walk abreast without their riders' stirrups brushing against their neighbour. But despite how steadfast the structure appeared, Silas hesitated. Just as the bridge was more considerable, so too were the waters that flowed beneath it. The current swirled the muddy surface with flecks of white.

Pitch had crossed already and stopped now for the very first time to see if Silas had followed at all from the signpost.

'Are you going to throw yourself off this bridge as well?' he called.

'Walk on,' Silas muttered to Lalassu.

He kept his eyes fixed upon the road ahead and did not allow his gaze to stray beyond the parapets and what lay below. The mere sound of the waters, the hush of them as they passed beneath him, saw him grit his teeth, the scratchings of his fear making themselves known against his insides. Still, he could not but wonder at what might occur were he to fall into this churning mass. The thought of it turned his stomach well enough, but might he recall yet more of the woman and the lake? Silas shook off the notion. Most likely he would repeat his unfortunate demise and drown most thoroughly.

The pale horse moved with her usual grace, and it was not long before they were stepping foot upon solid ground on the far side of the river.

'Well, that was rather dull.' Pitch met him with a wry grin. 'I quite enjoyed seeing you wild with terror earlier.'

Silas urged Lalassu on, ignoring the daemon completely, for his attentions lay elsewhere. Greeting them as they entered the village was the church, its rather magnificent bell tower reaching skyward, a cross at its pinnacle. At its base a sharply-pitched roof denoted the church proper with its slender arched windows and their stained glass just catching the hint of sunrise against their panes. But it was the scent of the place that pleased him most. Silas breathed in and the richness of the grave dirt left him dizzy with pleasure. He could not yet see sign of headstones but was convinced they lay there, in behind the buildings. And here rested peaceful dead. The soil did not wrench at him or send a sign that all was not well.

They passed beyond the church, leaving the quiet dead behind, and continued down the main street. It was a pleasant enough village, made up of a mixture of whitewashed houses with their dark beams, and sturdier stone houses with jutting chimney pipes. Only a smattering of the chimneys pushed faded white smoke into the air. Both types of abodes crowded in on the roadway where there was little passing traffic. A solitary man smoked a pipe as he sat upon his doorstep and made no secret of his scrutiny as the pair of riders moved along.

'Where is this inn you spoke of?' Silas sent his words over his shoulder, where Pitch once again struggled to urge Sanu into more than a lazy walk. It seemed her forwardness of earlier was well and truly done with.

'Within sight and this blasted horse chooses now to delay. I swear I shall roast you over the largest fire I can pile if you do not move,' Pitch snapped.

For a confusing moment Silas thought himself the target of Pitch's ire, but soon realised that special pleasure was reserved this time for Sanu.

'Gods, I am done with this farce.' Pitch slid from his mount, setting upon the ground as light as a sparrow upon an eave. He set off at a quick stride and easily made up the distance between Sanu and Lalassu.

'Pitch, what are you doing? You cannot leave Sanu wandering the streets.'

'I bloody can, and I just did. I assure you the Lady Satine's nag will not abandon me, so much as I might want her to. Come, come. Our destination lies ahead.'

He strode on, his steps carrying him a greater length than they ought, a handy talent to have when one was in a hurry to reach their destination. But as wonderful as a fireside chair and a pint of ale might sound, Silas was not about to leave Lalassu to such wanderings. He could make out the swinging blue sign that denoted The Moon Inn, a picture of a lake bright with the glow of a moon's fullest rays. It was as Pitch had said, just up ahead, sitting at a junction in the road.

'You be wantin' to stable them horses before you go to the inn, I'm bettin'?'

Silas turned in the saddle. The smoking gentleman from the doorstep had followed after them and stood alongside Sanu. The mare rubbed her forehead against his side, and he scratched beneath her coppery mane. He was a robust man with a squat, flat nose that ran at a crooked angle and weather-beaten skin that made guessing at his age near on impossible.

'Yes, is there somewhere you could direct me?'

The man's pleasant blue eyes twinkled. And the corners of his lips twitched with a gentle smile. 'Figures he'd leave you here to make your own way. Mr Astaroth's not one for such considerations.'

'You know Pit...Mr Astaroth?'

'Oh yes. He's ridden out in the Lieutenant's company more than once over the past year. Haven't seen him for a few months though, to be fair. Richards down at The Moon won't be much happy to see 'im. Didn't take much of a liking to the dandy with the cutting tongue and a sharp talent at the cards.' His laugh was throaty and warm.

Silas stared down at the top of the man's head. 'The Lieutenant?'

'Aye. Lieutenant Charters, a gentleman from Hereford way. He's got a family estate there. Man of means and good temperament. He's been coming to hunt in our woods since he was a lad. Caused a bit of a stir here those two when they first arrived together. Weren't exactly discreet, if you be taking me meaning.' The man's chuckle was ripe with suggestion. 'Had some of the townsfolk in quite a tizz, especially those ladies who thought they was in with a chance of mixing with some fine company.'

The man peered up at him, lips pursed. 'I'm talkin' out of turn. I'll stop now. Don't want to get myself into any trouble with that companion of yours. I've seen what happens if you rile him. Got a quick temper that one. But being in his company as you are, I'm sure you know that already.' His smile revealed several missing teeth on his bottom jaw. 'Just this way, Mr Mercer. We'll get your horses settled in and have you on your way to the inn in no time.'

'Thank you very much.'

They walked on. The shadow cast by Lalassu's great bulk covered the man entirely. Sanu plodded alongside him, following with far more vigour in her step than she'd ever shown for Pitch. Silas pondered the man's talk of the lieutenant. He'd known before now that Pitch and the man were acquainted, of course. When Silas had attended Baron Feversham on his first official appointment for the Order, the baron and his guests had been quite forward in their suggestions that the pair were very familiar with one another. And Pitch himself had interrogated Silas when he learnt of his meeting with Edward Charters at the marquess's ball.

But now with Cecil's lightly concealed insinuations it seemed highly likely the pair were indeed more than just hunting partners. Hardly surprising, Silas thought, considering Pitch's reputation. So why then did it leave him so unsettled to think of them together? He shook his head softly. It was no concern of his what Pitch did in his bedchamber.

'Name's Cecil, by the way. Pleased to make your acquaintance, Mr...'

'Oh, Mercer, Silas Mercer.' Silas grabbed at the distraction. 'Pleasure to meet you, Cecil.'

He led them down a narrower side road which stole The Moon Inn from view. Pitch had long since entered without a backward glance.

'Might I ask what brings you to Mordiford this fine early morn?'

With his thoughts elsewhere the question caught Silas utterly off-guard. He found himself blurting out a mostly-truthful reply, forgoing all caution.

'We're here on behalf of the Order of the Golden Dawn. I doubt you would have heard of it –'

'Ah, the spirtualists. Tellers of fortune, readers of the cards, and hunters of all things that keep folk up at night.' Cecil chuckled. 'I've got a wife who's mad for it all. Her sister keeps feeding her all the stories. She works down in London, lady's maid for some toff or another.' He stopped, casting an anxious glance up at Silas. 'Sorry, sir, I didn't mean to –'

Silas waved off the concerns. 'I am no toff, Cecil. I assure you.'

Cecil's chest crackled with laughter and too much of the pipe. 'Right then, sir. And Mr Astaroth is a member too then?' He seemed quite unconvinced.

'No, no. He is my escort for the journey. A guardian, as it were.'

Cecil shrugged. 'I can see that more likely than 'im reading tarot, I'll grant you. Slight he might be, but I'd not cross him. Now, here's the stables for you. Can I just say, that's a magnificent animal you have there.'

'She is a beauty, isn't she?'

'Aye. Though she's a fine mare too this one.' He patted Sanu's shoulder, and the horse lifted her head, as bright as Silas had seen her.

'They are both to be admired, indeed.'

They drew to a stop in front of the stables, a basic structure settled in between a row of single-level houses pressed up against one another. How pleasant it was to have a reasonable conversation, not worrying when it might grow sharp with barbs of sarcasm. But Silas could not help but worry at what trouble Pitch was already stirring inside the inn. And foolish as it may be, he was eager to question him about the lieutenant. Silas detected a vulnerability lay there and had to admit that he felt somewhat reassured to know such a crack in Pitch's armour could exist. Silas was all too human in comparison to this creature from a world of angels and daemons, mighty kings and berserker princes.

He dismounted, steadying himself a moment as his legs adjusted to the sudden firmness. Cecil stood on tip-toe to lift the reins over Lalassu's head, which the horse graciously lowered to aid him in his endeavour. The man was relatively tall, but still Silas stood a good head and shoulders above him. Not that it seemed to bother Cecil. For the first time no mention was made of Silas's stature. Pleased, he moved to Sanu and untied the saddlebag that he knew to contain their coin. Silas enquired as to the cost.

'Whatever you think's fair, I'd say. I'll give them a rub-down, and some chaff.' Cecil led a very willing pair of horses into the dimness of the stables, where stalls were packed high with fresh straw.

'Thank you very much.'

Uncertain what price to pay for the service, Silas decided upon two shillings and set them upon the wooden rail which separated the two stalls.

'Very generous of you, sir. You're a good man to be sure.' Cecil leaned down to tend to Lalassu's enormous hooves, and Silas stifled a sigh. If he had just paid too much, then Pitch would be sure to make it known. 'Can't say I picked you for a Mary, though. But you'll get no bother from me, Mr Mercer. Each to their own, I like to say.'

Heat filled his face. 'Mr Astaroth and I are just associates through the Order, that is all.'

Cecil did not look over from where he busied himself with relieving Lalassu of her saddle. 'Ah, righto. Must have been seeing things where this is nought to see. Don't mind me, I'm an old man and my eyes ain't what they used to be. But you might want to pass on some advice to Mr Astaroth. He set some tongues wagging last visit with him and the lieutenant, and they'll only tolerate so much 'ere. He'd best be a bit more discreet.'

Silas should have protested once more and made it as clear as the finest polished crystal that he did not indulge in any such untowardness, but instead he found himself lost in imagining just what vulgar displays Pitch stood accused of. His face warming at the scenarios his mind conjured.

'Me wife's going to go right mad with excitement when I tell her,' Cecil continued, 'that the Order has sent a strapping fellow to Mordiford. You here for the dragon or to charm the lady-folk out of their coin, Mr Mercer?'

'Dragon?' Silas said, alarmed.

'Tale as old as the village itself. A dragon falls for a young maid by the name of Maud, settles itself where the rivers Lugg and Wye meet so as it can watch over 'er. But the farmers don't much like its appetite for their flocks. We've had 'em here in the past, hunters that is. Each time a sheep gets found with its insides on the outside, everyone goes into a right bluster. Never mind it's likely a wolf or even a fox taking advantage of an ailing ewe, must be for sure a dragon.' Cecil got a belly-jiggling laugh out of that idea.

'Good lord, no,' Silas shook his head. 'We are not here for any dragon.'

'Ah, the ladies then, and the men for your companion. I'm betting you'll draw quite the crowd with your seances, muttering away to the dearly departed in the candlelight. Or are you a card-reading man? Fortune's your thing?'

There was no meanness in Cecil's words, but there was little doubt what he thought of the whole spiritualism movement. That is to say, not much at all.

'We are not staying long in Mordiford,' Silas said, his cheeks cooling. 'This is a rest stop, nothing more, as we head south. Your ladies are quite safe.'

Cecil returned to Lalassu's hooves. 'Not sure they'll be all that happy about that.' He laughed. 'Though I don't pay much mind to all that spiritualist tosh, at least you'll give 'em something else to talk about, save for the forest fae and those bloody bodysnatchers.'

Silas frowned. 'Bodysnatchers? You have issue with them here, too?'

'Too? You're talkin' like you've heard about it before.'

'I may have. We have travelled from the northwest and' – he hesitated – 'well, there was talk of some issue there with snatching.'

Cecil nodded, hoof-pick in hand. 'That's where it's said to be coming from, the northwest. Talk of a generous benefactor with lots of coin to throw about for the right corpse. Our grave keeper here, lad named Herbert, has been talkin' his mouth off after a few ales, says none of the younger folk should be dying anytime soon or he'd be tempted to dig 'em up.'

'That's the same story I've heard.' The encounter with the gravedigger left him uneasy still. 'Do you have any idea of the source of the rumours...who the benefactor might be?'

'Me?' Cecil snorted. 'No clue and no interest. Don't care much what they do with me bones when I'm done and buried. But tell me, Mr Mercer, if you ain't looking into the bodysnatchers, and you are headin' south, don't 'spose you could spread word you're 'eadin' in to the forest to see to those damned fae?' He patted Lalassu's rump, moving to tend to Sanu's hooves. 'Just say you're gonna chase the fae queen out, once and for all, you and I both know it ain't true cause she don't exist. But it would put a lot of minds at ease, and people might stop scarin' themselves silly.'

'Are you talking of the Forest of Dean?'

'The very one. I'm seeing a glint in your eye, Mr Mercer. Did I strike upon it? You *are* heading into the forest then?'

'We are.' There seemed no harm in mentioning it. By Sybilla's account the forest was massive. There would be no telling where exactly they were intended. 'Do the villagers truly believe there are faerie folk there?'

Christ almighty. Dragons, faeries, and bodysnatchers. How complex his life had become.

'Oh aye, the fae and all manner of monsters with them. And they believe it all right. So does every town and village that sits near it or in the forest itself.' Cecil's laughter rumbled. 'A dark woods at night does strange things to a man's mind, all sorts of tales come out of that place. Have done for generations. Fae queen rules out of the mines there, so it goes. Nothing like being deep underground to make a man mighty superstitious. They say you don't take a newborn babe through there lest you end up with a changeling, and best be careful where you step lest you find Jenny Greenteeth's lair beneath your feet. I grew up on the lore, much as everyone around here has.'

'There are mines in the forest?'

'Aye, prosperous ones too I'm told. On account of the bluecaps.' His grin was wide and careless. 'Surprised you look so confused, Mr Mercer, being an Order man and all. The bluecaps are the fae of the forest. They lend a helping hand to the miners sometimes, knocking on the walls to let 'em know of a cave-in coming, or showing them a vein of yellow ochre. Ain't that nice of 'em?'

Cecil, at least, was enjoying the folklore immensely.

'Very accommodating, indeed. But I can assure you we are not bound for any faerie queen's lair.' Silas smiled, mostly at Cecil's obvious and rather contagious bemusement at such a scenario.

'Careful as you go, you might not have a say in it. She'd think very highly of you pair, I dare say. They say she has quite the eye for an admirable man. Not sure I'd paint Mr Astaroth admirable, but it can't be said he can be easily overlooked.' He finished with Sanu's hooves and moved to a bucket that contained other brushes. 'I dare say though, even the bluecap queen would regret capturing Mr Astaroth.'

'I dare say you are right. Speaking of which, he will be waiting on me.'

'Alright then, Mr Mercer. You take care of yourself now. It's been nice talkin' with you. I'll be telling me wife that the Order might have some decent folk in them yet.'

'Do send her my regards. And thank you once again, Cecil.'

Silas gave the man a short bow and made his way out of the darkened stables back into the birthing day, his head abuzz with all the strange things he'd heard. Despite being certain that Pitch would declare Silas a gullible fool, he wished to tell him of what had been said. And hear him deny entirely that such a thing as fae existed. There were already far too many *naturals* in the world for Silas's liking.

Silas made his way to The Moon Inn, where the scent of fresh bread was now rich upon the air, partnered with a deeper hue of cooking meat. Stew, Silas suspected; beef, if he were to attempt a guess. And though the hour was far too early for such a dish, he hurried himself inside with his mouth watering. Sybilla might have pandered to Pitch's sweet tastes when filling the saddlebags, but Silas had been rather forgotten. He blinked, his eyes adjusting to the darker light within the building. There did not appear to be anyone else at all in the establishment, too early an hour even for the village drunk. A woman's laughter made her known before Silas laid eyes upon her. She sat perched upon an armchair by the window, her silhouette clear against the brightness of the day. She was petite. Her feet barely touched the floor, and her plain skirt hung just shy of her ankles. The pale yellow shawl she held had slipped from one shoulder, revealing a white blouse that was several buttons undone from decent. She was deep in conversation with whomever sat in the high-backed chair, the wings of the seat concealing them from view, but Silas suspected he knew who drew her attention so firmly. When a hand touched at her chin and traced its way down her neck headed for the swell of her pert breasts, Silas was certain.

'Mr Astaroth,' he said firmly.

The young woman squeaked and jumped to her feet, gathering her shawl around her. She was a simple-looking thing, a rounded face with brown hair braided to frame it, eyes ever so slightly too small for the face they were set in, a chin with a sharpness that didn't match the rotundness of her other features. But most disconcerting was the chubbiness beneath her skin, the swell of youth. She was barely a young lady. Silas glared at the figure in the chair, who had not bothered to show sign he'd heard Silas. Had the man no boundaries at all? The only mercy was that the inn was entirely empty.

'You must be Mr Mercer?' the girl said, padding on brisk feet towards him. 'It's a pleasure to meet you.' She bobbed in an unnecessary curtsy. With her closer proximity her flushed skin was evident, so too was the red, vaguely lip-shaped blotch upon her neck. 'My name is Mabel.'

'Good day to you, Miss Mabel.'

Her giggle confirmed her place on the leaner edge of youth. 'You're ever so tall and grand, just as Mr Astaroth said.'

'I'm sure.'

'Were you feeding the horses stalk by stalk?' Pitch called. 'I had intended to send Mabel to search for you, but we were rather distracted. Such wonderful conversation, wasn't it, dear?'

The girl in question blushed a brighter shade of pink, running her fingers along the tassel's of her shawl. 'It was quite wonderful.' She shivered, actually shivered.

Silas winced, deciding this must be the landlord's daughter Pitch had remarked on earlier. Poor child. 'I wondered if you might have some food at the ready?'

'Oh yes, yes. Mutton stew is in the pot right now. Can I get you a bowl?'

Silas nodded, though his stomach sank somewhat. He'd been altogether ready for beef. 'Thank you. And some tea, perhaps?'

'Tea. Gods what a bore,' Pitch said snidely, though low enough Silas suspected he was not meant to hear.

Mabel leaned into her whisper with a grin. 'He does enjoy his wine, doesn't he? I barely have time to fill the pitcher and he's ready for another serve.' She laughed gaily, as though it were the most amusing thing in the world. All at once she shivered again, blinking stunted lashes quite madly. When next her gaze lifted to Silas, her eyes widened in shock, and she stepped back as though noting how close she stood for the first time.

'I'm sorry, sir,' she stuttered. 'Goodness, a grand one, aren't you? I'll be getting that food right away for you.'

She left him so quickly that Silas did not have time to offer up his thanks.

'Come, sit, Sickle.' Now Pitch leaned forward in his chair, but with the window's glare behind him, he remained little more than a silhouette: one with sculpted lines enhancing a fine throat and the perfect set of the nose, tangled curls caressing the base of his neck, eyelashes so long and thick even the shadows could not hide them. 'Take that fucking coat off and relax, will you?'

Silas struggled to gather himself. Pitch was shameless in the way he toyed with them all. For that is what it was, Silas decided. These frivolous flights of fancy that overtook him. He'd witnessed Pitch's ability to enchant first hand on that fateful train journey to Leicester and Black Annis. He'd felt its touch himself when he stood alone with Pitch at Lower Broughton Farm. How Silas's body had betrayed him, reducing him to a whimpering dolt with a hardening between his legs and a hunger for the taste of Tobias on his tongue.

It was unseemly. Grotesque. And deeply troubling.

It was an enchantment the daemon used, no doubt, for it was ludicrous to imagine Silas harboured a hidden carnal desire for Tobias Astaroth. Dear god, the daemon had likely done the same to the poor lieutenant. Pitch was dangerous and beautiful, in equal and unattractive measure.

Silas smoothed at his coat. Though it was rather warm in the interior of the inn and it would have been pleasant to remove his coat to allow it to fully dry, Silas did not do so, determined not to allow Pitch to command him.

'She is but a child, Pitch. It is not right for you to enchant her so.'

'Mabel left her childhood behind some time ago, and I had nought to do with that. It is she who makes eyes at me. Who am I to let her suffer unrequited?'

'I would like to continue on as soon as possible.'

'You haven't even bloody well sat down. You are stiff as a rod, and not in a pleasant way. Sit down, man.'

Silas remained on his feet. He glanced towards the empty bar. Pots and crockery clattered behind a swinging door at the far end. 'You have a name here, already, it seems. The man who assisted me with the horses told me that you visited here frequently with the lieutenant, Edward Charters. That was the man I met at the marquess's ball, was it not?'

'What of it? I enjoy company.' Pitch surveyed the wineglass he held, the deep crimson liquid swaying side to side as he tilted the glass. 'The stableman has flapping lips.'

'It seems you caused quite the stir when last you visited here together.'

'I cause a stir simply when I enter a room, or have you not noticed?'

No sign remained of Pitch's punishing encounters with the boxer and the constable, his alabaster skin blemish free once more. His brilliant green eyes were unhindered by ghastly bruising. He was returned entirely to his beguiling self. But Silas was not about to indulge his ego further.

'You could not have caused much of a stir here though.' Silas waved at the empty chairs around them. 'Your talents have quite gone to waste.'

'Mabel would disagree, I assure you.'

Silas decided he was quite right in assuming that Pitch would not care one iota for the reputation of any man he dallied with. 'We cannot stay long here –'

'Correction, you cannot stay here long. I'll stay as long as I desire.'

'Pitch, that is not –'

'Spare me, mighty ankou. I'm in no mood for talk of your precious quest.'

'It is *our* quest, if you'll call it that.'

Pitch threw back the last of his wine. 'I'll call it my ball and chain, for that is what it is. We will go to your castle, don't fret so, Sickle. Stop acting like such a wet sack of Nephilim scat. Rest, fuck, drink yourself senseless. You are not the Lady's servant every moment of the day or night, despite what she'd have you believe. I have something I wish to do here, that is all. We will continue on, you have my word.' What that was worth, Silas could not say, but his stomach growled loudly enough for Pitch's eyes to dart to his belly. 'There you have it!'

'What do you wish to do here, Pitch? Tell me it is not to have yourself beaten in a ring once more. I shall not bother to scoop you up again.'

Pitch crossed his legs, his stovepipe trousers clinging to every curve. 'Nothing of the sort, and admit, won't you, that it stiffened you to see me that way. Barely dressed, ripe with sweat and blood.'

'Dear god, you are tiresome.' Silas pinched at his nose.

'Then rest. There are rooms upstairs which are not terrible.'

How wonderful a bed sounded in that moment. Silas sighed. 'Perhaps I will. But promise me, you won't do anything foolish. And if you consider such a thing you will speak with me first?' He braced for the irritation he thought might follow, but Pitch's smile was generous, his plump lips reddened by the wine.

'I have neither intention nor reason to do anything foolish.'

Though he knew that as unlikely as gold raining from the sky, Silas nodded. 'Cecil, the stableman, spoke of the Forest of Dean. He painted quite a picture, I must say. He believes there to be all kinds of folk about in there. Faeries, he said, "bluecaps" he called them.' Silas laughed jaggedly. 'Can you believe such a thing?'

He had hoped Pitch might snicker at the suggestion of such creatures, but instead he shrugged.

'Why ever would I not? Now unless you are going to fetch me another wine, could you please take yourself elsewhere? You do rather reek of foetid water and horse shit. '

Silas glowered but could find no energy to protest. He glanced at the kitchen, wondering at how long it took to organise a bowl of stew as his stomach growled yet again.

'Go on, I'll have them bring your food to you when it's ready. For the love of all the gods, find a washbasin and cleanse yourself. Even I would not touch you in the state you're in.'

'Fine,' Silas said, for he was truly quite tired and could see no reason they should not rest after a night spent travelling. 'I should like to leave before the sun sets, though. I don't wish to travel the entire time in darkness.'

'Afraid of the faeries, are we?' Pitch settled back into his seat. 'Or boggarts perhaps? Fancy another dunking in the rivulet, my dear Sickle?'

The whine of wood upon hinges filled the silent air. Mabel made her way towards them with a wide tray laden with two large bowls, the steam evident from their tops. Silas went to meet her before she travelled too far.

'I wonder if you might have a room I could rent?'

'Why certainly.' She chewed at her lip. 'Just the one, sir?'

He met her question with narrowed eyes. 'One room, for one person. Thank you very much. Mr Astaroth will take care of his own affairs.' Of that Silas was quite certain.

'Very good, sir. Take the stairs.' She nodded at a single wooden door at the back of the room. 'And you can have the first room on the left. I'll bring up some water so you can get rid of that smell on you just as soon as I deliver Mr Astaroth's meal.' She said it all rather breathlessly, her gaze darting towards the man in the armchair by the window, as though each second she stood away from him pained her. 'Here, you can take this now if you like. I'll be up shortly with the water.'

She set down her tray on the nearest table, and lifted one of the bowls. Thick, greasy brown liquid spilled over the edge. Silas reached for it, careful to stand as far from her as practicality allowed, mortified to learn that Pitch had not exaggerated his need to bathe. Mabel turned from him the moment he took possession of the bowl, and skittered to where the daemon waited.

Silas paused in his departure, watching as Pitch ran his fingers up her arm, eliciting a high giggle from the girl. It were as though Silas did not exist in the room at all, and he was struck by the most untoward sense of loneliness. He hurried away, before fatigue made a greater fool of him and he found reason to linger in the daemon's company.

CHAPTER 12

T he mutton stew was not half as terrible as it appeared. It was greasy beyond measure, certainly, but rich and salty and brimming with generous portions of carrot, potato, and mutton. Silas was not quite as pleased with his bed, however. Mabel had given him the largest the inn could offer, but it fell well short of accommodating his length, and the horsehair-stuffed mattress was so lumpy that he suspected he'd awaken with a terrible backache. In truth, he doubted he'd sleep at all. It was a cloudless day outside, and the strip of dirty yellowed muslin meant to serve as a curtain upon the single window in the stuffy room did little to keep the brightness at bay. Add to that the plethora of thoughts that chased one another in his head, and Silas assumed he'd simply lie here an hour or two, tossing and turning, before giving up entirely and joining Pitch in his wine.

He was happily mistaken.

He drifted off, deep into a dreamless sleep. There was no telling how long he slumbered, and he woke in a start, his hand slipping to search for the bandalore beneath his pillow. It was there, as he had left it. He sighed, letting wakefulness find him in full. His cock poked at the bedcovers, lazily aroused as it was prone on first waking. Stretching, Silas rose and made his way to the window. Conscious of his near-naked state, he angled himself beside it so he'd not be seen from the road. He wore only his undershirt. The rest of his clothes, all but his coat which Mabel had taken to lay out before the larger downstairs fire, were arrayed upon a chair placed near to the narrow fireplace where coals struggled to heat the small room.

He edged back the curtain. The sun hovered high in the sky. A smattering of cloud marching quickly across its face, pushed by the breeze that had risen. The village had come to life, with carts hauling hay and livestock below, and neighbours calling to one another as an assault of smells touched the air. Baking bread, most notably, and a fishier odour beneath it. He supposed there might be catches to be made in the river that cradled the village. He inhaled, savouring that most delicious of scents.

The air was redolent with the pungent earth beneath the headstones.

Silas exhaled – acutely aware of how strange it was to relish such a thing, and yet finding a comfort like no other. The only scent that came near to it was the waft of jasmine that accompanied Jane, and as pleasant as her perfume was, it did not burrow its way into his muscles, loosening them, nor trickle into his blood and make his heart thump more solidly.

He wondered if Jane thought of him in his absence, for he quite missed her brisk and useful demeanour. The air elemental was ever so sure of herself, and quite sensible. Despite her curious talents, Jane never caused Silas to feel the ever-present wariness that came with Pitch's company.

He made his way to his hanging clothes, hoping they had dried enough to be worn once more. Standing as undressed as he was, with the cool air teasing his nethers, would not do. Mabel was likely to knock upon the door at any moment with his coat, or worse, Pitch himself might decide to enter. Silas gathered up his clothes, assessing them quickly. They were warm to the touch, not a hint of dampness about them. The hum of voices and tinkle of glass whispered beneath the door. Whatever time it may be, the inn was fuller than it had been when they arrived.

Silas dressed, much of the fabric stiff and crinkled after his crude attempt at laundry. There was a cracked, mottled mirror above the dresser. He peered at his reflection. With his memories hidden, or gone, looking upon his own face always brought with it an odd sense of detachment. As though he viewed a stranger. He did not recall those light brown eyes with the pronounced ring of black around their irises, nor the solidness of the cleft chin. A chin that now held a distinct, rough fuzz of black. His peered more intently and ran his hands across the fledgling beard growing upon his face, the short hairs were sharp against his fingers. A curious sudden growth. His hair surprised him too. It hung almost to the base of his neck. Silas tucked the wavy black strands behind his ears. A month and a half ago he'd reawakened in his cottage at Holly Village with a clean-shaven face and neatly trimmed hair clipped about his ears. In the proceeding weeks that had passed his hair had not grown and there had been no need for a razor. But since Black Annis, much had changed. His hair seemed to grow an inch every night, and he would soon need the attentions of a decent barber. Even now he really should tend to the shadow upon his chin but had neither the implements nor the desire to address his unkempt appearance. It seemed the peculiarities of his reanimation would never end.

Silas pocketed the bandalore and made his way downstairs. He paused at the base of the stairs, not keen to enter the inn proper. The conversations coming from the bar were loud and many, sounding as though half the town of Mordiford was in attendance. He pressed his lips in irritation. He was in no mood for scrutiny, still muddle-headed from sleep, the mutton stew not sitting so well as he might hope, and his bladder urging him to find somewhere to relieve himself. He knew he should perhaps reunite himself with his coat before venturing outside, but he was not ready to face strangers. Or Pitch.

To his left he noted a shorter flight of stairs that ran downward from the level he stood upon. At the base of the stone steps, threads of light pierced through the slats of a wooden door. Here lay his escape route. Silas had taken a single step when a bright and soaring laugh rose above the chatter. The pretty notes danced high and were ripe with frivolity. There could be no doubting their bearer. Silas wondered if Pitch had left the bar at all, and suspected he knew the answer well enough.

He retraced his steps until he reached the door that led into the main room and peered through its pleasant red-stained glass inserts. It took little investigation to locate Pitch. The daemon was arranged, of course, at the very heart of matters. He stood in front of the armchair Silas had left him in, now surrounded by an entranced cluster of people. Unfortunately, Mabel was amongst them, an empty pitcher dangling from her fingers. Silas tilted his head so he might see the bar. A roughly-shaven man now tended there, scowling across the crowd as he towelled dry a pint glass. At least one onlooker was not quite so transfixed, Silas mused.

The group held fast to their pints and glasses, the scene painted a hue of pink by the red glass Silas peered through. Several patrons lined the window seat, while a solid woman with dark skin and copious wrinkles sat in the armchair Pitch had offered Silas earlier. Opposite her, where Pitch had previously lounged, a round-cheeked older woman in a grey smock stared fixedly at the daemon standing before her. Pitch enthralled them all with showmanship of a different kind. He reached for the woman's ear and, with a flamboyant flourish and much heralding of his own brilliance, produced a single red rose from seemingly nowhere to the general delight of his audience. Silas could not help but think of Cecil. If he had witnessed this he'd be no less convinced the Order were nothing but charlatans.

At least this was no boxing match. But was this what Pitch was so insistent he needed to do here? Play magician? Silas stepped away from the door, shaking his head, more convinced than ever that he needed fresh air. He made his way back to the stone steps. Their uneven surface threatened to unbalance him, and he made his way down their five lengths carefully. Finding the door unlocked, he pushed it open, and found himself upon the main village thoroughfare. Certainly not in any opportune spot to relieve himself. The inn rose high above him, the entranceway pressed into the rock wall that supported this section of the building upon a gentle rise. Dazzled by the light, he shaded his eyes.

'Mr Mercer? Is that truly you?'

He blinked in the direction of the voice, startled by its closeness, and familiarity. 'Lieutenant Charters?'

Pitch had not delayed here for parlour tricks at all.

'Edward, please.'

'Oh, I'm sorry, Edward. Of course.'

The man's background came back to Silas in a rush. Edward Charters had been discharged from service with the Royal Northumberland Fusiliers on account of the failing health that so bothered Pitch. During their conversation at the marquess's ball, Edward had confided in Silas after one too many brandies that he was quite ashamed at the thought of society learning of his fall from grace from the esteemed ranks of the Fusiliers.

'What a strange but delightful thing it is to meet you here.' Edward held out his hand in greeting and Silas grasped it. Edward's grip was firm and held for just the right respectable amount of time before releasing him, but as their hands slid apart, Silas thought he detected the faintest tingling upon his fingertips.

As Silas's eyes grew accustomed to the light, he took in Edward's appearance. There was no sign of his military medals, his chequered brown suit with its jacket cut to mid-thigh was sensible but seemed rather too large for his frame. He wore a burgundy tie and had a bowler hat perched upon his head, shading his face. He sported a longer beard than when they'd last met, as though he had not trimmed it at all in the passing weeks, and it was entirely more saturated with grey hair.

Silas could hardly help but stare, for the man did indeed appear unwell. He did not recall such a pallor at their last meeting, nor such darkness beneath his eyes. Granted, it served to highlight the unusual colour of his irises, like smoke lifting from a pile of burning leaves. Silas started at the sudden image that came to him. A great pile of orange and red leaves stacked high, flames licking at their base, the whisper of a woman at his ear. A flute played somewhere in the distance.

'Mr Mercer? Is everything all right?'

Silas shivered back into his senses. Edward watched him with no small concern.

'I'm sorry, yes, yes of course.' Silas blushed. He must have looked a fool, staring off into the ether. 'My apologies.'

'No offence taken. I was commenting on how strange it is to meet you in such a place.' Edward's smile was weak, barely able to hold itself aloft. 'Do you come here on Order business?'

'Actually I do, yes. But merely passing through. Our business is elsewhere.' He hesitated. 'You are here to see Mr Astaroth, are you not?'

The man's pallor grew ever sicklier. 'I am indeed. However did you know?'

'I spoke with him inside.' Silas swallowed. 'We are both staying here at the inn.'

Edward's subtle frown cleared. 'Of course, you must have met Tobias at Baron Feversham's, did you not?'

Amongst many other encounters. Now was the precise time Silas should speak of his association with Pitch. 'I did indeed see him there, though only briefly. He did not attend for long.' Blast it, why did his words fail him?

The weakened smile reappeared. 'He is not a patient man, I'm afraid. I'm sorry I myself could not attend. I just…I'm afraid I came over quite unwell at the time. How fortuitous we find ourselves all here at once. Perhaps we could all take a drink together when you return?'

'Perhaps, yes.'

Silas balled his fist. Damning the odd sense of guilt engulfing him. He'd done nothing untoward with Tobias. Save perhaps for that blasted moment at Lady Satine's farm. An indecent encounter if ever there was one, where his lips had pressed hard and hungry against Pitch's, heat running the length of his spine at the daemon's touch. But the damned fellow had manipulated the entire lewd act, he'd even admitted as much at the time. Silas should not be hesitating to inform the lieutenant of his partnership with Tobias Astaroth. He folded his arms. All the reasoning in the world did not shift the fact he felt rather like the proverbial third wheel upon a cart.

'It is a shame you could not attend the baron's,' Silas said. 'I believe it was a successful night indeed.'

He studied the man who had likely shared Pitch's bed. That in itself was hardly an astonishment, the daemon seemed to have bedded most of the country, men and women alike, but this particular man seemed to intrigue Pitch more than most. *A fine choice*, Pitch had once declared of him. As though selecting a stallion for the stud. Silas had thought at the time that it was an odd thing to say.

'So I was told,' Edward said. 'Thank you so much for your services. I left London the morning after the ball, I'll be honest. I thought perhaps my country estate would be more suitable for convalescence.' Edward glanced over Silas's shoulder towards the doorway, his teeth bothering at his bottom lip. 'I was quite pleased to receive Mr Astaroth's invitation to join him here. I've not seen him for some time, and I've not been out much of late. My mother does so worry that I'm not taking enough air and sunshine.'

It was not difficult to see where his mother's worries lay.

'It is a fine day for a sojourn,' Silas said gently. For that was how he feared he must handle Edward Charters. The poor man was fragile, thin ice near to cracking. 'I do recall you mentioning during our conversation that you had been plagued by a malady for some time.'

An ailment of the mind, the lieutenant had feared. A dream fever that left him terribly shaken and fearful for his sanity. It was the very reason he'd sought out Silas at the ball to begin with, in a desperate search for evidence that perhaps he was not mad at all, that perhaps it was a supernatural malaise that had struck him.

A flush of pink found its way to Edward's pale cheeks. 'You must think me quite deranged, for all the nonsense I spoke that evening.'

'Not at all. The mind is a strange beast, indeed. I hope you have found some peace since we last met. Do you consult a doctor?'

The lieutenant shook his head so fervently that his bowler was in danger of flying free. 'I have no wish to find myself in an asylum, I can assure you. My family worries too much for me as it is.' He wrung his hands and could not seem to keep his gaze from the windows above them.

'Do you have a wife?' Silas regretted the foolish words the moment they left him.

'I will not take one,' Edward said sharply. 'Though my mother would suggest matrimony is the true remedy for all my ills. She pushes me, despite what she knows full well. I do not want it. I could not bear it.' He seemed to take stock of his harsh reply, shaking his head. 'Oh, Mr Mercer, do forgive me. I thank you for your concerns, you are a gentleman, one whom I seem to act badly in front of each time we meet. I'm sorry.' He did not wait for Silas to reject his apology. 'If you'll excuse me, I should go to meet Mr Astaroth. He is expecting me, and I'm not sure if you know him very well, but he is not one to be kept waiting.' Edward grew rather breathless as he spoke, as though Pitch's impatience was quite thrilling.

'Actually, Edward,' Silas said, 'I must tell you that I do know...'

But what Silas knew seemed of no consequence to the man. The lieutenant's attention had left him, and turned instead to the doorway.

He tipped his hat, muttering something absently, and stepped around Silas to make his way to the door. He paused there a moment, brushing at his collar and fussing with his unkempt beard, before opening the door and stepping inside. Silas stared at the door as it closed.

'You poor sod,' he sighed.

For what else could it be but an enchantment upon the poor man. Whether he was sharing Pitch's bed or not, Edward Charter's was intoxicated. Perhaps it was the daemon meddling, or, worse, perhaps the chap's poorly disguised feelings were true. Either way Silas did not envy him for being transfixed by such a creature as Mr Astaroth.

Silas had to wait for a slow-moving cart to trundle by before he could cross the road. Once the way was clear he sauntered across, nodding to those who glanced his way. He was not sure what caused him to look back at the Inn, to search out the window where Pitch held court.

The daemon's audience was gone. Pitch and the lieutenant faced one another, hands clasped in greeting. Edward raised his free hand, reaching as though to touch Pitch's shoulder. The daemon warded him off, and his words must have stung, for Silas saw clearly the sweep of anguish that moved across Edward's features. He sank into one of the armchairs, pressing his hand to his face.

Pitch turned to the window, and his gaze fell at once to Silas – as though he knew himself to be watched. The daemon held himself tightly, unsmiling, his alabaster features hard and lifeless as stone.

Silas turned and hurried away.

CHAPTER 13

With much relief Silas found the privy set in behind the inn and went about emptying his much-maligned bladder of its load. Business done, he spent a moment considering his next move. If he'd been reluctant to join Pitch before he was doubly so now, and although it was not altogether proper to wander about without one's coat, Silas decided he would do just that. And where better to wander than through the headstones?

Following his nose, he found the heady bouquet of musty soil leading him along a narrow alleyway set in between the houses lining the street beside the inn. The scent did not dominate though, which pleased him greatly. Silas was in no mood for facing a lost soul, or a gravedigger up to no good. He made his way towards the cemetery, managing to avoid most of the foot traffic he could hear beyond the cover of the alley. He was not so lucky when he at last stepped out of the safety of the buildings, running into a pair of women who gasped at seeing him, one of them nearly losing the herb-filled basket she carried.

'My apologies, ladies.' He nodded his head, arms clasped behind his back in his best imitation of a gentleman.

'Oh my,' one of the ladies breathed, touching at the berry-red scarf about her neck. 'I'd heard new folk arrived at all hours this morning. I'm guessing you be one of them?'

'Indeed.'

'Where are you from then, if you don't mind me asking?'

Silas very much did, and as the women showed no sign of carrying on their way, he would do so instead. The high reach of the nearby bell tower and its jutting cross caught his eye. 'If you don't mind, I'm just on my way to light a candle for my departed mother.'

He did not like using his forgotten mother in such a way, but it was the first thing that came to mind. In a time when he could think more on such things, he would wonder about her and where she might be. Was she still living, or already swept up by the goddess Izanami's deathly kiss?

'Oh dear boy, I'm so sorry.' The lady with the basket crumpled with pity. 'Don't let us keep you then.'

Her companion nodded, all seriousness about her. 'Go on with you. Your ma will be waitin' on ya.'

Silas was left to his wanderings once more and very soon stood in the quiet graveyard. He planted his hands on his hips, filled with contentment. Thoughts of Pitch and his paramour forgotten. He could never have imagined, not in a thousand lifetimes, how such a place might bring such ease. Such sense of being where one ought. He could not stay here, of course. The compulsion to travel to Goodrich Castle still sat with him, a niggle he could not reach at with nails or ale. They must continue on, but while he passed the time he would do so pleasurably.

He surveyed the yard. Unlike the enormous Highgate Cemetery where the harpies had made their unfortunate presence known, these grounds were small enough that Silas could see their entirety from where he stood. There were no lavish monuments in sight, just simple curves of stone with their carved notations of death. All sat upright, no hint of leaning, and the lawn was cropped short by several goats that raised their heads at his arrival, chewing upon their mouthfuls before returning to their grazing, the bells at their necks tinkling softly. The sun vanished behind a bank of cloud that looked set to settle itself there, and the temperature took a downward turn. Silas shivered beneath his light coverings, regretting not stopping to gather his coat. He pushed his hands into his pockets, and something tickled at his skin. The bandalore's string shifted from its coil, brushing against his fingers like a cat's tail might brush its master's leg. Silas did not recall placing the scythe in his pocket when he left his room, but he smiled, not at all perturbed. Of all the uncertainty he'd faced, there was none to speak of here. The bandalore rested where it should.

A faint meow came from the far end of the graveyard, as though his imaginings of a cat's tail a moment ago had summoned the creature to him. There, perched upon the very last headstone at the northwest corner, sat a stout black feline. Its tail was remarkably long, in fact quite impossibly so, weaving about like a maddened serpent. The animal leapt onto a neighbouring headstone, then another, and another, setting a path towards him. Silas's hand wrapped tighter about the bandalore, but the scythe gave him no cause for concern, nor did his fingertips.

The animal moved closer, now just two headstones from him.

'That's quite close enough.'

He pulled his hands from his pockets and warded the creature back. The cat halted obediently, seating itself on its haunches and darting a pink tongue against its onyx coat. The serpentine tail swung like a grandfather clock's pendulum.

'Good kitty, well done.'

While it groomed, its honey-gold eyes never once left him. Silas was not sure he enjoyed such careful scrutiny.

'There is plenty of room here for both of us, you see. I'll leave you be, if you do the same for me. All right?'

He was not expecting an answer, of course, but he received one. The cat meowed with a long drawn-out curl of sound.

He raised his brows. 'I do apologise, but I have no idea if that is a yes or no. I'm not very adept at the feline language, I'm afraid.'

If the priest happened to step out of his church right now, he would think he'd stumbled upon a madman who spoke with the animals. The idea of it raised a smile to Silas's lips. There were far worse things a priest might think of him.

The cat leapt in a fluid motion onto the headstone nearest to Silas. He did not step back, though perhaps should have. As amusing as the creature might be, it still held sharp claws within those padded feet. But he was not hampered by ill-feeling here. His gooseflesh did not rise at the sight of the feline, as it had done when he laid eyes on the harpies in Highgate, even well before they made their vile transformations.

A sparrow flitted down onto the very same headstone where the cat rested. Silas gasped at the delicate creature's audacity, and blindness. Could it not see the predator that sat there? He made to wave the bird to safety, but stopped with his hand held aloft. The tiny creature hopped along the stone, moving right through the preening cat. Neither animal flinched. And only one of them bore a shadow. Needless to say, that shadow was tiny and birdlike.

'Oh,' Silas said simply.

He'd not see it quick enough. It appeared that cats too could be church grim. The feline in question lifted its head, as though it heard Silas's thoughts, and purred so deeply that the air seemed to vibrate with the strength of it. It jumped to the ground and wove between Silas's legs. It was marvellous how solid the grims felt. He could still recall the wetness of the hound's tongue against his cheek, the roughness of its fur against his palm. Silas crouched down.

'Might I pat you?'

For reasons he did not fathom, he felt obliged to seek permission from the creature. And he received it duly, with the black cat rolling onto its back, stomach bared for scratching. Silas laughed, delighted, and settled himself more comfortably against the headstone. He touched cautious fingers to the inky blackness of the cat's belly, and the purring rose a notch higher. They sat this way, with Silas scratching at the feline's preferred spot, for some time. The sun managed to evade its cloudy fortress after a while, and though the wind did strengthen, it did not grow unpleasant. He closed his eyes and rested his head against the stone. Silas did not think he'd ever come across a place so peaceful.

The wind toyed with his hair, brushing it against his neck. And soft drops of rain fell against his cheeks.

Do not linger here, ankou.

Silas's eyes flew open and he sat up with a jolt. The cat remained on its back, purring away. 'Who is there?'

More droplets found him, gentle against his face. He peered up at the sky. The sun still held its place, defying the white streaks of cloud that threatened it. Those clouds, pristine white as they were, did not hint at the chance of rain.

The Lady's Horseman. The stream spoke of you when it cradled you and we rejoiced. But the need for you is great. Hurry.

'Show yourself.' The pattering of rain came again. A sun shower, delicate droplets so fine it was a wonder the breeze did not blow them out of existence.

Heed our call, for the Verderer is lost.

Silas frowned at the word, at the oddness of the rain falling from a clear sky. 'The Verderer?' He peered about, searching for the speaker. The black cat had not yet stirred.

The keeper of the forest. The one who should guard us.

'I don't understand. Who are you?'

Naiads of the Forest of Dean. The river carried us here, against the current, but we grow weak so far from our source. Come quickly. The spirit of the forest is besieged.

Silas wiped at his damp face, pushing to his feet. Whatever a naiad might be, he hoped it not a liar, or an enemy.

'Tell me more of this Verderer.'

There was no answer. The pattering of moisture against his face ceased.

'Are you there?'

But the wind was already drying his dampened skin. The church grim eyed him sleepily, yawned wide enough to bare all its pointed teeth, and rolled over. Silas would get no assistance there.

He brushed at his shirtsleeves, and what little moisture had struck there barely dampened his palms. As much as it pained him to leave this tranquillity, there could be no doubt. They must depart at once.

CHAPTER 14

Silas left the black cat to its basking, beneath a sun that had long ago ceased to truly touch upon the animal. The grim flicked its tail against the headstone but otherwise showed no sign it had heard anything of the strange encounter. He made his way back to The Moon Inn, using the same clandestine path he'd taken to reach the churchyard. Silas was unable to rid his mind of the strange conversation.

The Verderer is lost.

In the strange way that other random pieces of knowledge came to him, he knew of such a title. Verderer's were indeed keepers of the forest, as the naiad had said. And they were very much human. They were chosen to administer forest law on behalf of whichever king or queen ruled England at the time. Verderers kept watch over royal hunting grounds, ensuring all was as it should be. It would seem that one had fallen foul of the Blight. Was this the teratism he was to face? Did the Verderer hide himself in the castle Lalassu had showed him? Silas frowned into his considerations, conscious once more of how certain he was of things that held an association with nature. He knew the Verderer protected the forest. Silas could distinguish between a wych elm and a hazel with ease. When he'd strolled with Jane in the gardens of Holly Village he had named the safflower or Queen Anne's lace they passed readily. Perhaps Sybilla's barmaid friend Clare, had not been far wrong in her assumption of him as a gardener. But what then of the castle he'd witnessed in his vision? Perhaps he was a landowner? He shrugged off the fantasy. Pitch had finer airs and graces about him than Silas. Silas Mercer was no more a gentleman than the farmer in the field.

There were greater concerns right now anyway.

He strode into The Moon Inn via the less conspicuous entrance where he'd met the lieutenant, and hurried up the stairs. Thankfully, he'd been unbothered on his travels from the church to the inn, and now the corridor was clear before him. He peered through the stained glass into the dining area. The crowd had thinned, though only modestly, and the chairs by the window had been taken by other patrons. Pitch and the lieutenant were nowhere to be seen.

'If you're lookin' to find your coat, Mabel's just taken it up to your room, sir.'

Silas turned to find himself addressed by a scrawny boy with an armful of chopped wood. His cheeks were smudged with soot.

'Thank you, but I was actually hoping to find where Mr Astaroth might have gone,' he said. 'He's the gentleman I arrived with.'

A curiously wry smile creased the boy's face. 'I be knowing who Mr Astaroth is, sir.' He jerked his chin towards the stairs. 'You'll be findin' 'im upstairs I dare say.' Pitch's location appeared to bring the lad much amusement, his darkened and chipped teeth showing themselves as his smile grew wide.

'Thank you.'

'Good day to ya, sir.' The boy trundled off down the corridor, and Silas swore he heard him giggle.

Upon reaching the top of the stairs, it became clear he should have enquired as to which of the six rooms on offer Pitch might be in. Faint noises came from several, the murmur of voices , the thud of footsteps, and a subtle, muffled groan from another. He had stood there a moment before he noticed that his own door was ajar. Movement within caught his eye. Mabel most likely, for the boy had just said she was in the process of delivering Silas's coat. The girl was bound to know which room Pitch resided in.

He stepped up to the door and moved to press it open wider so he might enter. Then froze.

Mabel knelt near the head of his bed with her forehead pressed against the wall, as though in some curious prayer.

'Mabel?' Silas stepped into the room.

She squealed, rising to her feet so fast she had to steady herself against the rickety bedhead. It squealed almost as loudly as she had. A thump resounded from the adjoining room. And then another.

'Mr Mercer, I was just, you see I've just...there it is...that's all...' Mabel positively glowed, her face the brightest pink. 'There.'

She jabbed a finger towards the chair set near the all-but-dead fire. Silas's coat hung there, most of its length spread along the floor. Mabel rushed past him, fairly shoving him out of the way in her haste to leave.

'Mabel, whatever is the matter?'

But there would be no answer from the flustered serving girl. She slammed the door behind him before he'd finished his question.

He frowned down at the space where she had been kneeling. The bedside table, little more than an overturned crate, had been shifted to one side. He edged closer and made out a significant gnarl in the wood, one with a hole at its heart big enough to allow light from the adjoining room to filter though. Silas knelt as Mabel had done. As his knees touched the floor, a muffled sound reached him. A grunt, followed by another heavy thump. A lighter sigh came next and Silas's face warmed. He needed no further investigation to understand what Mabel had been up to. The girl had brazenly intruded on his neighbour's privacy. Silas should speak with the innkeeper at once.

'This is not what I had intended when I sent word to you.' The words were panted rather than spoken, and Silas knew their owner immediately.

'But it is what you want, is it not?' The other speaker was equally breathless, though his words were harder to listen in on, as though he spoke into a blanket.

The answer was a groan of unmistakable intimacy. Silas braced himself against the wall. A slight push and he would be on his feet, well away from the peephole. Well away from impropriety. But as his own breath quickened, he could find no impetus to lift away. He lowered his head so that his eye drew level with the gnarl, held his breath, and almost choked upon it.

Pitch lay upon the bed, his legs over the edge, feet touching at the floor. He was clothed, though his shirt hung open and his undershirt was pushed high up his smooth, hairless chest. The lieutenant knelt between his bent knees, holding open the folds of Pitch's trousers. Silas's skin roared with heat as he saw why it was that the lieutenant's voice had sounded so muffled. The man's lips worked upon Pitch's cock, a member of generous girth, stark upright with arousal. Edward took Pitch fully in his mouth, sliding the shaft deep down his throat. Pitch squirmed beneath him, one arm slung across his eyes, his teeth bared as he bit at his lower lip.

'Edward, you should stop,' Pitch gasped.

Which was exactly what Silas should do, too. Rise to his feet and be done with this awful indiscretion.

The lieutenant paused in his efforts, his lips ruby red. 'I don't want to. I've never wanted to. And I don't think you do either, despite what you protest.' He must have tightened his hold for the daemon arched his back and hissed. 'Should I let go? Hmm? Tell me to stop, tell me you have truly tired of me.'

'Edward.' Pitch ground the word out between clenched teeth. 'I am trying to - ' Whatever he was to say flew into the air as a whimper, his body jerking as the man between his legs worked upon him.

'Trying to drive me mad?' Edward's lips rubbed at the very tip of Pitch's shaft and the daemon clawed at the bedcovers. 'I do that well enough alone. My god, Tobias, you're the only thing that soothes me. I need you back in my bed.'

Pitch exhaled and ran his hands through Edward's hair. He stared at the ceiling, and not down at his lover. 'No. I am no balm for you, believe me. My selfishness would astound you –'

'I don't care.' Edward peppered light kisses down the length of the daemon's rigid cock. 'I don't want to be left alone, Tobias. I'm so tired, but it is so difficult to sleep, without you. My dreams...' His voice cracked.

Pitch propped himself onto his elbows, at last looking down at the man who knelt before him. 'Does he still haunt you?'

Silas lost sight of the Lieutenant's face as the man lowered his head, pressing his forehead against the inside of Pitch's thigh.

'You and he both,' he said in a hushed tone. 'Though at least you are someone I can touch, please, and pleasure. When you fuck me, I can rest.' Edward lifted his head, shifting his hand to cup Pitch's balls, eliciting another shuddering gasp. 'I am sure he is my imagination gone mad. I think maybe he is my mind's vision of how I truly wish you to see me. Magnificent and desirable, like a gift sent from the angels themselves.'

His laugh was dry and wretched. All at once Pitch reached for him, grabbing at his collar and hauling him off his knees. Edward released a startled cry. The daemon's strength moved the man easily, and he cast Edward onto his back on the bed. Pitch stood and slid his own tight red trousers free, revealing the smooth, tight mounds of his arse. Silas's pulse was a mad beating thing.

'I should like to unwrap such a gift.' Pitch grabbed the waist of the lieutenant's trousers and tugged them free. Edward's jutting cock bounced against his belly as the daemon handled him roughly. 'But this must be the last time. I am no good for you.'

'Tobias,' the lieutenant breathed.

Silas leaned so hard against the wood his cheekbone ached. His own prick throbbed, his stomach was tight with need. Good god what possessed him? This was vulgarity of the highest degree. The air in his lungs was stale. He could not remember when he had last inhaled, but he could not tear himself away.

Pitch urged Edward further down the bed, until there was space for him to kneel upon it. He lifted and parted the lieutenant's legs, draping one over each shoulder, leaving the man most intimately exposed. The daemon settled himself in closer, his cock poised like a battering ram against the lieutenant's arse. Pitch slicked his fingertips with his own seeping juices and with no gentleness dove them between the mounds of rounded flesh. The lieutenant cried out.

Pitch leaned down, forcing the man beneath him to bend his knees so they almost touched at his shoulders. They both made sounds more fit for beast than man, and Silas could hardly breath for hearing it.

Pitch's fingers worked between the lieutenant's cheeks, driving in and out. The lieutenant whimpered, his face pinched with a mix of pleasure and discomfort. 'More,' he gasped.

'Once more. You were not made to endure heavenly gifts too long, my dear.'

'Just fuck me. I beg of you.' Edward's eyes were wild with lust, his hands white-knuckled where they grasped the bedclothes.

The daemon's fingers slipped from where they had buried deep, and the man he pleasured groaned at the loss. Pitch lifted the lieutenant's legs from their place over his shoulders, and drew them down to his waist. Edward wrapped his limbs about Pitch's hips with an ease that spoke of countless nights spent in just such a way. They settled in against one another so readily, as though the curves of their bodies fitted exactly.

Silas trembled at the intimacy. His heart thudded at the unbearable closeness. At the way Pitch lowered his lips to the lieutenant's with a soft urgency, at the way Edward gazed up at him, sweeping back the hair from Pitch's face. The men sucked and nipped and drove at one another. After what seemed an indomitably long time, Pitch grasped his length and eased it slowly into his lover. The lieutenant winced, pressing his shoulders to the bed as he was filled. He groaned and there was sweet agony and utter bliss in the notes. Gooseflesh rose the length of Silas's arms as he watched on. The daemon ground against the man beneath him, a dancer executing a move in slow motion, the roughness of earlier now vanished. The muscles in his arse flexed and tightened as he pushed himself deeper. He threw back his head, and the light caught at the sculpted curve of his neck. The lieutenant ran his fingers there, and Silas's thoughts raced unbidden to wonder at how that neck might feel against his own fingertips.

Edward whispered to Pitch, words too soft for Silas to catch, and the thrusting strengthened, violent pulses of the hip that proved more than Silas could bear.

He slumped back on his heels, finally drawing a breath. How his hands shook, and the weight between his legs ached. Silas wiped at the sweat that beaded on his upper lip, feeling utterly foolish and foul. And alone. Was there a person who existed who had looked at him the way Edward Charters looked at Tobias Astaroth? Never had Silas felt his lost past so keenly. He pressed his hands to his ears and squeezed his eyes shut, seeking to shut out the coarse sounds, and the memory of how Pitch's eyelids had fluttered as he kissed his lover.

'God, get a hold of yourself, man.' Silas knocked his fists against his temples, as though that might jolt the sense back into him. He set his mind back to their true purpose. Back to what it was that had brought him rushing back to the inn.

The warning about the Verderer.

The pleasured catches of sound grew more intense, more guttural. The bedhead suffered against the wall, marking the men's tempo. Silas got to his feet and doused his face at the washbasin.

He dried his face and threw the towel upon the ground. He was pathetic. Nothing short of a pervert. He left his room and took the stairs two at a time, leaving the rutting men drawing ever nearer to their climax. He burst into the dining room, drawing glances from the trio who smoked their pipes around the fire. Mabel was clearing a nearby table, and she dropped her head as he entered, but Silas had no time for her embarrassment when his own so mortified him.

'Wine, Mabel. And quickly if you don't mind.'

He wondered if his face was still flushed red, for she peered at him oddly before she nodded. 'Of course, sir. Right up.'

It was exactly four glasses later that Pitch sauntered into the bar. He might well have stepped out of the finest tailor's rooms for how preened and refined he appeared. His black jacket hugged tightly at his waist, his hair sat in tidy waves about his face, and his skin showed no hint of his exertions. Silas could hold his eye only a moment before his cheeks threatened to catch fire.

Pitch raised a pair of finely curved eyebrows. 'Were you thirsty, Sickle?' He gestured at the two empty glasses that Mabel had yet to clear away.

'Yes, actually I was.'

'Did you like what you saw?'

Silas spat his wine back into the glass. 'I beg your pardon?'

'My dear Sickle, are you going to deny you were watching me fuck the lieutenant? I could hear you breathing even as I came –'

'Now that is a lie, I was not there when you...' Silas stopped, seeing at once the trap he'd thrown himself into. The wine warming his veins was numbing his sensibilities.

Pitch's infernally attractive grin appeared. He lifted imperious fingers, which saw Mabel come scurrying. 'More wine for the table, if you please.'

The thought of it turned Silas's stomach. He'd had far too much already.

Mabel bobbed in the unnecessary curtsy she was so fond of. She could no sooner look Pitch in the eye than Silas could. 'Yes, sir.'

'Oh, and Mabel, the lieutenant will be staying the night here. He's sleeping now, and I don't expect him to wake before we are gone. Would you take care of him for me?' Pitch's features softened as he spoke. 'I'll pay for his night's accommodations and food. Be sure to see that he eats. We have had rather vigorous discussions this afternoon, and he'll need to gather his strength for his ride back to Hereford.'

The poor girl could not find a place to lay her gaze, and with a muttered reply, she dashed off to retrieve their wine, Pitch's coins held tightly in her hand.

'Does he know that you are leaving before he wakes?' Silas said. Did he just slur his way through that question?

'He does not. I should not have let this happen, but there you are. I am a selfish bastard and he has such a lovely prick, as I'm sure you would agree.' Silas blanched. Pitch's gaze grew distant. 'I did not realise quite how badly our encounters have ruined him. Edward is not a well man. I fear I rather sicken him.'

Silas frowned through his red-wine haze. 'Are you suggesting it is you that is making him unwell?'

Pitch ran his tongue over his lips. 'I am certainly not good for his health.'

'He thinks he is possessed, did you know that?'

'I do. But that is not the case. Not any longer, at least. And I'm sure once I put some decent distance between us his vigour will return.' Pitch stretched his arms overhead, arching his back just slightly. Silas was damned if he could push the image of Pitch's milk-white arse from his head.

'Not any longer...' Silas was definitely slurring. 'So it's true, the poor man was possessed. As it was with Clarence then, when the Lady Satine...used him?'

He could not hold Pitch's gaze as it fixed on him. 'Indeed.'

'By who?'

'Despite what you seem to think, that is no concern of yours.'

A surge of indignation struck Silas, and his inebriation gave it voice. 'You should tell him, you blasted fiend, he thinks he is mad.'

'Gods, does watching people fuck always get you this riled up?'

Silas glared, which was no easy task when the whole room swayed. 'I didn't...I hadn't meant...' he mumbled himself into silence.

'Next time I'll charge you for the show. Now, enough of all that. Where did you disappear to earlier? Sniffing graves again?'

'No.' The wine stuck to Silas's tongue quite unpleasantly. 'Well, I was in the graveyard –'

'Until you decided on some voyeurism –'

'Until I received a message...a call, actually.' He shook his head in a vain attempt to clear it. Bloody hell, he'd forgotten himself entirely. 'We need to carry on. With haste. When I was at the churchyard some strange creature of the water spoke to me, a naiad they named themselves, and told me that the forest is in dire need.' He stopped short of speaking of the Verderer, deciding he would do so in less busy company.

Pitch tilted his head. 'Well why didn't you just say so? You could have knocked on my door, instead of peeping through a hole in the wall.'

Silas swallowed hard. 'You seemed rather busy,' he said tightly.

'I was rather.' The daemon spoke from beneath dangerously lowered lashes. 'Tell me, did I rouse that old dead thing between your legs? I bet it grew most beautifully. Did you give yourself a thorough seeing to?'

'You are vile.'

The daemon's eyes glinted. 'And you like it.'

'Enough.'

'Very well, if you must be so dull and prudish. When do you wish to leave?'

Silas stood up, abandoning his unfinished glass. 'As soon as I gather my coat.'

CHAPTER 15

A short time later they were mounted on well-rested horses. Lalassu pranced about as though she had been at pasture for a week, not the hours it had been. Even Sanu had a spring about her, giving Pitch some trouble as he sought to mount. He swung his leg over her haunches, and Silas averted his eyes. He'd seen far too much of that arse this day. He paled to think back on what he had just done, his inscrutable crassness. Never would he have imagined himself capable of such an intrusion. Or such a lust for it.

'Come along then,' Pitch quipped. 'Was it not you who was champing at the bit to be gone?'

The daemon had already set off, leaning back with one hand set upon Sanu's rump to speak with Silas.

'I'm coming.' He instantly regretted his choice of words.

Pitch's lazy smile rose. 'Good for you.'

Silas busied himself with the reins, sinking deeper into the folds of his coat. They travelled down the laneway and past The Moon Inn. Mabel watched from a lower window, perhaps thinking herself hidden behind the folds of the curtain. Her attentions rested upon Pitch alone. He in turn paid her no mind, his own gaze lifting higher to where the lieutenant slept off his exertions.

Just the thought of the man caused Silas's skin to warm. 'Are you sure you would not speak with him of our leaving?'

He'd gone to inform Pitch that he was ready to depart, and had caught the daemon in a most vulnerable moment. One that involved all of his clothing. He'd stood in the room where Edward lay sleeping, watching over him in quite contemplation. Silas stilled his hand from knocking and disturbing the moment. He barely recognised the look upon the daemon's face, it was so foreign there, but he would have sworn to any who asked that Pitch appeared achingly sad. Pitch had laid his straw boater on the vacant pillow as though it were a bouquet upon a grave. Silas had slipped away quietly, leaving him to his silent farewell.

'I'm quite sure.' The daemon was returned to his cock-sure self now. 'We shared pleasant times together, I'll not deny that. And he served rather well when there was need of it, but he should be free now. It is done with.' He glanced over his shoulder, his gaze lifted too high to be directed at Silas. The Moon Inn alone held his attention. 'It is done with.'

Silas watched him as he resettled, swaying his hips with the movement of the horse beneath him. Served rather well? Be free? What on Earth did all that mean? He'd seen with his own, repugnant, eyes the intensity between the men. It had opened a tiny hollow in Silas's core. Edward did not lie beneath Pitch in servitude.

'Leave it be, Sickle,' Pitch said, as though hearing Silas's unspoken questions. And though he said it mildly Silas heard the telltale ripple of tension there.

He stayed silent for a long while, all along the main street where many stopped to stare at the departing strangers. Hats were lowered, papers were raised as whispers flowed. Silas expected showmanship from Pitch as they made their way along, but there was none to be seen. He stared ahead, sitting quiet in the saddle. Even the evident batting of lashes and coy smiles directed his way did not sway him from his thoughts. It was as though a statue, perfect and cold in its construction, rested upon Sanu's back.

His pose suited the day well, for since Silas had run from the churchyard, the sun had settled in behind clouds that crowded the sky until there was nothing blue left to see. The air held a chill, and he was grateful for the thickness of his coat. Mabel's cleaning efforts were most impressive, returning the royal-blue folds as near as they had been yet to their original brightness. A pity he had not thought to ask her to attend to the bandalore's fouled string. For soak and rub as he might, Silas could not delete the dark smudges there, and he did not enjoy the reminder they brought of his time in the mud in Black Annis's bower.

They moved well beyond the edges of the village, leaving the chatter and bustle behind before Pitch stirred.

'Did you have the saddlebags refilled?'

Cold dread touched at Silas. 'The saddlebags?'

'That is what I said.'

He glanced at his neighbour. Pitch's mood was too precarious to name. 'I'm afraid...I did not.'

A muscle flexed along Pitch's jaw but he said nothing. Which Silas thought might be worse than if he'd lost his temper.

'But I am certain there is still shortbread to be found in mine.' He twisted about and, with only a modicum of fuss, managed to keep his seat and undo the strap at the same time. Sure enough, and to his great relief, there was another muslin-wrapped parcel, which he withdrew and handed across the space between them. There was no thanks to be had from Pitch, and though his lack of manners was usually irksome, Silas felt he was in no position to spout on about proper etiquette.

For near on an hour, Pitch kept to his own thoughts and chewed his way through the shortbreads. Silas tried not to think too much on the sad state of his saddlebag and its lack of sugar-laden supplies, and sent up a prayer to whatever god it was that provided such things that they might come across a grocers or bakers in a village before Pitch's appetite built again. They passed by great expanses of freshly tilled fields, others sown already with barely sprouting rye and winter wheat. Sheep padded about their fields by the dozens, like enormous snowballs upon the grass. Lalassu kept to a quick-footed trot and was quite the marvel for how long she could sustain such a pace without need of rest. It was Silas who would call on her to slow for short distances so he might catch his breath and save his arse, and he wondered if she would stop at all had he not.

Sanu did an admirable job of keeping up, far greater than Silas had expected of her, though her passenger uttered not a word of praise.

'So, what does your murderer look like? Will he be carrying a bloodied knife to alert us to him?' Pitch sucked upon a strand of his own hair, slouched in the saddle with his feet hanging free of the stirrups. His eyes were glazed with his indulgence.

Silas took a calming breath before he spoke. 'A Verderer, is what I said.'

Twice already he had tried to relay to Pitch what he'd been told by the water spirit. Once as they gathered their belongings at the inn, a second time as they saddled the horses. Of course he sought the daemon's opinion on what it might mean, but he had also sought to fill the pregnant air between them.

'Well, it is likely they are a murderer as well, let us be honest,' Pitch said, swinging his legs against Sanu's forequarters in such a fashion that it would not have surprised Silas in the least if the mare turned and nipped him. 'We seek a teratism, and the last we encountered on this dull journey was definitely of the murdering kind.'

Silas yearned to disagree that the trip was dull, but what point in beginning such an argument?

'Perhaps a murderous nature is what determines why one soul will become a teratism, and another not? There is so much about the Blight I do not yet understand.' He spoke to the air, rather than Pitch, but hoped the daemon might have something to say. Silence greeted Silas's words. Settling taller in his saddle, he frowned at the road ahead. 'Can you tell me anything of the naiad that came to me in the churchyard? I suppose them to be something like Matilda, are they not?' He'd not yet met the water elemental who had led Pitch to Silas's rescue when he was set upon by the harpies, but intended a hearty thanks if the introduction should ever occur.

Pitch laughed, a snap of indignant derision. 'Oh please, when we return you must call Matilda a naiad. I should so love to be in your company when you declare an undine equal to a water nymph.'

'I will do no such thing, for you mock me quite clearly.'

'You are far too brilliant for me, Sickle.' He enjoyed his mockery, grinning like a fool. His green eyes were hard as they danced upon Silas. But his laughter was most welcome, for it lifted high and frivolous. The daemon's mood had soothed. 'Little wonder you are held in such good stead by dear Satty. Do you suppose she even notices I am gone?'

'Oh, Mr Astaroth, she most certainly does. I can assure you. You are nothing if not memorable.'

Pitch stared at him, and for a dreadful second Silas thought his judgement of the daemon's mood had been terribly adrift, that the quest to find the Verderer would end here, with Silas's own bloody demise upon a country road.

'You should know, Mr Mercer.' Pitch smiled, and if the sun had peeked from behind a cloud, it would not have been as brilliant. Silas's pulse thudded in his ears. 'I must say, I rather think I like you. You've not yet shit your britches, even when I've tried quite hard to make it so. And you're so full of contradictions that it may take me a few more days yet to be thoroughly bored by you. A gentleman, and a pervert. Death's whore, and yet so human that it is painful to look upon.'

They rode side by side, the horses having drifted in close to one another as they enjoyed a more leisurely pace. Silas stared at the man across from him. Christ almighty, those eyes made it hard to think straight. He did not much relish being called a pervert, but could he really deny Pitch's summary? But if Silas was contrary, he was not the only one. Pitch, he was coming to see, was far more layered than he first appeared.

'Seeing as I am quite so painful to look upon,' Silas declared. 'I shall do you a small mercy.'

'Which is?'

In answer he pressed his heels to Lalassu's sides, and the pale horse drove forward without hesitation.

The daemon let out a cry of surprise that stretched Silas's smile wide. Pitch roared at Sanu to lift her hooves. The curses grew faint in the background as Lalassu stretched her gait wider still. Silas's entire world was a smear of golds and blue and green as the landscape swept by. The horse strained beneath him, her breath hot and hard through flared nostrils, pulling them ever closer to the Forest of Dean, and the Verderer who was lost within her.

CHAPTER 16

Pitch took decidedly longer upon Sanu to near their destination. The coppery chestnut made a valiant effort to match Lalassu's breathtaking pace, and at times did so admirably, bringing Pitch near alongside Silas. He whooped and hollered with great gusto and vile language, reminding Silas of the spectators who'd watched on as Pitch had allowed himself to be beaten soundly in the barn at Bishop's Castle.

What a fine state of affairs they had left for poor Sybilla to deal with there. Between Pitch's assault on the constable and Silas's treatment of the gravedigger, she was likely viewed with even greater disdain than before. Silas pressed into his stirrups, leaning low against Lalassu's neck as she thundered beneath him, travelling her own path and leaving the road to gallop through a field rough with the scars of the plough. The horse did not slow, despite the unevenness of the ground.

How would those folk of Bishop's Castle feel to know it was an angel they turned their noses at and eyed with such open loathing? What poise the woman had to handle it with such grace. He could not imagine a daemon doing such a thing.

As though to prove his point, Pitch loosed his tongue upon his slowing horse. Sanu took the ridged ground more cautiously than Lalassu. 'You bracket-faced piece of shit, move your fucking arse.'

Silas cast a look over his shoulder, concerned for the chestnut's safety. He assumed he would need to call on Pitch to stop beating his horse. To his surprise no such sermon was necessary. Though Pitch scowled his pretty face into ugly wrinkles of simmering fury, he merely flailed the reins ahead of him, his legs steady at her sides. His tirade of ripe words continued, but it appeared it was Sanu's ears alone that would receive the harshest punishment, much to Silas's relief.

He shifted his gaze back to the way ahead and his stomach sank. A hedgerow approached, one he knew that Lalassu would guide them over. He was no fan of the jump. Each time, he was certain he would find himself cast from the saddle, landing head first upon the ground and suffering an appalling injury. Silas lifted his arse higher, grasping ahold of the pommel and stifling a squeal as Lalassu's bulk projected into the air. They sailed high over the hedge, and the downward journey was soon upon them.

The thud of hooves upon the ground was joined by Silas's own shocked exhale as his nethers met the swell of the saddle. He wobbled about in the stirrups, wincing, but he remained upon the mare. Catching his breath, Silas sent private thanks to Sybilla and her lessons in horsemanship. Though she insisted he must have ridden in his past life, Silas had no memory of it of course, and without her guidance, he did not doubt he would have spent much more time upon the dirt.

Onward they travelled, chasing the descending night. The shadows grew longer, the sky sickly pale with the vanishing of the sun. In the distance the lights of isolated farmhouses began to appear, near on the only sign of life they'd yet witnessed on the journey. Lalassu's chosen path had seen them avoid the villages and settlements along the way, much to Pitch's chagrin. Silas hoped that the horses saw well in the dimness, for though Lalassu slowed now and then to a walk, the pace moved mostly at a trot or slow rolling canter. Silas's body showed signs of fatigue far earlier than his mount's did. His buttocks were punished by the trot if he did not rise to it, or if he did, then his thighs protested vehemently. The knots in his wide shoulders were tightening with every moment that passed.

Lalassu abandoned her dedication to the fields and less well-travelled paths, and set them upon what must be the main road of the area, for it was wide with carriage-wheel ruts deeply imprinted. Silas was grateful for the walking pace and was considering dismounting awhile to walk alongside the horse when he spotted a small village ahead. Meagre to say the least, not more than a half-dozen houses clung to the sides of the road, with several more farmhouses positioned further out in the fields beyond. Though it was a suitable time for such things, he could not make out the flutter of candles behind the curtained windows of any but one of the houses. The majority sat dark and sullen in the dying day. What a strangely silent place it was, with no evidence of workers in the fields or in the apple orchard set behind the largest of the stone houses. The ground was painted red with the fallen fruit, only the most steadfast still clinging to the branches.

Silas ran his tongue over chafed lips. Perhaps there was cider on offer in one of these houses. A pint of sharp golden liquid would serve him well right now. Lalassu could not be halted though, and they continued down the road. The horse snorted as they moved past the singular house with candlelight, sweeping her head up and down as though something of the home bothered her. There was an emptiness about the place for sure, and there was no shifting of shadows behind the faded blue curtains upon the windows, as though the house was devoid, as all the others, of life. They were well past the cluttering of homes when Pitch called to him.

'For fuck's sake, Silas. Are we to have our balls in our mouth before your bloody nag decides to halt?'

Silas choked back his laughter. The daemon did not exaggerate; the journey was abidingly uncomfortable after such a time in the saddle. He was readying an answer when a towering fortress of great, deep shadow appeared up ahead. A barrier of woodland spread in both directions for as far as he could see in the weakness of evening.

'I think we have arrived.'

'Not a moment too fucking soon,' Pitch grumbled.

The treeline hugged the open fields and grazing land, like a wall of dappled green and yellow. The forest held the night within it already, and Silas saw even at this distance why Cecil's youth had been filled with supernatural tales of the Forest of Dean. He shivered despite his coat. One could imagine being watched from that darkness by the most terrifying of monsters and having only the hair standing upon one's neck to tell of their existence.

Lalassu dropped from a trot to a walk, as though she too was cautious about entering. The road they were upon would lead them straight into the inky black forest. Silas had been so eager to begin this journey, barely able to stand it whilst Sybilla set about packing their supplies, but now that he was here, on the very cusp, that eagerness abandoned him. He could not shake the sense of being watched, and though his fingers did not tingle with any alarm, his pulse quickened and his nerves jangled beneath his skin.

'Steady girl, we will wait on Pitch to reach us,' Silas whispered.

There was no need for it. Pitch and Sanu were just a few horse lengths behind, but Silas did not relish the idea of moving forward on his own.

'Don't tell me your nag has finally tired,' Pitch scoffed, riding straight past, Sanu blowing hard from her efforts. 'Come along. This is no small place, and I doubt very much your teratism is waiting at the entrance to greet you.'

Sanu took her rider into the gloom ahead. Lalassu bore Silas in a moment later. Against the deep greens and burnt oranges and yellows of an autumn forest, Lalassu was like a fallen moon passing low to the ground. The road grew ever narrower, as though pressed tight at its edges by the denseness of the wood. Just like the small township they had recently passed, the forest was altogether far too quiet. As though every living thing had shut its lips, or folded its wings. Silas peered over his shoulder and lifted his brow. How was it that he had only just entered the forest and yet that entrance appeared far behind him, at a much greater distance than their movement would allow for? And far narrower. He squinted. The road seemed more footpath now, incapable of handling the width of a wagon, or two riders abreast. As though new saplings had pushed themselves from the earth to block the way in the twinkling of an eye.

Lalassu flicked her tail in sharp sweeps back and forth.

'It bothers you too, doesn't it?' Silas patted at her damp neck.

It did little to settle his own nerves. Lalassu seemed so immovable, as though he sat upon a mountain, and nothing seemed to bother her. Until now. He was certain the environment did not please her. She came to a halt, and Silas quickly missed the reassuring heavy sound of her hooves upon the ground. Beneath the thick canopy of foliage, what slender light the early evening offered was all but banished.

'Pitch, wait.'

He and Sanu were now a darker blot up ahead.

'What for?'

Pitch's voice was deadened by the weight of the silence around it. Silas lifted his shoulders. The quiet was so rich and absorbing that one might fear one's own ears had fallen to deafness. He coughed, just to reassure himself it was not so. There were times when quiet could be tranquil, soothing even, but not here.

'Do you not feel the strangeness of this place?'

Pitch's answer was to slap at his own cheek. 'What I feel are the interminable bites I'm receiving from insects clamouring to suck at my blood. Can we not move along?'

Silas shook his head.

What sort of forest held no life amongst its branches or undergrowth? No rustling of leaves as a badger made its way, or chirruping of crickets marking the seconds. He rose in the stirrups, as much to ease the ache in his legs as to consider the view ahead. The creak of leather was deafening in the thick hush. Through the valley between Lalassu's ears, he peered beyond where Pitch waited upon Sanu. There was not much to see, as though a curtain of sheer black hung upon the road not much further from where the daemon sat. Silas longed for some sign from the bandalore or the merest tingling upon his fingers. Right now, he doubted a teratism existed here at all. There was an emptiness to the place that held neither life nor death.

A stagnant breath held too long.

'Fine,' Pitch sighed. 'If I am to wait for you while you are struck by terror, I shall do it on my feet.' He slid easily from the saddle, dusting at his trousers, unfastening his velvet jacket. 'Gods, I shall never get the reek of manure from these clothes, I'm sure.'

Despite the burn of his muscles and the ache at his hips, Silas did not dismount. He did not wish to be down where the trees might appear more colossal still. 'I am not struck by terror,' he returned, but it was a half-truth. 'But do you not find this place the least bit strange? There is far too much silence.'

'Would you like me to serenade you?'

'That is the very last thing I want,' Silas said, testily. 'I do not feel well here.'

'Perhaps then you should have spent less time galloping yourself stupid.'

'I am not sick from the ride.' Silas might have slapped that pretty face were Pitch closer. 'There is no life in this place. It is not right.'

'You're a creature of death. Perhaps you've lost your taste for the living.' Pitch cocked his head. 'You are frightened, aren't you, my little Sickle, by the big scary forest? Perhaps I can distract you with a firm hand and a fast tongue –'

'Don't be ridiculous.' Silas gathered the reins. 'Get back on your horse. We will continue to the castle.'

'Oh fuck, must we?' Pitch pressed at his crotch where his trousers hugged close. 'I am fearful that I might well burst my sack if I spend another moment on that nag. The intolerable animal trots so roughly just to vex me, I'm certain.'

'You are hardly kind to her.'

'And she is not kind to my most precious possessions.'

Lalassu nickered softly, ears pricking forward.

'Quiet, Pitch,' Silas whispered. 'She senses something.'

Sanu too lifted her head, pinning her attentions on the darkness before them.

'You consider yourself a horse master now, do you?' Pitch laughed.

'Shut up,' Silas snapped.

The daemon sighed, dramatically of course, but did as he was bid. Silas's breath sounded loud through his nostrils no matter how gently he tried to inhale and exhale. Both horses were still, not a twitch nor a swish of fine tail. Lalassu lifted her head, as though peering at the boughs about her. Never had Silas so desired to see an owl perched high there. It would be a welcome sight to see something where it should be. The sharp prick of gooseflesh ran down his back. It was as though each and every leaf held eyes, and every blade of grass fighting its way through the undergrowth watched them.

'There you go, there is life here yet.' Pitch raised a lazy hand and pointed into the forest.

Before he could shush him again, Silas saw what it was that had drawn his attention. Almost parallel with where they stood, deep in the forest, there came a strange trio of lights working their way through the trees: one as bright as the sun, another the shade of a blushing cheek, the third a brilliant hue of periwinkle.

'What is that?' Silas pushed his words through clenched teeth. 'Should we move?'

'If you wish to run and hide from harmless will-o'-the-wisps, then certainly.'

Lalassu shifted beneath him, pawing at the road. Without warning she jerked into a trot, nearly throwing Silas from his unready seat. The reins slipped from him, and he struggled to regain them.

'Remount, Pitch.'

'Your fear is getting away with you.' Pitch glowered. But Sanu was already upon the tips of her hooves, as ready to move on as Lalassu. 'Lucifer's balls –'

'Get on your horse, this is Lalassu's choice, not mine,' Silas barked. 'Mount, now.'

The lights raced ever closer, their glow setting the forest dancing. Silas was puzzled by Lalassu's signals. The horse was anxious, clearly, but showed no sign of racing from the approaching glow. The lights shot through the forest, not a sound betrayed them, no crack of branches or shuddering of leaves. Pitch shouted at Sanu to steady as his attempts to mount were thwarted by her restlessness. Barely had he found his seat and the lights were on them. Passing by with a blinding brightness that pained Silas's eyes near to tears. He threw up an arm in defence, but still Lalassu held her path and did not shirk at the encounter.

It was over in a moment. The trio of coloured lights crossed the road over them and continued their trajectory into the forest on the other side. He was ready to heave a sigh of relief when Lalassu turned about, and followed where the lights led.

'Oh gods, what is wrong with you, man?' Pitch shouted. 'You can no sooner catch a will-o'-the-wisp than you can a cloud.'

Silas had better things to occupy him than to answer. He ducked his head, barely escaping the low swipe of a sweet chestnut's boughs.

'What are you doing?' he hissed at the horse beneath him.

Pitch shouted his disapproval behind.

Lalassu's pace through the open fields had been frightening enough, but this was a whole new terror.

The terrain was treacherous for rider and mount, with partly exposed roots of great trees snaking across the ground and mounds of rocks appearing out of nowhere. Lalassu slipped and slid her way down a shallow embankment, a gully where perhaps once a rivulet had run long ago. The rocky crags grew more and more bold upon the landscape, the stone jutting high from the soil, at times reaching taller than Silas upon his steed. It was a strange maze of stone, which, had there been a roof upon it, it might have formed a network of tunnels so complex escape would have seemed impossible.

The only saving grace came from the will-o'-the-wisps up ahead. Their lights were bright enough that Silas could pick out enough detail on the forest floor to see where potential for a broken neck lay. It would not last though. Lalassu could not seem to gain on them, and the glow of the lights lessened.

Pitch hissed and cursed from behind, though really Sanu was doing an able job at keeping pace with her stablemate through the forest's startling landscape. Lalassu picked her way down a steeper embankment, and Silas leaned back in the saddle to offer her greater ease. Surely this must have been a river once, for the chasm was far wider than any they'd negotiated so far. The horse's considerable strides made short work of the distance, and now Silas moved his weight forward as she bore them up the other side. An odd tingling caressed his fingertips.

'Have you lost your mind, Sickle?' Pitch called. 'That is no teratism you pursue.'

'I told you, I am not –'

A note upon the air gave Silas pause. He strained to make sense of it beyond the crash of Lalassu's hooves through the undergrowth.

'Do you hear that?' he shouted. 'Is that a horn?'

'I hear only my spine jarring.'

The long drawn note sounded again from somewhere far behind them. There was no mistaking it this time. His fingers tingled up and own their lengths.

'Do you hear it, Pitch? It sounds like the horn of a hunt.'

The brilliance of the will-o'-the-wisps ahead was extinguished, three candles blown out suddenly. The darkness was shocking to the eyes, and Silas squinted to make sense of the path ahead. The horn resounded through the forest, still behind but far closer now, its solitary note clawing at the sky.

'A hunt is a damned sight more entertaining than this,' Pitch spat. 'Perhaps we should join them.'

Lalassu slowed her pace at last, but that did little to ease Silas's concerns.

'What if it is us who is being hunted?' he said, throat dry with the thought. 'I don't believe we were chasing the will-o'-the-wisps at all. We were following them.'

The pale horse jerked to a halt so suddenly that Silas bit his tongue. The coppery tang of blood followed.

She had stopped them before the highest rise of rock Silas had yet seen in the forest. And this one's purpose was clear. A gaping hole had been cut into the rock face, timber beams evident where they framed the entrance. One of the mines Cecil had mentioned perhaps. Sanu might make it inside, but he would have to dismount Lalassu to give her any hope of entering.

'If we are hunted,' Pitch declared, 'then let us turn and fight. Is that not what we are here for?' His eagerness buoyed his words.

'I don't think –'

A tug came at the hem of Silas's trousers. He cried out, kicking his leg at whatever held him.

'That's no way to treat your saviour,' hissed the most curious of voices, croaky as a frog. 'Do you want hiding or not?'

'Show yourself,' Silas demanded. His fingers prickled, the flesh there warm.

'What's wrong with you now?' Pitch said.

'There is something touching me.' Silas kicked out once more, but his boot met only air.

'Fool,' came the rough voice again. 'We seek to aid you. Or would you have the Verderer bring you down where you stand?'

Silas froze. 'What did you say?'

'I asked what is wrong with you.' Pitch sighed.

'Not you.' Silas peered down at his stirrup. 'There is something else with us. Show yourself, I say. What do you know of the Verderer?' The horn blasted once more, and the vibration of it shook the very trees around them.

'Linger here,' his assailant rasped, 'and you will learn to your peril what the Verderer is about.'

'Oh, that is a bluecap.' Pitch shifted in his saddle, not bothered in the least by the hub-bub. 'I thought I smelled something familiar. Nothing quite like the parfum of the fae, don't you think? Does your queen have enough stores of all things sweet and sticky to endure my appetite? I am quite famished.'

'Of course, of course, daemon. It's been a long while since the likes of you has graced our chambers.' Silas squinted, certain he'd just caught a glimpse of the figure who spoke to them. Part shadow, part shimmering of the air, that reached no higher than Lalassu's belly. 'Hurry along with me now. We'll keep you safe.'

Pitch sniffed. 'I'm fairly certain I at least do not need your protection.'

But Silas was still caught upon the daemon's words. 'The bluecaps, they are faeries?'

'They are fae,' Pitch said, as though that explained everything Silas needed know. 'Keep to the underground life mostly.'

The shuddering note of the horn sent a rumble through the ground. Silas spun to face Pitch, who made no move to dismount.

'Do we go with them? Is it safe?' He dug his fingernails into his palms, anything to ease the fierce prickling.

'Come, come, come, come,' the bluecap urged from somewhere beyond Lalassu's head. 'It is safe, much safer with us.'

'They are harmless enough.' Pitch shrugged. 'The miners don't mind having them about for the most part. But what is the point? Are you not here to slay this Verderer? And did the bluecap not just say it is he who approaches?'

Before an answer could form upon Silas's lips, there was the brush of something against his ankle. 'What the...'

A tree root pushed its way clear of the undergrowth, rising like a snake set to strike. Silas kicked out. A dull thud came where his boot met the wood, but the root pressed on, undeterred.

'I told you, I told you!' the bluecap trilled. 'The forest is ailing. Not itself. Come. Come.' The voice came from the mouth of the mine.

'I hope your queen is well stocked in honey, my dear fellow.' Pitch leapt from the saddle, grunting as he hit the ground. 'Or she shall not enjoy a daemon in her chambers.'

Silas lifted his feet in quicksteps, trying to avoid the serpentining organic matter that sought to wrap about his legs. The larger root was joined now by stragglier companions, finer veins that pressed themselves up from the Earth. 'What is going on here?'

'Something interesting, at last.' Pitch's fingernails illuminated with a faint fiery glow. He swept his hand towards the most menacing of the roots. There was the brisk and sure scent of burning. The woody serpent fell away, sliced through by the daemon's touch. 'Perhaps it would be wise to learn more of your foe before this fight begins. Let us go.'

Silas could not have been more relieved had Pitch declared he would see to the Verderer himself. The hail of the horn rang once more, the tremor escaping the ground to race up Silas's legs. The tingling in his fingertips sunk into the bone. The trees swayed about them as though struck by a sudden wind that did not touch his own skin.

'What of the horses?' he said.

Lalassu herself answered his panicked question. She pressed her muzzle to his back, urging him forward to where the bluecap hopped about in the shadows and beckoned them to follow. The mare's push set Silas stumbling forward. Lalassu turned on flicking hooves and, with Sanu close behind, launched into a gallop that set them back upon the very path they had just travelled.

'Where are they going?' Silas cried.

'Wherever they bloody want.' Silas started as Pitch took his hand. 'Now come along, Sickle.'

CHAPTER 17

S ilas entered the mine grasping hold of Pitch's hand like a child fearing he'd be lost at a fair. At least the press of the daemon's hand served to deaden the pin-prickling sensation at Silas's fingertips. It was beyond dark in the tunnel, as though he wore a blindfold, and the icy creep of fear made itself known upon the back of his neck. The slope of the ground led them ever downward, and with each step, Silas's feet grew more leaden. The sounds of chaos from without grew muffled.

'This is far enough, surely?' he said, when there had been a long while since he had heard the Verderer's horn at all.

The air held none of the crispness of the outdoors; it was heavy and stale. Silas reached out with his free hand and found the walls too readily. There was barely enough space for the two of them to walk side by side. His heart made itself known with a thump in his chest, and he struggled with thoughts of the day he had awoken in a box that hemmed him in on all sides.

'Everything all right, Sickle?'

Damn Pitch and his search for eternal bemusement. He knew full well how Silas's hand trembled.

'Everything is fine. I simply prefer to be able to see where it is I am being led.'

'Just a little further. Not far now. Just a little ways.' Their guide spoke from the stifling darkness, and the croaky voice echoed against the walls.

Silas stopped short, Pitch tugging against him as the sudden halt caught him off-guard.

'I can go no further.' Silas was dizzy with the creeping approach of panic.

'Well you must,' Pitch said shortly. 'For I am quite set on the idea of honeyed wine now, and none but the bluecaps make it so finely.' He pulled at Silas's hand, using only a fraction of the strength Silas knew him to have.

'No, I will not.' The panic flooded his chest, cruel and cold. 'I no longer hear the Verderer's horn. We should leave.'

'Gods man, pull yourself together. It is hardly the first cramped and lightless place you've found yourself in.'

'That is exactly the point.' Sweat ran damp and plentiful beneath Silas's armpits. 'I do not enjoy the memory at all.'

'I thought it was water you feared? Gods, you are entirely too delicate.' Pitch offered nothing in the way of comfort, which surprised Silas none. 'Here, would it distract you at all if I were to do this?'

He pulled his hand from Silas's, and found his way beneath the layers of Silas's coat. Pitch's fingers slipped beneath the waistband of Silas's trousers, heading towards the crease of his arse.

'No!' Silas cried, grasping Pitch's wrist with fervour. 'How would that be helpful in the slightest way?'

He wrangled the daemon's hand away, and Pitch's laughter found the dreaded walls. 'You will never know,' he replied, 'because you did not let me finish.'

Silas spun towards Pitch's voice, blinking into nothingness. 'Leave me be. Just leave me be.' His voice wobbled dangerously as he felt himself slipping into the embrace of utter terror. 'I will not stay here.'

'Sickle, easy now –'

'Leave me be, I say.' He swiped at the hands that felt for him. Silas knew not where he was going but only that he must. He stumbled in the darkness, where his fingertips met the hardness of the mine walls. The surface was smoother than expected, as though rubbed down of all its sharp edges. He turned so that the lay of the land flowed upwards, and set off as fast as his rubbery legs might carry him. A sigh came from behind him, a fluttering, pretty thing that could have come from one person alone.

'You are going to make me carry you, aren't you?'

Caught up in the certainty of his escape, and the rush of blood that roared in his ears, Silas paid Pitch no mind. He squeezed his eyes shut so that the darkness was of his making, and not some dastardly, inescapable monster forced upon him.

There came the sense of someone alongside him, the shift in the air that betrayed such things. Next came a touch at his neck, a press of fingers hard beneath his ear.

His knees buckled, his mouth opened with an unspent cry, and Silas fell into the waiting black depths.

'Does he stir yet?' Pitch's voice came from a distance.

Silas's lids fluttered open. The darkness had been replaced by brightness that stung so fiercely tears pricked their way free. He lay upon his back on a surface that was most comforting. For a precious, wonderful moment he thought he might be back in his own bed at Holly Village. The entire messy affair with the Verderer done with, or simply a horrid dream. His fingers no longer prickled, his heart no longer sought to rattle itself from his chest.

'He is quite large, isn't he?' A woman spoke over him, her melodic voice altogether enchanting.

'And in rather a need of company, I should say.' Ever careless, ever flippant, Pitch amused himself with his own words.

Peering through barely cracked lids, Silas rolled his head side to side, working to clear his muddled mind enough to make out his surrounds. There were no walls pressing in on him here. The space was open, and mesmerising in its beauty. The chamber, a grand domed space, was formed entirely from cobalt-coloured quartz, set in a striking tessellated pattern for the most part, but every so often a column of the near-translucent rock pushed forth, sending up an imposing shard that pierced the air like a giant's arrow. Silas pressed onto his elbows, staring in awe at the roof over him, one that reached so high he could barely make out its highest angle.

'You are safe here,' came the chiming whisper. 'We will keep you.'

Silas sat up, wiping at a tear that had pressed its way free as he grew accustomed to the return of light. There at his side stood a startling creature. She looked as though she'd been carved from the same crystal that pervaded the chamber. She regarded him through opaque eyes, their shape reminiscent of a perfect tear, her lips fuller still than Pitch's, her hair a crystalline imitation of dead straight strands that hung down to boyishly narrow hips. Striking as she was, Silas knew not where to place his own gaze. Her pert breasts, smoothed of all sign of nipples, rested almost directly in his line of sight. He dropped his gaze. But he'd not hide from embarrassment there, for she was entirely naked. His only saving grace was that she appeared as though a statue had come to life, one smoothed of the crevices and folds that were normally to be found between a woman's legs.

Silas lowered his gaze further still and found that he had been laid upon a plinth of sorts, one constructed from the quartz. But not all was entirely blue about this place, for the woman stood upon a carpet of green that rolled in swells around her, a layer of moss so abundant her feet were not visible for it. He recognised the foliage, with his usual puzzling certainty of the natural world, as glittering wood-moss. A glorious groundcover with its stems of subtle coppery-red and feathery fronds, and one that he knew to be impossible in a place such as this. Far from the heaths and moors.

'Come, you must try this wine, Sickle.' The daemon stood some paces away. 'It is even finer than I recall.'

Much delighted laughter followed his words. Not the daemon's own though, rather the titter of others. But Silas could not tear himself from the wood-moss, of all things. He was well aware of the naked, otherworldly woman waiting on him, but the moss intrigued him beyond measure for the sense of familiarity it brought. Silas watched the woman's feet shift amongst the delicate mesh of green. He had done just such a thing, he was beyond certain. Once, far from here, he too had set his boots aside to touch his toes to the coolness of Mother Nature's carpet.

'Sickle, I caused you to faint, not lose your ability to speak,' Pitch called. 'Get off that remarkable arse and join us.'

His shout sent Silas's memory scattering, the recall of his distant past fleeing beyond his reach once more. The woman smiled at him, but Silas could not do the same. Whether it was because of his frustration at losing such a memory or true concern, he was gripped by unease. He could not find the warmth in that smile she offered, nor in those eyes of hers that held no colour to give them life.

'Rest a while, ankou.' Her voice was the tinkling of sweet bells. 'We are most pleased to have you here, where we can keep you.'

Twice she had said that now, and Silas liked talk of being kept this time even less than the first.

'Where have we been brought to?' For all Silas knew he was no longer in the mines at all. He had no idea how long he might have been passed out. He set his legs over the edge of the plinth, planting his booted feet into the wood-moss.

After a weighty pause, the bluecap woman's etched smile widened. 'You are at the heart of the mines, in the court of Dela, queen of the bluecaps of the Forest of Dean.'

The soft caress of music filled the air, the quivering rise of a violin blended with the mellower tones of the harp. But whoever the musicians might be, they were hidden from Silas. As too was Pitch. There was no sign of the daemon. He might have taken any one of the multitude of tunnels Silas saw now branched away from this chamber. He seemed to be entirely alone with the woman.

'Can your queen tell me more of the Verderer?' The strangeness of his surrounds was but one worry. The teratism he sought to face was powerful. What creature had the might to cause the ground to quake at his passing?

'Of course. Shall I take you to her?'

'Sickle, where the blazes are you?' Pitch's summons came again. 'I shall be quite finished if you do not come along, right now.'

Silas cocked his head. There had been a strain against Pitch's words.

'There is plenty for all.' The woman leaned in to him and, before he could protest, pressed her crystal lips to his. A prick of something sharp came next, as though a tiny imperfection in the crystal barbed him. Silas sought to pull away. His heart thumped once, resoundingly. A shiver took him, and he wondered suddenly why on Earth he had sought to separate himself from this beauty. He leaned into the embrace, the sting against his lip increasing twofold. Painful truly, but unpleasant certainly not. His body stirred, a pressure between his legs as thickness rose and strained against material.

The woman withdrew her intoxicating touch, stepping back so he might admire her more fully. Silas gasped.

A statue no more, the crystal-carved woman was defined fully with flesh and bone. And what a remarkable face she had. He shook at the sight. For it was the very face he had seen as he tumbled into the water at the boggart's bridge.

Here stood the woman who had run to him across the manicured lawns of the castle grounds.

'Hello, Silas.' She toyed with a ribbon that hung from the cuff of her lilac jacket. 'I have missed you so. Shall we dance once more?'

CHAPTER 18

They danced through the glittering wood-moss, over the rise and fall of the ground, with the violins etching their gentle notes into the air. Silas could not tear his eyes from the woman he held. Her pale golden hair was caught up in an untidy bun at the base of her neck, as though she had not had time nor inclination to set it properly. It much suited the rosiness of her cheeks, bright with her exertions. Silas's hand was light against her back, his fingers warm against her own. Something bothered him about his fingers. They tingled so. How it vexed him, for he wished for no distractions while he danced with his...his...Silas shook his head, a pain taking hold behind his eyes.

'Dance with me before you keep safe and rest,' the woman said, her lips damp and alluring. But what of her eyes?

Silas spun his partner about in an ever-widening circle, her narrowed skirt fluttering against his legs. He grit his teeth. A thought had taken him and then slipped away. What was it he had been wondering?

He glanced about them. The world was alight with sapphire blues and an azure haze. The moss at his feet glittered as though diamonds had fallen amongst the delicate fronds. Was this still the chamber he'd woken in? The woman made a pirouette beneath his arm, returning at once to his embrace. How remarkable that their height was so evenly matched. Yet, how strange to find a woman of such stature. Silas performed another dizzying set of circles. So much of this was...curious...ill-fitting, but what of it troubled him most? There was a feature…a certain notable feature…

The clench of a headache came again at the back of his eyes. There it was! The eyes.

Silas snatched at the slippery thought, holding it firm. Her eyes. They were entirely wrong. Devoid of colour. A black ring marked her iris, an onyx spot denoted her pupil, but after that there was only white. Silas loosened his fingers where they clasped her fine pale hand.

'Do I not please you?' She tilted her head, but how odd and slow that movement was. 'Am I not as beautiful as you remember?'

'Yes…' Silas's brow wrinkled as he searched her face. 'I mean that is…you are beautiful yes…' His tongue was thick in his mouth, and his mind hummed as though bees made their home there. What did he recall of her, aside from the distant image as she ran towards the lake? He searched for her name, for a memory that held more than that one singular impression. Distracted, his toe caught upon a rise in the ground, and he fell against the woman in lilac. His apology died upon his lips. It was as though he had struck a piece of the quartz that formed the chamber itself.

She smiled. A dimple cut into her cheek. Perfect rows of white teeth contrasted against full lips that curved in a Cupid's bow. How familiar these lips were. Silas pulled his hand free and touched a finger to the pink swell. He knew these lips. He scowled against the interminable buzz that filled his head. These lips did not belong to her.

The pain struck once more and without remorse. Silas staggered, clutching at his temple, certain he would lose his knees beneath him. The woman's fingertips bit into his shoulder and clenched down so hard upon his hand that he caught his breath. She bore down on him, and all hope of staying upon his feet was lost. He dropped to his knees.

'Is he being troublesome, Your Majesty?'

The fuzziness about Silas's mind caused him to take longer than he should to recognise the speaker's voice, but when that recognition came, he could not have been more grateful. He sought to find his feet. At the daemon's side is where he ought to be, not here. The woman pressed down harder, and the sting that had come when her lips met his own now dug itself into his shoulder.

'I had thought he would taste sweeter than he does.'

Her words, lyrically spoken as they were, did not rest so easy upon Silas's ears now. He peered up at Pitch, who leaned against a pillar of blue nearby. He caught sight of the curve of his lips. A Cupid's bow. The knife stabbed once more into the softness of his skull. He coughed with the pain, his palm flattened against his temple as though that might stymie the agony.

'Dear me, he doesn't seem so well.' Pitch stood surveying Silas as though he were a cow on offer in a yard. 'But I did warn you that an ankou would have very little for you to devour. They are empty shells I'm afraid. All those heightened emotions you do so love to feast on are wiped from them when death makes them her whore. You won't find him quite as delicious as a terrified miner looking for escape, or a gracious one who the bluecaps have guided to a new vein of ore. Such a shame, for you.'

The woman brushed soft fingers through Silas's hair, but her grip upon his shoulder did not relent. 'But he did stir with thought of you, daemon, and that did please me.'

Pitch made a play at a bow. 'What use in being an incubus if I cannot twist those around me into delightful knots of longing? A pity you did not know him when he was fully human, for I have no doubt he would have given you ample to chew upon.'

Silas swayed as though intoxicated, but it was no crisp ale that skewed his mind. He listened in, as though from a distance, to Pitch's strange words. Talk of feeding and eating and devouring that pulled despair from the depths of his fog-filled mind. Did the daemon have no quarrel with Silas's predicament? Was Pitch to abandon him here to this? Whatever this might be.

'Perhaps, but he bores me now. Let him be kept safe with the others, for I am done.' The woman at last lifted her hand from Silas's shoulder. The thorny pricks withdrew from his skin, leaving it burning with memory of their touch. 'I am disappointed. I had thought feeding on an ankou would be more...challenging.'

'Well, at least you learned something new today.' Pitch's smile was laced with something Silas could not quite name with his thoughts so scrambled. 'It is indeed a day of firsts in this mine, I dare say.'

Silas rubbed at his shoulder, his free hand pressed to the ground so he would not topple. The entire chamber seemed to sway back and forth around him. Pitch offered him a hand. It took immense effort to take it. Silas's fingers twitching as though they had a life of their own. He was pulled to his feet, and his legs took some convincing to brace. If not for Pitch's steadying touch, he doubted he would have stood at all.

'Here is an idea for you, Your Majesty.' Pitch slipped one arm about Silas's back, while his free hand caressed Silas's cheek. 'Before you make him safe, how about I share one last dance with him? I can arouse him easily I assure you, and you may find something in him to feed on then? Thoughts, rather than memories of course, but what thoughts they will be. I can have him imagining himself spread beneath me – oh wait, perhaps you've a taste for subtler romance? A tender kiss upon a moonlit night, his hands wandering all over my body as he drives his tongue into my mouth. How would that please you?'

She still held the form of the woman in the lilac dress, the woman who existed in Silas's memory alone. He thought he understood the truth. The bluecap queen wrangled with the compartments of his addled mind, dipping into their contents at will. She had found his thoughts on Pitch's lips there, and his stomach roiled to imagine what else might float to the surface if this persisted.

'One dance, see what you can stir,' the fae queen declared. 'Then you shall pleasure me.'

Pitch inclined his head. 'Of course, Your Majesty. I would have it no other way.' The top of Pitch's head barely reached to Silas's chin, but he manoeuvred the much larger man as though he were light as the moss beneath their feet. 'Might we have the music a little louder?'

Silas did not see nor hear the queen's reply, but the cascade of music rose. The notes were more hurried than he recalled, the tune lifting its rhythm. Pitch pressed into him, his touch warm, his body the only thing capable of keeping Silas upright.

'Pitch,' Silas mumbled. The first words to cross his lips in what felt like forever.

'Just listen.' Pitch's voice was at his ear as he guided Silas through the shifts and turns of a dance he could barely fathom. 'It is not just your Verderer who is lost, this whole fucking place has gone quite mad.' Pitch tilted his head back and laughed, a sparkling sound amongst the notes. He leaned in once more, brushing his lips against Silas cheek. 'She has you in something of a rapture. The bluecaps do this to humans when they wish to suckle at them. It is their way. But they never do this to supernaturals. Do you understand me, Sickle? Our situation has finally become less dreary, for strange things are afoot here indeed.' He made a play of slapping gently at Silas's shoulder before he stepped away and twirled himself about. He returned to Silas just in time to keep him from tripping over his own feet. 'Shall I show you the full psychosis of this place?'

'What do we...' Words were cumbersome when one's tongue was the size of a piece of bread. Silas squeezed his eyes shut, feeling quite unwell. He sought greater purchase on Pitch's shoulder, desperate to hold fast to something he recognised. The daemon's hip ground against his thigh, his fingers delicate against Silas's back yet more reassuring than a metal girder. Silas's mind taunted him with a vision from the Moon Inn, Pitch's body as he worked it against the lover beneath him. He stumbled with the effort it took to wipe clear the sordid thought.

'Fight your way through the stupor, Sickle,' Pitch said, urgently. 'Focus on what is about you. Look up, but keep your fear hidden.'

Silas breathed in and drove his energies into lifting his chin. He opened his eyes. The room tilted and settled back upon itself.

'Steady now.' Pitch sighed against him. 'She watches us.'

The chamber rose above, a majestic assembly of quartz that shimmered as blue as the skies of heaven surely must be. Pitch hugged him tightly, and their dance shifted to a more intimate sway of body against body.

'Do you see how they keep everyone safe?' he whispered, and touched his lips to Silas's neck.

A shiver ran the length of Silas's body, and he was about to turn his attentions back to the daemon when a pattern within the quartz above caught his focus instead. Pitch's body tensed as he worked harder to keep Silas from swaying too far backwards.

'My god,' Silas breathed.

'Look away.' Pitch took Silas's chin and turned his head. 'Keep your calm.'

How was that possible? The blood in his veins chilled, and the wave of despair rode him high and hard. Overhead hung a massive pillar of sapphire-blue crystal, jutting from the roof like a cultivated stalactite. But this was like no other of its kind.

Embedded in the blue rock, with eyes widened by the horror of their demise, were the bodies of untold numbers of men and women. Packed against one another in a haphazard tomb.

Chapter 19

Fury found its way through Silas's shock. His skin prickled with the heat of his indignation. Was this how these monsters kept the humans safe? Never mind the terrible disregard for the dead. To cast them together as though these corpses were those of a slain herd was unforgivable. Silas felt as though his head might burst for the rage that swelled within. He fought to free himself of Pitch's grasp.

'By Gabriel's arsehole, did I not just tell you to retain your calm?' Pitch grabbed hold of the back of Silas's head and showed no gentleness in the way he wrenched it forward. He pressed his forehead to Silas's. 'Keep your trinket where it lies. Even if there are a multitude of lost souls here, they are not your concern right now.'

'There are none.' Silas was not in control of his faculties, and spittle flew with his words. 'They are all gone. But these bluecaps, you said they were harmless. They are murderers.'

It was a small mercy that not a one of these souls lingered here. How excruciating to find oneself trapped in such a place.

'The bluecaps are as far from murderers as I am from being a decent man. They are, normally, rather feeble like yourself.' Pitch's lips brushed his.

'Stop that, let me go.'

'And you would find yourself being stuffed into one of those quartz coffins, my dear.' He pressed soft weight against Silas's mouth. There was a salty sweetness on his lips. 'Insanity is rife here. Human massacre aside, do you see the marks upon my neck?'

Silas did, for at the angle Pitch held him, there was not much else to see but the alabaster whiteness of his skin. Tiny puncture marks were evident on his neck, four in all. 'I do.'

'One of the bitches sought to feed from me.' He laughed with light abandon, as though they were not surrounded by ravenous creatures and cruel death. 'Do you have any idea how unimaginable it is for a bluecap to try to feed upon a daemon?'

Silas did not but the question did not seem one begging an answer. Their slow sway to the music was intolerable, yet Pitch gave him no release, the arm he wrapped about Silas's waist holding behemoth strength. They were watched still by the fae queen, and she was not alone. Her bluecaps had joined her in great numbers. The queen remained shaped as she was from Silas's thoughts, while the rest held their crystalline form, with their sex rubbed smooth and their sculpted perfection giving off the impression that Pitch and Silas danced about in the hall of a grand museum, with ancient chiselled works surrounding them.

'And that wine, it was fucking horrendous. I knew from the first sip this place had rotted.' Pitch's breath warmed Silas's lips and fled up his nostrils. For those who stood shorter than the daemon, which was all the gathered assembly save for Silas, it might appear they were locked in an intimate kiss.

'How do we...leave...' Cursing his addled head, Silas fought his own tongue for purchase on his words.

'I am hoping their stupidity and insatiable appetite has not changed at least, for there is no way out of a bluecap's chamber save for the one they are willing to show you. A deal must be struck.' Pitch pushed his fingers into Silas's hair and let one hand fall way down his back to rest upon his arse. The music twirled frantically, and Silas could not help but imagine it was building to a crescendo. 'When they agree to allow you to leave, you do so without hesitation or question. No matter what you might hear.'

'And you?' Silas's lip actually grazed Pitch's with how close they were. The ache between his legs was a dull and distant pain.

'Never mind all that. Get that trinket of yours back into the forest, destroy that bloody horn-blowing teratism so I might have my honeyed wine once more.'

The violins scratched at the air, notes lifting to play at the crystal tombs that hung above, before dying into nothingness. Pitch pulled away and Silas could not save himself from falling. He landed upon his back. The glittering wood-moss cushioned his landing, but it could do nothing to protect his eyes. He stared at the macabre display above him, jaw tight with rage. He was not sure he could do as Pitch said – leave without a backward glance. Those dead above him should be at rest in their proper graves.

'Have you fattened him for me, daemon?' The mirage that encased the queen slipped away, the woman in lilac dripping from her like wax melting from a candle, returning the bluecap to her original form. Cold and pristine.

Pitch flourished his hands. 'He is a simpleton, I'm afraid. Attractive but vapid. There is nothing there that would much whet your appetite, Your Highness. Now, shall we return to sweeter things?'

'I will have that pleasure from you now.'

'Of course. And I will give much more, if you give me something in return.'

The queen's empty eyes fixed upon the daemon. Her assembled bluecaps shuffled and tittered. 'Of what do you speak, daemon?'

'A deal, Your Grand Majesty.' Pitch's charming smile worked its way forth, the cavern's blue mixing with the green of his eyes to alter them to a subdued violet. 'Show the ankou the way from your chambers, allow him to return to the goddess's service, and I shall remain here with you and allow you to feed from me as you see fit. '

The chamber fell utterly silent, the bluecaps returned to the statues they so resembled.

'You mock us.'

'I do no such thing.' Pitch tugged at his collar, the better to show off the tiny punctures upon his neck. 'I could have slain the guilty party with a wriggle of my finger.' He jerked his chin towards a bluecap who cowered behind a veritable hill of wood-moss. 'Yet they live still. Come now, when have you ever received an offer such as this? A daemon, an incubus no less, yours for the taking. You grant me sanctuary here, and allow the ankou free, and in return all that I am is yours to take, to feast upon. With no repercussions.'

'Repercussions?'

'Come now, surely you know that I could extinguish you all for feeding from me without my consent?'

A murmur went through the assembly and the oddest look swept the queen's face, his words seeming to confuse her.

'What daemon needs sanctuary in the mines?' The queen said with an imperious toss of her sculpted head. Her hair did not move with her, keeping its form as though frozen in its detail.

'One who has been exiled from Arcadia and forced into servitude.' Pitch pointed at Silas, a coldness upon him that matched well with the bluecaps. 'I am shackled to this ankou, reduced to no more than his whipping boy. I don't take kindly to servitude. Free him from me, and I'll sustain you and your kingdom forever. You cannot imagine how many pleasures and sufferances I have endured.'

While he spoke he made his way towards the queen. Silas watched closely. Pitch moved with a feline grace, exuding that mesmerising quality that Silas had seen on display so many times hence. That smile, the lowered lashes, the sensual swing of his hips, the voice sweeter than the honey he so coveted. Pitch weakened knees when he so desired. But what of a fae queen? Did she harbour the longings he relied upon?

The answer was not long in coming. Her azure eyes drank him in with naked hunger, her crystal fingers clenching at her sides. She was as spellbound as any other. Around her the bluecaps were restless once more, and their fervour sickened Silas. Pitch had overestimated his abilities here, surely, for they looked to set upon him like hawks on a carcass. Silas ground his fist into his palm. What nonsense did Pitch speak about, sustaining these mad creatures forever? Was Silas so repulsive the daemon truly could not stand to be at his side a moment longer? He wrestled unhappily with his thoughts. And it occurred to him he could do so quite clearly. He was not so numbed as before. His hands did as they were bid rather than flail about as though they staged a revolt against the limbs that held them.

'A deal with the bluecaps is binding, even for your kind. You would share your sufferings? Your pleasures? All the morsels of your being?' The queen still held herself with stately poise, but her voice betrayed her eagerness.

'All the morsels.' Pitch reached her. He stood taller than her, but they could be compared in the fineness of their limbs. Never had Pitch's delicacy been more evident than now. 'Shall we make this deal, Your Highness?'

'We shall.' She lifted sapphire-blue fingers to her lips and kissed them before sending them towards Pitch. Silas thought he saw the daemon brace as the monarch's touch landed upon his lips. There was no doubt at all of the shudder that ran through the daemon's body a moment later.

'Pitch?' Silas clambered to his feet. The world did not tilt and rock about him, though his head ached still.

'Go, Silas. It is done.' Pitch waved a careless hand over his shoulder. 'Remember what I said.'

That Silas should leave when he was told. It had been made clear, but with the moment upon him, Silas could not find the compulsion to leave.

'This way, if you will.'

A bluecap stood at Silas's side. The fae had not sculpted themselves with any particular sex in mind, stealing a little from both, with the swell of breasts evident beneath a face that held the more robust angles of men: a wider sweep of jaw and thicker press of nose all chiselled clear. Androgynous in a very different way to Pitch, whose manhood blended most disconcertingly with the more tender attributes of a woman.

'I am not sure that I –'

'Nothing to be sure about, you simply must,' the fae declared. This one too had the chime-like way of speaking that the queen possessed. 'Come now. You cannot undo a deal that's been done.'

Pitch offered his hand to the queen with a lavish bow. She accepted his gesture with a cool, unreadable look, and the pair set forth to wherever it was one shared oneself with these creatures. The very thought of it left Silas's mouth dry. He struggled to keep from staring up at the dead hanging above. What odds did they face here that one such as Tobias Astaroth must broker such an agreement? Silas was awash with confusion. He should move, he must move, but the notion of abandoning the daemon to so vile a place was perturbing. The fae sent to escort Silas grew impatient, tapping a small crystal foot. Silas scowled down at the bluecap, channelling his discomfiture into the look.

'I do not seek to impede on your precious deal.' He wondered if this creature was one of those who had corralled the luckless humans into the quartz tombs. 'I will leave, as promised.'

'Then do so now. It's been quiet in the mines for days. The Verderer chases away all who enter his forest. I am hungry. We are all hungry.' Though it was spoken without malice, and in the most practical sort of ways, the words were ice upon Silas's spine.

Nothing in the way Pitch held himself betrayed anything untoward. He was, as always, much like a peacock putting on his grandest display. The bluecaps closed in around him as he moved. He laughed gaily and even bent to kiss one of those nearest him. As he righted he cast a glance over his shoulder.

'Gods, are you still here you great bore? Go. Go now.'

If he had fired arrows at Silas, there would not have been more of a compulsion to turn and run. Silas spun on his heels, the echo of Pitch's warning-laden words following him. The fae skipped ahead, beaming now that Silas was at last following orders. But it was Pitch's directive the ankou followed, no other.

'This way, this way.'

The bluecap made their merry way across the chamber, leading Silas to where a plethora of openings were set into the rock face. The darkness suggested each was a tunnel. The fae chose one with a marking of crystal bulbs over the entrance, hanging like discarded Christmas decorations, and stepped inside. Silas had seen no sign of such tunnels when first he surveyed the chamber, yet here he strode along the length of one so high that he had no fear of striking his head. It was wide enough too that he was able to press back the whispers of anxiety that threatened. He could not be crippled by such fear, not now. The tunnel drove true and straight, and they carried on a cracking pace for what felt like boundless minutes. The striking azure blue of the quartz grew less and less as they travelled, rock of rust and clay taking its place, allowing only veins of the crystal to remain. But those veins threw off enough hazy blue light to keep the path visible. Silas squinted. The passageway carried on for as far as his eyes would allow him to see. He dragged at the folds of his coat, hugging it more tightly around him. The pinch of his trepidation grew more intense, and he was not certain when panic might grab ahold.

As they walked on, a faint sound reached them, the moan of a person discomforted.

'What was that?' Silas stopped still. 'Did you hear that?'

'It is the sounds of a feast. One I'm about done with missing,' the fae declared haughtily.

'What are you talking about?'

The disquieting sound came again, far in the distance, though from which end of the corridor he could not be sure. And there could be no mistaking it for any sounds of pleasure.

'I'm not partial to it myself. The good times taste best, so far as I'm concerned. But there are some, and Queen Dela is amongst them, that do enjoy the agonies the most.'

Silas's horror made him bold. He grasped ahold of a crystalline shoulder and jerked the fae about. 'That sound is Pitch? My companion? They are feeding on him now?'

All at once the walls pressed in, and Silas could not steady his breath.

'Course. I told you, we are near starved. Don't look so flabbergasted, we ain't savages. He keeps his flesh. It's just the emotions we want, and seeing as he's already lived 'em, I don't see the issue in sharing. The miners never bothered about it, though I 'spose they didn't have the entire flock eating their fill at once.' The bluecap shrugged off Silas's hold. 'Now, there you go. Be on with you. I can't be leaving till I see you climb.'

'Climb?' Silas frowned.

The taxed moaning would not leave them be, filtering down the tunnel.

'Right there, you blind?'

The fae cast their hand skyward. Silas lifted his head – and forgot, for a moment, the daemon's distress. Above, the roof of the cave was no more. A vertical tunnel struck upwards, a narrow construction that would only just accommodate his proportions. A shaft gouged from the earth to bear him aloft to the freshness of the air and the unpredictability of the forest.

On one side of the rock face a ladder clung, perilously narrow rungs of metal that would see him freed.

'Go on with you. Hurry along.' The fae stabbed a finger into his side and Silas cried out.

He clutched at his coat, expecting to find the tear of a knife evident, perhaps his own blood to follow. The fabric was untouched. 'Keep your hands off me,' he snapped.

'Certainly I will, so soon as you go.' The hard, fast smile held a peppering of cruel delight. 'Get on. Now.' The fae raised their hand as though to strike him again.

'Leave me be.' Silas glowered. 'Or you will know of it.'

The bluecap smirked. Silas took hold of one of the rungs, lifting himself so as to test his weight upon it. There was some relief in finding it steadfast in its anchorings. He cast a look back the way he had come, to where he had left Pitch in such foul hands. Pitch himself had warned him of this.

Leave. No matter what you might hear.

And what Silas heard was a man tormented. He clung so tightly to the ladder that his knuckles ached.

Silas hauled himself up another rung, consoling himself with thought of the barn fight in Bishop's Castle. The daemon enjoyed the torment. Silas drove higher. Another step, another return to stillness. A glimpse below told him the fae still watched. And so he climbed on. The air freshened, tinged with the fusty weight of the forest undergrowth, flowing down the shaft to meet him. Ever onwards he pulled himself, his hands roughened by the coarseness of the metal. A misstep saw his boot slide free of a rung. Silas's cry rang out. His back caught against the wall behind, reminding him too well of the confines of his position. Panic, so carefully kept at bay, now roared into him. Never had his heart thundered so. He wrapped himself about the ladder, his body shuddering so hard that his forehead met the metal with a painful strike. It was his own groans that bothered the air now, and his eyes squeezed shut as he madly sought to find shelter from a hysteria that was very near to rendering him senseless.

'No, no, no,' he whimpered, the bars of metal pressing into his shoulders, his lips grazing the rung. 'No. No.'

A whinny interrupted his panic-stricken mantra. A sound so out of place it jolted him from his slow dive into hysterics. Silas craned his neck. At the surface, a place not so far away from him now, stood the pale horse. Her neck lowered so she might peer down at him, the lengths of her mane dangling like precious ropes of salvation.

'Lalassu.' He nearly wept for saying it.

Silas found his courage, and his feet. He quickened his way upon the rungs. The mare nickered to him all the while, as though encouraging his journey.

He could make out the dripping boughs around her, hung with yellows and golds of autumn. The forest framed her graceful head. Her coat was luminous in a darkened world. He ignored the ache of his shoulders, desperate for the buoying strength the horse offered. He was within a hand's reach of the longest lengths of her moon-white mane and grinning like a madman when true awfulness arrived.

A man's agonised cry. Saturated with the torment of untold anguish. Not an agony of the flesh but of the soul itself.

It shook the earth and tore free the very rocks themselves. The shaft rained with dust and dirt. Silas cowered against the wall, blinking into the sudden chaos. Lalassu's neigh lifted high upon the air.

But he could not heed her call. Not with that cry ringing in his ears.

Silas hurried himself back down the rungs, back to where the bluecaps tortured a daemon.

CHAPTER 20

The downward journey was far shorter than the upward had seemed. Silas jumped clear with several rungs still to go, his breath leaving him in a gasp as he landed with a solid thump upon the dirt. The deep-set rumbling was more pronounced in the depths, reminding him of the Verderer's approach. That occasion seemed in another lifetime.

Silas ran the length of the corridor, zigzagging as the tunnel rid itself of pieces of rock and hard-packed earth. There was one small mercy, the ghastly cries had ceased. Though only from the air. They would remain for some time yet in Silas's mind. What awful misery had Pitch known to make such a noise?

Silas pressed himself harder. The length of the tunnel appeared double to what he recalled. He could only pray that it would lead him where he expected, and not to some dead-end of the fae queen's making. He shook off the disquieting thought and focused on his running. The hint of blue veining along the walls widened into sizable slabs of brilliant sapphire blue. He pushed himself harder yet, certain he was upon the right path. The length of his coat streamed behind him, the bandalore weightless in his pocket. Whatever shook the mines to their foundations was no lost soul, no teratism.

Dashing headlong into the chamber, he shot straight into the blaze of blue he'd so recently escaped. The quartz was as vivid as he recalled, but not so the glittering wood-moss. Silas stared at the carpet of ruin that spread out before him. Crisp and dry with death, the foliage crackled underfoot. He peered about, searching for a sign of where Pitch might have been taken. This hurried rescue was fraught with issues, not least of all that Silas was not certain the chamber would hold long enough for him to leave it again. Narrow black veins ran through the surface of the quartz. He could not tell if they were cracks or another substance altogether that permeated the rock. Either way, it did not bode well.

Silas cupped his hands around his mouth. 'Pitch!' A crude method, but all he had at his disposal. 'Pitch, where are you, damn it?'

A sound akin to the ice cracking upon a winter pond rent the air. If any answer came, he did not hear a word of it.

'Shit.' Silas spun around, not once but twice, at a loss as to where to head next. The chamber was considerable, and piles of quartz that had once been abundant with glittering wood-moss blocked his clear sight of the entire structure. A structure under considerable strain. Even as he hesitated, the black veining splintered through the crystal, a haphazard spiderweb that grew at an intensifying rate.

In desperation Silas chose the most appalling direction of all. He raced for the overhanging column with its entombed cargo. There was no sense to his choice, but his gut drove him onward. He scrambled up a rise of crystal, a roughly pyramid-shaped structure that would take him so near to the lowermost tip of the column that he might reach up and touch it. The very thought choked him. Breathing hard, Silas reached the peak, and saw what lay beyond. He pressed his hands to his knees, seeking to steady the thump of his pulse.

'Oh god.'

He had found Pitch. The man lay upon the cave floor, on his back in shallow water of the brightest blue. His vest was gone, his shirt ripped to expose his torso. Upon his skin were multitudes of angry red welts, hundreds of them Silas would wager. Silas raced headlong down the chunks of quartz. He barely missed landing upon his knees as his momentum got away from him, and the last step almost undid him. He blinked, his eyes stinging with the increasing dust upon the air.

'Pitch, do you hear me?' He stepped into the wide-spread pool of glacier-blue water. The thin layer of liquid covered the chamber floor almost entirely here and rippled with the vibrations that filled the rock.

Silas's gaze landed upon an unsettling sight, just beyond where Pitch lay. Another body, resting on its side, motionless in the water.

'Lieutenant?' Silas shook at the sight.

It could not be, this was sick illusion. A grotesque chimera of human and bluecap. The pelvis and legs were sculpted quartz, fine and slender with the sexless smoothness between the legs, but the torso was draped in the chequered brown jacket Edward had worn when he entered The Moon Inn. The head was a malformed oddity that was difficult to look upon. Half bluecap-carved stone beauty and half human. This monstrous imitation matched almost perfectly, down to the stubble upon the lieutenant's face and the darkness beneath his eyes. But Silas saw it for what it must be. A memory stolen from Pitch's head, just as the woman in lilac was taken from Silas's.

The air's fine dust scratched at Silas's throat, and he returned his attentions to Pitch.

'Can you hear me?' The faintest sheen of blue clung to Pitch's skin. They were not welts, he saw now, but massive numbers of tiny punctures, running all the way up his torso and his neck, as though he had suffered the attack of dozens of tiny vampires. The skin around each wound blazed red. His face was the only visible part of him that was not marked. 'Pitch, you need to get up.'

Dear god, he needed to be alive. Silas lowered his head to Pitch's chest, seeking a heartbeat, a rise of the chest.

'Fuck off.' Pitch swung his fist. The blow barely glanced off Silas's arm. A butterfly could have rendered more harm. 'There's nothing more to take.'

'Pitch, it's me. It's Sickle.' Silas coughed, mostly from the grittiness of the air, not least from the sudden unknotting of tension beneath his ribs. 'Can you stand? We must go.'

'Have you not had your fill?' He swung again, in time with the loosening of a massive chunk of quartz from the ceiling of the far side of the chamber. The effect was dramatic, as though his blow were the crash of thunder. 'What more do you want? I've nothing left.'

There was no time to reason with a delusional daemon. Silas gathered Pitch up in his arms and swung the flailing, cursing man over his shoulder. Pitch was light as half a bushel of hay. He had barely positioned the groaning daemon when a shower of blue hail fell from the cavern's ceiling, splashing into the icy blue water around him. Silas glanced up and uttered a curse Pitch would have been proud of.

The column full of bodies was as black as the inside of a chimney. And it rocked back and forth like an enormous pendulum. Silas fled, Pitch slapping at his back and demanding to be set down. He was no more than a few strides clear when the mammoth column snapped free, spearing into the ground with a rapturous crash that damn near rocked Silas off his feet.

Pitch struggled more ardently, his knee striking Silas beneath the ribs.

'Stop it,' Silas gasped.

'Then fucking well set me down.'

At least his reply was coherent.

'Can you walk?' Silas would not look back, he would not see what more terrible damage had been done to those wretched bodies he must leave behind. If such a thing were possible, if he and Pitch survived, he would find a way to mark this place for the gravesite it was.

'I don't bloody know.' Pitch coughed, his hips jerking against Silas's shoulder. 'What are you doing here, you imbecile? I told you to go.'

'I could not.' Silas ground his jaw. 'They were torturing you.'

'They would not be the first. And do you not see what it cost them?' His laugh was bitter enough to taste. 'This is exactly what I hoped for, and you've bloody ruined it with your fucking stupidity. Why does every god-created moron that surrounds me think themselves a saviour?' He dissolved into a coughing fit that threatened to unsettle him from Silas's hold. Just as quickly it was done, and he hung limp.

'Steady on, Pitch. I see the tunnel.'

By whatever miracle had drifted their way, it was true. Silas recognised the tunnel for the peculiar arrangement of yuletide-like decorations that marked its apex. He used the same zigzagging pattern that had favoured his return to the chamber, and they were soon rushing beneath the rocky ornaments and into the depths of the tunnel. Silas's lungs ached with overuse, a cramp of muscle bothering his side. But it was not long now and they would be back at those rungs to follow their passage to freedom where Lalassu waited.

The earth protested, shudders joined the booming collapse of the main chamber. With thighs trembling, Silas could not sustain his quick pace, dropping back to a rapid walk. The darkness was thicker than he recalled, and soon he saw why. The black veining so evident in the main chamber had spread here too and all but extinguished the azure haze that might guide them. But still, he recalled how very straight this passage was. All they need do was continue as they were.

'Pitch, we are almost there.' The daemon was silent, and very still. He only moved as Silas did, dangling like a downed stag upon his shoulder. 'Pitch?' Silas coughed.

The dust gathered thicker here upon the air, and it was not long before he hacked as hard as Pitch had done. The fits doubled him over, and his eyes watered with their ferocity. The grit made his throat swell and clogged his nostrils.

'I need to set you down.'

There was no reply, and Silas did his utmost to handle the daemon with care. But with his lungs squeezing so tight, he feared he would lose consciousness too before long. He sought out the wall so he might steady himself. His fingers glanced against the rock easily. He must have staggered more off-centre than he first imagined. Silas grabbed the collar of his coat and pressed it over his mouth, seeking what isolation he could from the grit which hung so dense about him. He peered ahead and could have shouted with sheer glee for what he saw. The rungs of the metal ladder, glinting with light from above.

He pushed away from the wall and straightened.

His head met at once with the solidness of shuddering rock. The roof of the tunnel was mere inches from his crown. Either he was dragging them along the wrong path, or the tunnel had lost half its size.

'Fuck.'

The pressure at his head grew weightier and he was forced into a stoop. The tunnel was closing in on them.

All around, the ground continued to rumble as though giants awoke at the heart of the Earth.

He grabbed at Pitch, shaking him hard as he dared. 'I need you to wake now,' Silas coughed. 'Right now.' The rough handling did not so much as elicit a moan from Pitch, at least not one Silas could hear above the calamity of his surrounds. He grabbed Pitch, looping one arm around the limp man, and dragged him along the passage. Silas was forced to angle himself sideways. It was ludicrously slow. The sharp tips of panic's claws dug at him as the curve of the tunnel's surface bore down, forcing Silas into a trembling bow. The ground shook anew, a stronger tug at the earth that sent its shockwave through his entire body. A scream perched itself at the base of his throat as he realised they were about to be pressed into a dirty tomb.

Silas tilted his head, all he could manage in the circumstances, to seek out the ladder.

He swept his free hand across his eyes. Not certain he was seeing clearly through the haze and sting of gritty air.

But there it was. A wave of snow white swept down the shaft. Now it touched at the ground, sweeping across the stones and piling debris, covering them as completely as a January snowfall. The torrent headed for them, the paleness of the moon's touch upon it, and as it slid ever closer, he saw that it was not so white as he imagined. The glimmer of sea-green flashed its way clear.

'Lalassu.' Silas coughed and cried, dropping to his knees. There was no space for him to remain upright now. A whimper escaped him as the tunnel walls groaned with the pressures upon them. Silas lay on his side, pulling Pitch to him, seeking to shield the daemon as their world shrunk. 'Hurry, Lalassu.'

He threw his leg over the lifeless daemon, and ducked his head as the white waved reached him. Thousands upon thousands of fine strands wove their way into a rapid and silky cocoon around them, sliding beneath their bodies as though they carried no weight at all. Drowning out the horrendous sounds of the collapsing world that surrounded them. Pitch grunted, moving for the first time in a while, struggling to shift his hands from where they were trapped against Silas's chest. The shroud drew tighter, and Silas's arms were pinned against the daemon's damp back. He shut his eyes fast. This was every bit as claustrophobic as any coffin. The journey need be swift if he were not to soil himself with terror.

Lalassu dragged them forward, and Silas braced for the discomfort he was certain would come. But the roughness of the ground did not bother them. There were carried upon a thick blanket of horsehair that allowed no trespassers of stone. That did not save them from being thrown about though and rolled so that Pitch now lay atop Silas. The mine's collapse was a dull roar about them. An implosion of soil and rock and wood.

Their horizontal journey shifted abruptly to vertical. They were lifted up the shaft, two blinded men bound and near gagged. Pitch's curses were muffled in the layers of Silas's coat, though his dissatisfaction needed little deciphering.

When Silas's wits were at their very end, his grip on his panic slipping, the momentum shifted once more. Horizontal again. They flew a short distance and then came crashing down upon a surface that yielded beneath them. Thunder boomed from somewhere near by. They landed with Silas once more on his back, Pitch nestled atop him.

The fine strands slipped away, unravelling the protection they'd offered, and Silas found himself gazing up at a night sky illuminated by a crescent moon. The air was hazed with the settling dust, a false mist that gave an eerie weight to the night. Silas rolled his head to one side. The moonlight was enough to show him the mineshaft in ruin, filled to its very brim with scores of rocks and snapped timber. A haphazard crypt now. Pitch moaned, coming too in the silence.

'What the fuck just happened?' He wriggled his way free, his elbows unkind against Silas's ribs.

'Lalassu saved us.'

He pointed to where the delicate strands of Lalassu's mane slipped across the ground, whispering away like a woman's gown upon a dancefloor, trailing back to where the massive horse stood calmly a few feet away. Pitch rolled off him, taking no care with the more delicate parts of Silas's anatomy. He drew himself into a seated position, knees raised, his head resting between them. With a grimace Silas got to his feet, wiping his hands against his stained and torn trousers, and made his way to his horse. He pressed his face against the width of her neck, thankful it was her rich scent now that filled his nostrils, and not the harsh rub of grit-filled air.

'Thank you,' he whispered.

Words far too simple for the miraculous feat, but just how did one thank such a creature? He inhaled, eager to clear his senses entirely of the horrors that had just befallen them.

A vigorous slap met the back of his head.

Silas spun around. 'What the blazes was that for?'

'You would not need to thank that beast if you had not decided on being a fucking hero.' Pitch glowered, fastening the few buttons upon his shirt that had survived his assault. 'I told you to go. I told you to fucking leave me. Next time, you will do as you are told, or so help me, I'll tear you apart myself.'

Silas blinked. 'Fine. All right then.' He bit back a harsher retort. Pitch's cry still rang far too loudly in Silas's head. The man had been in a pain Silas could not imagine.

'Fine. All right then.' Pitch sniffed, repeating Silas's own words. He seemed taken aback by the acquiescence. 'So, where is my bloody horse then?'

'I do not know. I'm sorry.'

Silas rubbed at his arms; the air had cooled notably since they'd entered the mines. And the trees about them were far more barren than he recalled. Their crooked, grey limbs gave them a skeletal look. Lalassu nickered, her breath whitening the air. The animal's magnificent mane draped as it should against her neck. Not a knot or caught stone in its strands to betray what had just occurred. Her velvet lips nuzzled at him, and he stroked her, a smile upon his face. The serenity of the moment was pure heaven in comparison to what had just occurred. The ground did not rumble, the dust did not choke him, and he soothed himself with knowing the dead men, woman and children now rested in a place more akin to a tomb than a prison. How he longed to mount Lalassu and ride clear of this forest at once.

'Do you think you could pull yourself away from the seduction of your horse?' Pitch snapped. 'I suspect they heard that collapse in London, let alone wherever your Verderer prances about in this forest.'

As sharply as the words might have been delivered, Pitch was right in saying them. So far they were fortunate; there was no hint of the horn's cry on the air. Thank goodness for small mercies. Silas did not fancy meeting the Verderer so soon after the ordeal with the bluecaps.

Gathering his reins, he drew himself up into the saddle, the length of his coat slipping across Lalassu's rump. The pang in his thighs was most unkind.

Silas grimaced as he settled. 'You will need to ride with me, until Sanu returns.'

The punctuated refusal he expected did not arise. Pitch merely raised an imperious hand, seeking assistance to mount. He sprang easily from the ground, managing the height with only the mildest of support from Silas before he found his seat upon Lalassu's haunches and settled with barely a grievance. The daemon's silence did not much please Silas. There was a distance in his gaze that had not existed before, a distraction in his manner. Pitch's body may have suffered little in the mines, but Silas was not so sure about his head. Pitch did not anchor himself with hands to Silas's waist, and though worried he might slip, Silas chose not to press him into doing so. Lalassu moved on with no urging from Silas and relaxed into a gentle but energetic walk. Her lack of urgency told Silas that wherever the Verderer might be, it was not nearby.

They left the ruined mine behind them, and Silas saw that it was not just the trees at the edge of the mine shaft that appeared different to how he recalled. All about them the boughs were either stripped entirely of their leaves, or the leaves that clung fast were crinkled and curled with dryness, the bland brown of encroaching decay rather than the intense gold and flame colourings of autumn. Lalassu led them down into the strange passageways that marked the terrain so uniquely. They travelled through sections of the forest floor that might have been tunnels once, now though their roofs were eroded by the elements, leaving only the rocky walls behind. It was like travelling through a natural labyrinth.

All the while, Pitch was silent behind him.

Silas cleared his throat. 'Did you suffer much harm?' Stupid question, really. The daemon's agony had peeled through the chamber, but he could stand the silence no longer. Silas tensed, ready for the blow to the back of his head he thought might follow.

'Not so much as the bluecaps.'

No strike came.

Silas dared another question. 'What caused the collapse? Was it your doing?'

Pitch made a brittle sound. 'Indirectly, yes. Though even I'll admit I did not imagine it would be so thorough. That will teach them I suppose to intrude too deeply where they are not welcome.'

'I don't understand.'

'As you so often don't.'

Silas bit at his lip. 'Might you help me understand?' he said gently. 'I heard your cry. It was...well, I shall not pry as they did, but it pained me to hear.'

Lalassu's hooves cracked the underbrush. There was a long pause before Pitch spoke. 'I'm so terribly sorry to have inconvenienced you.'

'That is not how I meant it.' *And you know it,* Silas wished to say. But he kept his tongue. 'I'll bother you no more with talk of it.'

Their journey continued, plunged back into quietness.

After some time Pitch rested a hand upon Silas's hip. 'If you must know, the fae queen sought to involve herself in a past that was not hers to look upon. For her troubles she was forced to watch her precious bluecaps melt from existence before the same fate befell her. I cannot say it was not fucking wonderful to see. My curse is quite the thing to behold, would you not say?' He did not wait for a reply, pushing on breathlessly. 'Now, Queen Dela will bother no one. And the Lady's precious Horseman is safe.'

Silas winced, recalling the pool of ice-blue liquid he'd trodden in. Dear god, what curse brought on such carnage? 'I must thank you, for what you endured for me. You must have known what agony it would cause –'

'No bloody idea, actually. Like I said, the bluecaps never touch supernaturals. This is a brand-new madness here, Sickle. But let us be clear, I endured nothing for you. I followed the Lady Satine's orders, that is all. And you nearly ruined the entire bloody thing with your pig-headedness.'

Silas set his sights beyond the barb. 'But there is much I don't understand –'

'Hardly a new dilemma for you.'

'So, you are cursed with more than just a vanishing tongue. Is that why you do not wish me to speak that name I've heard you utter in your sleep? Is it too close –'

A hand wrapped over his mouth. It tasted of sweat mingled with a sweeter tang upon the skin.

'Stop. Now,' Pitch whispered. 'I mean it. Do not test the powers at work here, Silas, for I assure you, you and I will come off second best. I do not understand how it is that you should have heard that name, let alone utter it, but I beseech you, do not do so again. Are we clear?' Silas nodded, absurdly conscious of how soft Pitch's skin was. 'Especially here, in this place. There is a rot at work here, make no mistake of it.'

Pitch removed his hand, and Silas licked at his lips, taking in the taste of him. How ridiculous it was to savour such a thing at this time and place.

Lalassu halted. They were deep in one of the sunken passageways, and Silas had to lift his chin to see up and across the forest floor. Nothing untoward appeared. He readied to urge Lalassu forward.

A tingling started anew at his fingertips.

A vibration moved through the ground beneath them. For a startling moment Silas feared they had not moved far enough from the mine site to escape the crumbling earth. The Verderer's horn sounded, the blast of its note so near that Silas winced.

'He's here.'

'Then face him.' Pitch breathed against Silas's neck, the unexpected caress drawing a shiver.

Silas's mouth was dry. He dug his hand into his pocket, where the bandalore's string rose to meet his fingers. 'Are you ready?'

'I will be if the need arises.'

Though Pitch spoke with his usual aplomb, Silas was not so certain of his readiness. The encounter with the bluecaps had dulled him, the glint in Pitch's eye not quite so bright as it had been. Nevertheless Silas nodded, and squeezed his thighs to send Lalassu forward. Usually, she needed the very slightest of encouragement, but here she did not stir. Silas pressed again, shifting his weight forward in the saddle.

The pale horse remained as she was.

'Well?' Pitch said.

'She will not move.' His fingertips pained him as badly as they had before entering the mines, the sensation sharp as the prick of a blade's tip.

'Then kick her harder.' Pitch shifted against Silas as though he readied to do it himself.

Silas placed a quick hand on his knee. 'Wait.'

A low sound came from Lalassu's chest, as near to a growl as a horse might make. The rumble of hooves grew ever louder, and Silas wondered if the approaching party was about to thunder over the top of them. He hunched his shoulders, trying to stoop so that his head was brought below the lip of the stony rise about them.

Pitch's hands pressed to Silas's shoulders, his body weight against Silas's back as he eased himself up.

'Stay hidden,' Silas hissed.

'I'm not cowering here like a...' Pitch's grip tightened on Silas's shoulders. 'You should see this.'

His strange tone drew Silas upwards. 'What is it? Oh...my...'

The moon's dappled light illuminated a horse and rider racing through the forest from the direction of the mineshaft, passing by not more than fifty yards from where Lalassu stood. The light glanced against a coat of red. Sanu ran headlong through the forest, travelling at far greater speed than she'd ever done with Pitch as her rider. A dark shape leaned low against her shoulders. Silas peered through narrowed eyes. He thought he glimpsed something of Sanu's rider that seemed familiar. There. A hint of wavy strands upon their head, slender arms reaching over her neck. If Silas had seen it any other day, he would swear it was Pitch who sat upon the mare.

But it was what followed after that left him truly confounded. Sanu was not alone.

The pale horse galloped close behind. Her rider's blue coat flailing behind, their dark hair wild about their head.

'How is this possible?' Silas stared at his own image upon the very horse who sat so quietly beneath him now.

'My bloody stupid horse is an illusionist it would seem.' Pitch laughed crookedly. 'Not so fucking useless after all then.'

The pair veered off sharply right, heading away from where Pitch and Silas sat in their makeshift hiding place. But the pounding of heavy weight upon the earth did not relent, growing ever stronger. Silas winced, curling his fingers into his palms. The skin did not tingle so much as burn.

Trailing in the wake of the horses ran a crowd of low shadows. Silas's eyes widened. Perhaps he had been struck too many times upon the head in the mines, for it looked to him as though it were wolves and stags running together. Three wolves that he could discern, with at least two stags right at the heart of the pack. And neither paid any attention to the other. They set their sights on the horses ahead.

The bandalore jerked hard in his pocket, dragging the coat against his shoulder.

Pitch touched at Silas's chin, urging him to turn his head. 'Your Verderer, I would guess.'

At the back of the unlikely pack ran one more.

A horse as black as the tunnel Silas and Pitch had just been hauled from. And upon the steed's back, a rider with a towering crown of stag horns and a flowing cape that reached far behind him, cutting a whirling path through the crumpled leaves upon the forest floor.

Chapter 21

The glimpse of the Verderer was brief, Sanu's frantic pace taking the strange party out of sight before Silas could discern anything of the horseman's features. The sounds of their passing slipped beneath an oppressive silence.

'Why are we still just sitting here, like shags on a rock?' Pitch said. 'That is your Verderer, is it not?'

'Yes.' He could barely stand the sharpness beneath his fingertips.

'Then by Lucifer's crack why do you not draw your trinket and attempt to strike him down? Let us be done with this forsaken place. I would very much enjoy a change of clothes.'

Silas shook his head. 'She led him away, did you not see? And Lalassu would not budge.'

That changed a second later. The pale horse set off, and her sudden movement caught Pitch off-guard. He swore, gripping Silas's waist tighter.

'Fine, then what does your nag tell you we are to do?'

'Lalassu doesn't *tell* me anything, it's not that way.' The prickling of his fingertips was most perturbing. 'I'm just...there is a certainty that comes over me.'

He lifted a low-hanging branch of birch so he would not be struck in the face. The leaves fluttered free from the branch.

'And what are you certain of now then?' Pitch minced his words with a heavy dose of sarcasm.

Silas hesitated. 'Nothing in particular, only that we should allow Lalassu to lead us.'

The moss upon the rockery around them was not so vibrant as that which they'd passed earlier. In fact great sections of it were brittle and yellow as hay. Patches of white at Lalassu's feet caught his eye. A closer inspection revealed the parched skeletons of what might once have been rabbits. Silas twisted a strand of Lalassu's mane about his aching fingers. How he longed to hear the chirrup of the crickets at the very least, something that might tell him the forest yet lived.

'Wonderful.' Pitch patted Silas's thigh. 'How I wished for nothing more than a pony ride through the woods.'

'If you have nothing useful to say,' Silas snapped, 'then do shut up.'

Pitch laughed, and though Silas was riled, he could not ignore how the lilt of it brightened the sullen surrounds.

'I do enjoy it when you attempt to be forthright. It's so sweet, and pathetic.'

Lalassu led them up out of the natural maze, climbing a gentle slope that took them back onto the forest floor proper. Silas sighed at Pitch's reply. Perhaps he should have left the mine when he was told after all. How quiet this journey would be. Peaceful even, if one did not take into account the looming encounter with a teratism that seemed to have corrupted not only the forest but those who lived within her. He glanced down to where Pitch rested his hands against Silas's belly. The ankou could not fool himself. A quiet journey was not what he desired. He had plunged back into the mine without a second thought when he heard the daemon's distress. Perhaps Silas would blame loneliness for such an unfathomable attachment. He was a dead man risen to a world where he knew no one, and no one knew him. He did not even know himself. Pitch was a constancy in his life where few others existed. He scratched at his chin where the hair was rough and in need of a trim, thinking on that strange hybrid creature he had come across in the bluecaps' chamber, one with a twisted body of fae and human. He wet his lips before venturing a question.

'I saw that the bluecaps used the lieutenant's image against you –'

'Did you indeed?' Pitch's hands withdrew from Silas's waist. 'Your appetite for voyeurism knows no bounds. The queen had a particular taste for role play as she fed. How much did you see?'

It was not a question Silas was expecting, nor was the strange waver in Pitch's tone.

'I saw nothing.' He bristled. 'It was long over when I arrived, only the ruins survived. But that is not why I brought it up. It's just that I know you share a deep...connection with the lieutenant. Do you suppose she taunted us with those we are closest to?'

He thought of the woman in lilac. And of who she might be.

Pitch scoffed. 'Connection? If you mean by way of our cocks then I suppose there is one. But I hardly swoon over the man. I suspect Dela simply wished to stir memories of intense pleasure. The bitch got rather more than she bargained for I would say.'

He denied the lieutenant so wholeheartedly it only made the lie more blatant. Silas had seen all too well the intensity between the men.

'I do not mean to intrude –'

'And yet you continue to do so.' The daemon did display a peculiar sensitivity when it came to Edward Charters. 'I have had quite enough of grinding my balls against your cantle. I think I shall walk after all.'

And with that he pushed himself free of Lalassu's back, landing on the ground before Silas could utter a protest.

He glared down at the tousled waves of hair upon the daemon's head. Lalassu would not be reined in, as fervently as Silas tried, continuing on as though Silas did not ride her at all.

'This is foolish,' he said. 'You need to remount.'

'I need do nothing of the sort.' Pitch shrugged. With his ruined, stained clothing he had something of the vagabond's look about him. 'And unless you choose to gallop that flea-bitten lump away, I can keep pace easily.'

Which was quite true. He watched Pitch move – one step taking him much further than seemed reasonable – and was reminded of Jane's airy strides. Thinking of Jane brought with it an ache of melancholy. How delightful Holly Village seemed now, and how far away. Jane's sensible, congenial nature would have been most welcome in the circumstances.

He lamented the Lady Satine not making her his guardian instead of the petulant, unsettling daemon.

Silas adjusted his coat over Lalassu's hindquarters. The bandalore's weight had transformed once again; no longer could he feel its tug within the pocket.

Lalassu bore them down a wide slope, into what might be a further extension of the long-dried river bed they'd come across earlier. Her broad legs scattered the great piles of dry leaves that had accumulated in the depression. The foul reek of decomposition fled from the shifting leaves. Silas wrinkled his nose.

'Gods, is that you, Sickle?' Pitch slid easily down the bank, his barely-fastened shirt flying out on either side, exposing the hard muscles at his stomach. He made a wide berth around Silas and his mount. 'You need a change in diet if so –'

'Of course it is not me. There is something dead here. There.'

He pointed to the brush tail of a fox which poked from beneath the mulch.

From beyond the swell of the bank came the crack of a bough breaking.

A small cry followed. Lalassu tossed her head, bunching beneath Silas.

'Pitch,' Silas called. 'I think there is someone –'

'Brilliant you are, ankou.'

The daemon raced past him on light feet, dashing up the bank as though he flew the distance and slipping from view over the top.

'Pitch,' Silas hissed, standing in his stirrups so he might see where he had gone.

A shriek, a very human shrill of distress, came from the forest above. 'Set me down, now good sir, or no good will come of you!' a strained voice demanded.

A moment later Pitch reappeared at the top of the slope. Clutched beneath his arm was a figure with long wheat-coloured hair and a dark brown dress that trailed the ground. He carried his struggling captive down the bank, her skirt scraping the ground clear of leaves as it swept by.

'Who do you have there?' Silas called.

'Damned if I know. But she should not spy on people from the branches if she does not wish to be manhandled. I would have cracked her neck, but could not bear the thought of the lectures I might receive from you if I did so. Defenceless humans and all that rubbish.'

He dumped the woman unceremoniously at Lalassu's feet. Her shadow was evident at once. The stranger was no natural. Lalassu nuzzled at the untidy mess of hair that had tangled about the woman's face.

'Get off, all of you, there's no time for this,' she rasped, clambering to her feet. The woman battled with the folds of her skirt. Her dress was plain in its fabric, a coarse weave that held multitudes of darned lighter patches. 'I don't know how you got so deep without any harm coming to you, but you have no place in this forest.'

She had a gaunt face with a myriad of lines that suggested many hard years lived. There was a handsomeness about her though, a strong chin and fine nose that tilted pleasingly at the tip. Her eyes were bright too, the moon's light caught at their grey depths.

'Is that so?' Pitch scoffed. 'And who might you be to decide such a thing?'

She shoved at her tangled hair, glaring at the daemon. 'Someone who knows when a place ain't right. If you have half a mind to match that pretty face, you'll be moving on from here.' Her gaze darted to his chest, barely concealed by his shirt only thanks to the two paltry buttons that could be fastened. 'If you're headed for Goodrich, turn back. Now.'

'My my, isn't she a fiery hag.'

Silas dismounted. Lalassu pushed her muzzle into the woman's hair again, evidently none too concerned about the new arrival.

'Goodrich?' Silas said. 'You speak of the castle?'

'I do. Keep yourself far from that place, lad.' She pushed at Lalassu's snout, her frown momentarily lifting into a smile as the horse insisted on exploring her pale yellow hair. 'That's enough of that now. Or I've a mind to set the bees onto you.'

Pitch snorted. 'You think you control such creatures?'

'Of course not, silly boy, but I've a tongue that can speak to them well enough for them to listen.'

'Do you indeed?' Pitch lifted one elegant eyebrow, much amused. 'You imagine yourself a sorceress, then?'

'Nothing of the sort. I'm a witch, thank you very much,' the woman sniffed.

'Oh look, Sickle, another one driven mad by the forest.'

'You would know about madness,' she snapped. 'Grabbing a defenceless woman like that.'

'I thought you were a witch?' Pitch cocked his head. 'Hardly defenceless then.'

'I'm not that sort of sorceress,' she sniffed.

'Of course you're not. True witchcraft hasn't run in human veins since your grandmother's grandmother was a twinkle in the night-soil-man's eye.'

She scowled hard at him. 'You talk a lot of rot, don't you? I'm a healer, if you must know. I work with what the forest provides to cure ailments. Though I doubt there's enough St John's wort in all the forests of England to fix that smug mouth of yours, boy. Now get on with you.'

Silas placed himself in front of Pitch before the daemon could reply. 'Please, madam. You need to leave this forest –'

She squared up to him, near on half his height. 'You might be a large man, but that doesn't mean I'm scared of you. Either of you.' She shook a finger at them. Upon her wrists were many bracelets, some woven from grasses, others entirely floral, the largest of them all a cuff-like creation of twisted wood and holly leaves.

'We mean you no harm,' Silas said. 'But it is not safe in the forest. You need to leave. Quickly.' He would not tell her of the bluecaps incited to madness and torture. It was a miracle she had managed to avoid being listed amongst those in the crystal tomb.

Her heavy-set eyebrows knitted together, and she searched his face. 'What makes you say that then?'

'There is no time to explain it now –'

'There is a lunatic ghost about that needs putting down,' Pitch declared, stepping around Silas. 'I'm surprised it skipped your witchy notice that the forest is a half-dead thing and quieter than a tomb.' He pointed to the fox's rotting corpse. 'And unless Mother Nature has given you the skills of necromancy, there is not much healing to be done here.

So go on then, get out.' Pitch moved to grab her arm and was met with a swift slap to his cheek.

Pitch's laughter crept dangerously low. Silas hurried to step between them once more.

'Madam, there is no need for that, we have only your best –'

'The name's Ottelie.' She glared at Pitch. 'And you should watch your tongue, young man, or I'll sew up those plump sweet lips of yours. And I'm no seamstress.'

Pitch's lips curled with a venomous smile, his eyelids heavy. 'And I am no young man. Do go ahead, crone. Amuse me with your efforts.'

'Enough.' Silas gave Pitch a shove that rocked him back on his heels. 'Please, madam, we cannot escort you from the forest, for we must continue on –'

'To put down a lunatic ghost?' The woman's hands shook as she brushed hard at the folds of her well-worn dress. 'Are you boys on the drink then? Because you'll get yourselves into a right mess here.'

'If only,' Pitch sighed.

'We are not inebriated, I assure you.' Silas said, casting a wary glance back the way they had come. The standing about had him on edge. 'We are here to set things right within the forest.'

'Are you now?' Ottelie eyed him, clearly curious but still wary. 'Well, I'll tell you, I'll not abandon this forest. She has kept me safe for many a year when those beyond her borders would like to see me burn upon their stakes. And she's ailing terribly now. I'll not leave her.' Lalassu nudged at her shoulder, her breath shifting the woman's hair. Ottelie's scowl softened and she caressed Lalassu's velvet nose. The horse lowered her head to the long pocket stitched to the front of Ottelie's dress, nostrils flaring as she sniffed deeply. 'That would be my special blend you're smelling there. Been pressing that poultice to my face every time I cross his path, and I'll swear black and blue it's working. Forest is keeping me safe as she can, even while the Verderer makes a ruin of it.'

The ever-present tingling in Silas's fingers ripened. 'You know of the Verderer?'

'Course I do. Lord of the forest, he is.'

Pitch moved as though to speak, but Silas silenced him with a look. 'Lord of the forest?'

178

She nodded. 'You don't know much for someone claiming to be fixing things.'

Silas cleared his throat. 'I have the means to assist you, but I would ask that you tell me all you know of this lord. It would aid us greatly.'

She darted a glance at Lalassu before she answered. 'He is the original Verderer of this forest, once living and breathing, like you and I. But he ain't so anymore. Not for a long time. Any who have the sight can catch a glimpse of him if they look right.'

'He was human once, you say?' Silas pressed.

Ottelie tossed her chin, regarding Pitch. 'Perhaps back when my ancestors were lying with the night-soil-man, I suppose.' She returned her attention to Silas, who hung upon her every word. 'He got himself killed protecting his master on a hunt, run through by an injured stag. Bled out on the forest floor, and the spirit took him then to aid her. I'm not entirely sure what that makes him now. But if you ever see a man upon a coal-black horse, with the horns of a stag upon his head and –'

'A long cloak of ash leaves upon his back, then we have seen the Verderer,' Silas finished. 'We saw him not long ago, with a pack of wolves and stags. A strange party indeed.'

'He's not as he was,' Ottelie said darkly. 'Stay well away.'

'Bastard is busy chasing my bloody horse,' Pitch grumbled .

A shadow passed over Ottelie's face as she studied Pitch. 'Thought you looked familiar. Caught a glimpse of a chestnut leading him on a merry dance a little while back. Tried to get in a warning to you, but he was too close to risk it. Things are topsy-turvy all right here in the forest. I was on my way to the mines when I came across you. I heard a god-awful row coming from that way earlier, and I'm worried the fae have got themselves into some trouble.'

'Oh they are beyond trouble now.' Pitch studied his nails. 'I assure you.'

'What does he mean?' Ottelie demanded of Silas.

He glanced at the ground. 'I'm afraid that all was not well in the mines.'

'And by not well,' said the daemon, 'he means the bluecaps went stark-raving bonkers and required elimination.'

A whimper escaped Ottelie and her head dropped, her pale hair sweeping forward to cover her face. Silas heard her whispering but could catch none of it.

'Madam, I understand how it must pain you to hear such things,' he said, aware of the derisive groan that came from Pitch. 'But there was quite a foul scene to behold. The bluecaps had entombed people within the crystal, the miners I fear, and some of their families as well.'

Her grey eyes shimmered. 'Truly?'

Silas nodded gravely.

'The forest is wounded far deeper than I knew,' she whispered. 'So you say you can fix this then?'

'We certainly intend to try.'

'Eventually.' Pitch sauntered towards the far side of the bank. 'If Silas ever decides to find his nerve.'

To Silas's relief the woman paid him no mind. 'Who are you then?'

'I'm Silas, that is...Tobias. We've been sent on behalf of the Order of the Golden Dawn.'

'That don't mean much to me.' Ottelie sniffed, wiping at tears that fell for the fae.

'Me either.' Pitch shook his head.

Silas glared at him, exasperated with the daemon's nonchalance. 'The Order deals with matters of the supernatural nature...which we believe is what you have here.'

A spirit of the forest had taken hold of a lost soul, and in turn the Blight had taken hold of them both. What did that mean for the teratism created?

Ottelie laughed, a sound like the crack of an egg. 'Well I won't be arguing with you on that one, Mr Silas. All has gone topsy-turvy in the forest, like I said, and I'll tell you that the heart of it is in the bloody castle.'

'Why do you suppose that?' The hairs on his arm prickled. Pitch might denigrate her witchcraft, but certainly the woman had knowledge of things.

''Cause I can't go near the place without losing my guts. Being anywhere near it just makes me feel...hollowed out inside. Like my heart can't bear to keep beating.' Ottelie's grey eyes were fierce with her disdain. 'You want to fix things, that's where you need to be going. I've never seen hide nor hair of no one about the place. It's been like a grave there the whole time, but the front gate is shut fast. You won't be able to just waltz over the bridge and –'

'Bridge?' Silas said. 'There is a moat?'

'Dry as bone. Hasn't had a trickle in it for over two hundred years. Place has been in ruins since it got bombarded in the Civil War.'

'Shame,' Pitch declared. 'You would have enjoyed a swim, wouldn't you, Sickle?'

Ottelie folded her arms. 'Can he do anything more useful than mouth off?'

'Unfortunately, yes. Otherwise, I'd have no need of his company,' Silas muttered. 'He can be quite helpful when he sets his mind to it.'

'Hope it's set then, because I think you're going to need it. Let's see if we can get you to that castle. I'll show you where the walls are at their lowest. You might get in, if your innards don't try to force their way up your throat like mine do every time I'm too near that blasted place.'

Chapter 22

Ottelie refused to ride upon Lalassu's back.

'She is beautiful, there's no denying it, but I prefer to feel my feet on the soil, thank you just the same.' And she could do that very well, for her feet were bare, so blackened by the ground and constant brush of undergrowth that Silas had mistaken the darkness for shoes of some kind.

'I certainly do not,' Pitch said. 'Let's get this over with, shall we?' He stood at Lalassu's side as Silas mounted, raising an imperious hand for assistance.

Lalassu set off as soon as he was settled, setting a brisk but manageable pace for the woman walking alongside. The moonlight waned as wispy clouds seeped across the night sky. The horse took them up a steep embankment that was saturated with a blaze of yellow and burnt-orange leaves. Lalassu's weight pushed her hooves deep into the soft covering, and Pitch leaned against Silas's back as they shifted forward to aid her climb. Ottelie was first to reach the top of the embankment. Given how sure-footed she was, Silas had no trouble believing the woman had begun her life in this forest. It was there in the way she caressed the trunks as she passed by and how she stooped low beneath a branch without setting eyes on it, as though every bough was committed to memory.

As they made their way, the branches grew ever barer of leaves. They were forced to manoeuvre over downed trees more often, the descent of their boughs hacking a path through the foliage around them, allowing more of the moon's light to reach the ground. It was as though a storm had passed through this area, causing havoc amongst the foliage. Silas suspected there had been no such storm, at least not one in the shape of the weather. He rubbed at his stomach, a swell of nausea bothering him.

'Hungry?' Pitch leapt upon the movement like a hawk. 'I'm famished.'

'How could you eat at a time like this?'

'Quite easily.' Pitch wrapped his arms around Silas's unsettled belly. 'It is hardly the Hellfield.'

Silas certainly hoped not. He barely felt ready for an encounter with a singular foe, let alone a battlefield of them, but Hellfield or not, the idea of putting anything in his mouth left him quite unwell.

'Oh my.' Ottelie regarded something upon the ground. 'There is too much of this, 'specially this close to the castle. I worry all the birds will have fallen from the sky by the time this is done.'

It took no time to see what she referred too. The corpse of a bird lay with wings spread, a scattering of speckled brown feathers framing a chalk-white skeleton that all but glowed with the moonlight upon it. It was a considerable size, and from its talons and beak Silas would guess it to be a bird of prey.

They left the bones behind and continued on. Pitch patted Silas's stomach like he was marking the rhythm of a silent tune.

'Will you stop that?'

The daemon substituted patting with a caress that took his fingers over the lip of Silas's trousers. 'Would you prefer this?'

'I'd prefer you don't touch me.' Silas tugged at the collar of his shirt, a pressure at the back of his throat bothering him.

'Fine.' Pitch pulled away. 'But if I slide off, I shall blame you.'

The moonlight held a strange hue here, no longer a wondrous pristine white cast down upon the forest but a dirtier ash grey. Silas's stomach roiled, and he wondered if he might have to lean from his saddle and be sick. He blew out a breath, fiddling again with the material at his neck.

'You're feeling it then?' Ottelie appeared at Lalassu's side. 'Sickening, isn't it?'

'It is not pleasant,' he said. 'What do you suppose –'

A sudden and awful cramp tore through his gut. Silas buckled forward. The bandalore dug into the crease of his leg, as though it sought to burrow itself into the bone.

'Sickle? What is it?' Pitch's hands found his shoulders.

'The bloody castle,' Ottelie said. 'He's feeling it hard. It always starts right about here, but I've not had it hit me this bad.'

Bad was rather the understatement. Silas's stomach was being squashed in a vice. And he shook as though with a monstrous fever. He pressed his face into Lalassu's mane. 'Oh god, it is wretched.'

A firm hand patted at his back. 'If you throw up,' Pitch declared. 'Do it on the horse, and not me.'

'Here,' Ottelie snapped. 'Help me get this on him.'

Ottelie grabbed at Silas's arm, seeking to tug his hand free of where it entwined in Lalassu's mane. Pitch reached around him, and a firmer hand prised his fingers from the horsehair. Silas dared not raise his head, for he feared the slightest movement would bring him undone, but he didn't protest when his arm was pulled down to his side, where Ottelie could reach him more easily.

'A fucking bracelet?' Pitch growled.

'It is more than that.' She slipped something around Silas's wrist. He groaned, tilting his head a fraction so he might see what was being done. 'It is rowan wood to ward off evil, and holly for protection.'

'Let me guess, passed down for generations?' The daemon sniped.

'Exactly. Now how's about you stop being such a cunt and let me do what I need.'

'My my, such insults. Be my guest.'

'Do you feel nothing, Pitch?' Silas grunted.

'I can't say it is my favourite place,' he said. 'But compared to the mines, this feels like a summer jaunt to the seaside.'

Ottelie's lips moved against the back of Silas's hand as she muttered. They were words he could not make out for the most part, but those he did were unrecognisable. Another vicious wave struck him, and he let out a startled cry.

'What have you done?' Pitch wrestled with Ottelie for hold of Silas's wrist. 'Take it off. Now.'

'Give it time.' Ottelie slapped at him. 'Things are worse before they are better.'

'And I know first-hand there are things that cannot be made any worse.'

'That would explain a lot about you then.'

The vice released its grip on Silas, the barbed clench shifting to more endurable aches of muscle. He sighed. 'I am all right,' he said, Lalassu's mane muffling his words.

'Sickle?' Pitch's hands were firm on his shoulders as he sought to pull Silas upright.

'Slowly, slowly,' Silas admonished, not certain the respite would last. He was far from comfortable, what with the prickling in his fingers, the bruise he was certain was forming where the bandalore drove at his hip, and the still-niggling nausea, but it was a good way from where he had been a few moments earlier. He touched at the wood around his wrist, careful to avoid the points of the holly leaves wrapped about it. For an article that was generations old, the leaves were astonishingly green, and the wood too seemed as though it had just been snapped from a sapling.

'You might be needing some more wards. I've got half the forest sewn into my clothes, and I still can't abide the place.' Ottelie frowned up at him. 'You seem more settled though. Are you all right then?'

'Thanks to you, it would appear so.' He swallowed, the hint of bile in his spit.

'Perhaps when all is said and done here, and we are sitting by the fire with a hot mead in hand,' she said. 'You can pay me back by telling me just who Mr Silas of the Order might truly be?'

Silas inclined his head. 'Of course.' Of course he could do no such thing, for he did not know himself.

'Gods, what I wouldn't do for a mead.' Pitch released a drawn-out sigh. 'I don't suppose you bake too, witch?'

'I am a witch now, am I?'

'If it gets me teacakes and spotted dick, I'll call you the Queen of England if you like.'

While they irked one another Silas gathered himself, rubbing at the back of his neck, rolling his head side to side, up and down to ease the tension there. And it was as he lifted his gaze that he saw the castle set upon the swell of a hill. The jut of ruined stonework was evident above the tops of the trees.

'We are almost there,' he said.

Ottelie nodded. 'Are you all right to carry on?'

He chewed at his lip. There was one true answer but he would not utter it. 'I am.'

'This way then.' She set off, with her skirts bundled about her knees, one hand protecting the pocket sewn in the front of the dress.

Silas pressed his heels lightly to Lalassu's sides, and she bunched muscle and sinew beneath him, launching them forward. She could move no faster than a tentative trot would allow, for the ground was treacherous with the bulge and invasion of tree roots. Far more so than anywhere else in the forest they had travelled. The strange ash light grew stranger still. It was as though the castle sucked the colour from the world, leaving it drab and half-hearted. The slope of the land rose, enough that Silas expected Ottelie's pace might slow, but she carried on with no sign of diminishing speed.

Pitch soon joined her on the ground, finding it impossible to keep his seat with no saddle to keep him from sliding back off Lalassu's rump. And not much pleased about it.

The landscape had taken on a foreboding atmosphere, and the closer they drew to the castle, the more so it became. Though the sheer numbers of closely-clumped trees still gave them some meagre cover, the greenery was all but wiped from every branch, every shrub. Lalassu halted, where there were trees enough to afford some protection for her considerable frame. Silas jumped down, taking a moment to steady himself against her.

'Stay here, girl.' He pressed his hand against her warm chest, taking what reassurance he could.

Pitch and Ottelie made their way ahead, and Silas left the pale horse to follow. The spasms of knotting muscle at his core were bad enough to cause him to wince, and he was thankful for the witch's bracelet. Without it, he wondered if he'd be able to ride at all. Ottelie and Pitch took turns using the shielding girths of oak and ash to draw closer to where the castle perched upon slate-coloured bedrock. More than once he saw Ottelie bend and wretch, Pitch leaning as far away from her as he could without breaking cover. Silas held back, waiting until he could move to the next point where an ash would keep him hidden. He peered up at the castle. Here was the vision in Lalassu's mane now made real. Rotund towers made up the two corners that Silas could see, with arrow slits along their length that were far too narrow to even imagine gaining entrance through. The castle was clearly damaged, with not a scrap of its wooden roof remaining upon the entire structure and most of its walls no longer horizontal along the top, undulating instead where stone had broken free. But it was not half as damaged as Silas might have hoped. The walls rose high, a dangerous climb if they attempted it. He could see a lower section of crumbled wall that might be where Ottelie suggested they enter, but from where Silas perched, it still seemed a formidable climb.

Pitch waved him forward, and Silas dashed across a short open space to join him and Ottelie behind a natural outcrop of stone, the same type the castle set its foundations on. Pitch was giving him the oddest of looks.

'What is it?' Silas asked.

Ottelie was ghostly pale, her lips such a dull pink he wondered if she would faint. 'He said you have an issue with swimming, which is going to be a problem, I'm afraid.'

Silas frowned. 'What are you talking about?' He pressed up on his knees to take a look. 'Oh god.'

The moat Ottelie had spoken of, the one that had not been full in over two hundred years, was churning with murky brown water.

CHAPTER 23

The aqueous barrier swirled and churned with currents that smashed against one another in a chaotic dance.

'This is impossible.' Ottelie crouched with her hands pressed at her waist, looking set to heave once again. 'It was dry a day ago.'

'It is not dry now,' Pitch said. 'Come, Silas, I will carry you across. It is rough water, nothing more.'

'Nothing more?' He laughed in the way people do when they are quite beyond terrified. 'Are you mad?'

'Some would say so.' Pitch's reply did nothing to sooth Silas's nerves.

The pale light cast by the moon barely reflected upon the surface, the roiling waters sucking the light into their depths. His heart thudded just considering the idea of stepping foot in the moat. He turned away, his gut every bit as riotous as the water before him.

'We will have to go to the front gate,' he insisted.

'And what?' Pitch said.

'Can you not' – Silas fluttered his pained fingers – 'you know, make us a way in?'

'That would hardly be the quietest of entries. The element of surprise is always useful.'

'Likely whatever is inside already knows we are here anyway.' Silas was being unreasonable, he knew it, and Pitch's face said he did too.

'That's not a certainty. Come on, if ever there were a time for you to get over your silly aversion to water it is now.'

Silas glared at Pitch, incredulous. 'Silly aversion? I died by drowning, I'd say I have every reason in the world not to want to step foot in there.' He ignored Otellie's shocked expression, jumping ahead before she could question him. 'Pitch I have no doubt you are as adept at swimming as you are everything else. Why don't you go ahead and scale the walls and then –'

'Please do not say open the front gate.'

'Open the front gate,' Silas nodded. 'What is wrong with that plan?'

'Aside from giving me far too much to do, it would mean you are left unguarded. And your little sickle would be out here when it might well be needed inside. And by the time you could get it inside, what if it was too late? You are the one who has gone on about getting to this fucking castle, and it is you who was sent on this quest to destroy lunatic ghosts. So hurry up and do what must be done. If I do not change out of these trousers before long my arse will be chafed out of existence.' Ottelie coughed, but Silas couldn't tell if it was borne from ill-feeling or laughter. 'Get on my back, and be quick about it.'

'What?' Silas spat.

'You will get on my back and I'll swim us across. Is it that hard to understand?'

'Then it is you who will be drowned. Have you not noticed my size?' He could say no more, for the mere thought of sinking into those foetid waters brought on a fresh new terror.

'Ariel's balls, you are a dolt. Have you quite forgotten the barn incident?'

Silas tore his gaze from the troubling waters. 'I could hardly forget. You were most cruel...' He didn't add the rest of what he was thinking – *throwing the constable about with a mere flick of your fingers.*

'Now now.' Pitch blinked prettily. 'Flattery hardens me and we do not have time for that. The point is that you know I am not entirely the delicate and beautiful creature that I appear. I will carry you, Sickle. Have no fear. Take off your coat though. I don't wish to work any harder than need be.'

Silas stared at him, dumbfounded. Ottelie tugged at his sleeves. 'Right then, I'll look after this. Let's get you on your way. The Verderer comes back here most regularly.'

'Right then.' Pitch repeated and discarded his shirt the way a courtesan might shed her nightgown. 'Shall we get on with this?' He looked this way and that and, apparently satisfied that no one lurked about, dashed the short distance across open grass to the moat. He stepped into the frothing water and sank low until only his head protruded from the grim wetness. He jerked his chin, signalling Silas to go.

'Off with your coat, lad,' Ottelie urged, wincing as she lifted her arm. 'Be quick about it. Don't think I can stand much more of being here.'

Silas shook himself from his stupor, shrugging out of the reassuring folds, and shifting the bandalore to his trouser pocket.

'That a good luck charm then?' Ottelie folded the coat over her arm, holding it tightly against her troubled belly. 'Your trinket I mean.'

'Ah, of sorts, yes.' He wondered how much a reanimated body could take of this, the trembling, the harsh tingling, the near-constant aching of muscles at his core as the foulness inside the castle messed with him.

'On you go.' Ottelie touched at the bracelet around Silas's wrist. 'That'll be helping you too, don't forget.' He wished it might numb him more. 'Good luck, boy.'

Ottelie made a hasty retreat, skirts aflutter, disappearing in behind the nearest tree of bulk.

'Come on,' Pitch hissed.

Silas took a short, sharp breath, cursed the insanity of the venture, and ran to join Pitch. His boots filled at once with water far colder than he was ready for. He edged forward until the water was midway up his thighs, the pressure thudding against his legs, seeking to topple him.

'Pitch, I don't think I –'

The daemon swam up to him, the water spitting and swirling about his neck, the strands of his hair pulled about like miniature serpents, and he took hold of Silas's hands. 'I shall not let you be overcome.' He spoke with a calmness, a gentleness that seemed to caress Silas's ears.

He nodded and allowed Pitch to pull him down into the waters. His breath was rough in his throat, the icy water covered his body with painful gooseflesh. Pitch turned, keeping so close to Silas that their bodies were in constant contact as he offered his back.

'Hold on, Sickle,' Pitch said. 'Quickly.'

The idea was preposterous. Never mind the likelihood that Silas would descend into a wild panic before long, he was near on double the size of the slight daemon. But he found himself reaching for Pitch all the same. The rough waters slammed about them as he wrapped his arms around Pitch's neck and the daemon pulled them deeper. The ground fell from beneath Silas's knees, and he bit back a whimper. Hands touched at his legs and he jerked, thinking for a moment that something nefarious came at them from the depths. But it was Pitch, his seeking hands finding the backs of Silas's knees and slipping beneath them.

'Do you know how envious so many would be of you right now, Sickle? Riding me as you do.' Even now the man's arrogance could not be held at bay. 'Hold fast.'

Silas interlocked his legs so that his calves rested against Pitch's belly. He felt a fool, a giant child upon a parent's back because he was too weak to walk any further. The water splashed at his face and pushed its damp tips into his ears. Pitch shook his head, spitting against the liquid that was determined to force its way into his mouth. He swept his arms ahead of him, drawing them back in a wide circle, propelling them forward despite the best efforts of the current. His entire body worked against the pressures around it, and Silas felt the shift of his muscles like they were his own. Each time Pitch widened his arms to stroke, his shoulder blades glanced against Silas's chest, and the arching of his back as he kicked out lifted his arse against Silas's groin. Drifting into something of a trance as the daemon moved beneath him, he barely noticed the sting of water in his eyes, the bitter taste of it on his lips. Silas's fears were a distant annoyance, a vague clamouring that he could barely hear over the dull thundering of the water.

He watched as though he still sat safe upon the bank while the currents menaced Pitch. Violent waves splashed his face, and the strong pull dragged them off a straight path, but inch by inch Pitch hauled them closer to where slate-coloured rock formed a natural platform beneath the wall Ottelie had chosen for them. Silas wrapped his arms tighter about Pitch's neck. How was it that even with such a dunking, his hair smelled so delightful, like warm brandy and teacakes?

'Silas.' Pitch coughed.

'Mmm?'

'You are strangling me.'

The curt reprimand snapped Silas from his reverie. And the bedlam rushed in at him. The cold needled into his marrow, the riotous dance of the water overwhelming his senses. Pitch had toyed with him, charmed him stupid, and encouraged him to travel where the ground disappeared beneath them and the depths sucked at Silas's feet.

He would drown out here. His panic raised its bothersome head. His legs slipped from Pitch's waist.

'What are you doing?' Pitch's words bubbled with the water. 'We are not there yet.'

But terror does not reason. Cold streams of water stabbed at his nostrils and forced their way past his teeth. Silas kicked out, searching for something solid. His foot glanced against something beneath the surface.

'Fuck's sake,' Pitch grunted. 'Get ahold of yourself.'

But Silas didn't want ahold of himself, he wanted ahold of the rocks that loomed ahead. Unbreakable. Unmovable. In place for time immemorial. He pulled his arms from Pitch's neck.

'Silas, hold on, you idiot.'

But only an idiot would remain here, where darkness sucked at their toes. Silas made a wild lunge for the rocks, only to find it was he who was stone. A whirlpool took its hold, sucking him under as though he were but a leaf. Silas screamed into the rough embrace, and the water stole his sound, snatching it away and roaring its defiance back at him. Fingers wrapped about his wrist, and he was dragged upwards. He broke through the surface and landed with a breathtaking thump against blessed stone. He lay there, his feet still hostage to the churn of the current, his lungs greedy for all the air they could steal.

'Perhaps I underestimated your silly aversion.' Pitch rubbed at his neck where dark patches marked his skin. 'As much as I enjoy a rough handling, it is not the time for it here. You had best be able to climb because I do not relish the idea of being scratched bare while dragging you up this wall.'

Silas pushed onto his elbow, the panic ebbing away as quickly as it had risen, and not a small amount of grim embarrassment replacing it. He lay on an outcrop of rock that spread out from the foundations of the wall. The damage Ottelie mentioned, from an assault upon the castle during the Civil War, was starkly evident, with pockmarks all the way up the brickwork, chunks of stone gouged clear by weaponry.

'I can climb,' he said.

Even if the damage did not appear sure to provide sturdy enough hand and footholds, Silas would have forced himself up and over unaided, rather than cling like an oversized monkey to Pitch's back. He'd made a fool enough of himself already.

'Very well then. Shall we?' Pitch set straight to the task, the water still running from him. His lithe body moved with surety up the vertical obstacle, more akin to a giant spider than a man. And if Silas did not set off immediately, he was in danger of finding himself entirely alone on this side of the wall. He spared a glace back across the moat and gaped. The water was not half as unsettled as it had been on their crossing, nor half as high. The brown surface was barely disturbed by ripples.

'Pitch, do you see the moat now?'

He paused, halfway to the lip of the wall, and looked over his shoulder. 'Well, that is curious I suppose.'

'What do you imagine might cause such a thing?'

'Did the witch not say the Verderer was both soul and spirit? Man and nature. Water is as natural as any other element. Maybe it rebels against us.' His foot slipped, setting loose several pieces of stone. 'Come along now, before squirrels start pelting us with their nuts.'

Pitch continued on his way and was drawing himself over the rough-hewn edge before Silas had climbed more than a foot off the ground. He winced at the scrape of the stone against his fingers. Silas discovered he had some knack for climbing. He was doubtless too slow to find his footing, wary of making any move before he was certain he was anchored firmly enough to venture higher, but he found his way with little effort, the strength in his legs never waning, and though it was not pleasant to dig his tingling fingers against the rub of brick, his focus upon the task at hand gave him a little respite from his bodily ails.

He reached the shattered brickwork, dragging himself into the cradle like depression that had been created by a long forgotten attack. Silas searched for sign of Pitch while he caught his breath. How dark the interior of the castle was, as though the roof were not destroyed at all and still cast its shadow down upon the floors. He could just make out

Pitch waiting on him, standing at the base of a pile of rubble that was the remnants of the collapsed wall they had just climbed. There was a gap as long as Silas was high between his perch and the top of the pile.

'Jump down,' Pitch called in a harsh whisper.

'It's quite a distance,' Silas hissed.

'And you are a supernatural being. Jump.'

Silas set the other leg over the width of the wall, pressed his hands to the bricks, took a measured breath, and jumped. He would never admit that a squeal might have found its way up his throat as he plunged the short distance to the pile below. His boots met the rubble with a none too subtle thump that sent several smaller pieces of the ruin tumbling deeper into the heap. He scrambled with no elegance down the debris. A sudden and breathtaking twist of his troubled gut surprised him, and he staggered, landing upon hands and knees at Pitch's feet.

Silas cursed beneath his breath, not least because of how painful the tingling in his hands had grown.

'On your feet, Sickle,' Pitch said, speaking low with warning. 'Keep your wits about you in this place. I do not think much of it, I must say.'

Cradling an arm about his stomach, Silas pushed to his feet and was met with a formidable sight. The shadows he'd seen from atop the wall were not darkness at all. Rather, they were the heavy swathe of ivy that hung so thick from all the walls that only the merest of passageways was discernible through its depths. It may have been the casting of the unnatural ashen light upon the place that was to blame for the deepened hue of the leaves, making them appear as though they had been dipped in tar.

'Which way?' Pitch said. 'And so help me if you say you don't know —'

'This way.' Silas moved first, taking the passage that lay straight ahead, urged on by the curious certainty that came to him so often now. He strode across the only patch of open ground in sight where the soil was parched so dry it had cracked open with thirst. He quickly met the leafy wall of foliage that seemed intent on clogging all the corridors and hesitated but a moment before pressing into the wall of ivy. With a twisting from side to side, he plunged deeper, hands sweeping ahead of him to force a way through. There was no trick of the light, he saw, for the leaves were indeed inky black. Their points jutted like arrowheads, and their vines were thick as Silas's fingers. As they moved deeper he would find one wrapping about his wrist or slinking about his ankle.

'Bloody hell, I am so tired of nature,' Pitch muttered. 'I hope to the gods you have chosen the right way or I'll fucking scream.'

'It is this way, I'm sure of it.' Silas grunted, straining to pull his foot free of where it snagged at something by the ground. He rocked back on his heels.

'So sure you must stop?'

'Shut up. I'm caught upon something.' As the words left his lips, the ivy slithered over his shoulder and burrowed its way beneath his armpit. 'Pitch, I fear we may be in some trouble.' The pressure at his ankle rose higher, the vines finding their way up the length of his leg.

A violent rustle of leaves and curses followed. 'You don't say.' Pitch's voice squeezed from him. 'I'm being violated by a plant.'

Silas sought to turn to him, but the ivy would have none of it. The length that had wrapped about his shoulder slipped lower still, finding its way around his middle, to where his stomach pounded with the ever-present ache. As he busied with trying to free himself, the vine reached his pocket and set the bandalore bouncing madly at his hip before he realised what it intended.

'Shit!' He moved to reach for his pocket. The ivy moved faster, spinning itself about his wrist and jerking his arm behind him. 'Pitch, it's going for the scythe.'

He wrestled against the ivy as it sought to encase him, an attempt that saw him jiggling about in a useless struggle, a puppet caught up in its own strings.

'I say we forgo the element of surprise,' Pitch said hoarsely.

The darkness slammed back against a sudden glow of light, the blaze of a summer sun that pummelled its way into the swamp of ivy. A hiss came upon the air, the crack of wood as it snapped beneath the force that descended upon it.

There was a squeal, the high pitch that comes from the depths of a strong fire, and heat burned warm against Silas's side. The hold of the ivy relented, whipping away as Pitch's energies consumed it. Silas went at once to his pocket, where his fingers were met by the feather-light touch of the string. The bandalore at rest in the depths. Pitch pushed his way around Silas, an easy feat with the space between them no longer choked by the plants. He tugged at a vine that clung to his neck, the glow still evident upon his fingers.

'Straight ahead, right?'

Silas nodded.

Lifting his hands before him, Pitch threw away all pretence of sneaking about, fingers and palms aglow, the vines withering, crumpling, and dying before him. Whatever lay ahead, it knew of their arrival, for it was being announced with all the commotion of a forward charge. So be it, Silas decided. He had no intention of turning back. The urge forward drove at him, as gripping as any compulsion he felt when the dirt of the graveyard called on him.

Pitch broke into a run, cutting his golden path through the ivy. The damage was done silently; there was no scent of fire, no odour of smoke. Pitch's flames were not of any Earthly design. They slashed a careful path, cauterising the vines and creating a macabre, beautiful archway through which Pitch and Silas ran.

The mournful note of the hunter's horn rang clear. Somewhere beyond the castle walls.

'Faster,' Silas urged.

And Pitch obliged, lifting his pace easily and drawing ahead, taking the light with him. Silas forced his legs into a faster stride, his chest straining to take in the air that would sustain him. Endurance was not handed to an ankou, it seemed. He would work on that, if they ever escaped this infernal place.

Pitch came to a sudden halt up ahead, the brightness slipping from his fingers. Silas panted his way to his side. It was as though his own fingers burned with Pitch's flames, so intense was the sensation that came upon them.

They had reached the castle's central courtyard, a rounded space that held a well at its centre.

And more terrible things.

'Oh dear lord, what is this?' Silas breathed.

The well was a simple circle of cut stone, but above it hung a far more complex object. A prism of glass, high and wide enough that Silas could have stood upright inside. It was shaped like a chandelier's pendalogue and reinforced at its edges with silver strips of metal. Hanging inside, with no visible supports, was the strangest of creatures. It resembled a stag, one with a great beard of white hair upon its barrel chest and a cluster of narrow horns upon its head, all of the same formidable length, touching their tips to the glass that encased the creature. Its hooves had grown so long that they curled at their tips, and its tail more resembled Lalassu's than a stag's. But it was the creature's face that set Silas's pulse racing. The head was stretched long and wide, and sections of the fur were either missing or had never existed at all. The skin in these patches was smooth, hairless, robust with the pinkness of an infant. But it was the eyes that told the most.

Silas stepped forward, drawn as though pulled by chains.

'Stay back.' Pitch touched his arm.

But Silas shook him off. 'He is here.'

A stag's rounded brown eye, wide and unblinking, watched from one side of the face, and from the other, a pupil of green, the warm richness of juniper.

A man's eye.

Watchful. Fearful. Glistening with the tears he shed.

Silas took a ragged breath. Nature and man.

The Verderer was not the creature they had spied on the hunt. He was here. Imprisoned with the spirit of the forest.

Silas moved so quickly that even Pitch could not lunge fast enough to catch him.

'Damn it, Silas,' he shouted. 'Do you know what you are doing?'

'Setting this right.' Silas wrenched the bandalore from his pocket. The scythe released a note so forlorn it pained him. 'Something terrible is being done here, Pitch.'

He swung, the bandalore transforming from wooden trinket to death's blade in the time it took to reach over his shoulder. He raced at the prism.

The blast of the horn shattered the air, and the all too familiar rumbling erupted beneath Silas's feet. A howling of wolves rang out for the first time, sounds of hunger and wrath. Every corridor echoed with the approach of the hunt. Silas swung his blade.

CHAPTER 24

T he scythe's point glanced off the prism, sending Silas stumbling back with the momentum. There was not a crack upon the surface, nothing to show for the blow he'd delivered.

'Your talents lie with dead things, you fool.' Pitch spat his words, his hands aglow. 'Do not waste your strength.' His legs were set wide as he twisted about, glaring at each of the corridors in turn. With the bouncing of the echo, it sounded as though they were to be attacked from all fronts.

'Then you open it!' Silas shouted back. He swung a second time at the prism, under the solemn gaze of the forest spirit and its lost soul. Again he achieved nothing more than a painful twinge at his wrists. The hammer of his blade must have caused a terrible sound within the prism, but the creature did not flinch.

'There are more pressing matters at hand, my dear,' Pitch returned.

But Silas disagreed. Here was where the forest's mortal injury lay. The spirit's gaze had not left him once since they entered the courtyard, the creature's head turning so that the stag's eye followed his moves. Silas peered closer at the glass that made up the prism. There was movement there, like water moving beneath the ice. He pressed his palms against the smooth surface. An unseen force slammed against his chest, a bitter, acrid taste filled his mouth, and he nearly staggered off his feet in his haste to move away.

He was barely upright, and the hunt was upon them, spewing from the passageway behind. The wolves first, baying like hounds possessed.

For that is exactly what they were. Froth gathered at their jaws thickly, spraying against Silas as the first leapt at him, amber eyes widened so that the whites showed. He threw up the scythe before him, there came the sharp crack of wood against bone, and the animal was thrown clear. It was a small deterrent; the wolf bared its teeth and gathered to strike again. It leapt, snarling, baring claws grown long and curving as a hawk's. Silas struggled to bring the blade close, the long length of the scythe making it unwieldy in such close quarters. His talents may well lie with dead things, but surely the sharpness of the blade would help him here? It may have, but he could not set it in place quickly enough. With an anguished cry, Silas abandoned his attempt to strike and lifted the scythe's shaft before him, squeezing his eyes against the jaws that barrelled at him.

An anguished whelp sounded. Silas opened an eye. The animal lay before him, a smoking hole at its chest, amber eyes lifeless. The waft of burning flesh wrinkled Silas's nose. He spun to face Pitch. For the shot could have come from no other.

'Thank you.'

Pitch was surrounded by four tremendous stags, wide of chest and muscled of haunches. The glow of Pitch's hands set off the red tint to their coats. Each was graced with antlers so thick and wide in parts that Silas imagined Gilmore could have seated himself there without issue.

'Consider that a favour.' Pitch smirked. 'Now get off your arse and deal with the teratism so we can leave this bloody place.'

'Pitch, look out!'

Silas shouted his warning too late. The largest of the stags raced at the daemon, head lowered in its charge. Pitch turned, heeding Silas's warning, but even his quick movement was too slow. The tips of the creature's antlers drove into him, sinking into his flesh as though it were the softest butter. The daemon's roar was monstrous.

'No!' Silas cried.

Flames danced from Pitch's fingers. He swept his hand against the stag's throat, and his daemonic flame made slight work of the animal's thick neck, slicing its head clean from its body.

'Fuck.' Pitch grasped hold of the antlers with both hands and tore them from his body. Blood poured a dark curtain down his side, and Silas gagged at the sight of the twin gashes in once smooth pale flesh.

The daemon kicked at the head with a force that catapulted it into one of the other creatures, knocking the considerable animal off its feet. The beast within the prism bayed, an achingly forlorn cry.

'Pitch, are you –' A blow landed against Silas's shoulder, followed by a searing pain there.

He gasped, throwing his hand to the place. The smoothness of an arrow's shaft met his fingers. 'Blast.'

He spun around. The hunter, a man whose height matched Silas's, stood with bow raised, a crown of antlers upon his hooded head, his cloak covered in death-crinkled brown leaves of the ash. His was mostly shadowed beneath his hood. Only one feature gave hint that a man existed there at all.

An eye as green as juniper.

The hunter, the Verderer, released his arrow. Silas threw himself clear. But he was no expert in such things, and his landing was a calamitous thing that saw him crash upon his injured shoulder, snapping the shaft. The arrowhead burrowed deeper. The tenderness was eye-watering, and Silas delivered onto the air a ghastly spray of curses. The Verderer cared little for his woes and was already nocking his next arrow before Silas had drawn breath.

On hands and knees, Silas scampered in behind the shelter of the well.

'Stop fucking hiding,' Pitch shouted. 'Kill the bloody thing. I cannot keep them from you forever.'

The castle had set its full weight against the daemon. Stags and wolves surrounded him, taking turns to dart at him, drawing his fire but shifting at the last moment to avoid its burn. He was a bloodied mess of taut muscle, and the outlandish tattoo on his back seemed to shift with the suddenness of his movements. The ivy that had plagued them in the corridors pushed its way through the cracks in the courtyard's stone floor, snaking about Pitch's legs. As fast as his fire seared the vines, another grew to find him, wrapping his legs in a cocoon of the thickest black.

Silas wrapped sweat-laden palms against the rough shaft of the scythe. The Verderer drew his arrow, the creak of the bow sounding. Silas breathed out, steadying himself. *Kill the bloody thing.*

He thrust to his feet, abandoning his shelter. The Verderer fired. Silas swung the scythe. The shot was wild, he knew only that the arrow barrelled straight for him, and that he held slender hope his blade might protect him somehow.

The hope was not so slender. The blade found the arrow.

There came the clang of metal on metal. The arrow's tip meeting the scythe, and glancing away. Silas ran at the Verderer, scythe aloft. Ready for the blow he hoped might bring down the teratism.

If that was indeed what faced him here.

The blade and his fingertips said so, but confusion held him. The Verderer seemed to exist in two places at once. Both here, with imposing menace, and within the beast imprisoned in the glass cell. That eye, with its deepened shade of juniper green, the very richness of the forest itself, could not be mistaken.

Silas's foe cast his bow over his shoulder, the weapon seemingly swallowed by the leaf-drenched cloak, and withdrew a short blade from somewhere at his hip. Pincers of dread found Silas. Now he would see if Sybilla's training held itself in his mind. He threw his utmost into the sideways drive of the blade, aiming its tip at the Verderer's side.

Their blades met, the hook of the scythe catching around the shorter weapon. The Verderer disengaged them with a violent flick of his wrists, sending Silas staggering. He hurried to find his balance once more, and this time when he threw his strike, he feinted low. The Verderer's short sword moved with him, and Silas thrust the scythe high to where his foe's chest was exposed.

The gamble ran in Silas's favour. His blade sliced deep through the Verderer's cloak to what lay beneath, and the teratism uttered his first sound. One of startled agony. Silas did not delay with delivering another blow, swinging wide to send the curve of the blade in behind the lost soul that jerked and contorted with the taste of death's cut upon its flesh. The tip dug deep into the Verderer's back, and he arched back with a howl that lifted to unearthly heights. Silas could see little else but the single pained eye beneath the shadows of the hood, no sign of the mouth that made such god-awful wailings. Silas dragged the blade deeper.

He thought his ears might shatter for the keening the scythe wrought from the creature. The calamity of it took up all the space in the air.

It seemed an interminable length of time before at last the Verderer fell to his knees, his cloak of leaves spreading around him as though he were a toppled tree. The lost soul swayed about, total blackness now beneath his hood. He toppled forward, his face planting upon the stonework. Silas panted, and his shoulder burned with a fierceness that might buckle him if he thought on it too much. There was not a part of his body that did not pain him.

He set the scythe's shaft against the floor, leaning his weight against the makeshift crutch. The teratism had been downed. Yet still his fingertips burned with notice of a lost soul. He stared down at the fallen Verderer. Where was the sign of the soul he'd seen on Black Annis's demise? The momentary glimpse of the woman she'd once been, before the foulness distorted her beyond recognition?

'Is it done?' Pitch stood on the far side of the well, his alabaster skin contrasting horribly with the wide, dark stain at his side. His pant leg was black with its flow. A dim glow remained at his fingers, the ivy reduced to a dusting of ash at his feet. Several wolves and two powerful stags, one smeared with the blood of his downed fellow, stood at the entrance to the passageways. The wolves held their tails between their legs, and both they and the stags set their heads low as though fatigued beyond measure. Silas was surprised to see there had been no more bloodshed. Only the single gruesome decapitated corpse remained.

'It is done.' Silas wiped at his brow, unsettled despite his words. 'They did not attack again?'

'No,' Pitch said gruffly, poking his finger at the gorier of his wounds. 'Dreary of them really. What point in killing if there is no fight involved? None have ventured close since I took their brother's head.'

The retreat was yet another oddity that did not sit well with Silas. 'There is a strangeness afoot here, Pitch.'

The desolate wail of the creature held within the prism rang out.

'Damn it, Silas,' Pitch cried. 'You said it was done.'

Pitch flew at him, his pace such that Silas could barely keep his eyes upon him. The daemon rammed his shoulder into Silas, setting them both on a course for the ground. The hiss of a blade cut the air.

With the air knocked from his lungs, Silas could not utter the cry of surprise that came with seeing the Verderer back upon his feet.

'Get up.' Pitch handled him roughly, Silas's shirt tearing at the collar as he was dragged to his feet. 'If you cannot fucking finish it, I will.'

'I did finish it,' Silas gasped. 'Wait, this is not right.'

Pitch ran at the Verderer, letting loose a war cry and a blast of daemon fire. His flames hit the mass of the creature and were twisted upwards, as though glancing up a wall. The teratism sliced his blade at Pitch's back, sending the daemon wildly off course. Pitch screamed an abysmal curse, barely stopping himself from crashing headlong into the brickwork. Silas bit at his cracked and dry lips, shuddering.

'It is only me,' he whispered.

Pitch could protect him, but he could not take Silas's place. He could not win the fight against a lost soul gone rabid with the Blight's touch. That fight was for the pale Horseman.

'Stay down, Pitch,' Silas cried.

He lifted the scythe. The weight of it was not much, but the wound at his shoulder made it so. He was tiring. How was it that the Verderer still stood?

The Verderer's eye was upon him again, his bow at hand, setting his arrow into the notch – as though the confrontation played out again from the very start and the scythe had never made its mark.

The howl of the entrapped spirit caught at the air once more. A chill ran the length of Silas's spine, sinking into him.

'This cannot be,' he muttered. He glanced back at the prism. The spirit raised its heavy head. This time the eyes of man and nature found him. It struck him then. The Verderer was not in two places at once at all.

'Silas!'

He spun about. Pitch threw a blast of light at the arrow set on a course for Silas's chest. The contact exploded the slender portion of wood into tiny specks of bright ash.

'The prism,' Silas shouted. 'We need to destroy it.'

'Kill the bloody teratism first –'

'Can you shatter that prism, Pitch?' Silas shouted.

'It's highly fucking likely.'

'Then do it, now.' Silas twisted, sending the blade to rescue him from another arrow. 'What lies before us is merely a phantom, a projection. We must release the spirit of the forest, for that is where the Verderer truly lies.'

CHAPTER 25

Tobias Astaroth did as he was told. And it was a wondrous sight to behold. He was a vision of grisly beauty, gliding past Silas with the fierceness of his emerald gaze fixed upon the prism, the set of his shoulders accentuating every curve of muscle there. Despite his wounds, which were ghastly abuses of flesh, Pitch moved as though they did not exist. As though to be so battered were nothing at all.

Silas was pulled from his misplaced considerings by the sudden jerk of his arm. The scythe lifted his hand, and the blade found yet another of the arrows that seemed to come from nowhere at the Verderer's back. Silas scowled. Did the blade act despite him? He relaxed his hold, bracing for the next shot that came. His hands shifted right, in time for the familiar clank of metal against metal to ring once more. Silas imagined his grin must appear maniacal, but he could not help it. This discovery was too wonderful. He'd been too distracted by Pitch, his mind moved from the heat of the moment, to realise that the scythe guided him. The blade reacted to a threat before Silas had a chance to notice it.

Buoyed by the discovery, Silas grew bold. He edged in closer to where the teratism, or at least the shadow of one, moved on swift feet about him. A hurried glance over his shoulder told him that Pitch had reached the prism unimpeded. The wolves and stags still watched from across the courtyard, their wary stances unchanged. None had tried to prevent the daemon from reaching the curious structure and spreading his hands wide against the panes of glass.

Radiant yellowed light poured from his palms, so bright Silas could not have kept watch even if he had the chance to do so. He turned back to the Verderer.

The teratism had no such trouble keeping his one-eyed gaze upon the daemon. He'd readied his bow in the quickened way he had, and its aim was set clearly upon Pitch.

Silas dove at the Verderer and brought his scythe down upon the creature's outstretched arm. His shoulder screamed in protest. The teratism let out a growl that a wolf would envy and lashed out at Silas, swinging wild as a drunken boxer. They were matched in height but Silas found himself unexpectedly quicker. He dodged low to escape the blow, crouching with the scythe's shaft against his belly. He cursed the length of the weapon, not for the first time. For if it were shorter and more easily wielded, he might have raised it in time to be spared the shock of a strike against the small of his back. He cried out, arching at the new pain that came. He could not make out where the agonies across his body started and ended, though the arrowhead buried in his shoulder fired most stunning of all.

'Goddamn it.' He whirled about, his anger pushing him to send a counter blow the Verderer's way. This time when he swung he found his wish most curiously granted. The scythe shortened to half the length it had been a moment ago. Far more reminiscent of a sickle.

The entire courtyard was aglow, as though a forest fire burned its way into the castle.

Silas struck out with the shortened weapon. The tip of the blade sank deep into the Verderer's chest. The moan that left the teratism seemed to rattle the entire castle. With both hands fast upon the shaft, Silas ground his teeth against the throb of his shoulder and dragged his blade down the length of the hapless creature's shadowed chest. Christ, he was tired. To the very marrow.

The Verderer sank beneath the folds of his cloak, buried beneath the leaves, his antler crown rapping a sharp note against the stonework.

A tremor started beneath Silas's feet. He staggered away from the fallen teratism. The creature would rise again, he was sure. But he was not certain the strength remained in him to fell it once more. He breathed hard, his breast soaked with sweat.

206

The spirit of the forest was the key. It held the true heart of the Verderer.

Silas blinked, shading his eyes against a sudden glare. The daemon stood with light streaming from his skin, as though a million candles burned beneath it. He stood upon the rim of the well, his hands pressed to the prism. The silver girding reinforcing the structure was no longer silver at all, rather the red heat of a horseshoe fresh from the forge.

'Can it be done, Pitch?' Silas grimaced at the pain in his shoulder. The rumbling throughout the ground was strong enough to move the arrowhead within him, and it was far from pleasant.

'Of course I can fucking do it.' But the daemon sounded laboured, anguished if Silas were to name it truly. 'I will ruin their game yet.'

He threw back his head, the lengths of his damp hair glinting in the firelight. If he cried out, it was silent, only the widening of his mouth to betray any torment. The glow became too much for Silas to bear. He lowered his head and covered his eyes.

Glass shattered with all the force of a thousand mirrors cracking at once. Silas threw himself to the ground, covering his head for fear of the shards that surely must be sent from such a blast. All at once his mouth filled with that same bitter, acrid taste that had come when he touched the prism. How utterly foul it was, and how his body repulsed it. Silas retched, convulsing in spasms that made him dizzy with their intensity. Yellowed liquid burned his throat, propelling from his mouth.

But his mind lay with the daemon at the centre of the blast.

'Pitch?' He raced his convulsions to cry out. 'Pitch?'

Silas dragged himself to his feet, the weight of his bones almost more than he could stand. Pitch lay beside the well, his arms cradled about the stag in the most curious of embraces. Stiff lengths of the silver girding jutted like crude plants from the ground, the broken glass resembling pieces of ice scattered thickly over the ground. Silas attempted to stand and found the world far too unbalanced for such a thing. He dropped to his hands and knees, wincing at the bite of stone against his skin. The shuddering ground hampered him as Silas edged closer to the daemon.

'Pitch, Pitch, can you hear me? Are you all right?'

'Wonderful,' Pitch groaned against the stag's neck. 'Though I do miss my clothes...and would kill for a tartlet.' He pushed himself onto a bloodied elbow.

'Pitch, your skin!' Silas cried.

The daemon's faultless covering of white was run through with darts of smoky grey, as though his blood had taken in the ash borne of the burning ivy. Another great spasm shook the ground, rattling debris from the walls around them.

'End this, Sickle. Go. Move your arse.' Pitch released the stag. The beast's chest rose slowly with deep, troubled breaths, the rounded eye of the animal hidden beneath a lowered lid.

A commotion came from behind.

Silas glanced around to find that the Verderer was on his feet once more. Silas's entire body protested, so heavy with exhaustion he could not imagine finding the strength to lift a finger let alone death's weapon. But the commotion came not from the teratism alone.

The stags and wolves had made their move. But it was not the one that Silas feared.

They drew themselves into a line, setting their masses between the Verderer and the ruined prism. The wolves sank low, predators summing up their prey, the stags at their back providing a formidable barrier with regal heads held high, their crowns of bone spreading wide and considerable. Silas edged closer to Pitch, dragging the scythe with him. The blade retained its smaller form, something to be thankful for, for it made movement all the easier. His hands touched at warm, slippery wetness. Silas found his palm covered in the crimson of the daemon's blood. The ground shook as though a giant stamped their feet, and the castle loosened its bricks onto the courtyard.

'Do what you must, Sickle. Let it be done,' Pitch wheezed.

It was difficult to look on him, with the dark veining at his neck and the repulsive gashes at his hip.

'God, Pitch, your wounds.'

'For fuck's sake, Silas,' Pitch hissed between clenched teeth, 'I am not important.'

The castle suffered another assault against her foundations. This one large enough to rattle free a massive section of wall near to where the

Verderer lay. The crash of brick upon the stone overwhelmed Silas's ears, and the dust plumed so thick upon the air that it choked him. The wolves and stags broke ranks, scattering like phantoms into the hazy depths of the passageways.

Silas raised the scythe. The sickle. The vibrant pulse at his fingertips left him with no doubt of what must be done. Death called on him, the goddess's bidding all too apparent.

Strike down the spirit, and the teratism at its heart.

Goodrich Castle was tearing its walls down around him. Sickle held the blade over the beast's chest, where lichen grew within the dirty white beard. He raised his arms, his heart leaping to the back of his throat.

With an exhale he dealt the death stroke.

Metal moved surely through coat and meat, barely catching at bone, and Silas did not flinch.

The stag's eye opened. But it was not the soulful brown of an animal's gaze. Fixed upon Silas was the eye of a man. Green as the very forest he had tended over since the day he'd bled his life into its soil.

The Verderer.

The guardian of the spirit of the forest.

The iris bloomed wide, swamping the white of the Verderer's eye before wilting again, shrinking until only the soot-black pupil remained.

The scythe wrenched from the flesh, moving with a will of its own. Even as his gaze remained locked upon the stag, the scythe altered its shape within his grasp, curling itself back into rounded discs and dirty string.

Silas watched the stag, mesmerised. Death graced the animal with silent efficiency. It had been a clean, true kill. A job well done. Contentment wrapped him to her bosom. And he might have just been crowned King of England for the sense of accomplishment that held him.

Silas raised his head. Through the dust clouds that surrounded him, he saw the apparition of the Verderer as he once was. The man who had roamed this forest with the notion of protecting it, not turning it upon itself. As the Blight had turned him. A slender man, with gentle green eyes and a tumbling beard the same off-white as that of the stag. The spirit of the forest that had claimed him the day his blood had spilled into the soil he so loved.

The Verderer paid Silas no mind. He had eyes only for the stag, and if sorrow ever had a face, then this was it. The grief was palpable, pricking at the back of Silas's own eyes. The Verderer reached for the stag with hands roughened and dirtied by his living years, but those hands had long since made their last touch upon this world. The Verderer shivered, faded, and at long last, the lost soul found his way.

Silas slumped onto his heels, returning the bandalore to its pocket. He sank his empty fingers into the coarse depths of the stag's coat, brushing at the lichen that coated it. The grey-green covering graced the stag's muzzle too, all the way up to the eye socket that had held the juniper green gaze of the Verderer. There was no hint of the eye now, the sunken hollow taken over by the lichen.

A violent shudder took the castle. A blast of sound followed, and the well water sprayed from its circular confines in a twinkling column that reached for the heavens.

'Get up, Sickle.' Pitch grabbed him roughly. 'The castle will not survive this.'

The water rained down in sharp, frigid drops, hammering at them as though it sought to drive them both into the stones. Puddles of blush red formed where the liquid met Pitch's blood. Silas made it to his feet, just as another powerful rent came. Beyond the well the floor lifted, blocks of stone sent skyward by a blast that tore the ground open. A cavity great enough to have swallowed Silas entirely, with room perhaps for Pitch as well.

The daemon shoved at him. 'Go!'

'Wait!' Silas struggled against him. Something about the stag caught his eye. A shift of a delicate leg. 'The spirit.'

'Forget the fucking stag!' Pitch shouted. The riot that surrounded them sought to bury his words.

'It lives,' Silas cried. 'I'm sure of it.'

The agonised earth roared in protest at the forces that sought to tear it apart. He saw it again. The tilt of the stag's head as the animal roused. Silas threw off Pitch's grasp; he crouched at the beast's side and gathered his arms beneath it. He tilted his head so as not to find himself with an antler piercing his temple and readied to lift to his feet. A blast shook the courtyard, one that saw him stagger as he tried to negotiate the weight in his arms. Pitch was ready with a none too gentle, steadying hand.

'Gods have you lost your mind? We are leaving.'

Silas would offer no protest. Not once he had secured the stag. He lifted it over his shoulders in the way of a hunter, draping the body against the back of his neck. Despite the size of the creature, it was not weighty, a good thing considering the angry pulse of the arrowhead embedded in Silas's shoulder. Once the stag was settled, he pushed to his feet with a grunt.

And stared in horror at what lay beyond the well.

The cavity was not done with its widening. And it sought to consume the courtyard. The stones that had formed the well, set in place so long ago, were ripped from their resting place, tumbling down into the sweeping maw of the fractured Earth. Overhead, it was little better. The reaching lengths of brick swaying formidably.

'It is coming down!' Silas cried.

'Go, go, blast you.' Pitch wrenched on Silas's arm, dragging him forward so quickly he was almost toppled.

The daemon hurried him towards the passageway the Verderer had appeared in.

'Is this the way?'

'I have no fucking idea.' Pitch swatted at the smaller lumps of rock that fell upon them, as though they were no more than irritating insects of a summer's night, his flames deflecting the pieces that dared draw near. 'It's as good a choice as any.'

The roar that came from behind deafened Silas to anything else Pitch might have said. There was a dragon awakening, surely. A savage beast that would tear them limb from limb. Pitch pushed at him, a hand to the small of Silas's back urging him ever faster. They raced down the wide passageway, the castle walls towering high above them. Silas struggled to find air clean enough to catch his breath upon. Ahead, a most marvellous sight – an imposing gate of Cimmerian wood.

'I see the gate,' Silas cried. 'Can you bring it down, Pitch?'

Silas squinted. He swore a figure stood in the shadows that clung to the doorway. A trick of the light, surely.

'We will not make it,' Pitch said, his voice hoarse with the air's pollution. 'On your knees, Sickle.'

He gave no choice in the matter, taking Silas's hand and dragging him down. An easy enough feat when Silas had the stag to contend with. Pitch set himself on his knees in front of Silas and laid his hands upon his thighs.

'What are you doing?' Silas eased the stag from his shoulders, leaning back so he could slide it down his back and set down the creature as gently as haste would allow.

'Don't move. I'm not sure I can hold this long.' Pitch closed his eyes.

The shimmer of gold around his hands raced the lengths of his arms and embraced his mauled torso. The black veining was not quite so evident as before, turned storm-cloud grey beneath the shimmer. The glow found its way along his neck to light his face with radiance. Pitch was haloed by the daemonic energies that swirled so restlessly beneath his skin. Silas had witnessed such a sight before, when the harpies descended upon him, but that display was pale and insignificant compared to this one.

He stared, open-mouthed. Eyes fluttering against the brilliance.

Flames rose from Pitch's back, twin streams that flowered from between his shoulder blades, rising up like twin rainbows of gold, shielding them from the downpour. The flames gave off no heat that Silas could feel upon him, but they did serve to brighten the air so that every swell of muscle, every jagged edge of pierced flesh upon Pitch's exposed body was highlighted. The awful holes rent by the stag's antler upon his stomach pulsed light, as though a miniature sun rested within. The castle rained bone-shattering pieces down upon them. And not a one came close to inflicting harm. The sections struck the flaming barrier and shattered against it, reduced to particles so fine they could have been mistaken for sand.

All the while Pitch did not move, did not utter a word or sound while his body burned with the inferno. His wounds bled anew, the pump of blood from the largest a horrid ribbon of burgundy. Silas kept his gaze fixed on Pitch's face, despite the glare. The sight brought a knot to his throat.

The daemon was as beautiful as he was unfathomable. Watching on through narrowed eyes, Silas imagined the blazing arches to be the very wings of an angel.

CHAPTER 26

The destruction seemed never-ending, the groans and screams of protest coming from the long-standing walls searing their way into Silas's ears. And all the while Pitch held them under cover of infernal safety, the power that flowed from him repelled anything that dared strike. But their security came at a price. Silas noted the slump of Pitch's shoulders, the drop of his head. They both knelt in a pool of his blood. Silas saw clearly the vile darkness that had taken a place in the veins bulging along his neck and arms.

Goodrich Castle tore itself apart around them.

He slipped his hands over Pitch's where they rested on his thighs. The daemon trembled. Silas adjusted his hold, needing to offer more. He entwined his fingers with the daemon's. There was a barely perceptible movement. A gentle fastening.

Together they knelt. And Goodrich Castle fell.

At long, long last, it was over. The castle had no more layers to rid herself of, no more weight to shed. There was a heartbeat of silence, broken by a sharp, pained gasp from Pitch. At once the fiery ribbons withdrew, secreting themselves between the daemon's shoulder blades and vanishing from sight. The sudden loss of light was almost as painful as the glare. Pitch toppled forward, and Silas rocked forward to steady him. He threw his arms about the daemon, taking care not to press too hard to his back, lest the flames had burned him there.

'Pitch? Can you hear me?'

Without the firey barrier of protection, he found himself in the embrace of the dusty air. The grit rubbed at his eyes and weighed upon his tongue. Silas blinked, the world hazy with dirt and the echoes of light.

'Lord save me, I cannot believe it.' A cry came from the white glow. 'You've survived such a thing.'

Silas could not turn with Pitch's weight against him. He did not wish to, for fear the slightest movement might cause the man pain. 'Ottelie? Is that you?'

'It is lad, it is. Good gracious, what a sight you are.'

Silas peered up. Ottelie's brown skirts swept about her, sending the dust scattering as she negotiated the considerable piles of rubble that formed a circular lip around Pitch and Silas.

'Are you all in one piece?' Ottelie said. 'By the maiden, why do you have a stag at your feet?'

'It is wounded. As is Pitch, most gravely I fear.' He ran his hand against the back of Pitch's head, hoping a gentle touch might stir him. The rise and fall of the daemon's ribs was evident, the laboured breath of a man who had worked himself hard. 'Pitch, can you hear me?'

Silas still saw those arches of flame when he blinked. A glorious sight.

'Yes,' the daemon groaned, leaning all his insubstantial weight against Silas. 'Are you hurt, Sickle?'

His voice was raspy, as though the fire had found its way down his throat.

Silas shook his head fervently. 'No. You saved my life.'

'As ordered.' Pitch's arms hung at his sides, his hands against the dirt, a puppet with cut strings.

'Bloody hell, what happened in this place?' Ottelie reached them at last and peered at Pitch with a wrinkled nose. 'He's quite the mess then, isn't he?'

'Go away, crone. Let me sleep,' Pitch growled and Silas's heart leapt. To have the daemon so helpless, so still, had frightened him as much as the teratism they had just faced.

'Got a perfectly fine bed you can sleep in, young man,' Ottelie declared. 'You need those wounds seen to.'

Pitch made a sound, barely a whimper. With a tentative touch, Silas shifted the hair that had fallen across Pitch's face. 'Are you in great pain?'

The answer seemed obvious of course, with such horrendous rents in one's flesh there must come agony, but there was little obvious about Tobias Astaroth.

'Just let me sleep...I'm so tired.' An odd sound made its way up his throat, a choked grunt, as though an internal affliction bothered him.

'Here, let him go, Silas,' Ottelie said. 'I'll deal with him.'

Silas's arms tightened about the daemon's body. 'Are you sure we should move him?'

'What else are we going to do with him?' Ottelie tutted. 'You'll both float away on a stream of his blood if you don't move soon anyways.' Something must have shown on Silas's face for her scowl smoothed clear and she touched a hand to his shoulder. 'Come now, we will see him well. You have done your part here, now let me do mine.'

He did not let go of Pitch immediately. But the woman was right. Silas's trousers were warm and damp and it was not just the sweat of exertion that covered them. He nodded. 'I will get him on his feet.'

Ottelie clucked her tongue. 'You can barely get to yours.' She slipped her hands beneath Pitch's arms. With impressive dexterity, she lifted him to standing. 'Good grief, does the boy not eat? He's a bag of feathers.'

Despite her declaration, she grunted as she manoeuvred his arm about her shoulders. Pitch's protest was as weak as the hand he raised against her, his unsteady gaze seeing him do no more than swipe at the air in front of her face. As she settled him into place at her side, Silas got to his feet, wincing at the heavy wetness of his blood soaked clothing. Was there any blood left in the daemon? Pitch's chin dropped to his chest, consciousness leaving him once more, but Ottelie paid him little mind. Her mouth fell open, her eyes set upon what had until now been hidden mostly behind Silas's bulk.

'I did not see her for what she was before,' she breathed. 'That is the spirit of the forest at your feet, Mr Mercer.'

Silas nodded, though his focus was on the man who leaned against her, limp and intolerably silent. 'Evil intent was worked upon the spirit, and the Verderer who lived within her. Both the stag and Pitch will need your healing strength, I fear.' And he too, but the throb of the arrowhead was distant and untroubling, as though his flesh had numbed around it.

Ottelie sucked her breath between her teeth. 'The Verderer is to blame for this carnage?'

'I am not sure the blame is to be laid with him, though it is he who wrought such damage upon the forest, yes.' Crouching before the animal, Silas found a warm brown eye upon him. The stag made a low sound and attempted to lift its head, revealing more of its broad face to him. The anguished eye of juniper existed no more. A swathe of lichen had made its home in the empty socket. 'The Verderer had been corrupted, and is no more.'

Nor was the mysterious prism that bound them both.

'Corrupted? Well then, it is true that nature's greatest weakness is man.' Iron coated Ottelie's words. 'What possessed the lord to betray his forest?'

Silas sought grip upon the bulk of the stag, readying himself for the lift. 'I cannot say.'

'Can't? Or won't?'

'I do not understand much of what happened here today.' Silas huffed his way to his feet, one arm beneath the stag's thick neck, the other wrapped against the animal's tail end. Squeezing it so that its four hooves touched at one another against his thighs. Pitch might have been a bag of feathers but the beast was certainly not. Thankfully, the animal did not protest the move, but the arrowhead shifted beneath Silas's skin in a discomforting way. 'What I am certain on however, is that Pitch still bleeds and the stag cannot stand. Please, let us go. They need your attention.'

The woman stared at the beast in Silas's arms. Her eyes sparkled with unshed tears. 'Little wonder I felt my heart crack along with this castle.' She sniffed and at last looked away. 'Now is time indeed to repay the forest for its protection of me, I only hope I am up to the task. I'll do what I can Silas, you have my word.' She turned and picked a path through the rubble, seeming to have no trouble at all with manoeuvring Pitch along, as though he were but an oversized doll. He was every bit as limp as one. 'Do you see his veins? Grey as week old ash they are. What could cause such a thing? Anything you know might aid me.'

Silas paused at the summit of the rubble pile they climbed, as much to consider his answer as to catch his breath, but all thoughts were scattered

at the sight he beheld. Around the circle of bare earth where Pitch had
protected them lay what remained of Goodrich Castle. An enormous
depression scarred the earth, all but consuming the remnants of the
structure, as though quicksand was taking its time to eat the brick and
beams that had stood so long upon this spot. Already peeking through
the debris, poking their leaves to the moonlight, were the hints of wild
grasses and the dark leaves of the ivy's vines. Barely had the castle fallen
before nature was reclaiming its territory.

He glanced at the creature he carried. Perhaps all was not lost for the
stag, if the forest converged so readily.

The narrow bridge that had laid beyond the gate was mercifully intact,
and short. Silas lifted his chin to peer over the low-set parapet. There was
nothing to be seen of the waters that had tormented them on the way
across, though the moonlight did glitter as it touched the bed, betraying
the dampness that remained.

Lalassu stood on the bank with ears pricked towards him, her coat a
ghostly, wonderful sight to behold. A pair of horses waited alongside her.
It took a moment for Silas to recognise the shorter of the pair. His eyes
widened. It was Sanu, but she had been transformed. The mare tossed
her coppery head, nickering at their approach. He could scarce believe his
tired eyes. She was not the steed she had been on entering the forest. The
red horse held her head aloft, with a proud curve to her thickened neck.
Her mane, a lighter red than her coat, hung nearly as long as Lalassu's
now, her tail trailing on the ground behind her. Sanu's bulk rivalled
Silas's horse more closely. A barrelling to her chest that had been absent
before, and added inches to her fine legs that brought her to stand just a
fraction below the pale horse. She remained more delicate though, just
as Pitch was to Silas.

Marvelling at the transformation, Silas was slow to take notice of the
black horse at Sanu's side. When he did, his skin prickled.

'That is the Verderer's mount,' he said. 'Is it not?'

'Seems he rode him a while, but to whom the stallion truly belongs,
I do not know. One of the miners perhaps? I've a mind to suppose he
might be staying with me. Found the poor sod wandering about as lost
as I was while I waited for you.'

The black horse lifted its head at her words as though it knew she spoke of him directly. The horse seemed far too fine for any miner's mount. The coal-black coat rippled as the horse shifted its weight, the trimmed tail and mane suggesting it may have once stood in a gentleman's stables. Its origins might be unknown, but there was no doubting its eagerness at Ottelie's approach, nuzzling at her arm as she waited on Silas to join them.

'How far must we travel?' Silas asked.

'Not far,' Ottelie replied. 'At a walk perhaps a quarter of the hour.' Her brown skirt held darker marks where Pitch bled upon her. 'We will place the spirit on the red mare, you will be needing to ride with the lad. He's not quite with us and won't stay in the saddle on his own.'

How he would have relished a protest from the man in her arms, a vulgar dismissal of their plans. Pitch hung silent.

'Of course.' Silas set his teeth, readying for the pangs that would come with lifting the stag onto Sanu's now much-raised back. The horse stood as a statue, with not so much of a flick of her tail to betray her a living creature. Silas grunted, trying to ignore the dig of the arrowhead and the twinge of sore muscles as he settled the creature over Sanu's broader haunches.

'Careful now.' Ottelie fussed.

'I will be nothing less,' Silas hissed through clenched teeth.

The stag showed as few signs of life as Pitch. The pair of them were all but devoid of consciousness. Once it was done, Silas returned to where Ottelie braced Pitch against Lalassu's side.

'I will take him now,' he said.

Ottelie nodded absently, her attention still upon the stag. 'That won't do. Slip straight off it will,' she muttered, making her way to Sanu, and leaving him to manage the rag-doll daemon alone. She lifted her skirts as she went, tearing at the yellowed petticoat beneath, and setting about using the strips to secure the stag more surely to the saddle. Silas was a word away from requesting her return so she might assist him when Pitch shifted about.

He moaned, and appeared to be attempting to remove himself from Silas's hold. His weak struggle would have been farcical were it not so concerning. He was slippery with blood and sweat, and it was no easy feat to keep him upright.

'Pitch, it is all right. You are in no danger.' Silas grappled with the restless daemon, his hands searching for a place upon the lithe body where he might find a firmer hold. Muscles shifted beneath his fingertips, warm and wet.

'Let me sleep,' the daemon groaned, all at once pressing in hard against Silas, as though he thought himself climbing into bed. His knees buckled. Instinct took hold and Silas swept a hand beneath his legs and lifted him. The witch was not wrong. Pitch was light as a bag of feathers, but in his state he was as slippery as an eel and far too unpredictable. Silas would not risk him falling from the heights of Lalassu's back should he lose his grip. There was nothing for it. Silas would make his way to Ottelie's cottage on foot, with a daemon in his arms.

CHAPTER 27

The further away they drew from the castle, the crisper the air became. The dawn was still to come and the sky held a white tinge, a paleness that matched Lalassu's coat. The creatures of the wood were unsettled. Birds that should have sung to a raised sun already warbled in the branches; a deer or two dashed through the stark landscape of skeletal tree trunks, and half-covered shrubs whose leaves hovered between rotten browns and water-deprived yellows. Silas thought he spied a fox travelling with them, glancing in and out of what low shrubbery had not been totally stripped bare by the Blight's influence on the Verderer. The bushy plume of the creature's tail was evident as it moved, seemingly unconcerned about being spotted.

He adjusted his hold on Pitch, ensuring his head was not about to slip from where it lay in the crook between Silas's shoulder and chest. The man, still snoring softly, reached for the lapel of Silas's coat, clutching it tight. Silas's breath caught and something whirled in the pit of his belly. He assured himself it was only because he was much relieved to know the daemon was still capable of movement at all.

It was not hard to know when they arrived at Ottelie's home, for it was the only place evident in the forest where the foliage still claimed its lushness and greenery. An oasis in a beleaguered landscape where all else had been reduced to shades of its former glory.

Ottelie's cottage sank into its environment so well that Silas might have walked straight past it in a healthy forest. What small evidence there was of the cottage's framework had been claimed by the woods. The slope of its roof was covered entirely with a thick bed of moss from which tiny mushrooms sprang, and the walls were enveloped by jasmine grown so thick that the cottage puffed like a cotton bud. The front door, built from mismatched columns of birch and a solitary window with a sunshine-yellow curtain, were the only obvious indicators an abode existed here at all.

'Here we are. Take him inside and settle him in. You'll have no trouble finding a resting place, for there is but one.' Ottelie dismounted, leaning to pick from the greenery that spread at her feet, a delicate plant with tiny yellow and white flowers. 'I'll need some time to gather the herbs, and I wish to see the spirit settled.'

Ottelie came to stand beside Silas. 'Open your mouth, lad.' She tapped a finger at Pitch's lips. He grumbled but parted them enough that she could pop one of the flowers into his mouth. 'Feverfew. That will help with the pain for now. I'll mix something stronger.'

'What of the stag?' Silas said. 'Let me assist you in bringing him down.'

'No need. Go on. Go on.' She rubbed at her eye, leaving smudges of moss green against her skin. 'We have things under control enough, see?'

He could not help but see. Sanu sank down onto knobbled knees, first the front, then the back, so that the stag's legs dangled an inch above the grass.

Lalassu whinnied, tossing her head. And Silas nodded, as though he understood, for he thought he did. They were all safe here. Pitch muttered and shifted in his arms, attempting to roll over as though he were at rest in a feather-filled bed and not balanced in someone's arms.

'Hold on, Pitch. We are not there yet.'

The daemon's curse, soft and hoarse, gladdened Silas to his very core. Here was sign that his guardian might live to drive him mad yet. Ottelie urged him away, still bothering at her eye and mumbling about needing a decent bath before long. Silas hurried to the door, and after some fumbling with the latch, which he could not see for Pitch's body, he had them inside.

The interior was every bit as small as he imagined. The room was dominated by a grand hearth fashioned out of the very earth itself, a clay-like soil packed tight to resemble a mantel. A low fire burned, the heat most comfortable. A crude wood-framed bed, quite massive considering the meagre size of the room, pressed its head against one wall. The mattress barely contained the straw it was stuffed with and the blanket was of the same fabric as Ottelie's dress.

The only other option for resting oneself was in an armchair. Its upholstery looked to be fashioned out of the rough, sectioned bark of an oak tree and hardly a comfortable place to convalesce. There was little decision to be made, the bed it would be. Silas set off, trying at first to avoid the delicate covering of tiny purple flowers that formed a rug of sorts on the floor. But with his view encumbered, it was inevitable he'd find his feet clomping upon the delicate spread. Much to his astonishment, Silas's heavy step caused no damage at all, the seemingly fragile florals holding his weight. He took great care as he laid Pitch upon the bed, supporting his head until it rested on the mattress, before moving to try and pry the daemon's fingers from his lapel. The arrowhead made itself well known in Silas's shoulder as he moved and he exhaled sharply.

'You said you were not hurt,' Pitch whispered, eyes shut tight. He'd not let go of Silas's coat.

'I'm not. Not as you are.'

'I've known worse.' He spoke through pale lips and skin tightened with the discomfort he denied. 'Fuck, what is this shit she put in my mouth?' His lips curled with ill-taste, and he at last relinquished his hold on Silas's lapel.

'It should help the pain, she said.' Silas sat himself gently upon the bed. The straw poked at his backside.

'Bloody woman is delusional,' Pitch muttered. 'And her bed isn't fit for pigs.'

Silas smiled for the first time in an age. He slipped a finger beneath the tendril of hair that clung to Pitch's cheek, teasing it from the sweat that anchored it there. Not so long ago that skin had beamed bright as a chandelier. The odd tightness came to his stomach once more, and Silas withdrew his hand.

'It can do no harm, surely, whatever she might offer.' Silas's gaze flicked to Pitch's fingers, still wrapped fast against his coat sleeve. He noted with much relief that the greyness of Pitch's veins had all but disappeared, returned to the more normal hue of blue green. 'That was...remarkable...what you did at the castle.' Silas's pulse stuttered just thinking on it. 'But it has taken much from you, hasn't it?'

'Are you worried for me?' With his eyes still closed, Pitch smiled. 'How quaint. Fear not, my Sickle, I will heal, with no need of the witch-pretender's nonsense.' He lifted his hand and found Silas's cheeks. The touch was silken, disconcerting, and Silas made no move to shift away. 'And you, my Sickle. How very brave and daring you can be when you are not trembling like a leaf. It was quite the sight, I must say.'

Silas's skin flamed beneath his touch. 'There is so much I wish to speak with you about.'

'I'm quite sure there is.' Pitch had not yet opened his eyes. 'But can it wait until I am no longer tasting blood and punctured as a pincushion?'

'Of course.'

Pitch's fingers traced a path along Silas's neck. Christ. Ottelie's fire was built far too strong for such a small room. He reached for something, anything, to say that might halt the downward path of the daemon's fingers and the upward trajectory of a traitorous part of Silas's anatomy. 'I will need Ottelie's assistance too I fear. The Verderer's arrow found me.'

The fingertips halted their caress. 'You have a cut? How dreadful for you.' Pitch's eyes rolled beneath their lids.

'Well, the arrowhead is still in my shoulder. So yes, it is rather dreadful.'

Pitch let his hand fall. He cracked open his eyes, the glint of gemstones evident between the lashes. 'You still have it?'

'Yes. Not as painful as one might imagine though.' Silas waved a vague hand towards the sight of the injury, the air returning to the room now that Pitch no longer touched him. He stood up with a grunt.

'Wait, show me.' Pitch sat up suddenly and set an iron-tight grasp upon Silas's arm. He tugged him downward. Silas toppled rather too easily onto the bed, planted face down upon the rough mattress. Straw jabbed at his chin. A weight settled upon his back. Pitch had him straddled.

'What on earth are you doing?' Silas cried.

'Lay still.' Pitch's meagre weight rested upon the small of his back. 'I promise it will be quick.'

'What is wrong with you? I would have Ottelie see to –' Pitch dug his fingers into the wound. Silas yelled the air from his lungs. 'Damn it, Pitch. You bastard!'

The sting was keen but fleeting. There came a squelch like boots in mud as the arrowhead was dragged from Silas's body.

'It is done.' Pitch dismounted and dropped heavily onto the bed alongside Silas. He panted as though he'd just wrestled with a Goliath. The trickle of blood from his wounds ran anew as he studied the arrowhead in crimson-tipped fingers. The metal seemed unremarkable, the colour of smudged charcoal, with two of the prongs cut with jagged edges.

'What has come over you?' Silas admonished.

'Nothing and no one recently, which is a terrible shame.' He attempted to laugh at his own crude joke but the jerk of his ribs pained him visibly. So be it, Silas decided, he'd offer no sympathies.

'I dare say Ottelie would have dealt with the removal rather less painfully.' His shoulder throbbed with a dull ache. He hoped the woman had a good supply of fresh hay at the ready, for her bed was a wreck of red stains.

'I dare say you are right.' Pitch brandished the arrowhead, though the gesture was somewhat lacklustre, as though it were too heavy to hoist very high. 'But a little discomfort never killed anyone. You have come to the rescue, my dear. For the second time I might add. What a knight you are.' His smile faded. 'I thought everything had been destroyed when the fucking world caved in on top of us but here we have it. Our strange little treasure.'

A seriousness fell upon him, and dread held Silas anew. The only thing worse than a vulgar daemon was a serious one.

Silas propped himself up on one elbow, careful not to position himself too close to the dreadful wound in Pitch's side. His knee touched at Pitch's leg and he considered edging back. 'A treasure?' Silas kept his knee where it was. 'It's a simple arrowhead is it not?'

'The only thing simple here is you, Silas.' Pitch ran his tongue over his lips. 'Now pay attention because I am far too tired to bother with telling you this tale twice.' He curled his hand over the arrowhead, and laid his arm across his eyes. 'You'll find no forge in the British Isles from whence this arrowhead came. Actually, you'll not find one in this world at all.'

Silas stared at the man's lips. 'Not forged in this world? Then where?'

'In mine,' Pitch said.

CHAPTER 28

Ottelie's voice reached through the silence, the witch singing quite sweetly somewhere beyond the thin walls.

'You speak of Arcadia?' Silas's voice was tiny, and he wondered if Pitch would hear him at all. Arcadia. The land of angels and daemons. His heart thumped ever harder. Pitch's jaw flexed as he shifted himself, his teeth clenched.

'I'm sorry,' Silas said. 'Do not talk of it now, save your strength - '

'There is none to save. I need a distraction anyway,' Pitch winced. 'Healing is more bloody painful than injury, it appears.' He cast the arrowhead over the side of the bed where it rolled like a chunk of coal in between a trio of cane baskets, out of sight.

'Should we not keep that? To take it to the Lady Satine?'

'Are you riding off now?'

'No.'

'Than it will be fine there.'

'If you are sure - '

'I'm sure it won't grow legs and run off. Yes.'

'Very well...' Silas moved on before the daemon's temper rose any further. 'What more can you tell me of it?'

'Depends how far I am allowed before I get all tongue-tied.' He exhaled. Silas remained silent. 'The metal used to forge that arrowhead is called nekhri. It is mined from the Siltron Ranges which run mostly through Arcadian territory. There is a small portion that the Exarch

227

Azazel claims for Elyssiam, but there have been rumours for a long while that he has mined his mountains dry. I have no fucking idea what that is doing here...in your shoulder...on the Verderer's arrow, but Silas, I must say, this dreary quest we've been sent on has just become far more interesting.'

There were at least half a dozen words spoken just now that Silas could not fathom and he struggled to decide which one to ask upon first.

'Elyssiam?' Silas might be lying upon the bed, but he had the surest sense of falling.

'Home of our sworn and eternal enemies,' Pitch said lightly. 'The stronghold of the Watchers.'

'I see. And the Watchers might be...who exactly?'

'Fucking ridiculous name, don't you think? But it is what Samyaza and his merry bunch of traitors called themselves after they started their little Angelic rebellion and appropriated a portion of Arcadia. Over time the name has come to include any who take up residence in Elyssiam. I mean, the Watcher...how pretentious. What was he watching? His cock inflate?'

Silas stared at him. Christ almighty, if he were not overwhelmed before he certainly was now. 'So this Samyaza...he led a rebellion?'

'Did the Verderer deafen you?'

'I'm just trying to understand,' Silas said shakily. 'None of this makes any sense.'

'To you, I suppose it would not. Yes, Samyaza was a naughty but terribly powerful angel, who led a rebellion against Enoch's rule. He fancied the throne for himself, though he would be bitterly disappointed in his personal success in achieving that goal. However it is thanks to him we still have the Hellfield. A delightfully blood-soaked stretch of territory where the surviving Watchers and all those traitors who have since fled Arcadia to join their cause, fight beneath Azazel, a self-important toad of an angel, who took over leadership of the Watchers when Samyaza fell. His army is impressive, I suppose, but pales in comparison to the daemon warriors who defend Arcadia's front lines.' Pitch paused. He pulled his arm from across his eyes but still held them shut fast. The press of his knee was warm against Silas's leg. 'If not for the Dominion and their Daemonkind legions, I have little doubt dear Lord Enoch's Ophanim throne would have fallen long before now.' He touched at his lips, and one brow scrunched with a frown.

'Are you all right?'

'I am.' He seemed uncertain though and fell quiet.

Silas waded through all he'd been told, losing himself in the fantastical tale. 'Daemons and angels living as one still astonishes me, humans have that part of the lore so very wrong.'

'Hmph.'

'These Dominion sound formidable.'

'They are.' Pitch sliced the words thin.

'Are they the same as the Princes of the Hellfield you have spoken of? The offspring of the Kings of Daemonkind?' He recalled the conversation they had after the encounter with the boggart, where Pitch had spoken bitingly of the *seven princely spawn who do all the actual hard work upon the Hellfield*. Six, now that the Beserker Prince seemed to be no more.

'Yes...gods.' Pitch's grimace contorted his entire face.

'You cannot speak more of them?' Silas was enraptured and repulsed at once. Wanting to cover his ears and hide from all this, while at the same time willing to lay here for hours and listen to what Pitch might say.

'I do not *wish* to speak of them. It is neither here, nor there.'

Silas would disagree, but certainly not out loud. He could not help but dare another question. 'Enoch then...he is the ruler of Arcadia?'

Pitch seemed happy enough with the change of direction and nodded, eyes still closed. 'He is indeed, our great and benevolent Lord, ever surrounded by his almighty guardians, the Seraphim.' Pitch coughed upon that last word.

'Seraphim?' Silas clung to the familiar word. 'The boggart spoke of such a thing. He said that the Beserker Prince had brought one down - '

Pitch's eyes flew open. 'Damn it, Silas. I know what that shithead said, I was there.' The daemon sucked at his teeth. A flicker of something unreadable crossed his face.

'Is the pain too much?' Silas asked quietly.

A bitter smile found Pitch's lips. 'Is that not the whole point?'

Silas had no answer for a question so cryptic. Pitch seemed to gather himself, his face smoothing with bland disregard, as though the entire situation bored him. Gory wounds and all.

'I think I should go and find Ottelie...'

'No. Don't go.' Pitch's eyes fluttered closed. Silas did not like how dull the gleam in them was. The man needed tending. But if Pitch wished Silas to remain, a dozen wild horses could not have dragged him away.

'All right. I'll stay. But perhaps you should rest awhile, we can continue later.'

'I don't want to sleep,' Pitch said tightly. 'Keep me awake.'

Awake? He was clearly exhausted, sleep should have been foremost on his mind. But Silas nodded. 'All right then. So if the arrowhead is this...nekhri metal...why is it here?'

It was so much easier to ask such an enormous, frightening question when one was distracted. And Silas was very much so. Pitch wheezed a little when he breathed, and his cheeks were oddly hollow. Sweat beaded on his brow, and Silas hoped it was from the heat of the fire, and nothing more troubling. He opened his eyes and Silas glanced away, aware of how intently he'd been studying the daemon's face.

'There is something you should know about the Severance War, Sickle. That is what we call the mayhem that Samyaza's rebellion became. You'll be delighted to hear, I dare say, that the war did not begin in Arcadia, but somewhere rather more close to home. In fact, close enough that you would have slipped in Angelic blood should you have chosen to take a stroll in the English countryside at the time.'

The excessive warmth of the room chilled at once.

'Here?' Silas whispered. 'You are suggesting this war began here?'

'I'm not suggesting, I am telling. The Severance War had Earthly origins.'

Now Silas fell quiet for entirely different reasons.

'Gods, your face.' Pitch laughed and winced at once. 'It is truly priceless.'

'The angels fought...upon this land?' Silas bit into his words to stop the tremor in his voice. If warmth still came from the fire, he did not feel it.

The daemon rolled his head to face him. The emerald in his eyes was lighter, closer to that of grass blades than gemstone. 'I'm not certain how much more I'll be able to tell you before I choke on my own tongue, but I must say I'm enjoying the idea that Satty will be furious about what I've already said. Obviously she intended you to be kept in the dark. Do you want to know more?'

'I'm not sure,' Silas said, truthfully. 'This is all quite overwhelming.'

'No more so than being woken in your coffin and shuffled off to Holly Village, I suspect. And considering recent events, you should know these things. But first, I want something from you.'

'What is it?'

'Will you lay - '

'Not this again.' Silas pushed back, the sudden jerk sending a sharp pain through his wounded shoulder. Straw pricked at him through the bedclothes.

'Good gods man, what did you think I was going to suggest?' Pitch said with a note of genuine surprise. 'If I were seeking to fuck you I would choose a time when my insides did not leak upon the bed.'

Warmth filled Silas's cheeks. 'My apologies.'

'Accepted. I merely wish to sit up a little as my nose is bleeding into the back of my throat and it is not pleasant. I was hoping to lay my head in your lap.' Silas stared at him. 'There are no pillows. If you don't wish me to throw up on you, you'll allow me to put my fucking head in your damned lap.'

His eyes did not brighten but at least there was some fire behind his words.

'All right, all right. Don't work yourself up.' Silas grit his teeth against the ache that came with shifting his body. He sat up, positioning himself on his knees and sinking back onto his heels. Ottelie's bed was sturdy, it did not once protest such a weight moving about, but he was very near to the edge and would have to keep his wits about him if he did not fancy tumbling onto that strange rug of flowers. He lifted Pitch's head gingerly, manoeuvring his thighs beneath him and lowering the daemon's head onto his lap. Pitch grinned up at him the whole while, save for one moment when he grew so pale and his lips so pinched Silas feared he may pass out.

'Comfortable?' Silas said gruffly. The heart-shaped bow of the daemon's lips was more pronounced when viewed from above, and the top of Pitch's head was alarmingly close to Silas's crotch.

'Quite so,' Pitch declared. His sweat-dampened hair clung to Silas's trouser legs. 'Now where was I?'

Silas knew exactly. His pulse still thudded because of it. 'You were saying a war between angels began here, on Earth.'

'Right, yes, that's where I was.' Pitch cleared his throat, green eyes settling on the straw-packed roof. 'Samyaza was a formidable angel. The gods get all carried away with their creations every now and then, and won't admit when they've made a right cock of it.' He spoke through tight lips, his disdain like a crackle on the air. 'Samyaza was a right cock. He was supposed to have served as Lord Enoch's Angelic right hand but decided he didn't much like the idea of being in servitude for all eternity, and convinced a few of the Archangels they didn't either. Now of course, this merry band needed somewhere secluded to unify their discontent. Somewhere they could walk unnoticed, where the inhabitants were an ignorant lot and easily deceived.' He paused, running a fingertip across his lips. Silas held his breath. If the daemon's tongue was stolen now he would be driven mad with the suspense of it. Pitch continued. 'What better place than this? And with the Blessing of two of the Celestials...the intolerably stuffy name given to Arcadia's gods...the Watchers were able to hide their forays to Earth rather well, and conduct their war-mongering without notice. Samyaza and his rebel brood spent their mornings discussing their plans to overthrow Lord Enoch, and their afternoons fucking about with the humans until their great Angelic cocks could stand no more.'

Silas stiffened. 'I beg your pardon?'

Pitch clucked his tongue, which was still in full use. 'Oh, did I offend your sensibilities, my sweet Sickle? Well, it offended many in Arcadia to, so I suppose you are in good company. To fornicate with creatures so lowly and base as the humans, is one of a great many taboos of my world. Right up there with one of Lord Enoch's precious Seraphim debasing their Angelic selves with those of Daemonkind.' He paused, his attentions turning inwards, the gold flecks in his eyes dulling further.

'Pitch?' Silas prompted, worried at the evident slip of the daemon's mood.

Pitch blinked rapidly, as though clearing out whatever thoughts had overtaken him. 'Anyway, it turns out Samyaza was rather good at breaking taboos. His cock would become one of his greatest weapons, thanks to the goddess Morrigan who had made it quite clear that she was ready and willing to break from the Celestials entirely. From Samyaza's seed, she brought forth the Nephilim, a monster race born of angel and human -'

Silas went still, a chill brushing at his neck. 'Monsters born of angels and humans?'

'I'm fairly certain that's exactly what I just said.' Pitch gave a feeble shrug. 'Giants, to be exact. Even you would pale alongside them, my little Sickle. But despite divine assistance they were rare. Most killed their mothers whilst they were still in the womb, and so ended their own fleeting lives, the rest did not take a breath after they were born, but enough survived to become Samyaza's warriors in the Severance War. Enoch was blind to the births until Samyaza had created enough Nephilim to give him reason to shit his divine britches. They are the major reason the war was not ended long ago. They keep us locked at the Hellfield, neither side can advance, neither will retreat.'

The blood roared in Silas's ears. 'Do any among mankind know of this? That giants walked the Earth once? There is no remnant of them now, surely.'

'There are whispers of them in your holy books, but they are counted as story and nothing more.'

Silas took a couple of slow, deep breaths, very very glad he was already sitting down.

'So the arrowhead,' he said. 'What are we to make of that? Tell me that you do not think Samyaza has returned to create more of these...these monsters?'

'He's dead, so no, I do not think that. He did not live to see the Severance War pass its first century. Enoch's lapdogs got him when he returned to the human world one time too many with his cock hard, ready to try and fuck another monster into existence. The Seraphim destroyed him.' That word again caused him trouble. 'They tore him into three pieces, one for each of them, and it is said that Samyaza bled so profusely it flooded the entire world.' Pitch sneered. 'Likely that detail is merely histrionics. Lord Enoch does so enjoy embellishing his tales with a grandeur undeserved. But the defeat of Samyaza was true enough. The Nephilim bloodline was ended, Earth was under Arcadian protection, and all was well once more with the plain, dreary life of humankind. Azazel was Samyaza's chief commander, and he very quickly took his master's place, named himself Exarch of Elyssiam, and continues to this day to piss off everyone in White Mountain.' He waved his hand carelessly. 'White Mountain is...well, think of it as Arcadia's Buckingham Palace with ten times the corridors, and infinitely more stiff rods up arses.'

'Good God,' Christ almighty, Silas was dizzy.

'If only there were just one, and they were all good,' Pitch said quietly.

'I'm sorry.' Silas whispered.

'What for?'

'For what you must have seen and endured in a place such as the Hellfield.'

Pitch's cheek fluttered, and his breath hitched. All at once he seemed desperately frail and drained. He stared up at Silas, his lips parted. But whatever words he might have been considering were swallowed. A scowl swept away his frailty. 'I don't want your fucking pity.'

He moved as though attempting to sit up. Silas pressed a hand to his shoulder. 'Pitch, for goodness' sake. Stay still.'

The daemon moaned through clenched teeth. 'Fuck, is that bitch growing her bloody herbs from seed?'

'Lie back,' Silas demanded. 'Please.' He braced his hand across Pitch's chest, holding just firm enough that the daemon slumped back against him. Breathing hard. When it seemed he would not try to bolt again Silas withdrew his hold. Pitch's skin was worryingly warm and clammy, his chest skimmed with sweat. 'We will not speak of all this anymore, you must rest. I think you have a fever. Ottelie needs to see to you now.'

'Hmph. The witch won't have the herbs for this poison I do not think.'

'Poison? What do you mean?' He slid his fingers beneath Pitch's shoulders. He was lithe, near to the point of too slender, but solid as a chunk of stone.

'You enjoy watching me, so I'm sure you saw it.' Pitch traced his fingers through the bloodied skin beneath the tear in his belly.

'Pitch, speak your mind - '

'There was something in that prism, and when it shattered it was released, burrowing into the blood of this fine body and leaving it putrid. Tell me you did not study me well enough to notice the stain it left upon my veins?'

Silas dragged his gaze from the lazy path of Pitch's finger. 'I saw it, yes. I think that I tasted it too.' The acrid tang in the air had made him retch. 'That was a poison?'

'Indeed. Though it was not one intended for my blood, so I shall heal, albeit fucking slowly and painfully. But there are others who would not fare so well, should it blight them.' Ottelie's fire was far too kind to the sharp angles of his face, brightening the hollows. Pitch was right, Silas did like to watch him. It was maddening, and entirely inappropriate.

'Blight them...' he replied absently. Pitch's words took time to sink in. 'Oh, Christ. The prism contained the Blight?'

'My clever ankou.' Pitch lifted his hand and pressed it to Silas's cheek.

Silas was far too preoccupied to ward him off, and only vaguely conscious of being grateful Pitch had not used his bloodied hand. 'The prism was built to...*create* a teratism? My god, they trapped the stag to get to the Verderer's lost soul.'

'How adorable you are when you furrow your brow.' He traced Silas's jawline.

'Who could do such a thing?' Silas ignored the flattery, and the touching, his mind a whirlwind of thought. 'And the arrowhead...Pitch...what is going on here?'

'All kinds of nefarious things, I would say.'

First an arrowhead from an unimaginable world, now a cage filled with the Blight. He sat stunned, and distracted enough that he did not push Pitch's hand away. Silas's skin tingled beneath the soft pressure against his cheek as the daemon explored it. Somewhere beyond the walls of the cottage Ottelie still sung merrily. A tune too jovial for the moment.

'We must speak with the Lady Satine,' Silas muttered.

Pitch let his hand fall from Silas's face. Even that small movement forced a whimper from the injured daemon. Bloody hell, he was paler than before. Silas shook off thoughts of Goodrich Castle, and focused in on the here and now. His hands hovered helplessly over Pitch's traumatised body, a flicker of guilt taking him. He'd drawn Pitch into conversation too long.

'Well, even if Ottelie cannot deal with the Blight, I'm sure she has something to make you more comfortable,' Silas said. 'I'll fetch her.'

Pitch's hand darted once more to his face. Silas did not have time to shirk away before the daemon's fingers sank into the rough stubble at his chin.

'Don't bother the witch,' The daemon whispered. 'You could assist me far more ably in subduing the pain, Silas.'

Ottelie's pleasant singing came from nearer this time.

Silas should have pried Pitch's hand away but dear god those pools of green were mesmerising, dulled as they were, gazing up at him as though *he* were the one who was difficult to look away from. 'Pitch, if you are working your enchantments upon me I must insist that you cease it at once.'

The daemon tilted his chin, exposing more of his slender neck. 'It would be a waste of my charms to use them here where they are clearly not needed. Come now, I only require a little attention. Pleasure does wonders for the incubus blood. It is a wondrous high and a natural painkiller. You would be returning a favour, that is all.' The coy tilt of his smile caused an odd thrum to add itself to Silas's heartbeat. Pitch's fingers brushed his lips. A dart of something hot and intense ran the length of Silas's spine, spilling into the slumbering length between his legs. Causing it to stir.

'Pitch,' Silas growled in warning. He was certain he was being meddled with, certain he did not truly wish to lean in closer.

'Surely you are too exhausted for such false modesty?'

Silas stayed Pitch's hand with a firm hold upon his wrist. He should wrench himself free entirely. 'I don't want...' The protest died on his tongue. What was it he *didn't* want? Christ, he was tired. Pitch had that much right.

He loosened his grip and the daemon did not hesitate to touch him once more. He cupped a hand to Silas's cheek, and damn if he did not find himself leaning into the daemon's palm. Silas swam in emerald. The pulse at Pitch's wrist beat against his grip. Had Silas actually leaned down closer? Pitch seemed nearer than before, his faded-pink lips not so far out of reach as they had been. Silas ached to lie down, drained by all he'd heard and seen.

Nephilim, rebellious angels, Hell Princes and traitorous gods, all brought far too close for any comfort by one blasted arrowhead.

How he wished to escape from the Forest of Dean and all the secrets it was pouring forth. Even if just for a moment. With Ottelie's voice trilling in the background, he recalled the way the flames had streamed from Pitch's back. How safe he'd felt beneath those firey arches. Protected, and no longer so desperately lost. Alone. Pitch's hand slipped around the back of his neck, tugging him down. Closer.

Silas abandoned resistance. If the daemon meddled with him, then let the bastard play. Pitch's lips parted. His breath rich with the same sweet and bitter scent Silas recalled from the farm. It was intoxicating. Likely quite actually so, but Silas shoved back his concerns. He hunched over the bleeding man, closing the inches between them, his throat tight with want. Pitch's fingers worked into the damp strands of Silas's hair. The heat of his breath caressed Silas's lips. And, bloody hell if that warmth did not send a pulse straight to Silas's cock.

'Right then lads.' Ottelie burst into the room. 'The spirit is most improved.'

'Shit!' Silas cried, and the room descended into chaos.

CHAPTER 29

S ilas flew back and toppled himself off the bed. Pitch screeched a violent protest as he lost his fleshy pillow, and let loose with a flurry of curses that would make a docker blush.

'Flipping heck, sorry lads,' Ottelie blustered. 'Didn't mean to intrude...how about I come back...later...when you're done...'

Her entrance into the cottage might have been swift-footed, but her attempt to exit was not so. She back-peddled so hastily she almost lost her grip on the bowl she carried, sloshing a substance bright as a blueberry over its lip. Her hair was loose and messy across one side of her face. 'But I'm glad to see you faring well, Tobias.'

'Not as well as I might have been.' Pitch lay sprawled on the bed framed by the spread of bloodstains, his chest heaving. It turned Silas's stomach to realise he had lost himself while sitting in the daemon's blood.

'Ottelie, please do not leave,' he said, 'tend to his wounds. I will go and see to the horses. We need to prepare for our return journey.'

Good god, he had lost his mind. Pitch was gravely injured, a castle had been destroyed, a fae kingdom decimated and teratisms were being deliberately created, yet Silas stood with a swollen cock and his heart drumming with ill-placed desire.

'You're not going anywhere for a while, I can assure you,' Ottelie declared. 'You are both in need of a decent sleep and a warm meal. Have my bed, I was intending to stay with the spirit this day anyway. I'll even

238

get some fresh straw for you, so you're not in quite the bloodbath. Once I've seen to *both* your wounds I'll leave you in peace a while. You men deserve your relaxation, considering what you've done for the forest. And you have no fear here, do whatever you wish to one another, I only ask that you aren't too noisy about it. The hawfinch's have just hatched some chicks in under the eaves and I'd rather you don't scare them off.'

Silas could not have widened his eyes more if he tried. The awkwardness of the moment was excruciating. 'No, no, that's not - '

'Damn you, witch. I had almost undone some of his knots, now you've tightened them again.' Pitch broke into one of those grins of his that had Silas's head spinning, hard as he tried to stop it. 'You should tend to Silas first. I've no need of your concoctions. I will heal sure enough alone. But it will be more pleasant with honey, or teacakes if you have them. Both will dull the ache...though not as well as rough hands and a stiff –'

'Drink,' Silas interjected, glaring at the daemon. 'Perhaps you have some ale or cider?' His cheeks were tiny bonfires. 'I am rather parched.'

Ottelie's grin was lopsided and most perplexing. 'I'm quite sure you are. It is a wonderful idea. A celebration is in order after all. But it could wait, if you like, until you are done with your *own* celebrations?'

'You misunderstood what you saw, I'm afraid.' Silas shook his head. 'Tobias is my guardian. I was concerned for him, checking his wound. That is all.' Oh, dear god, he might as well have a shovel in hand.

Ottelie inclined her head, mirth simmering in her gaze. 'I see. I didn't realise that his mouth had been injured, my mistake.'

Silas willed the cottage to burst into flame, or collapse about them. 'That is not what - '

'Now, now. I am just playing with you.'

Silas had had quite enough of that for the day. Thank god his mortification had toppled the tentpole between his legs.

'He is so delightful when he is abashed, don't you think?' Pitch shifted onto his side with great care, the tear in his belly glistening.

'He is, but we've had our fun now. Silas, I'll tend to your...guardian's...wounds, and then we shall raise a toast to the work that you've done here. However it was done. The spirit of the forest lies recovering in my smokehouse, and I can hear the birds heralding the dawn for the first time in over a week, it is wonderful. Be sure to send my thanks to that Order of yours, will you not?'

'Of course, of course.' Silas nodded like a man possessed. 'The moment we return.'

Which he wished was occurring as they spoke.

The woman nodded, sweeping a hand through her wheat-coloured hair, pulling it back from her face.

Silas uttered a low cry. 'My goodness. Your eye.'

'Yes.' Ottelie touched her fingers to her temple, letting them slide down to where a coating of green-grey lichen covered the socket of her right eye. The flatness there told Silas that her grey eye was not hidden beneath, but gone entirely. 'You are not the only ones to have had a surprising day.'

'The would-be-witch is the new Verderer then?' Pitch sniffed. 'As good a choice as any I suppose.'

'I'll take that as a compliment from you, Tobias.'

He found his most radiant, beguiling smile and she giggled like a girl rather than the woman of age that she was.

'Are you all right, Ottelie?' Silas asked. 'That must have pained you.'

'I am the best I've ever been, my lad.' Her smile was no less radiant. 'The forest has chosen me as its guardian. A living Verderer this time. I intend to do it a damn sight better than that last unfortunate fellow, I assure you. You'll find a much better welcome next time you pass by. Now go on with you, the cider's in the well just beyond the smokehouse.'

She stepped aside to allow him to pass. Silas took his leave, trying his utmost not to stare too long at the spirit's mark upon her face. He rushed from the oppressive air of the cottage to the briskness of a slow-rising morning. The door swung closed behind him.

'Now wipe that smug look from your face,' he heard Ottelie say. 'He's a good lad that one. Don't be giving him any trouble, because it seems to me like you're made of it.'

Pitch's laughter rang out, utterly careless and delightful as church bells on a wedding morn. 'Well I am hardly to blame for that. We are as we are made.'

'Still, if you have the devil in you, it doesn't mean you can't cast him out.'

Silas hesitated outside the closed door. Lalassu lifted her head from grazing to watch him.

'I would not be so certain of that,' Pitch returned. 'Now are you going to soothe my ills or not?'

Ottelie's reply came after a pause so lengthy that Silas thought perhaps he had missed it.

'I'm not sure I have the skills needed for all of them, my friend. I'm privy now to a few things I was not before the spirit gave me sight. Back at those mines, you suffered, you poor lad. The forest heard your pain when the bluecaps set upon you. She reached deep, the queen, didn't she? And she found much unhappiness to feast on.'

'Careful, witch. You're liable to bore me to death.'

'All I wish to say on the matter is that the forest, and I, are deeply sorry you suffered such a loss. For it was grief she dragged out of you. A sorrow sharp as I've ever seen.'

It were as though every bird in the forest who'd just started to sing again, fell silent once more. There was not a sound from within the cottage either. Silas's breath sounded intolerably loud in such quiet.

'The forest should best bother itself with things of greater import,' Pitch said, his voice cool and bristling with warning. Silas pressed too hard against the door, if he were not careful he'd find himself toppling back inside. There came the tapping of an implement against wood, Ottelie stirring her insipid concoction perhaps.

'Well, I just want you to know that you have a place to come, should you need space to do your grieving properly.'

'And I would like you to know that you and your spirit should keep your eyes and ears and mouths shut, lest someone shut them for you more permanently.'

'Easy there, Tobias. You know I mean no harm. Let's say no more of it.'

Deep and wallowing silence followed. The birds in the branches held their breath. The crickets stilled their wings. Silas glanced at the door, and considered entering, lest the witch had stirred a temper best left undisturbed.

'By the gods that salve stinks,' Pitch coughed, at last. 'Use it before the stench kills us both. Or are you too overwhelmed by my fine figure to move?'

Ottelie was not overwhelmed at all, with Pitch soon protesting the chill of the compress. The witch remonstrated his childish wailings. Silas moved on from his spying place.

He took himself to Lalassu's side, to the solid warmth of her. And he stood there a long while. Wondering on the fate that had taken him from drowned man to ankou, and then here to this place where he was beginning to understand that there was so very little he understood. In the midst of birdsong he stroked Lalassu's storm-touched coat, struggling to comprehend how he found himself in the midst of a world where angels and daemons, giants and fae existed. He shivered at the notion of a force so dark it could turn a forest upon itself and his pulse quickened to think on the arrowhead from an impossibly distant Arcadian mountain.

But most of all, and most entirely, one thought alone captured him.

He could not stop wondering at who Pitch had lost.

Silas leaned into Lalassu and the horse steadied herself for him. What tremendous grief had brought the alluring, infuriating, and seemingly immovable daemon to his knees? The sorrow had been rent from him in the mines, let loose in cries that Silas was not certain he could ever forget. He pressed his forehead against Lalassu's wide neck. It pained him, perhaps more than it should, to know Pitch suffered so. But it also stirred something within him. An ache of a different kind.

A desire to know if anyone grieved for Silas the way Pitch grieved for an unknown soul.

Silas stepped back from the pale horse, and under her watchful eye made his way towards the well as Ottelie had instructed. Moving past the smokehouse where an ageless spirit now rested, saved by Silas's hand. A hand that wielded death's own blade. How deeply fantastical his existence was.

He found the well, and pulled up a basket holding two amber bottles brimming with cider. The glass was achingly cold. Silas pulled the stopper from one of the bottles and with a furtive glance towards the cottage, took a deep swig. He was not ready to go back in there yet. He needed more distance between himself and that harrowing conversation.

Between himself and that arrowhead.

Between himself and that damned daemon.

He took another gulp. The tart liquid stung the inside of his mouth, making his tongue curl. He wondered if he enjoyed cider in his past life, for he certainly did not relish it now. But if ever a man was in need of drink and forgetting, it was Silas.

Tomorrow he would face whatever troubles drifted his way. Most likely they would not so much drift as run at him like a herd of enraged bulls, but he would worry on that when the time came. He might go as mad as that Beserker Prince otherwise. Silas raised the bottle once more.

'Sickle, where is that damned drink?' Pitch's voice flowed from the cottage, his impatience as sour as the cider. 'The witch seeks to mummify me in her ghastly concoctions. Have you abandoned me, you dead bastard?'

The cider must have hit its mark for Silas found himself chuckling. Maybe his sanity *had* left him when he rose from the grave. For despite everything that had happened it had not occurred to him to abandon the daemon. Hell, he'd thrown himself into a collapsing mine rather than do so when the opportunity had presented itself.

Silas pressed the stopper back into the bottle. The peacefulness of the recovering forest was pleasant but he found that he was not relishing the solitude quite so much as he had imagined.

He made his way back to the cottage, warm with the drink.

The pale horse watched him as he went, her eyes the colour of the last light of the day. And hidden in their depths, the path that lay ahead.

Exclusive Excerpt

THE SKRIKER - PITCH & SICKLE BOOK THREE

The figure strode from the woods with eyes of fire, and a pair of scorched rabbit carcasses dangling from one hand. Whisps of smoke curled from their burnt hides and their heads were orbs of charcoal each. The scent of their scalded flesh reached Silas where he stood by the paltry fire. He was hungry enough that the waft was not altogether unpleasant.

'Supper is served,' Pitch declared, swinging his bounty carelessly.

He strode into their makeshift camp like a terrible ghost, skin white as snow and eyes tiny blazing suns. Christ almighty it was a sight. One that tightened Silas's chest, and caused his heart to stutter beneath his ribs. He coughed, stoking absently at the fire they had set to ward off the evening chill. Three days ago they had left the peacefulness of Ottelie's cottage, despite her protestations it was too soon to do so. After near on a week spent recuperating, Pitch was a mess of restlessness, and could not be swayed from his determination to leave the Forest of Dean and return to Bishop's Castle.

'I trust you did not set the woods ablaze as you hunted rabbits?' Silas scowled down at the fire. It was not a kind thing to say, he supposed, considering the daemon had seen to it that they would not go hungry that evening. But then again it was because of Pitch that they had no supplies to begin with. Ottelie had provided bread and eggs and an astounding array of sweet treats and cakes that should have sustained them for a week. There was a half a loaf of bread and one egg remaining. Pitch's appetite was monstrous. Perhaps if he ceased his endless tapping of feet in the stirrups, or the knocking of knuckles upon the pommel he might have conserved some of his energies. His agitation was exhausting to lay witness too.

'They are hares, not rabbits, Silas. And perhaps if I had burned this bloody wood down it would see us reach our destination sooner rather than much later,' Pitch replied. 'Or does your nag intend for us to forever wander the forests of England alone, pissing against trees, and sleeping on the dirt?'

Silas took a breath before he replied. One of them at least must stifle their temper, and the daemon had no talent for it. Especially not of late. 'Pitch, we have discussed this already. Many times.' He bit his lip, pausing before he spoke again. 'I do not decide Lalassu's course. I agree it is strange that we have not yet passed through a town, but there is reason for it, I'm sure. And we must act accordingly.'

Which was to say, Pitch should not have depleted their stores by sunrise of the second day, but Silas was hardly going to broach that subject once more. He did not favour another vicious tongue lashing. It seemed the further on their journey went, the more turbulent Pitch's mood became. It was likely he would have had them ride day and night if the choice was his. He muttered angrily beneath his breath when Lalassu stopped, late in the evenings, to afford them some rest. But when he was not cursing their need for sleep, he was mostly silent. Far too much so for someone who enjoyed the sound of his voice most other times. The modicum of calm the daemon had seemed to embrace while he recuperated in the cottage, slipped away with each mile they travelled. And that intimate moment between them, lips within an inch of touching, grew more dreamlike with each passing day.

A pair of smoldering hares landed with a thump at Silas's feet. 'I caught them, you will skin them,' Pitch said, lofty as a king.

Silas looked up in alarm. 'I beg your pardon?'

DK GIRL

'Why do you insist on saying that when it is clear you heard me very well?' Pitch replied, his irritation wrinkling his forehead.

He kicked at a jutting log, sending sparks flying from the fire, bringing it to life. There had been a lot of that of late, too. Lashing out at random objects: a low hanging branch receiving a punch as Sanu took him beneath it, a rock in a brook where they had stopped to take water being sent flying with a well placed kick. Silas had the sense of being near to a pot ready to boil over. But if he dared asked if all was well, the glare he received could have peeled the skin from his bones.

'I'm not sure I know how...' Silas bent to take the hares in hand but Pitch was there before him. Their hands met, a brief brush, before Pitch snatched the dead animals away.

'Damn it Silas, must I do everything?'

Pitch had not called him Sickle in two days.

'I did not say I wouldn't do it,' he protested. 'Here, give them to me.' Silas reached for one of the carcasses that Pitch clutched about the neck. The daemon slapped at his hand, a sharp whip of skin against skin hard enough to wrench a gasp from Silas. 'What was that for?'

'Need there be a reason?'

'For god's sake, Pitch,' Silas shouted. 'What is wrong with you? Give me the damned rabbits.'

This time when he sought to claim the dinner bounty Pitch pivoted on his heels, twisting to avoid him. A hiss came from him as he turned, and Silas would swear he saw the daemon wince.

'They are fucking hares, you imbecile.' Pitch spoke through gritted teeth. 'Leave it be will you? I'll do it. Just keep the fire going.'

He shrugged into the faded brown leather coat that Ottelie had provided him. His own clothes were ruined beyond repair after Goodwich Castle. She'd sequestered an entire outfit, a white flannel shirt, a blue vest with tin buttons, and, most impressively, a pair of his favoured fall-front trousers, along with near-new lace up boots. A farmer's garb. Though how the new Verderer had managed to source items that fit Pitch near perfectly was a wonder. The daemon had complained at the lack of a corset among the items but otherwise seemed quite pleased.

Silas had not been in such dire need of replacement clothing luckily, he doubted any nearby countryman could match him in size. Ottelie had laundered his dusty, ash and blood stained clothes and returned them to him as good as new.

'Pitch...please tell me...is there something wrong? Are you in pain? Perhaps we should rest here for a day — '

'No. We keep on.' He snapped. 'If you dare coddle me Silas I swear I shall separate you from your balls. Do you understand?'

Silas did his best to match Pitch's glare, but concern tugged at his brow. 'I'll keep my balls just where they are, thank you very much. And I am not coddling you, I am asking you a question. Just now when you moved, I saw that it caused your difficulty. Is it the wound in your stomach? Ottelie said it was too soon for you to be on horseback — '

'It is not the wound on my stomach. Don't bother yourself with my well-being.' He turned and began to walk away.

The words burst from Silas like a flight of swallows. 'It *does* bother me. You've eaten all we have and a rabbit is hardly — '

'It's a bloody hare.'

'A hare then, damn it.' Silas balled his fists. 'But I know it is not enough for you. You've said as much before. Do you need...that is to say...would...it's just that I know —'

'Gods, what is trying to dribble from your mouth, man?'

'Company.' Silas spat it. He did not dribble. 'You need...company. You said once that what you drew from others was a natural painkiller for your kind.' What Pitch had said exactly, eyes heavy with need, was *pleasure does wonders for incubus blood*. 'So I just thought that perhaps...you needed...'

His words faded like the smoke curling from the dead hares. Good God what had come over him? His face roared with heat despite him being turned from the fire, but he could not chase from his mind the bittersweet scent of Pitch's breath as they had drawn so dangerously close upon Ottelie's bed. A kiss. That was all he was offering of course. What harm in that, if it would restore the daemon from insufferable to barely tolerable?

The fire spat and crackled behind them, and Pitch stood in silence for far too long. Silas shook his head, ready with a curt withdrawal of the ludicrous offer.

'Do you *want* my company, Silas?' Pitch's voice slunk low, nearly lost beneath the soft night sounds of the woods. He stood perfectly still, like a hunter lying in wait.

Sweat beaded on Silas's brow. He felt lightheaded, Pitch's question pounded in his ears. 'It's not like that...I was just...' Silas faltered. He was *just* taking leave of his senses, surely. If his heart thumped any harder he'd have a broken rib to contend with.

'How very noble of you, Silas, to stoop so low, but have no fear, your virtue is safe.' Pitch held so tight to the carcasses Silas thought he heard a crack of bone. 'You cannot sooth what ails me. I dare say you'd be less use than a teacake.'

Silas's lips parted in a silent gasp. If he'd thought the daemon unwell before, he was certain of it now.

Pitch made his way to where the stump of a felled tree formed a perfect table on which to lay their supper. As Silas watched, lost for all words, the daemon dug his fingers into the ruff of a narrow neck and with the flick of a wrist tore away a strip of the hare's hide. The wet ripping sound sent a shudder through Silas's body.

'Go and tend to the supper,' Pitch said coolly. 'And stop gaping like a fool.'

With a scowl, and making a point of not jumping immediately to follow the curt command Silas moved back to where the fire weaved and shone, thankful for its heat now as it chased away the chill that gripped him. Lalassu and Sanu watched on from just beyond the clearing, working their mouths against cropped grass.

They ate in silence a little while later. The meat was pleasant enough once roasted, the company less so. Silas sat on one side of the fire, Pitch on the other, gnawing at his meat as though the creature still lived and he sought to ensure otherwise. His hands were unwashed, stained with the blood and muck that came from a disembowelled body. It did not make for pleasant dining surrounds, and Silas found he could eat no more than a few mouthfuls of the stringy meat.

'Would you like the rest of mine?' Silas raised what remained of his hare, impaled upon an oak's discarded branch. Pitch sucked noisily at a cracked bone, stealing the marrow.

'Hmmph.'

Silas supposed that to mean he would care for the leftovers and he rose to his feet, grunting as his saddle-weary joints protested. He handed over the portion. Pitch snatched the stick without a look or a word and bit into the pink flesh. He had already stripped his own carcass bare of meat but was clearly not sated. Silas hovered, likely longer than he should have.

'You are blocking the light,' Pitch spoke through a mouthful. 'I'm sure you're enjoying the view but I'd prefer you move.'

The view was distracting, certainly, flames always favoured Pitch's complexion, but worry curdled in Silas's stomach along with the portions of hare. The daemon was withdrawing into himself, placing a distance between them that Silas did not understand. Nor relish.

It was lonely where he stood. And he realised it was likely the first time he'd felt that way since they had encountered one another.

Without a word he left Pitch to his gorging and after tending to the horses - a gesture more beneficial for himself than the horses who needed no real fussing over - Silas searched for a place to settle for the evening. Somewhere not too far from the fire. Lalassu nudged him towards a patch of moss-covered ground beneath a considerable oak. Without the mare's encouragement the hidden natural bedding would have gone unnoticed. As he settled down for the evening, with a saddle for a makeshift pillow, gathering his coat about him, and shifting the pocket so he would not lie upon the bandalore, Silas kept his eye on Pitch.

The daemon lay on the far side of the fire. It was only the whiteness of his skin that marked his position, huddled in the bulge of the dead roots at the foot of the stump he'd used as a butcher's block earlier. The wood was still sticky with the hares' blood, its entrails glistening in the firelight. Silas did his best to sleep, but his mood did not lend itself to the calmness needed for such things and he tossed and turned as the night deepened. Pitch's odd behaviour was but one thing to worry over. He rolled onto his back and touched at the pocket where the arrowhead nestled with all its vast implications. He had asked Pitch who should carry it, as they prepared to depart, and the daemon had told him with much vexation that he should cast it into Ottelie's well.

'I don't wish to see the fucking thing again,' he'd declared downing the very last of the Verderer's cider.

Perhaps Silas should have seen then that all was not as it should be with the daemon.

'No...no...' Across the way Pitch, struggled with his dreams again.

Silas sat up, debating the merits of trying to rouse him. The daemon had slept fitfully for several nights now. Mostly restless, as though no position he found made him content. He mumbled in his sleep, but the words were usually too distorted to make any sense of.

'I didn't know...' This time though he spoke clearly, if not for the fact his eyes were shut, Silas might think him awake. 'He should not have been there. Raph...Raph!'

The name, all too familiar now to Silas, rose from Pitch with its ever-present weight of anguish. The daemon fell still. And though Silas waited for some time, he said no more and did not move again until the sky lightened and they rose to begin preparations to depart.

They rode on some time later with the overcast day greylit and damp. The twitter of birds as they rose to meet the morning, mixed with the creak of leather from the saddles. Silas wove the loose reins about his fingers, seeking some distraction from Pitch's notable silence.

A half hour after they had set off from the campsite the farmhouse came into view. It was some way up ahead still, just visible at the end of the forest-shadowed track they followed. A small affair, a main house with a red tiled roof surrounded by rather meagre fields that looked in need of a till.

'About fucking time,' Pitch sighed, the first words he'd spoken since they left the campsite. 'Move your arse now, Sickle.'

Silas started at the return of the moniker, and was wholly unprepared for the dimple-inducing grin that was shot his way. For whatever reason Pitch's mood had swung more favourably towards light. He clucked his tongue and urged Sanu into a canter, and Silas hurried to follow.

"*Ancient Aliens*" meets "*Resident Evil*" with a
pinch of "*Predator*" - Goodreads Review

'*Brilliant start, Kick-Ass heroine more plot twists
and turns than you can take in. An absolute
pleasure to read, a real page turner more please.*' -
Goodreads Review

About the Author

Danielle K Girl is an Aussie who lives in stunning Tasmania with her three furkids, cats Luffy, Sweetie (@sweetiebyname) and Ren.
Her idea of heaven is a farm full of rescue animals, with a vegie garden that sprouts peanut M&M's and chocolate wheaten biscuits.
When she's not keyboard-deep in mysterious, beguiling worlds, she is binge watching K-Dramas, listening to K-Pop or hiking through the beautiful Tasmanian wilderness.
Join the newsletter - Get a FREE D K Girl novella!
If you'd like to receive DK's monthly newsletter, and be first to know when a new book is ready, then you are in the right place.
Head to, https://daniellekgirl.com/subscribe/ and score yourself a
FREE Dystopian novella
in the deal.
Find D K Girl online:

https://daniellekgirl.com/

https://www.instagram.com/daniellekgirl/

Lightning Source UK Ltd.
Milton Keynes UK
UKHW011646031022
409847UK00004B/1088